Trans Am

ROBERT RYAN

review

First published in Great Britain in 2001
by Headline Book Publishing under the author's name Rob Ryan

First published in paperback in 2001

This edition first published by Review in 2005

Review is an imprint of Headline Book Publishing

10 9 8 7 6 5 4 3 2

ISBN 0 7553 2561 3

Typeset in Cochin by Palimpsest Book Production Limited,
Polmont, Stirlingshire
Printed and bound in Great Britain by
Mackays of Chatham plc, Chatham, Kent

Headline's policy is to use papers that are natural, renewable and
recyclable products and made from wood grown in sustainable
forests. The logging and manufacturing processes are expected
to conform to the environmental regulations of the
country of origin.

HEADLINE BOOK PUBLISHING
A division of Hodder Headline
338 Euston Road
London NW1 3BH

www.headline.co.uk
www.hodderheadline.com

For the founders and volunteers of the National Center for
Missing & Exploited Children (NCMEC):
www.missingkids.com

Trans Am is the final part of a trilogy of novels based on classic Children's stories transported to a US noir setting. Some characters reappear from *Underdogs* (Tenniel and Bowman) and *Nine Mil* (Shepard and Wuzel), but, like the others in the series, *Trans Am* can be read alone.

Trans Am is loosely based on the story of *Peter Pan*. The theme of lost children intrigued me. I read the original JM Barrie novel, play and its later additions (such as *When Wendy Grew Up*) and all that came to me was: *we read this stuff to our children?*

Apart from naming the hero Jim Barry and a few other nods to Peter Pan, this is mainly a story of a mother who loses her son, and the lengths she will go to get him back (and of another mother who will contemplate breaking the law to save hers). It's not a journey to an American Neverland. Quite the opposite, in fact.

For research I travelled to Arizona and New York City. In the latter I found a club called 'The Air Strip', a strip joint which was housed in a building between the cargo warehouses at JFK. Beside the stage where the girls danced, airport-style screens displayed the flight times, so customers could be sure to catch their plane. I spoke to the owners of this establishment, who told me about other clubs in Queens and New Jersey that used girls as described in this novel, and which were run by various East Europeans. I hasten to add that 'The Air Strip' (which was actually only a topless club, in line with Rudy Guiliani's stipulations on nudity and alcohol) was completely above such behaviour. Besides, the owners frightened me.

In Arizona I spent some time at a new age spa, where the masseuse really did tell me she thought that heaven was a place where they played Elton John all day long. Many of the staff appear in bit parts in *Trans Am*.

I also visited the Grand Canyon, like every other American that day, it seemed. It is over-crowded, but as with many monuments, the visitors cluster in one spot. If you ever get there, go to Shoshone Point, like Coogan and Wendy. It is neither signposted nor mentioned in the official guides. If driving, you have to clock your milometer at 1.25 miles east of Yaki Point. Here, there is a clearing next to the road, a locked gate and a sign saying you can only use 'this facility with permission'. That refers only to the picnic area at the end of the trail. The red earth path runs for a mile, and at the end is a rocky promontory, jutting out over the canyon itself. It is much higher than the usual viewpoints and you can look down on eagles, flapping their way between the walls. It is a magical spot. Make sure you bring your head for heights with you: it's a long way down.

When I wrote *Trans Am*, *Blackhawk Down* was not a major motion picture. I needed Coogan to have a military background, but Vietnam had been used in *Underdogs*, and I wanted him younger than that war would have made him. The (then) little known debacle in Somalia seemed perfect. He was also once a trumpet player, but somehow he took up the guitar instead. Shame, because at one point I could do a pretty mean 'Round Midnight' on the horn.

The ending with the helicopter did happen to an unfortunate father some years ago. The image of what occurred and the devastation he must have felt stayed with me. I also thought I had to address the fact that there is only one way a boy can live forever, and it isn't Peter Pan's.

As with the other two novels, there is a film reference threaded through the book, in this case *Taxi Driver* and other Scorsese films. I wanted The Creep to have a Travis Bickle like moment of epiphany (and a bloody shoot out). The Creep, you'll be pleased to hear, isn't based on anyone I know, but on a story a Federal Officer told me in New York.

I am grateful to Headline for re-issuing *Trans Am* and the companion novels. Thanks, as always, to Martin Fletcher for guiding the new editions.

Robert Ryan
London

PROLOGUE

Toots Turtleman edged forward onto the long finger of the promontory, his feet slithering on the frozen rocks, scrabbling for a hold. Ahead of him was one of the most famous views in the world, or at least part of it, but the way few visitors ever saw it, glistening with diamond-hard ice particles, as if it had been dusted with confectioner's sugar.

He looked over to the left at the valley, felt the familiar whirls in his head, the clash of senses as optic lobe, semicircular canals and cerebrum all sent different messages, screaming at each other: it can't be this big, that far down, this complex. It is, he reminded himself, and it's beautiful.

If the walls and buttes were merely sprinkled with frost, the opposite side of the canyon was thick with a layer of snow and ice that wouldn't be gone until May. He shuddered as a sprite of cold wind curled up from the sheer walls below and ripped straight through his thin jacket. The sun was falling already, as if the effort of rising even so low in the sky had exhausted it, and soon it would be bitterly cold. But he wouldn't be here to feel that.

Toots remembered how it started. Wished he had never shared the dream, the dream they had turned into a nightmare.

He should have known. He pulled them all in and they came, mostly, he had to give them that, but all they did was gripe and snipe. It's the best chance you'll ever have to get your pride back, he told them. It's like a second time around. Make it sweet. Make it beautiful. Make us rich. Yeah, they said, but what about this? What about that?

Hey, Toots had said: they forgot us, didn't they? They are ashamed of us. They think we got our ass kicked, and they want us buried. You a Vietnam vet? Well here, take our sympathy, look at this wall we built for your fallen brothers. Gulf? Jesus you guys got a rough deal. Let's have a congressional investigation. And maybe some compensation. But us? We get the heads turned, the eyes downcast. God that was a mess. But they are wrong, he insisted. The mission was accomplished. We got the targets, we fought a whole town to a standstill. A whole fuckin' town. No, a city. A ragged-ass city, for sure, but a city. Sure we lost guys. They lost more. We did well. So let's show them what Chalk Five can really do. Let's stick it to them.

One by one, as they got drunker and drunker, they all told him in a different way he was crazy. They would all do time, or worse, they kept saying. All too yellow to try. He could see them all now. Nash. Fuckin' Nash, always so smug, superior, like he had read the book when you couldn't find page one. Coogan. Fucked up. Had this thing about boys. Jones. Mr Normal, retreated into some suburban let's-go-to-the-mall-kids middle age. Flint had a new wife, guy was in lurve.

Maybe they were right. Perhaps he was crazy. He had set it all up, the timetable, the hardware – one dry run, one hit. All those dollars. Hundreds of thousands. No takers.

His head was full of noise, of static, of tumbling thoughts, voices pulling him this way and that. The headaches would come back soon. Then the black gloom, the dark place where his soul shivered in fear. He didn't want that.

He looked at the birds again and tried to will himself into their minds, feel what it would be like to have such mastery over this hole in the earth, floating over a mile-deep ocean of free space without fear. He still remembered the feeling of falling, and spinning, the terrible jolt as he hit the earth, when he put his trust – his life – in the hands of a man-made bird.

Toots looked down again, tracing the tiny pathways criss-crossing the rocks of floor, as he had done a thousand times before. He wondered if it was true what they said. That you were dead before you hit the ground down there. He also considered whether it was true about the light, the eye-watering glare of death from which old friends emerged to help you pass to the other side. A friendly luminescence, the complete antithesis of the Bible-black tendrils that would wrap round his heart with increasing frequency. Toots hoped there was light.

Another glacial gust hit him, tugging at his clothes, as if encouraging him. There was only one way to find out what was true and what was not. He took a deep breath and stepped forward into the cold, clear air.

PART ONE

ONE

London, England

Harry Darling tried to wind the clock back as he stared at the photographs laid out on the desk in front of him, back to when he had a rank, men under his command, a sidearm and a burning sense of duty. Not to mention a notion of right and wrong, black and white, before grey bled into the picture, blurring the line between the two. That was what he was dealing with now. The days when the grey came into his life.

He had spread the eighteen six-by-eight black-and-whites before him as best he could, crowded and overlapping, some threatening to fall from the desk top onto the floor. They offered varying degrees of clarity, here pin sharp, showing every pore in the face, every whisker missed by the morning shave, there displaying the fuzzy, snatched furtiveness of old pornography.

He stared hard, waiting for the heady rush of unwelcome memory, but time would not move. Stubbornly his reality stayed put, stranding him in the front room of his rambling home in a suburb of North London, with the rumble of cars doing the evening rat-run rather than the squeak of armoured vehicles, the smashing of glass from the recycling collectors, not from the systematic looting of property, the footsteps above him the headlong, almost-falling-over run of a one-year-old, and the more confident steps of his older sister, not the scrabble of panicked figures trying to escape wicked, arbitrary death. Bath time soon, the clomping reminded him. He should go up.

'Anything?'

The voice on the other end of the phone jerked him back to the reason he was trying to make this temporal transference.

'Give me a minute.'

Darling redoubled his efforts, squinting now at each visage in turn, trying to get just a flash of an image, of the man in the picture in a different context, a machine pistol at his waist, that carnivorous look in his eyes, the strange misshaped nose, the smell of fear and death and atrocity steaming off his body, framed in the lenses of high-powered binoculars, the freshly painted skull and crossbones on the wall behind him glistening red and obscene. Still nothing came.

It had been too long. Now he wore pinstriped suits and had to force himself to go to the gym once a week to keep a cap on his weight, creeping up because of corporate dinners and informal interviews. Once he had had thirty men under his command, now he had three hundred, but being a personnel director in the City was a tad different from army life. He was trying to make the jump to an alien world he no longer had access to.

'Roy, look I'm sorry, but—'

'It's important, Harry.'

He heard a squeal of joy from up above and wanted to get off the phone. Roy Krok was also from that other world, one that didn't recognise or care for his kids, the kids he swore he would never have after he had seen the pain, and the agony, they could bring. It had taken him five years to realise that he was unlikely to experience in Highgate the kind of suffering he and Krok had once seen. Now he was sorry he had waited so long, especially when he saw fathers twenty years younger running around the park, while he worried about his knee giving out whenever he kicked a ball to his son. 'I know, Roy. I know.'

'You don't sound convinced.'

'Who are you these days, Roy?'

'Who am I?'

'What are you?'

'Same old, same old. State Department.'

'So why are you in New York?'

'This is where the most visa fraud is. Immigration and Natu-ralization Department, one of the busiest in the country.'

'So you're on visa fraud now?'

A touch of evasiveness. 'Um. It's a means to an end.' The tone suggested Harry shouldn't be asking these questions down an unsecured line.

Darling knew Roy Krok would be working for some strange sounding little unit within the State Department, one that was a shape and name shifter, coming up with new goals and acronyms every six months. It kept the prying eyes on their toes – 'One thing about the Freedom of Information Act,' he remembered Krok saying, 'Is you gotta know what question to ask and who to address it to. So we keep changing the address.'

'Roy, I have to go. I wish I could help.'

'You still can, Harry. Look, you're the only guy we know who saw him.'

'Bollocks.'

'Excuse me?' He could picture Krok at this moment, shirt sleeves rolled up, playing with the cigarette he wouldn't be allowed to smoke, big bullet head still shaved close, the stubble of fair hair flecked with grey now. He would bet he wasn't spreading around the girth, though.

'Bullshit. He was around for months, almost a year. I only saw him through some bins, Roy. Binoculars. I simply do not believe you can't find anyone else who knew what he looked like.'

'OK, I'll rephrase that. You are the only reliable guy we have – impeccable credentials, no axe to grind. Credible witness. Not someone who could be accused of a vendetta or hysteria. There are no photos of him, Harry – he had the last guy who took one beheaded—'

'Roy – I found the bloke.'

'Oh, yeah. Shit, Harry. I know I Fedexed a whole stack of photos, but I got a gut instinct about five of them, and there are two who smell real bad. I want you to come over.'

'Over where?'

'Here. I want you to stare them in the eyes.'

'As in a line-up?'

'No, more casual than that. You'll bump into them on the street, in the elevator, on the subway. Full back-up from us. But when you see him, smell him, you'll know. Either that or you ain't the same guy I knew.'

I'm not, he wanted to say. Far from it. He wasn't sure those senses that Krok was talking about even existed any more, if they ever did. 'I should have got a sniper up there and shot him. Nobody would've known.'

'Man, nobody this end would have blamed you. But you didn't. British officer, rules of engagement, and all that bull-shit.'

'Is this official?'

'If he's here he has committed visa fraud.' There was some-thing in his voice told him it was still personal. And that Roy was in a hurry. Why rush at it now, he wondered?

'Is that all you can get him on?'

'It'll get us to the plate. Get me up to bat. I just need to be sure. If we go with the wrong guy, the real one'll just slip away, straight down into the sewer like the turd he is. Look, you won't have to travel coach, and we'll VIP you. Meet you on the tarmac airside—'

'Collect me at the gate, Roy, I don't want all that melodramatic black limo stuff.' He realised he had fallen straight into it.

There was just a hint of suppressed elation in Krok's voice: 'Is that a yes? You'll come?'

He thought about taking leave for a week or maybe even two just as the salary review was imminent, about abandoning Sarah with the kids when Jessie was about to start nursery school and hesitated. Then he looked back at the photographs and felt a sudden jolt. Number six. The bulky, balding guy getting out of a cab, face blurred, features indistinct. But maybe. Strip away seven years and twenty pounds, it could be him. He grabbed his nose and squeezed his nostrils, as if trying to prevent the smell that had hung everywhere back then from entering, the cloying, choking smell of burnt hair and bone, the one it took thirty minutes under the shower to scrub away.

He closed his eyes and, finally, he did flash on that day. Just for a second, he saw the Warrior personnel-carrier in front of him lift as if pulled on a string, the percussive slap of the mine's detonation reaching him a moment later, followed by the rolling thunderclap of high explosive punching his ears. The vehicle left the ground and started to rotate, slowly displaying its underside, before landing on the roof with a sickening, crumpling sound, bouncing once, and coming to rest, the creaking and groaning of torn metal mixed with the unbearable shrieks of the injured inside.

That was when he had scaled a wall and scanned the village ahead for the minelayers and seen that man, the one who might be on the table in front of him now, standing before the spray-painted symbol of his murderous paramilitary unit, suitably crimson on the whitewashed wall.

'Harry? You still there? Is that a yes?'

'I suppose it is,' he found himself saying.

T W·O

Scottsdale, Arizona

The building was on one of the new roads that spring up around Scottsdale every few months. The community simply kept growing, sending new tentacles into the scrubby desert, or subdividing existing block systems to create new housing and malls. Wendy drove around several junctions before she got the right address. Solutions Inc was located in a new two-storey adobe-style structure between a bookstore and a bank, with a small parking lot around the back.

She hesitated before turning in, so long that she jumped when someone honked her to get a move on. Too late to stop now. She parked up, checked herself in the mirror, and prepared for the blast of the summer heat as she left the air-conditioned cocoon of the Saturn. She hoped Pete was all right, that Duke was looking after him OK, then put him out of her mind. This was mostly for him, after all.

Wendy walked briskly towards the entrance of Solutions Inc, knowing if she hesitated she would start melting in the heat, her prim two-piece spouting unladylike dark patches. And she had to be cool and controlled for this one, something she hadn't been for a long time.

The receptionist led her straight through a maze of what looked like hastily constructed offices, with electrical and computer and telephone leads snaking haphazardly across the floor. It wasn't what she expected. She had imagined clinical, steely. This looked like an overworked tax audit office.

She was led into a cubicle where a forty-ish woman in a white overall stood up and took her hand. 'Miss Blatand.

I'm Marion Volker. Thank you for coming. Can I get you something? Coffee? Soda?'

She declined. The rituals of pouring coffee or opening a soda would fluster her. She could feel the woman's eyes examining her as it was, making her jittery. 'You must excuse the mess out there. Business is . . . well, booming. Which is good news for you. Demand has never been higher.'

Wendy managed what she hoped was a positive smile. Volker picked up a form she recognised, one that was the size of the Phoenix yellow pages. It had taken her two days to fill it in, and a lot of phone calls.

'I'm afraid I couldn't complete all the sections on my grandparents. About illnesses.'

Volker flicked to that page. 'Yes, but they both lived until they were into their eighties. Very good. I have to be honest with you, Miss Blatand, but three, maybe even two years ago we would not have been seeing you. You are twenty-nine, and we find that demand drops off considerably after thirty. Also you . . . well, you already have a child. You know, college students are our most common applicants.'

'That's what I want the money for. To go to college.'

'Well good, that's nice to hear. Anyway, those restrictions do not apply in this case,' she lowered her voice conspiratorially. 'You are blonde blue-eyed of strong Swedish stock from – uh—'

'Minnesota.'

'Minnesota. You are what the market wants right now. It's a terrible cliché, and I wish we could help some of the . . . darker women who come in. But it's market forces. Now, Wendy, can I call you Wendy? Wendy, are you clear about the procedure?'

'I did, you know, read the literature you sent.'

'I am afraid by law I am obliged to go through it again, and get you to sign a release.'

'Sure.'

Volker started the litany, trying hard to keep the I-speak-your-weight tone from her voice. 'For three weeks you will have to inject your stomach with a drug called Ergon. What this does is put your ovaries into a state of stasis. Basically they won't be working, and none of your egg follicles – you know what they are? Good. None of your egg follicles will ripen. Then you will inject FSHs, what we call follicle stimulating hormones, into your hip. Your eggs will then start to ripen, like a clump of grapes. Eight days of that, and then HCG, human chorionic gonadotrophin, and boom, your eggs are ready for collection.'

'Does that happen . . . here?' Wendy waved her arm around the office.

'Good grief, no. You think we move the telephones off the desk and clear a space every time one of our donors comes in? You will go to the Solutions Fertility Facility, which is three blocks away. We have to put you under, and then the eggs are simply hoovered up, fertilised and implanted. But the last bit needn't worry you, Wendy. Now, I am also obliged to tell you by law that some research – not backed up by subsequent studies – but some research suggest the chemical stimulation of the ovaries increases the risk of ovarian cancer down the line. We can refer you to the papers in question if you wish. Do you have any questions?'

She knew about the cancer scare, had decided that the five years she smoked from seventeen to twenty-two were probably more of a risk. 'Yes. It said in your literature about . . . gifts.'

'That is right. Gifts. Our standard fee to you is seven thousand dollars per session. We don't recommend more than four sessions, incidentally, and reserve the right to refuse further extractions at any time. Is that clear? Now, the question of gifts is between you and the client. It has become a . . . convention for girls with certain attributes – let's say blonde hair and blue eyes for the sake of argument – to be offered bonuses if the eggs take. You may find several clients contacting you and offering these various inducements. These can be . . . considerable. I only have one comment. Get it in writing, and get it looked over by a lawyer. Anything else?'

'Do they get to interview me? The women I mean.'

'Usually both wife and husband, but I don't think you have anything to worry about there. You have no prior convictions do you?'

'I'm sorry?'

'A criminal record of any kind.'

'Speeding.'

Volker laughed for the first time. 'Well, I suppose speeding could be a genetically inherited trait.'

'Why do you want to know?'

'Increasingly clients are asking about the donor's circumstances as well as their genetic profile – do they drink, take drugs, steal, have promiscuous sex? Not all our behaviour is a product of our environment. So I am afraid that we try to exclude anyone with a criminal background.'

'I'm a single mother.'

'I know—'

'But my mom wasn't, so it hardly runs in the family.'

'Relax. It isn't a criminal offence. Not yet, anyway. And the explanation in here about your boy—'

'Pete.'

'Pete, and the tragic death of your fiancé will satisfy everyone.'

Wendy felt herself blush. Her so-called fiancé was shacked up with her sister somewhere in Chicago as they spoke. After a stupid, stupid party he had managed to have sex with both of them consecutively, without the other's knowledge, something that won him a hundred-dollar bet, and got them both banged up. She and Joanna had always done everything together – sports, books, dating, their periods and, it subsequently seemed, their ovulation. Even Mr Superstud could only marry one of them, and he chose Jo. Wendy had left before Pete was born and moved south, falling down the country like a pinball, bouncing off cities and towns, until she came to rest in Tucson.

'So when do I start?'

'As soon as a client selects you from the candidates. Which won't be long. But before that, one more little formality. I am afraid where the academic records are incomplete, like yours, clients do like to see an IQ test. It won't take long.'

Fifty minutes later she was back in her car, with the air conditioning up full blast, trying to unscramble her brain, to block out shapes and words and squiggles that had filled it during the test. Four cycles at seven thousand dollars, twenty-eight thousand, plus 'gifts', which she knew could at least double that. True, the thought of all those needles made her queasy, but what the hell, it was the kind of money to get her and Pete out of the trailer park for good.

THREE

Federal Plaza, New York City

As the man stepped onto the Plaza from the recently reopened
Jacob Javits building the heat hit him hard, a soggy wet blast of
fume-laden fug, pressure-cooked in the glass, steel and concrete
that surrounded him. He slipped off his jacket and loosened his
tie, aware that his shirt was sticking to his body already. The
air was like a wet sponge that had been microwaved, scorching
his throat.

Shouldering through the irritable lunch-time crowds turning
out from the city admin buildings all around, he took the
steps up to Broadway and squeezed through the newly erected
steel-and-concrete planters that studded the frontage of the
complex.

He crossed the Great White Way and strode beneath the
clusters of neon signs advertising all kinds of dubious legal
advice and translation services, and struck off down Chambers
Street, glancing up at the twin towers of the World Trade
Center to his left as he crossed Church, then turned right on
West Broadway, passed Odeon, where the usual well-heeled
expense-account crowd were tucking into lunch, and slipped
into Lagoon, the new Australian/Polynesian diner. After a second luxuriating in the iced stream of air funnelled across the
entrance, he was shown to a table, ordered a Tahitian fajita,
then went out back to the call box, leaving his jacket on the
chair to indicate occupation.

He found the piece of paper in his billfold – it was a
different number each week, sometimes e-mailed to him first
thing Monday, other times whispered in a cryptic call. He

dialled and waited, four rings, then hung up. Then he dialled again, and the receiver at the other end was picked up. He could hear the steady breathing somewhere down the line – it was a New Jersey number he had noted – but nothing was said. He cleared his throat. 'One-one-seven. Eleven-fifty-five.'

There was no reply so he repeated it.

'Two-Sixty Madison Street. After six,' came back. Seeex. Like a cartoon Mexican.

'Madison?' he asked with some astonishment. Christ, they were going upmarket.

'Madison *Street*.'

'Where's tha—?'

But the line was dead. Two-Sixty Madison Street. He felt the little tickling in his stomach, the sensation that always came when he crossed the line, the mix of anticipation and dread he swore he would never court again, but there it was cajoling him, seducing him. He felt himself stiffen at the prospect, and walked quickly back to the table, adjusting himself as discreetly as he could. He took out the mini-street atlas of New York from his jacket pocket and found Madison on the Lower East Side, heading for Alphabet City. Downtown this time.

His hand was shaking slightly when the food arrived, and he clumsily knocked some of the flatware on the floor. Calm down, mustn't get flustered. Got to get through the rest of the afternoon without thinking about it. About her, whoever she was, lying in a darkened room, not knowing – how could she even guess? – what he had in store for her. Would she be blonde or one of those wild, gypsy-looking brunettes? Hairy or smoother, big-breasted or pert? The options scrolled before him like a sexual-preferences menu. He didn't mind. The variety was what made it interesting.

He looked down at the stuffed maize tube, the steam curling off it into his face, and suddenly realised he wasn't hungry.

FOUR

Bloomsberry, New Jersey

Jim Barry couldn't believe his wife was making him do this. A forty-mile drive after work, just so they could coo over someone else's baby. After a trip to the liquor store for champagne and the mall for flowers and baby clothes, it was getting on for seven-thirty by the time they left Bloomsberry and turned north, heading for the State line that would take them across into New York. In the back of the Lexus sat Tommy, trying hard to put the Yankee stickers into the book straight. Yankee stickers. He was barely five and someone was poisoning his mind. Jim didn't want to bring up a Yankee fan. There were enough of them already, like locusts. Like particularly smug locusts, he corrected himself.

'Who gave you the book, Tommy?' he asked, not wanting it to sound like an issue.

'Mike Crichton,' he replied.

That figured. Dick Crichton's boy. It was some kind of subtle attempt to undermine him. They had to choose new uniforms for their ball team and Jim wanted them based on the Mets. Dick was all for pinstriped Yankees. Maybe this was part of his campaign. What was irritating was that Dick had only really become a full-on Yankees fan in '99, the season when they won twelve consecutive World Series games, twenty-two out of twenty-five, and Giuliani crawled up their collective asses to regain his flagging popularity. Jim had stuck with the Mets. It had been pain and pleasure in equal measure. Sure, you couldn't point to any glittering prizes. Certainly not a subway series. Instead you had to revel in the small victories – Piazza carrying on with a swollen thumb, Dunston, stealing bases under everybody's noses, or Melvin Mora's record in throw-outs. For a Mets fan God had to be in the details, otherwise you'd end up a baseball atheist.

He remembered what he should have been doing and hissed to Belle: 'I wanted to go through pitching with Tommy tonight.'

'I thought practice was tomorrow?' said Belle, as casually as she could. She was not in the mood for a fight. She had the envelope on her lap, toying with it, secretly thrilled. She didn't want Jim to dent her pleasure.

'It is. This is practice for the practice, you know that. Couldn't this have waited?'

'Look, Saturday you have a match with Chesterville, don't you? And on Sunday my mom is over. Besides, Mamie was so pleased when I told her you were coming. She always liked you.'

'Why they wait so long to invite us, then? I mean, most new parents invite you over to see their little darlings when the umbilical cord is still attached. How come we had to wait months?'

'I told you. Doctors were concerned about her immune system. Mamie didn't want to take any chances. Shoot, Jim, you remember how precious we were? Always worried Tommy wasn't going to make it through the night? Called out the doctor at every cough? Worried about rolling over on him if we co-slept, and Sudden Infant Death syndrome if we put him in a crib? Cut them some slack, Jim. They waited a long time for this.'

Jim grunted noncommittally. All he wanted to do right now was be out there throwing and catching and batting and running. He had sworn that he wouldn't deny his son the opportunities he had missed. His old man, he hated sports of any kind. The other kids just didn't believe it. He's a writer, Jim would explain to anyone who would ask why his dad never helped out. Yeah, he remembered one of the other dads saying, so was Hemingway, but he wasn't no pussy.

Well, nobody was going to accuse him of that. So he'd enrolled a Bloomsberry side in Pocket League, a kind of pre-Little League for New Jersey and New York States and set about creating a team around Tommy, who had one hell of an arm for a five-year-old.

'We nearly there, yet?' asked Tommy.

'No, son, but I tell you what – Uncle Morgan has a scale model of Wrigley Field.'

'Wriggly?'

'Wrigley. I told you, like the gum.'

'Not wriggly like a worm?'

'Tommy, we went though the grounds last week. Let's do it from the top. Shea Stadium.'

'Mmmmts.'

'Pardon me?'

'I'm tired.'

Jim glanced in the rearview mirror and watched the boy close his eyes and instantly feign sleep. He felt a sudden stab of irrational anger, as if he wanted to smack the boy. Tommy lacked concentration for such things. He was sure that when *he* was five he could do not only all the baseball grounds, but when they were built, too.

Belle could see the tendons strumming in his neck and she touched his knee. 'Jim. He's five. He's had a long day. You've had a long day. Me too. Relax. He can do it when he wants to—'

'I know, that's what makes me so mad. He keeps deliberately messing up the names – Mickey Mangle it was last week. Pete Wose. Wouldn't say it right. Deliberately.'

The sun was dropping in the sky now, and the fields and white houses around them had taken on a warm, orange glow. It looked beautiful, he thought, like America was meant to look, bathing in God's own sunshine at the end of a perfect day.

'Jim. It doesn't matter. The baseball.'

He shot her a glance, a quick hard stare, one he hoped that

warned her not to blaspheme like that. It Doesn't Matter. Like she knew jack shit about baseball and why it did or didn't matter. But she just smiled back, a smile that was superficially warm and conciliatory, but she was savvy enough to know this was flirting with danger. If this blew up, it wouldn't be their first snit about the national sport.

He decided to let it ride. Belle was great at indulging him, but it seemed there was a line he shouldn't cross. He knew there was some kind of razor wire behind that grin when she wanted it to be. They had left their trenches and were dancing in no-man's land. At any moment the flares could go up and the shelling would begin, followed by hand-to-hand combat. Time to let it drop.

He nodded his head towards the envelope. 'What's that?'

She couldn't help the toothy smile that expanded across her face. She poked a thumb under the edge of the flap and ripped, pulling the remittance advice form out and flipping it open. 'Oh my God. Ohmigod.'

'What?'

She held it in front of his eyes, and he had to brush it aside so he could see the road. 'Tell me.'

'One hundred and twenty-two thousand dollars.'

'Ohmigod.'

'Oh, yes, I know it's small apples compared to what Si wants to stuff in your billfold—'

'No, no. It's . . . wow.'

'Wow,' she repeated. Wow and it was all hers. Her book, 'The Maximum Child: Releasing The Full Potential Of Your Offspring' had been on the *New York Times* bestseller list for fifty weeks now, and was still selling. It was almost like a dream. Thirty months previously *New York* magazine had featured her in an article on 'boosters' – the new breed of motivational therapists who specialised in counselling already-gifted children to make sure they didn't squander their talent and burn out.

A publisher subsequently approached her with an idea for

putting her ideas down into a self-help manual for people who felt their child was better-than-average, which turned out to be most people in the Metropolitan area. It was essentially a guide to compartmentalising – helping your child separate and order their thoughts, rather than have to cope with the over-active, free-association stream of images and concepts that plagued so many gifted children. The Edison effect it was called – after the genius whose random juxtapositions had generated so many groundbreaking innovations. Her job was to calm the constant brainstorming, help them separate static and signal, and focus. OK, they may not invent the equivalent of the telephone, but it might help them excel in one field rather than be spordically brilliant in many.

Now she was based in the exclusive Institute for Child Enhancement on the Upper East Side four days a week, and charging three hundred bucks an hour to repeat verbatim what was in the fifteen-dollar book to star-struck parents and their precocious children.

'Well done,' said Jim, trying not to sound patronising. He must keep the irritation out of his voice. He had always hoped to be the first in the family to publish. True, hers was just one of those improvement manuals that always sells to the gullible, and his would be a novel, but still, the shelf at home held a dozen proudly displayed copies of 'The Maximum Child', and no work by him.

'Ye-es,' she said slowly. 'If it keeps on coming, maybe I could give up ICE. You know, I had one couple in today wanting to know why their daughter seemed to be the only Asian in America who wasn't a violin prodigy. Three hundred dollars for me to tell them that, hey, somebody's got to be in the audience.'

The truth was, much of the time it wasn't the kids who needed talking up, but the parents who required talking down. Now and then she felt like saying, what this child needs is a couple of hours a day to kick a tin can round an empty lot or watch *Dawson's Creek* and eat junk food. But, it seemed, doing nothing was a luxury most kids didn't get these days. 'Next left, up here,' she said.

'I know.' Snappy.

The Starkeys' house was a handsome turn-of-the-century grey stone structure, two storeys, with detached garage, set well back from the road, with close to an acre of grounds around it. Morgan, however, had done his best to ruin the lines of the house, in a way that simply would not be tolerated in the city. The original wooden windows had been torn out, replaced with triple-glazed sealed units; rotating solar panels, like some junked props from *Babylon 5*, studded the sides, and hot-air recycling pipes snaked over the roof tiles, in between the metal vents that could be opened in high summer to cut down on air conditioning. Out the back, he knew, were composting bins, methane generators and a vegetable patch. The Starkeys were slowly becoming eco-bores.

Morgan Starkey had worked with Jim Barry on *Our Thing*, his magazine – their magazine – when it had been a cross between the old 1950s *Esquire* and *George*. And sold about fifty thousand copies. Jim had decided that the injection of some tasteful European-style raunch – more upmarket than the *Maxim* and *Loaded* boys who had just come farting and leering onto the scene – would do wonders for their circulation. It did more than wonders, it so incensed Morgan and his newly discovered green ways, that he resigned. Jim had bought him out and his old pal had moved across the State line to try and create a low-impact lifestyle.

Now Condé Nast wanted to buy into *Our Thing*, which was bound to make Morgan mad. Had he stuck with it, accepted the rising nipple count, he would be seeing five, six mil now. Too late, old buddy. Shouldn't have been such a prude.

But Jim was worried about Condé Nast's intentions. Why did they want another magazine when they had killed *Details*? Did they have plans for it that he should know about? He shouldn't really care, but he was still proprietorial enough to feel protective about his two big stories. One was the murky Nazi background of a major fashion house – in its previous incarnation it had designed the SS uniforms, so it was alleged. Would Condé Nast run something that might damage an advertiser? He hoped so. The second one was more up their street. The inside story of the hit on Zeljko Raznatovic, better known as Arkan, in Belgrade. Great story – even though you knew the ending, it generated a kind of *Day of the Jackal* tension – and the writer was a fabulous young reporter. He wondered if they might want to lift it for one of their more established titles.

Still, if he got even a fraction of some of the figures that had been tossed around, he should fret about what Conde Nast did to his magazine. Maybe he could use some of the windfall to fund Morgan when he finally got that 'hip eco-mag' as he called it off the ground – a lifestyle magazine where every aspect was designed to be as guilt-free as possible, from the kind of investments and clothes it recommended (no closet Nazis here) right down to the paper and the inks used, without sacrificing good taste and having to wear shoes made from banana leaves. He wasn't too sure about *Stalk* as a title though – it sounded like a self-help manual for perverts or a marijuana-growing tipsheet.

Whatever he called it, Jim knew the time was wrong for such a mag right now. The shaky economy of the last three years had meant nobody gave a fuck about anything other than saving five cents on the dollar – green issues were less important than greenbacks. But with the property market taking off, the Dow and Nasdaq recovering, and unemployment down, maybe, in a year or two, it could work.

Jim pulled the Lexus next to the natural-gas-powered Chrysler that Morgan drove, and stepped out. Tommy had passed from feigning sleep to the real thing and Belle motioned for Jim to leave him be for a while as she gathered up the flowers and he grabbed the Mumm.

Morgan was already out of the house, looking lean and fit now he had dispensed with all those Manhattan lunches, hand outstretched, a grin wider than the Chrysler's grille filling his face, pumping their hands, ushering them in for the big unveiling. His skin looked a little grey, maybe he was baggier around the eyes, but recent fathers always seemed washed out, probably from rhapsodising about nothing but the product of their loins. Barry knew there wouldn't be any magazine or ballgame or even ozone-hole talk tonight. He put on his best coochie-coochie-coo face and followed Belle inside.

Morgan had the table now. His turn at the figurative mike. They had eaten the first course – rod-caught salmon from British Columbia and Mamie was at the wood-fired range finishing off her signature chicken dish – organic, no doubt lived a life of such indolent pampering that it was a poultry version of Ivana Trump, thought Jim – with one ear on the table conversation. There had been a little ripple of tension in the air when Jim and Belle had arrived, a slight thickness, as if they had walked in on an argument, but that had dissipated quickly.

Morgan and Mamie's kitchen/diner was full of local antiques, everything wooden and polished and scratched and chipped, well worn but well loved. It felt comfortable, more homely – and that wasn't meant as an insult – than any of those *Metropolitan Living* shiny, shiny installations Belle found herself lusting after. This was a place you could fold into. Perfect for reforming the bonds of friendship that had loosened and frayed over the last year or more.

Morgan continued his soliloquy. 'OK, so after that I took her to the Rainbow Room. I know, I know, cheesy or what? But I was out to impress. I'd been earning real money for two months at this point, and it was my idea of being a high-roller.'

Jim poured himself another glass of merlot, swilled it round his glass and smiled to himself, lining up his own next story.

'And we have a dance on the revolving floor and don't put too much work the podiatrists way. I wouldn't say cutting a rug, exactly, more like giving the carpet a small trim. So Mamie decides after the second number that it's a good time to powder her nose. We still said things like that back then. This being before you get to the "Hey, Morg, I gotta take a crap" stage of a relationship—'

'Morgan,' squealed Mamie in horror. 'I have never said that to you.'

They all laughed while Morgan took a mouthful of the wine. There was a time when the group had been bigger. Perhaps a dozen, a group of young couples all in publishing media, who met for barbecues and went upstate for weekends or out to the beach together. Then some had kids and fell away, and, for the most part, somewhere along the line, one by one, they changed partners, which put fractures in the collective psyche. With new faces in the group, suddenly stories of the early days were deemed to be too exclusive, tainted by the unspoken presence of the earlier companion. Until there were just the four of them left who all went back to the same point, in and around Madison, and who still shared the marital bed with the person they had wooed back then. Jim and Belle and Morgan and Mamie.

So Morgan's story – one of a library of perhaps twenty – had a ritualistic quality, like a well-loved piece of prose, brought out and mulled over every now and then whenever this original quartet convened. Like a reading from a very secular version of the Talmud or Koran. Jim smiled a secret smile to himself again as he decided he would tell his duck fart story. That always went down well.

'So,' Morgan continued. 'I see Mamie coming back from the Ladies' Room to our table, which is aways from the dance floor. And as she comes I see the waves in the crowd, the movement of heads, swivelling, marvelling at that loose-limbed walk, sexy and confident and at that moment I just felt like the proudest guy in the world. That was *my* woman they were looking at. I would be taking her home that night.' Another hiatus. 'It wasn't till she reached the table I saw why they were all staring. She had left her skirt tucked into her pantyhose.'

The four of them chortled, even Mamie, who had, as always when this ignominious tale came out, blushed to her roots. As the laughter died they heard the baby squawk over the monitor. 'Shit,' said Mamie, slamming down a spatula. 'Just in time for the entrée.'

The heat of the day had been cut by a shower by the time Wendy got back from Scottsdale. Driving down the undulating Mango Road, on the eastern edge of Tucson, skirting the south side of what the locals insisted on calling the Rillito River, although she had only seen water running in the wash once since she arrived, Wendy turned off the air conditioning, lowered the window and sniffed. The air carried the aroma of warm rain on hot earth, moisture that had either evaporated or been hungrily sucked away by the soil. Although not as greedily as once, maybe. This summer was wet. Most days the afternoon thunderheads built up over the jagged profile of the Santa Catalina mountains before her, towering higher and higher, like some bizarre meteorological version of Marge Simpson's hair. Then came the deluge, the monsoon as they called it round here, rain or hail pounding the desert as if trying to punish it for some heinous crime.

The result of the downpours was all around, the green ground cover where there was once over-grazed scrub, the barrel cacti throwing out two, three crimson flowers each, the orange of Arizona poppies, and the purple/violet of desert asters run rampant. The thirst-quenched wilderness was blooming. Still not enough water to fill the Rillito, though.

She made the turn into Quality Street – a sick joke on someone's part – and into the dusty lot of the trailer park that was, currently, all that sat on the two-hundred-acre lot. Twenty trailers, randomly scattered over the land, hidden from the road by a row of junipers and saguaros, otherwise certainly an eyesore. They wouldn't be here for too much longer. This land, nudging the very edges of Tucson City limits, had been part of the disputed Gadsen Purchase of 1854, and had recently been ceded back to the Mexican government by a court in Madrid. They in turn had leased it to a Dallas company who were currently seeking permission to build yet another 'adults only' retirement community, with maybe a drying-out clinic – the real Arizona growth industry – as an adjunct.

In the meantime, some of the new arrivals who serviced all the existing communities, spas, clinics and bars now had cheap trailer homes to live in, generating some income for the new owners while the exact boundaries of the land were defined.

Wendy pulled up in the lot and looked over at the trailers. Duke and Pete were playing catch out front. Duke had opened the door of her unit and the Chili Peppers were blasting out, loud and distorted, which was why he hadn't heard her drive up. She could detect another sound, another guitar playing a different tune, almost lost in the pounding of the Chilis. The guy opposite, the axeman whom she heard every now and then but rarely saw.

Duke was in a grubby singlet and cargo pants, and she couldn't help admire the way his arms glistened with sweat. He was twenty-seven and, she knew, more or less total trouble, but there was no doubt he was easy on the eye.

Pete missed the ball and went sprinting past her trailer into the back lot after it. She had tried to rope it off into a garden of sorts, even planted a tree where they had buried Noodler, Duke's dog that had been hit by an SUV illegally pounding the scrubby tracks that criss-crossed the area, but the desert had its own way of doing things, and she gave up trying to tame it and now let it run wild. Suddenly, jarringly, Pete screamed and she found herself running over to the trailer, even though she had heels on she could barely walk in.

'Pete, what is it?' she shouted.

Duke scratched his backside as she came by and said: 'Oh, Wendy. Hi.' He showed no inclination to go and find out what was wrong with the boy.

'*Mom.*'

Torn between the two of them she gave Duke a quick sardonic smile and sprinted, ankle-threateningly, to look at her son. She tried to keep a cap on the panic bulletins being flashed from her cerebrum – snake, tarantula, scorpion. 'What is it, honey? Let me see. Oh, just a few spines. We'll get them out. C'mon.' She looked at Duke, who was taking his own goddamn time coming over, but her relief meant she couldn't be angry. 'Hi. You OK?'

'Yup.'

They walked into the trailer together and, as casually as she could, she turned down the music before she headed for the bathroom.

'How'd it go?' he asked.

She rummaged through the chaos of the medicine chest. 'What?'

'The interview.'

'Oh that.' She'd decided that her plans to do a little body-part harvesting was no business of Duke's. How much money it involved certainly wasn't. As far as he knew it was a clerical job. 'Kinda OK. They'll let me know.' She emerged with the tweezers and ointment. 'Thanks for lookin' after Pete.'

Duke shrugged. ''S OK. Look I gotta split now. Said I'd help get an MD-9 ready for inspection. Will I see ya later?'

She carefully pulled out the first of the cacti spines from Pete's thumb, dobbed at the tiny sphere of blood, and applied some of the antiseptic. He just stood there staring with those big ice-blue eyes, each one cradling a large globule of tears, almost hidden under the blond fringe. She must get his hair cut.

'I . . . I'm real tired, Duke. I mean . . . bushed, y'know.'

'Hey – don't put yourself out.' He ambled over and pulled a beer from the refrigerator. 'I thought you might be workin' tonight anyways.'

'Tomorrow. But . . .' She hesitated to ask again. 'Look, Sherry has let me down again and . . . I wondered . . . wondered if you could . . .'

'What?'

'Look after Pete.'

'What again?' he asked in amazement. 'Like twice in two days? Shit, it's not like we're married or nothin'.'

'Duke, I wouldn't . . . I'm desperate.'

He raised an eyebrow as if an idea had just occurred to him. 'How about I drop by later and we talk it over? Sure I can think of some way of doin' it.'

She sighed inwardly. Dropping by later meant rolling up at midnight and humping her brains out, regardless of whether she was awake or not. And she was tired. But what the hell.

'Great,' she found herself saying. 'But not too late, eh?'

He gulped down the rest of the beer, letting it spill over his chin and down the singlet and let out a belch. 'Darlin', I never come late, never come early you know that. Always right on the money. Deadeye Duke.' He winked suggestively as he left.

After he had gone she switched the CD over to Mary J Blige, and fixed her and Pete some tacos and beans, which they ate on their knees while he watched *Pokémon – The Next Generation*. She knew she should stop him watching TV and eating, but it was hard to have strict rules with Duke as his only real male role-model. Duke should be better than this – shit he was a qualified helicopter pilot, but after that big bust-up at the Canyon he seemed to have lost heart. She knew he hadn't really tried to find another job. 'They layin' us off all over. The new lepers. Hawaii, Niagara, all those fuckin' Sierra Club types tryin' to get us banned from flight-seeing anywhere. Even New York now – used the excuse of that chopper strayin' into La Guardia airspace to scrap half the round-Manhattan flights.'

He had neglected to mention that the collision had brought down a USAir 727, killing all on board.

Trouble with Duke was, his desire to fly helicopters was fired by old Vietnam movies, *Apocalypse Now* and *Platoon* and

Tour of Duty. On screen it was manly, maverick work, chopper pilots were a brotherhood, a secret society mere fixed-wing fly-boys would never gain entrance to. So now that it had been taken away from him, he had a chip on his shoulder like a genuine Vet who had been given a raw deal.

Despite his small tantrum when she shut off the TV, she managed to get Pete into bed by seven, giving herself four or five hours before Duke came back. Wendy poured herself a glass of the Cabernet that Cecco had given her from the bar, put her feet up. She thought back to the meeting at the clinic, and of all those chemicals and injections, wondered what effect it would have on sex. Shit, that was what she meant to ask – would her sex drive rise or plummet? And should she have sex at all? It would all be a waste of time if she got banged up during the process. She'd have to call that Volker woman and ask. Mustn't dwell on it for the moment, or she'd never get to sleep.

It was all a means to an end, she reminded herself. An escape route, an escape from the torpor that she had allowed to overwhelm her. Torpor and self-pity, a powerful narcotic. They said being pregnant scrambled your brains for a while. Well, somehow, it had lasted five years with her, five years without focus or direction. Maybe that was over now.

Wendy was about to hit the remote for the Mary J to repeat when she heard the guitar player across the way start up long, fast, sinuous runs, hesitant at first, then gaining in volume and fluency, part blues, part jazz, then dropping into a standard. She knew the tune. Most of what the guy did, she didn't recognise at all, but this one . . . Love for Sale, that was it. Love for Sale. Well, she certainly knew how that felt after today.

It was late by the time they got away, and Belle drove because Jim felt a little like Tommy had before, dozy, except his heavy lids came courtesy of the half-dozen glasses of wine he had downed. Ironically, Tommy himself had woken up and was full of beans, listening to a Harry Potter download on his MP3 player.

Jim was just letting his head drop when Belle said. 'Whaddayathink?'

His head jerked and he felt something go in his neck. 'Ow. Shit. Got to get some massage on this. Been stiff since last week's practice.'

'It's meant to be for the kids, not you, y'know.' She thought grown men swinging and pitching in front of what were almost babies faintly ridiculous.

'Someone's gotta show 'em the moves.'

Yeah, and indulge in a little fantasy where the people throwing balls at him are not some three-foot high kids but Cy Young or Sandy Koufax or Bob Gibson – names he mentioned so often as perfect pitchers, they even stuck in *her* mind, never mind Tommy's. She wondered if she should bring up the question that had been raised at her book-circle meeting the previous night, but decided not to. Was it up to Jim alone who was in the squad, anyway? Other fathers sometimes helped out, although few with the zeal of Jim, it was true. But maybe she could appeal to a group of them, when Jim might be a little less inflexible. 'What about Dick Crichton?'

'Dick? He only comes to one-in-two games, always pulling that pressure-of-work shit. He's a fuckin' civil servant.'

'Jim, do you mind?' He shot her a puzzled glance. 'The language?'

She knew Dick Crichton mainly as one of those men who spent most of his time giving your tits furtive glances, thinking neither you nor your husband would notice. She liked him, he was a big, muscular guy with a nice kid whose wife had, so they said, gone off with his boss, so maybe she felt sorry for him too, but she liked people to look you in the eye, not the chest, when you talked to them.

He pointed to the back seat with his thumb. 'He's got phones on. Besides I heard one of the kids call another a toothless cocksucker the other night.' He glanced over to make sure none of this was leaking through the headset, but Tommy

ROB RYAN

was engrossed. 'What did I think? I think I'd forgotten how all houses with kids in 'em smell of shit, and that everyone except the parents can smell it. And God, didn't Morgan look rough when you got up close? I swear that was some of Mamie's make-up under his eyes.'

'You also forgot what we both looked like at that stage. Three and a half months, fourteen weeks of sleeplessness. We could have got a part in one of those terrible zombie films that were your idea of a date movie.'

'That was art. That was George A Romero.'

'Yeah. A guy kind of art, if you ask me. Like that other one . . . what was it? Mel Gibson? You made us see it three times?'

'*Mad Max*? *The Road Warrior*?'

'Right. So tell me, I always wanted to ask you this one, but, you know, we were in love back then, I didn't want to ruin the mood.'

'We're not in love now?' he asked warily, wondering if she was using Mel as some cunning ruse to break the news to him. After the way their friends had been decimated, he was beginning to accept it was inevitable their turn would come. Then there were two, maybe.

'I'm teasing you. So tell me this – *The Road Warrior* is all about a world shortage of gas. Yeah?'

He nodded. 'Yeeeah.'

'So why does everyone rev their engines quite so much if it's so damned precious? They must burn a whole tanker's worth just opening the throttle of the bikes. Vrooom, vrooom.'

He laughed. 'You're right. That is definitely a chick's take on *Mad Max*.'

'So what about the baby's name? Ariel?' she asked suddenly.

'Ariel? I wanted to ask. What kind of a name is that?'

'Two thoughts. It's *The Little Mermaid*. Disney.'

'Disney? Still, I guess it could've been worse.'

'What, *Pocahontas*?'

'I guess. Or? What else?'

36

'It's Shakespeare.'

Knowing Morgan they both said together: 'Shakespeare.'

Jim would have liked to stop for another drink now, the buzz was going, but he shouldn't. He had a meeting in the morning with Jack Hooper, the lawyer who was dealing with the Newhouse people.

'Anyway,' she said, 'did you look at the baby?'

'Course I looked at it,' he said, 'Morgan insisted I let it piss all down my shirt. Look.'

'Didn't you notice?'

'What that it didn't have a diaper on? He said it'd be OK, she'd just pissed and pooped a stack.'

'No, didn't you notice about the kid? Ariel, we must start calling her by her name.'

'No, what?' Incipient sobriety was making him tetchy. Was Belle going to pull out some psycho-shit about the baby's Environmental Awareness Index or Daley's Cognitive Stage Acceleration. Or was it something more basic? Did he miss something? Six fingers? A third eye?

She risked taking her eyes off the road and staring at him. 'Jim. The kid looked Mexican.'

He found the address on Madison easy enough. Most of the street consisted of those big, ugly brown towers that dominate the south-east tip of Manhattan and most of FDR Drive, but this was a run of three lonely walk-up tenements, last survivors of a previous housing era. His one was four storeys, dingy and run down, whereas both of its neighbours had been spruced up, a lick of paint, a bit of carpentry on the stoop.

His contacts clearly had the whole place, probably on a short term lease, maybe before some developers moved in, possibly before it was torn down. The windows were so dirty, you couldn't tell if there were drapes or not. Some lacked glass – pressed oil cans or packing cases did duty instead. It was the architectural equivalent of the alcos and crackheads who had started colonising Avenue D, the façade shrieking all the details of a dissolute, damaging life. The only new thing on the entire frontage was a doorbell, which he rang.

The man who opened the door looked at him with mistrustful eyes. He was tall, over six-two, but rake thin and stooped. His cheekbones protruded in his face, giving him a dangerous, half-starved look, but it was easy to guess his problem was deeper than three square meals a day. The only luxuriant thing about him was a big black moustache. He raised his head in a what-you-want gesture.

'I'm expected.'

'Name?' asked Mr Moustache in heavily accented English.

He just snorted. 'Ask Schmee.'

'Ah. The Creep,' he said, daring him to make something of the insult. 'Yes, you are expected.' Moustache laughed as if at some private joke, causing his facial furniture to shake, before standing aside. Not so private, he reflected. He knew it was what they all called him. The Creep. Funny thing was, away from all this, when he thought back to the depths he mined in these rooms, he agreed with the nickname. It was another man, a different human being, one that made even his own flesh crawl. He went inside, trying not to take in the smell, mildew and damp, mixed with bodily secretions ancient and new.

'What's in the case?' Mr Moustache pointed at the attaché he was holding.

'Ask Schmee.'

The guy shrugged, as if it were too much bother. 'Top floor. Blue door.'

The Creep sighed. Always the hard-man peacock display to put up with. He walked slowly up groaning stairs, the carpet long faded to black and semi-liquified, coarse sacking showing through. It wasn't the best venue he'd ever been to, he had to admit. Still, he knew, next week it could be some swank place on the Upper East Side or the upstairs room at the club in Queens. You never could tell.

On each landing someone sat in a chair, smoking, only half interested in him, reading a newspaper in the gloomy light, one of them oiling a gun he had stripped down on an old McDonald's tray he had on his knees, springs and bullets dotting Ronald's long-faded *Bug's Life* promotion. The man looked up. He recognised him. Tarr, the one with the arms full of tattoos. 'Hi,' Tarr said. He ignored him. The Creep, he reminded himself. That's what they were thinking. He shouldn't take it personally. Maybe what he liked to do to his girls did seem strange. It was none of their business, so fuck them.

There were three doors on the top floor, and despite extra light from a grimy pane in the ceiling, he couldn't tell which one was supposed to be blue.

'First left,' Tarr shouted up after a few seconds. Still he hesitated, steeling himself, listening to a heart pounding wildly. He was panting, there was no air up here, just an atmosphere made of superheated treacle, so viscous it was hard to suck into the lungs. He counted to three, turned the handle and stepped in.

This was one of the rooms with drapes, but they barely covered the windows. The filth on the glass inside and out did the better part of shutting down the light to a twilight grey. He heard a familiar scuttling and scratching, looked at the brown stains and crushed carapaces that peppered the walls where someone had gone on a killing spree. Roaches.

She was over in the corner, on a bed that complemented the windows perfectly, worn ticking, a few meagre blankets, a pillow you wouldn't want to put your head on.

He went over and touched her and she jumped. Slowly, gently he helped her to her feet and pulled off the rags that covered the bed. The stains, most of them old, a few freshly secreted, were a codex of neglect, filth and degradation. From the attaché he took a sheet that glowed blindingly white in the setting, almost like a shroud, and laid it across everything including the pillow. Standing next to him, she kept her shoulders together, her arms folded across her breasts. She was hiccupping out long, pitiful sobs. He held her face, cupped it in his two hands and looked at her, trying to see if she was pretty, guess the age. Old enough, he figured. 'Get undressed and lie down,' he said.

For a moment he thought she would resist, which surprised him – by the time he got them, they were normally compliant. After a few more sobs she began to do as he said. This was the stage he liked them at – broken but not hardened, bruised but not yet scarred by the succession of men who would come through this room for the next six months, year, two years. She shrugged off the slip dress she was wearing and was naked underneath. A body almost as pale as the sheet, save for the odd red weal here and there and the dark bush of her pubic hair.

'Lie down.'

She stood shivering, like a rabbit caught in the headlights. He grabbed her shoulders and pushed her down. He realised she had seen what else he had in the case. He felt a little angry. They were for later. When they knew each other a little better. 'Just relax. Be better for both of us,' he said, as he started to undo his belt, wondering if she actually understood a word he was saying.

Jim rolled into bed next to Belle, who grunted irritably. She had emptied her mind of all the worries about Morgan and Mamie and their high-volume baby, and had just been dropping off into that wonderful half-slumber, and here he came, an hour after she had plumped the pillows and brushed her hair and cleaned her teeth, jabbing at her with his hard-on like some jousting mediaeval knight. You would have thought he could get the aim right by now, rather than continually trying to slide up her ass. Or maybe that was the idea. She hated the way what was once a great taboo had become part of the mainstream and you were belittled if you wanted sex to resemble something other than severe constipation. She had tried it once – not with Jim, although she would never tell him that – and she couldn't see what all the fuss was about, apart from the fact it was pushing the boundaries. Well, her boundaries had been sore for a good two days afterwards, and she didn't want it again.

She arched her bottom up to allow him to slide inside the designated space and said, 'Don't worry about me. I'll enjoy it.' Jim buffeted her for a few minutes, reminding her of that bad plane ride she had back from Chicago once, and then came in a quick judder. He kissed her ear, rolled over and was snoring within three minutes. She, on the other hand, had been thoroughly woken. Furtively she slid her hand between her legs to see if it was worth some attention, but Jim's little performance hadn't done much for her arousal. She wondered if she should present Jim with a table of his sexual performances like baseball stats. Innings started, orgasms achieved for one or both, points added for a simultaneous number. She bet she could come up with a way that would make him pay more attention then a lazy hump-from-behind because he couldn't be bothered to clamber on top. Well, maybe every couple came down to this after a while.

She tossed and turned, trying to get comfortable, poking him when his snuffling got too bad, and thought about Mamie trying to cope with that baby. She didn't envy her.

Belle knew that soon she and Jim would have to face up to whether they wanted a sibling for Tommy. A girl, please Lord, a girl, something to cut the jock testosterone levels in this house. The thought of three big lugs lounging in front of the TV, flicking from sport to sport, was just too depressing. But whatever sex it is, she thought as she drifted away, give me a baby who sleeps.

FIVE

JFK Airport, NYC

The plane landed right on time, and Harry Darling stretched his legs, luxuriating in the fact he could hardly touch the seat in front. He had forgotten just how fast a transatlantic flight went if you turned left when you entered the aircraft. He looked at his watch. Almost midday New York time, which meant it was . . . five o'clock back in London. Kids would just be having dinner, noisy, messy, chaotic, exhausting but fun. At least, when you didn't have to do it every day. His wife assured him the novelty did wear off.

The pilot announced a delay to the gate and Darling slumped back down in the seat. Within minutes the temperature started to rise as the sun beat down on the skin of the plane. He was now doubly glad he wasn't crowded in cattle class. He bet Roy was gnashing his teeth landside, waiting for him to get through. He was fairly sure he wouldn't be allowed a chance to check in, shave, enjoy the skyline. It would be straight downtown and to work, looking at photos again, planning how they could get him a look at the prime suspects.

He touched his jacket and felt the bulk of the package in his inside pocket. It was his talisman, a simple watch, a Sekonda, cheap, reliable. Except this one hadn't worked since 2.55 p.m., Tuesday August 5 1999. It had been half melted in the fire that had killed the entire Simatovic family. Grandfather, father, wife, son, daughter and unborn child, and three others who remained unidentified.

He remembered standing by as the medical team bagged up the bodies, carefully trying to sort the twisted, blackened remnants into whole people, their breath coming heavy through the masks. He had bent down and picked up the watch, wondering why it wasn't on a wrist. Maybe loot, dropped. Maybe an attempt at bartering for a life or lives, with a pathetic twenty-dollar watch. Whatever, he had pocketed it, because he never wanted to lose the feeling he had in that room. As he had stepped outside he looked up at the wall where the leering skull and crossbones were still glinting at him. It had been the perfect way to cover their retreat. Torch the village with the inhabitants tied up inside. The bastards knew the Brits would try and get them out rather than give chase. Because they still had some human decency left.

He had clenched his jaw so hard in frustration, part of his front tooth had chipped, a serrated surface he still worried with his tongue whenever he was stressed or anxious. 'Sergeant,' he recalled saying. 'Get some paint and obliterate that fucking monstrosity.' It might have been a futile gesture, painting out the skull, but it had made him feel better.

'Ladies and gentlemen, once more welcome to JFK,' the purser announced. 'We have been given clearance to the gate.'

Immigration was surprisingly painless, not the long snaking lines he recalled from his first trips to New York. He retrieved his baggage, skirted the Department of Agriculture beagles, handed over the white Customs slip promising he had no food on his person, and passed through the glass sliding-doors where Roy exploded all over him.

'Harry, Harry, how are you? You look great. Good flight? Here let me take that. I told you we should have picked you up on the tarmac. All this bureaucracy – it's for regular folk, Harry. This way, we're on the roof, have to take the elevator. Look, I hope you don't mind, but I thought before you went to the hotel – you're in the Sherry, they do us a good deal – could you come down to the office with us and we'll go over the battle plan, if you will? That OK?'

Roy was just as he had imagined. Older, sure, but the service kept him hard and trim, and Harry suddenly felt slow and lardy next to the guy. 'That'll be fine, Roy, but do we have to sprint to the car?'

'What? Oh, yeah. I'm just chomping at the bit. Thanks for comin', I got a lot to fill you in on. Five days, it ain't a lot.'

They had slowed down to a more sedate walk, and Harry was able to converse almost normally. 'Roy, forgive me, but who are you now exactly? Just so I know.'

'Right now? Right now I answer to the Assistant Secretary for Intelligence and Research.' He laughed. 'I suppose we are a sub-division of INR. They had a competition on G-Web to give us a name.'

'G-Web?'

'G-Web. I guess there's no reason why you should know about it. Back in the Nineties? When the Bureau hired all those computer nerds? To fight white-collar computer crime and viruses? Well, a couple of them set up this unofficial site for disgruntled Feds. You know, like the one airline pilots have? Where they can beef about the job anonymously? Report near-misses, that kind of shit? G-Web is the same. It's a chance to say your director is an asshole and Washington sucks without getting canned.'

'And they allow this?'

'Hey, it's a steam valve, Harry. Block it up and a coupla guys liable to explode. Besides, it's also a helpline. You know – I got this case, anyone throw me a lead?'

'So what won?'

'What?'

'You said about a competition? I thought you guys were the men in grey? How come they know enough about you to have a competition?'

'This isn't public access. It's run and used by the kinda guys whose job it is to know every dirty little nook and cranny in Washington. Those boffins made sure it was real hard to access unless you know the right passwords.'

They reached the elevators and went in, Krok punching the button for the rooftop car park.

'Roy – what won?'

'Oh, S.O.L.V.E.'

'Solve?'

'Es-oh-el-vee-ee. S.O.L.V.E. Special Operations and Logistics in Volatile Environments.'

Darling laughed. The Yanks always liked to dress things up in such portentous terms, gave them some kind of spurious authority to go poking their nose in where it wasn't welcome. Mind you, the Brits wrote the book on that.

'What? You don't like it?' asked Krok in mock horror.

'It's just a little . . . a bit like U.N.C.L.E. or S.P.E.C.T.R.E., isn't it?'

The intense aroma of sun-baked rubber and plastic welcomed them to the rooftop, rows of cars glistening in the midday sun. 'I guess. Maybe that's why everyone here loves it. Makes 'em feel like . . . what was the guy? Napoleon Solo. Hell, if you can't have a little fun with this whole business, what's the point? Over here.'

They swerved left and the lightness left Krok's voice as he said: 'OK. I gotta level with you. The reason I was so damned pushy to get you here is that we are being shut down.'

'Shut down?'

'The last of the Ames' chickens come home to roost. All so-called intelligence functions under the State Department are being centralised to DI, and the Directorate doesn't give jack shit for what we've been doing.'

Aldrich Ames was a CIA operative who had been arrested more than a decade previously, but the shock waves of the case were still rippling through the community. This mole should have been picked up – or at the very least relieved of his duties – well before he caused the death and torture of operatives in the old Soviet Union. But the CIA culture which said that one of their own – not even an incompetent drunk like Ames – could not possibly be a traitor meant he went undetected for too long.

46

The fact that the first the new CIA director at the time heard of the Ames case was what he read in the paper didn't help. Since then the US intelligence machinery had been through dozens of reviews to try to restructure it into something for the modern world. It looked like Krok was deemed surplus to requirement.

'What will you do?'

'Oh, push paper around in Washington. Point is, I'd like to wrap this thing up, if nothing else, before we get shipped out. Wrap it up, or at least give ICTY over there something to chew on.'

'They are very slow chewers these days, Roy. We're part of the last century, remember. How long you got?'

'Six weeks. That's us here.'

He pointed across the lot towards a town car, darkened windows, but otherwise unremarkable. As they approached, the driver got out. Black, grey suit, shades, bulky, but again unremarkable. 'That's Steve Schatz. Please, no jokes about the name. He's real good.'

They were about ten yards away when Schatz seemed to stumble, as if he had stubbed his toe. Except he hadn't been moving. Krok stopped, then dropped Harry's case. Schatz spun round, as if looking to see where a blow had come from. Darling gasped when he saw the big patch of dark spreading across the grey fabric of the suit. The guy had taken a heavy round in the back, one which would have catapulted any normal man over the car in front.

Instinctively, Krok took stock of their position, moving his body slightly to protect Harry. They were a short sprint shy of the nearest vehicles for cover, and it was a long, bright, exposed run back to the elevators. He put a hand on Darling's shoulder and pushed him to a crouching position.

The first shot, the one that hit Schatz, must have been silenced, but the next ones weren't. There was the flat bark of a sub-machine-gun, and this time Schatz went down, sprawling over the bonnet of a Ford, bits of flesh and blood hitting the windshield seconds before it crazed into a milky web.

Roy realised they had to go back, he tried to spin Darling round when a shotgun blast ripped his legs from under him, shredding his trousers, and tearing the flesh from one calf like the meat off a ham bone. The second round hit his waist, chomping a bite of flesh and guts, spraying it across the oily concrete.

The air was filled with another sound, a jet taking off, almost drowning out the flat snapping sound of the next two shots that threw up a mist of dust and grit, momentarily blinding Harry. His very old, rusty instincts made him reach for the gun in Roy's hand, a Glock he noticed. He stood up and spun, squinting into the harsh, bleached daylight, trying to pick out the assailants. He could see one beyond Schatz, threading between the lines of parked cars, too far for a convincing shot. Another near the elevator, cutting him off. Then another and another. Five, six. Jesus, he was surrounded. He could see weapons being raised. He thought about his kids just finishing their yoghurts, their faces a beguiling mess of smeared dessert. He raised the Glock and fired at the elevator man, hitting him, he reckoned, seconds before a fusillade from every point of the compass tore into him, snuffing out his life.

The New Jersey docks had a breeze, a light wind blowing between the stacks of containers, taking the edge off the soupy heat that embraced the rest of the town. Hoek and his group of six helpers walked between stacks of big battered metal boxes, all with their paint flaking off, the stencils and logos faded and worn by a thousand loadings and unloadings, a hundred voyages strapped to open decks, corroded by salt air and, occasionally, pounded by waves. This was the dog end of the complex, where cheap rubbish was dumped. Hoek laughed to himself. Rubbish it might be. Cheap it wasn't.

He walked through the dark, grimy canyons created by the slabs of corrugated metal, and emerged into a small clearing, a kind of industrial piazza, closed on three sides, with the fourth open to the river, where men took their breaks away from the prying eyes of the Port Authority. The floor was littered with the evidence, mounds of polystyrene cups and fast-food containers and candy wrappers. On the dockside, a single container had been laid down by the overhead crane so it was separate from all the others, back to the harbourside, front facing into the square.

Two men stood on either side, one Hoek didn't recognise, another he knew was Mason, their man in the Port Authority, a bull-necked bruiser with skin like lemon-rind. Mason was looking impatient. Fuck him.

'We been here an hour already,' he said testily to Hoek. 'It's not like we ain't got a real job to do.'

'How long has *this* been here?' Hoek pointed at the scratched and stained yellow box.

'I dunno. Ten, maybe twelve hours.'

'Why the fook wasn't I told?' Hoek stepped forward, his podgy face bunched up with anger.

Mason took a step back, banging his shoulder on the edge of the metal box. 'I . . . I only just found out myself. Like I said . . . an hour ago. It must've got mislaid in inventory.'

'Mislaid? I don't pay you to mislay things. Open it up.'

'I—'

'*Open it up.*'

Mason had an image of a snarling animal, someone who might reach forward and tear his lip off with his bared teeth. He signalled for the locks to be undone.

Hoek stood back, his heart pounding. Twelve hours. Not that he gave a shit about the cargo, but twelve hours meant the chance of discovery, of awkward questions.

As the two metal doors swung back a thick blast of stale air hit him, ripe with overtones of excrement and sweat, and following behind it a great wave of babble, of voices and gasps, and screams and yelps as the previously interred people sucked in the sweet outside air.

There were sixteen of them, standing in the detritus of a long confined sea voyage, the discarded clothes, the overflowing buckets, the empty ration packets. All were wide-eyed and unkempt, puzzled and angry and relieved in equal measure. Most of them were shouting, a few of them in a language Hoek recognised.

One of his men sniggered: 'They look like that Michael Jackson video—' he began, but Hoek silenced him with a look, before retreating a few paces and turning his face. They stank.

'Hose them down,' he said to Mason. 'And sort them. The decent women send over to the club later. The men—'

There was a piercing scream, a wail of anguish. He furrowed his brow and saw movement in the line spread across the open doorway. It parted in the centre and squeezed out a pathetic woman who held a baby in her arms, limp and lifeless. She proffered it to the onlookers, as if one of them could raise it from the dead. Her eyes caught Hoek's and burned with pleading, with stupid, irrational hope. Hoek shook his head. He had specified no babies and children, simply because the wastage was too high. No doubt she had paid extra cash in Rotterdam to be allowed to bring him or her.

He walked over to Mason and pulled him away. 'Weight it down, dump it in the river,' he hissed angrily. 'This is not good. These people are not in good condition. I paid for chemical toilets. I want you to have a word with your man in Rotterdam.' Hoek leaned forward, and Mason could smell the over-sweet cologne. He gripped Mason's upper arm and squeezed, a reminder that there was strength under the layer of fat that had settled over his big hands. 'A very strong word.'

Hoek's cellphone trilled and he pushed Mason away before he answered: 'Yes? OK? How did it go? Very good.' That was it. No superfluous statements, no discussion, just the barest information which suggested to him that a certain incident at JFK was going to make the evening news.

'The men I want filed past me, one at a time before you move them out. OK?'

Mason nodded. Always the same. Anyone would think he was looking for someone.

S I X

Federal Plaza, NYC

The man showered long and hard in the basement facilities, scrubbing at every surface, trying to rub away the smell of that place, the pestilence he had felt writhing in the bed below them, seeping through the sheet like a bloodstain. He had burnt the cover afterwards, of course, simply swung by one of the vagrants' camps across the river and stuffed it in an oil drum.

He must give it up.

The thought always came to him the moment he had finished and, before the last of the jizz had pumped from his tubes, regret and remorse set in. Even before the women realised it was all over, and would start trying to compose themselves, to rid their mind of what they had been through, wondering if all the men were going to be like this, he was making plans for his retirement, sure this was the last time. The thought became a feeling, a rage, a determination, a new resilience to conquer these urges, not to be their slave any more.

This purity of purpose usually lasted a day, once his depleted testosterone levels had climbed once more, his balls filled with fresh sperm and his brain with old thoughts. He knew that. By tomorrow he would be willing to do anything to get another two hours with one of the girls, the women, the seeming endless stream of new faces and bodies that he could call upon.

But for now, as he rubbed himself dry in the empty, tiled space, the slaps of the towel making a lonely echo, all he had was pity and hatred. Hatred for the people making him do this. If they didn't lay the goods before him, tempt him, surely he wouldn't fall so easily. Or would he seek them out anyway? Which came first? It was hard to remember. Had they approached him or him them? He was fairly sure it was their move, their suggestion. Yeah, that made sense. He had something they wanted, after all.

He picked up his clothes and headed for a cubicle, hung up his shirt and pants, laid the towel on the toilet seat and sat down, head in hands. He reached forward and bolted the door. The Sig was kept in a holster at the rear of his trouser belt. He reached up and eased it out and studied it. Maybe this was the only way to stop. He could leave a note, blame it on the pressure of work upstairs, his secret would die with him. He slipped the gun into his mouth, grimacing at the oily, metallic taste, flicked off the safety and felt his finger tighten.

SEVEN

Bloomsberry, New Jersey

Belle waited until Jim had finished a rushed sandwich and changed both himself and Tommy into their Mets replica kits before she raised the topic. She was sitting nursing a strong black coffee, watching their little bonding rituals, smiling at how cute her boy looked. Thank God Tommy didn't need any of her b.s., she thought. But then, she always felt spectacularly blessed to have a normal kid – neither prodigy nor punk – after her one day at the Davies Assessment Center in Newark, the penance for all the spoiled brats she encouraged over at ICE.

At Davies she got to see the real, raw side of a kid's psyche – instead of not paying due attention to their tennis lessons, these kids had been fucked by their grandparents, or had been left watching twelve hours of television a day for four years, or casually beaten every time they broke a set of rules that seemed to shift and fade like a mirage whenever they tried to tie them down. Kids who, ultimately, would end up shot or OD'd or just scrapped by society, doing twenty-five to life in some Federal Penitentiary rather than dates at Carnegie Hall. Her job was to help them compartmentalise their thoughts and feelings, to put what they had been through into perspective, to lock it away in dark corners so it wouldn't poison their entire life.

Fifty dollars an hour, a panic button, an armed guard seven paces away, scared and scarred kids, parents who should have been sterilised at puberty, it made her feel sick and grubby and misanthropic. Which was why she could only manage one day a week – she just didn't know where the regulars got their strength from. They made her feel weak. She had to remind herself she was a rich, successful, best-selling author. Maybe that was the problem, the one that those stuck there five or six days a week never hit – that passing over from the Neverland of the Institute of Child Excellence to the Never-Had-a-Chance-Land of Davies, the culture shock was just too great.

Finally she said: 'Jim, the other night at our Book Circle, Marta asked if, well, maybe if her boy could come along to practice.'

He was busy loading the big canvas bag from under the stairs, filling it with gloves and helmets and face masks and balls and bats, both wooden and aluminium, inhaling the beautiful smell of leather and sweat and oil. Even at this level, the very bottom rung of a ladder that ended in the vertiginous heights of Shea Stadium, it was a powerful stimulant.

'It isn't a regular practice,' he said warily. 'We got a game coming up. Does he play?'

'Well it's not a national sport in Hungary. Baseball. I don't think. Probably whup your ass at chess though.'

He stopped loading the bag. 'What?'

'The Sebastyens? They're Hungarian. You seen him around – stocky guy, drives a Range Rover. Got that big house on Thurloe with the helipad?'

He had him now. Seen him at school, nodded to each other a few times. Big man, thinning hair, looked like he enjoyed the good life. Strange-looking face. Something odd about it. Misshapen. Hungarian. He'd only been in the town six months, some kind of venture capitalist. They came first, then the kid joined them. He tried to remember what the boy looked like. 'He the scrawny one? Pronounced overbite?'

'That's him. She – Marta – says he's having trouble integrating at school. With his accent, n'all and . . . well, you're always telling me that baseball is the cornerstone of the American way of life.'

He zipped up the bag. 'He's small.'

'You said size doesn't matter.'

'It doesn't – but practice does. I haven't got time to start helping a complete rookie at this point. Maybe next week, huh? I tell you what – he can come and watch.'

'Watch? That's a big deal?'

'Yeah, watch. Johnny Bench used to say he learned most about the game just by watching, by looking at how the pitcher changes speed, angle, spin, the way the batter anticipates the attack—'

She realised he was about to go into a cornball revelry and said, 'I'll tell Marta to bring him over, shall I?'

Jim raised one shoulder, a kind of half-shrug. 'Come on, Tommy, we gonna be late. Yup, do that. He can sit on the bench tonight and Saturday.'

'But you'll let him have a go?' She put an edge of hardness into her voice. She wanted a positive response on this.

'Sure, sure. Listen, call Dick will you, ask him if he's going to come over and give me a hand?'

She waited until she heard the car drive off towards the ground on the far side of town, and called Marta to tell her to take Petyr along. Then she rang Dick.

'Hello?'

'Dick?'

'Yes? Who's this?'

'Belle. I . . . Jim was wondering if you're going over tonight.'

His voice brightened. 'Damn right, I'm just getting Mike's kit together.'

'Great.'

'Yeah, I missed a couple recently. But Jim's real psyched up about the game on Saturday – if I ain't there tonight I reckon he'll chew my ass off.'

'I know, he gets more excited than he does about any Mets game. For five-year-olds.'

Dick suddenly became defensive. 'Yeah, but five-year-olds aren't sulking because they've been on the bench for too long or they didn't get the same kind of deal as the catcher. It's like

57

pure sport, Belle, before the greed takes over. You should watch it now and then. Gives you this kinda warm glow.'

Her bones ached at the thought and she said: 'I'd rather get my warm glow in a hot bath, thanks. I don't need to give Jim another excuse to lecture me on the rights and wrongs of the designated hitter. Listen, Dick, there is a boy coming over just to watch tonight. Petyr. He's the Sebastyens' boy. You know them? Stefan and Marta? Nice couple. Well, I only know her, really. She joined our Book Circle to improve her English, and we're reading Milan Kundera in her honour.'

There was a pause at the other end. 'Isn't he Czech?'

'Um. Technically. But Marta agreed it was in the ballpark.' Damn even she was catching the baseball-metaphor syndrome. 'Besides, he was the only East European any of us had heard of. Anyways, about their son. Thing is . . . he's kinda . . . actually I wouldn't say this to Jim, but the kid's kinda weedy, you know what I mean?'

'I know what you mean. They used to call me that at school.'

'You? I can't imagine you were ever weedy, Dick.' She realised as soon as she said it it sounded like gross flirtation. Christ, she thought, how do you say well-put-together without it sounding like a come-on? 'I mean, you're a big . . . well . . . you know—'

He laughed at her discomfort. 'Yeah, I know there is a lot of me now all right. But really, I was bullied at school – my old man sent me to boxing lessons to toughen me up.'

'I think that's kinda what Marta wants for her boy – not boxing, you could blow him over with one good puff, but something physical.'

'What's his name again?'

'Petyr.' She spelled it out for him.

'Well, they ought to ditch that straight off. You wanna fit in, lose the foreign name. He'll be Petey before the end of the week. Don't worry, I'll keep an eye on him. Do some catch.'

'Thanks, Dick.'

She hung up feeling relieved. It made a change talking to someone who wasn't quite the zealot that Jim became whenever you mentioned his precious Pocket League.

'OK, this one's got tequila, pulque and mescal, mixed up with my secret formula of fruit juices. Whaddayathink?'

Wendy looked at Cecco, Nunca's head barman, and at the frothy drink he was holding out. It was seven o'clock, and the evening rush, if you could call it that, was just starting. Nunca was a Tex-Mex joint on Interstate 10, just north of Tucson, part of a collection of gas station, genuine Indian craft shop, auto shop, and family restaurant.

The bar of Nunca occupied one half of the space, with dining booths in the rest. Everything was decorated with a melange of Hopi and Navajo imagery, overlaid with kitsch Mexicana. Outside were three huge multi-armed saguaro cacti which had cost Burt, the owner, a small fortune. None of them looked too happy, but Burt was eager to tell anyone who would listen that they came with a one-year guarantee from the TransPlant Company.

Wendy was wearing the Nunca uniform, a kind of beaded Indian top with denim shorts cut too high for her liking. Every time she turned to get a drink she could feel those eyes on the bottom of her cheeks. Tonight two cowboys were tucking into the chicken-strip fajitas when she heard one mumble, 'I dunno, she ain't young any more, but she got a nice butt.'

She had whipped around and glared. Being told she had a nice butt should've bothered her she guessed, but didn't, but suggesting she was getting old – she wasn't even thirty f'Chrissakes – that would get her goat every time. They were dusty farm hands, weathered and scuffed, like they could afford to be picky or critical. Besides, her new shoes, built-up sneakers with a platform that almost gave her vertigo when she put them on, were hurting, which made her testy. She should have known better than to wear them to work, cutting edge of bartending fashion or no.

She took a sip of Cecco's concoction and swilled it round her mouth before spitting it out. 'Coyote sweat,' she finally announced.

Cecco, a young Mexican, hollered like he had been stung. 'Wendy, you ungrateful bi— it's an acquired taste.'

'So, I hear, is coyote sweat,' she said. 'Honestly, we can't serve that. Here – try it on the Lone Ranger and Tonto if you don't believe me.'

The two cowboys looked around to check she was talking about them. 'Gentlemen, wanna try a new drink?'

'Sure.' They wiped the salsa from their mouths with napkins and she poured a finger each of the crimson mixture into the glasses and passed it over. They both knocked it back and shuddered. 'Shit. I mean . . . shit,' said one, his mouth puckering like an asshole. 'Do we get a free beer after that?'

'No, you get a warning about talking about my butt.' They grinned at each other. 'No good denying it. I heard it. I heard everything, guys. Even the crack 'bout my age.' At least they had the decency to look a little uncomfortable.

She switched back to blank-faced, who-gives-a-damn waitress mode. 'You all set?' They nodded and she cleared the plates and gave them another beer for the hell of it. Burt could afford it, he had major shares in the Mesa Grande Rehab place up the road, where celebrities came to be told it wasn't their fault they filled themselves with shit – someone, anyone, anything else was to blame. That'll be fifty grand please.

The Mescaleros finished and Elton John came on. Wendy whipped round in time to see Cindy creeping away from the CD player and back to her station. 'Cindy, I told you about sneaking that shit on.'

She came over. Plump, blonde, around thirty-five. Cindy had an angelic face somewhat bloated by a lifetime of too much protein and animal fats. Her family were ranchers and butchers.

She had only just opted out of the business, and was going to college in Tucson.

'Oh, Wendy, I love him so much. Just once a night. That's all I need.'

'I bet you say that to all the guys.'

Cindy pursed her lips. She was married, with two kids, had only ever been with her husband, whom she snared while they made out to Elton John, and had a resilient strand of religion running through her.

'Listen, the customers come in here for a few beers, they wanna hear something upbeat, y'know, Los Lobos, Rangewars, Sidewinders, Rich Hopkins, that kinda thing. Not "Candle In The Wind" – they'll all be sobbin' into their brews soon.'

'"Crocodile Rock" is up next.'

'No it ain't, Cindy. Beck is up next, trust me.'

'Ah, shoot, I guess I'll have plenty of time to listen to him when I'm gone.'

'Gone where?'

'Both Ralph and I are sure Elton John is the kind of music they have in heaven.'

Wendy waited a second to see if she was joking, then said: 'I'll be damned.' If there was any justice, that is. Still, she mustn't be too hard on Cindy. It was her going to college to re-train as a beauty therapist that had given her the idea of doing something similar. With so many spas opening up, massage was the thing, and if she could raise twenty thousand dollars, then she could put herself through school and get a decent job that didn't involve waving her ass at salsa-stained cowboys. Hot stone massage, shiatsu, she could learn them all, go to Miraval or Los Oinos or one of the other swanky resorts that catered to New Yorkers and Angelinos who thought that having to choose new drapes was the epitome of a tough life.

She turned to make sure she got the Elton John off the player but Cecco was in her face again. 'Wendy, what you think of this?'

It was yellowy this time, and she had to stop herself making any horse urine jokes. She sipped. And sipped some more. 'What's in . . . no, don't tell me. I'd rather not know. Not bad. You know, Cecco, I reckon you could serve this without risking a lawsuit. Is there lemon in there?' He nodded. 'It's a bit sharp. I'd cut it with a little sugar.'

'OK. I'll give it a try.'

'No, try serving that guy over there with his tongue stuck to the bar. I think he needs a drink real bad.' She turned to the cowboys, ready with the waitress hustle she had picked up so easily. 'Can I get you folks another?' with the sort of inflection that suggested it would be a personal affront if they said no.

The evening slotted into a kind of rhythm as the bar filled, the after-work crew replaced by Interstate drivers who needed a break, some locals out in search of a hangover, a few groups celebrating birthdays and the like over in the booths. Gordon, one of the waiters, had replaced the Beck with some thumping dance anthems, French house music he claimed, not the softer Lauryn Hill she liked, but it gave the evening an agreeably hard edge, made the routine of bending to get the beers, sweeping up the glasses, pouring a draught and fetching the food orders seem more like an aerobic class. And all the time Cecco was there, asking her about his new drinks. 'I'm going for Tucson-Jose Cuervos Mixer of The Year, Wendy,' he finally confided in a whisper. 'I gotta come up with something new.'

She sipped something that looked as if it had crème de menthe in it and grimaced at the taste. 'You sure have. The lemony one was better.'

'Not masculine enough,' he said.

'You wanna be able to drink it, not run drag-racers on it.'

'Wendy. Phone.' It was Burt, with a disapproving tone.

She went to the back office, where Burt hovered impatiently while she picked up the receiver. 'Hello?'

'Mom.'

Her heart jittered. 'Pete?'

'Mom. I woke up and . . .'

'What? What's wrong, Hon?' Thank God she had taught him to dial the numbers written out above the phone.

'I'm all by myself, Mom. I need a hug.'

'By yourself?' She felt her stomach take the express elevator down. 'Oh, Hon. Where's Duke?'

'I . . . I dunno. Mom, I'm scared.'

'OK, OK, now listen.' She tried to keep her voice level. Didn't want to spook him, make it worse than it was. Twenty-five-minute drive, tops. Fifteen if she didn't mind running the shocks on the bumps. Don't panic, she told herself, with an authority she didn't trust. Her skin suddenly became prickly, clammy, as if she was going to vomit, and her chest suddenly felt as if corsets were back in fashion. 'Look, he's probably just gone out to get some beers. OK? Just go back to bed and I'll be right there.'

'There's a monster under my bed.'

'No there isn't, Pete. That's just a story.'

'Duke said there was.'

Stupid fuck-up bastard. 'Duke is . . . Duke is wrong. Hear me? Duke is wrong?'

'I heard it moving. That's why I woke up.'

Probably one of the many pocket mice they got around the park, maybe even a cottontail hopping under the trailer. 'No, that's nothing. Look, switch on the TV and I will be there in five minutes. Understand? OK. I love you, sweetheart, just stay cool. I bet Duke is back before I am.' She hoped so, because then she could waste no time castrating him on the spot.

'Wendy—' began Burt.

Her facing burning red with anger, she wasn't going to take any shit from the boss on this one. 'I know, I know – my kid is all alone. I'll try and get back – OK? Come on, it isn't up to the rafters exactly, is it?'

'That's not the point—'

'No, the point is my boy, Burt.'

After asking Cindy to switch to covering the bar, and Gordon to work Cindy's tables, she stopped off at the staff area and changed the shorts for her regular jeans and sprinted out to the Saturn.

That no-good Duke. Babysitting, you would have thought, was not as difficult as flying a Bell Ranger helicopter, but now it seemed like he couldn't do either without a major screw-up.

She pulled onto the highway and accelerated down the road, past the prison, with its warning signs – 'State Correctional Facility. Do Not Pick Up Hitchhikers' and hung a left onto Mango Road, the long, undulating blacktop that would take her home. Ahead of her she could see the mountains, a lone crackle of lightning illuminating the peaks. Other cars' headlights flashed into the sky and they negotiated the long, shallow dips that made up the road – it was like an automobile rollercoaster, following the long ridges of sand that corduroyed the desert here. Usually she took it easy on the wavy surface, but tonight she floored it, feeling the wheels almost leave the humps at the apex, before crashing down again.

She hadn't gone half a mile when she saw more lights, this time blue ones, and heard the quick impatient squwark of a siren. State Troopers or Sheriff she couldn't be sure. Damn, of all the nights. She eased off the gas, braked, rolled to a halt and reached for her purse and the documentation within. Time to turn on the helpless female-in-distress act. It was only then she remembered the stream of high-octane cocktails she had been sampling all night.

Dick and Jim made sure all the kids had gone to their nice Bloomsberry homes, cleared up the playing field, consoled the shortstop that he wasn't the klutz his old man reckoned he was (at the same time making a note to let the Saperstein kid try out for the position), dropped Tommy back to Belle and ended up back at Dick's, where Dick had bundled Mike to bed and cracked open a cold one for both of them.

'How do you think it went?' asked Jim.

'OK. No, better than OK. Good.'

'Good enough for Chesterville?'

'I dunno. They got some eight-year-olds, you know. Should be in Little League.' The idea of Pocket League was to mop up the years five to seven, when the kids were big enough and sensible enough to practice and play, but before they could get in an official Little League side.

'I know, I'm gonna have to say something about that. More and more older kids appearing. It was no more than two in the squad.'

'Maybe we should just say none. You know, there's dozens of Little League teams to choose from – they got no excuse for muscling in on our action.'

Jim nodded, and felt a wave of tiredness hit him. The two hours he had spent sparring with Hooper over what sort of proposal to hit Condé Nast with for *Our Thing*. Jim had decided he wanted twelve million, Hooper reckoned eight plus bonuses to stay on as Executive Editor. Jim wasn't sure he wanted to stay on once it was someone else's baby.

Dick said: 'What did you ball out the Raub kid for?'

'Ah, nothin' much. He was obscurin' the back line of the batter's box – you know, kickin' dirt over it. I told him technically it was illegal, but he said he saw all the batters do it in the majors. I told him not to be a wise-ass.'

'Smart, though, eh? And a hell of a pro-spitter.'

Jim laughed. 'I know. He'll be corking his bat next – best keep an eye on him.'

'You see the Sebastyen kid?'

'Yeah. Kinda little, don't you think, for his age?'

'We could let him have a few knock arounds, a bit of fungo, though. Just to get him going.'

'I guess.' There was a silence while they both took a hit of beer.

Jim willed himself to broach another subject. 'Dick, how are you doing? Generally, I mean. I only ask because Belle asked me to ask you if—'

'I'm fine. I've almost forgotten she was ever here.' He flashed a wan smile. 'Don't get me wrong, it was tough at first, after she went. If it hadn't been for Mike, I'd've probably climbed in a bottle of Jim Beam and gone for a long, slow soak. But I found hangovers and a kid bouncing in at six a.m. really don't mix. He kept me, you know, focused. That and the job.'

This was more than he'd said about the situation in six months. Which he guessed was a good sign. Jim was relieved, you could never accuse the guy of oversharing, but he didn't really want an Iron John hugging session with the guy, not today. 'Belle meant anything she can help with. You know – drapes, whatever it is wives do.' Jim realised that Belle would kill him if she could hear him – and remind him that this wife wrote bestsellers as well as bringing up a kid and with just one caregiver as support.

'What, she'll come over and nag me, just in case I miss it?'

'It's an idea.'

'Thanks. No, tell her thanks, but I'm fine. How is Belle?'

How was Belle? Great, he was tempted to say, absolutely on a roll. And starting to throw her weight around. Now she was seeing royalty cheques, she was beginning to think of more staff – a cook, maybe. He groaned inwardly. Good staff were like some rare illicit commodity in this town – envied, lusted after, traded, bought, the price escalated as demand outstripped supply. Jim quite liked the idea that Belle did it all with just Thereza, the little Puerto Rican girl who picked up Tommy from school and cleaned the house. Although he had heard that, as with all market forces, the latest wave of East Europeans and Balkans were cheaper than the traditional suppliers of drudgery, so that might be an option. 'Fine. She's fine,' he finally said.

'Well, as I say, tell her thanks. Mike goes off to camp soon, and I'll have some time to straighten things out.'

Jim scanned the immaculately kept room. 'Seems pretty

straight to me now.' He pointed at one of the prominently displayed photos on the pine-clad wall in front of them. 'Is that Allbright?'

'Yeah. Mads. It was taken when I was seconded to her security. Spent the whole time looking under her bed and in her closets before she could enter a room. I tell you – that is not a glamorous assignment.'

Then it hit Jim. Mike. To camp. 'He'll miss the Springtown game then?'

'What?'

'Mike. He'll miss the Springtown game.'

Dick could sense the hostility. 'I . . . I thought I'd told you.'

'No.' There was a prickly, snitty edge to Jim's voice.

'Well, it's only one game.'

'Sure.'

'And he's getting coaching at camp, he'll be even better when he comes back.'

'Mike is our best catcher by a million miles right now, Dick. He's the only kid who can call a pitcher.'

Dick felt a little surge of pride in his boy, but suppressed a grin. He didn't want Jim to think he wasn't taking this seriously. 'Maybe that's because the others haven't had a chance. This could be the time to let some of the other kids have a pop. You gotta rotate, Jim, some of the dads were saying—'

'Oh yeah?'

'I mean, just casually, nothing in it, Jim. Just you know, you tend to field the same team—'

'The *best* team. The best.' He knew some of them thought the element of competition should be suppressed at this stage, it could wait for Little League. Bloomsberry was a town haunted by Doing The Right Thing For Its Kids. Just fourteen miles from Manhattan, it was stuffed full of people with – he had to admit – a profile just like his. Media or Wall Street, mostly white, affluent, with one or two kids, left-of-centre politically, people who might have been punks or Goths or grungers at some stage of their lives, but now wanted to live in a town where Frank Capra was the Mayor and Steven Spielberg the Chief of Police. It was true, with its rows of neat New England-style houses behind picket fences on tree-lined streets and its neighbourhood cook-outs and Memorial weekend barbecues, it could stand in for the All-American dream town. Which was why so many commercials were shot here. Shame about the assholes who lived in those houses, he sometimes thought.

'That's not always the point, Jim,' said Dick.

Jim finished his beer and stood up. 'It is for me. I'll see myself out.'

Dick shook his head, wondering when the guy was going to grow up.

They put Wendy in the Spartan waiting room at the Sheriff's office in La Cholla. It was a slow night, she was the only one around, which meant she had the big, echoing space all to herself. Wendy sat on the bench with her head in her hands. The moment they shone in the flashlight and its built-in air-alcohol-monitor registered fumes, and the red light started winking, she knew the rest was inevitable. They asked her to perform a Field Sobriety Test when, through nerves, she had fumbled her licence and dropped it out of the window. Walking a line, touching her nose, that kind of shit. That had gone OK, until she tripped over her new shoes and ended up grabbing onto one of the deputies to stop herself falling and, catching him off balance, had pulled him down on top of her in a messy tangle of limbs and curses.

When they said she could choose a breath or a blood test there had been a scene on the highway, where she totally lost it, screaming about her child. It must have made her look even more like a lush out for a late-night drive. Not only has she been hitting the bottle, she's left the kid at home, too, and now she's come up with some crazy story about a missing babysitter.

In the end one of the deputies agreed to drive her car home

and check on Pete, while she came in the back of the cruiser to the hospital and gave a sample – it was that or a breath test, which was notoriously unreliable. Now she was simply waiting for a ride home. The techs had all gone for the night, and the blood alcohol results wouldn't be through until the next day. If she was over the .10, she was totally fucked. Driving Under the Influence. Two hundred and fifty dollar fine, lost licence for at least ninety days and publicity. Stupid. She must remember to punch Cecco in the mouth, however the blood level came out.

Wendy heard someone approaching outside and looked up. It was one of the arresting officers. The yellowy hall light gave him a jaundiced look.

'You OK?' he asked.

'Been better. You get to Pete all right? My little boy?'

He opened his mouth and closed it again. Then she realised it wasn't just cheap illumination making him look sick. 'What? What is it?'

'Ma'am,' he cleared his throat, as if the words were jamming up in there. 'We checked your trailer. It was empty. Your kid's gone.'

She sprang to her feet and tried to scream, shout at him, tell him that was impossible, to look again, but the only sound that came out was the sound of a frightened woman she didn't recognise.

The club was outside the entrance to La Guardia Airport in Queens. It was not an original idea, there had been one outside JFK for a while, but if a concept was worth anything, it was worth stealing. This one lacked the upscale appeal of the JFK one, it was simply a large barn-like room, with a bar at one end, a stage at the other, and seven dance stations scattered around the floor. The girls stripped on these small tables, through which a pole passed, running up to the ceiling. At each station small monitors hung down, displaying arrival and departure times for La Guardia, so punters could see how many dances they could

stay for before they risked the gate closing. The place was called
The Landing Strip.

It was a slow day, which is why they had shut early, at
midnight. Near the stage Schmee sat with his employer, while
a desultory pack of minders and runners milled around, waiting
for the after-hours show.

Schmee looked across at Hoek, who was lighting a cigarette,
he watched as the flames highlighted the dark marks under his
eyes and the strange, little silver snakes that ran up the side of
his nose. Schmee wondered if the man was tired of all this. He
certainly looked weary all of a sudden.

'Any fall-out on JFK?' Hoek asked suddenly in that raspy
bark of his.

Schmee shook his head. He guessed the FBI and Airport
cops and Transportation Feds would still be analysing the
crime scene. 'No. Still a mystery to them. Nobody will connect
them to us.'

Hoek nodded. Schmee knew his stuff, it was why he employed
him. Behind those unemotional, lashless eyes lay a brain well
used to screwing up official organisations, throwing people off
the scent. Schmee had been running the Port Authority Docks
racket, bringing in Germans who needed their slate wiped clean,
a fresh start. Especially those whose Gauck Authority files were
tagged IM, unofficial collaborator, which marked them down
as a Stasi informer. They were not the most popular people
in the reunified Fatherland. Often they were snubbed by the
friends and neighbours they spied on, and had no choice but to
start again elsewhere. But, now the files had been in the public
domain for a good few years, this supply had been drying up.
When Hoek had come on the scene, with his more desperate
human cargo, they had seen that a merger was the best business
option. But there was no doubt who was in charge now.

'Will there be more?' asked Hoek. 'Others who know me?'

'I don't know.' Schmee fiddled with a nail distractedly. He
knew there would be. There would always be someone. Maybe

not this week or next. But maybe next month or next year. Look at all those old Nazis who thought they had beaten the system, who were sure they would die in bed surrounded by adoring grandchildren who knew nothing of what had happened in Latvia or the Ukraine or Poland. And then one day . . . 'It is possible,' he said honestly.

'You know they nearly got Tokavitch? The chain-saw guy? You hear that? That would have been something, eh? To see him on trial? They think I did bad things? Shit. OK, find out what their next move is, if it is me they still want. Use The Creep.'

'I don't know how much further I can push him.'

'The Creep?' Hoek laughed. He knew the type of man. He was pathetic. 'Till he breaks. I'll see them now.'

Schmee got up and headed for backstage. He had come a long way from the Stasi to this. He just wondered how long the luck would hold out. He had been suggesting to Hoek that it was time to move bases, away from New York. The city was too high-profile, too clean, and Hoek was getting paranoid now he felt the government was after him. A break in the country, that was what he needed. He pushed the curtain aside and stepped through.

There were six of them in the small, cramped space backstage, scared, thin, and pale. Two of them struck Schmee as right straight away, a redhead and a badly dyed bottle blonde. He touched the latter's face and she stared back, a veneer of defiance occasionally slipping to show the fear, the vulnerability, behind. A decent hairdresser and she would be fine.

He told them to take their tops off, and they did so, quickly, already aware that it was useless to argue. They wore a motley collection of underwear, from the black and would-be sexy – and might have been, had they not been so worn and frayed – to shapeless old grey numbers. He took a large ink marker and wrote a number on their skin, one to six and nodded at Anna, the hard-faced woman who passed as a mother hen round here. She was more fighting cock than mother hen, he couldn't help thinking.

He indicated they should come out one at a time and went back to join Hoek. 'Any good?'

Schmee shrugged. 'Couple.'

They came out as directed, and Hoek looked each of them up and down, asking one to turn around, another to remove her skirt, some he just waved away. When the last one had scurried off he looked at Schmee. 'Two and five.'

The blonde and the redhead. 'That's what I made.'

'OK, tell Anna those two as dancers, the rest can work the rooms.'

'There is one more problem,' said Schmee.

'What? Here?'

'One of the Americans.' They had two or three girls who weren't imported working the club, girls who couldn't perform at the regular joints for one reason or another – drug habit, excessive tattoos, attitude problem.

'She was working a scam with the barman. Ernst. A German, I am sad to say. Fellow countryman.'

'Ernst?' Hoek asked, then, knowing full well the answer: 'Didn't you introduce him?'

Schmee sighed. A friend of a friend. Never do favours, he should know that by now. Favours always blew up in your face. 'Yes.'

'What did you do with him?'

'East River.'

Hoek frowned. 'Without my say-so?'

'It was a matter of honour. He let me down.'

Hoek half smiled. Honour, yes. These Germans were still big on such things. 'How?'

'Gas mask.'

'Of course.' Schmee liked the mask, a remnant of his old Stasi days. The old anti-biological warfare face mask was slipped onto the victim then the oxygen supply shut off. Sometimes, if you wanted them to talk, you turned it back on. Not this time, though. 'And the girl?'

'Upstairs.' There were two floors of private entertaining 'suites' up above, where much lucrative business was done, although never with the dancers, and only for well-vetted clients with very specific tastes.

'OK, put her in one of the rooms. For a week or two. Teach her some manners.' Schmee got up to attend to it and Hoek had a thought. Just to be sure she suffered. 'Oh and, Schmee? Give her to The Creep.'

EIGHT

Federal Plaza, NYC

No more, The Creep decided. What had brought him to sitting there waiting to bite the bullet, his finger an eighth of an inch away from sending the projectile into his brain? He had to stop. He would not call any more. Simple.

But every day the thought of all those new women, ones he hadn't yet seen, newly initiated into the truth about how their life in the Land of the Free was going to pan out, at least until they were no use any more. All over the city, little hot spots of vice and degradation, glowing with the fires of pure lust, stoked by men like him. Two, three days that was all he could go before the worms in his stomach started crawling, writhing, reaching down into his groin, sending those signals to his brain. Maybe she's eighteen, nineteen. Slim, beautiful, perhaps even a little willing.

The last one had been disappointing, maybe that's why he felt so bad afterwards. He had had to slap her around a little to make her come round, understand what he required. That was probably it. He hated abusing women like that – it was so much better if they entered the spirit of things.

Then they rang him.

'Mr Hoek is pleased. Wants you to have a bonus.' He recognised the voice as Schmee, the case-hardened edge of the accent giving him away. 'The number to call is – you got a pen?' He said he had and took it down, then replaced the receiver without saying anything further.

He took a deep breath, looked around the office, but the shoulder-height blue fabric-faced screens meant nobody had seen him go pale, a little flustered. No, never again. But would a bonus be special? Might they have provided something a little different for him?

Before he changed his mind he stood up and headed out to find a public call box, where he could ring the number and get an address.

Sebastyen brought the kid over himself, come the next practice. Jim wasn't best pleased to see him, not when he still had his mind on the defeat of the previous weekend. He was running over the two line-up cards, trying to work out where he had gone wrong and Sparta's coach had gone so right. 8–3. It was humiliating.

'Mr Barry. Stefan Sebastyen. Thank you for this. For taking on my boy, he said how nice you were to him.' Jim looked Stefan over. Yeah, as he had thought, he had that well-fed affluence that many immigrants to America aspire to. Back home he was probably from a poor family, where food was restricted and repetitive. Here, in the Land of the Free, the Brave and the Full, he could celebrate his elevated station by a little gluttony. Nice suit, though. Well cut.

All around Jim the kids were starting to limber up for practice. He was keen to do a debrief, but when he had them all to himself, when the only parents left were those who understood what was at stake, who wouldn't mind their precious darlings being chewed over by the coach. Guys like Raub and Perl who, after the weekend fiasco, had vowed to take a more active role.

Nice? Jim suddenly thought. He didn't remember being nice to the boy. Dick was pretty encouraging, more than he thought entirely necessary, given the kid's low potential. But maybe Sebastyen was getting the two of them confused. 'It's nothing,' he said eventually. 'You understand we may not be able to include him in a competitive side just yet.'

'Oh, sure, sure,' said Sebastyen. He held out his hand and Jim took it. 'But I said to Marta, his mother, if we want to raise our son as an American, he has to learn baseball. Everything he needs to know is in the game.'

Jim found himself nodding enthusiastically. 'You're right, Stefan. I wish all the folks saw that.'

'Maybe it takes an outsider to put it in perspective, eh? I'll pick him up later.'

Jim looked down at the kid who returned his gaze steadily and broke into a big smile. His two front teeth were missing, which gave him a helpless urchin look. Oh, shit. Just a boy who wanted to join in the greatest sport that humans have yet invented. Who could blame him? 'OK, kid,' Jim said, ruffling his hair, 'We'll see what you can do in a minute. In the meantime, I got some ass to kick.'

The deputy had done it deliberately, of course. He'd told Wendy that her kid wasn't in the trailer. Which was true. He hadn't said they had located him in another trailer on site, sound asleep, and being well looked after. Bastard. That was his little twist of the knife, no doubt, for her being an unfit mother.

Wendy accepted the coffee from the man opposite her and sipped it gratefully.

'Sorry I ain't got anything stronger,' he said.

'That's OK, Mr . . .'

'Coogan. George Coogan.'

Coogan was, she guessed, around thirty-five, -six, although the salt-and-pepper hair made it hard to pin down exactly. He wasn't tall, not as big as Duke, but reasonably well built, broad-shouldered, although he sometimes held himself and moved stiffly, as if afraid of snagging a nerve or something. She looked around the trailer. One wall at the far end was covered in tapes and CDs. Another was dominated by a huge map of the entire United States, covered in red dots, with a little scribble of writing next to each one. The furniture was spartan to say the least, just one couch and an armchair to sit on, a Sony TV and video, a small hi-fi, and a desk covered in papers and books. In the centre of the room was a music stand and, at its base, two guitar cases and a small amplifier/speaker combo.

'So they said he was missing and I freaked,' she explained. 'I figured . . . well, I was afraid he'd been snatched. They waited five minutes to tell me you'd found him.'

Coogan took the armchair and swivelled to face her and sipped his own coffee. 'I didn't exactly find him. I heard him yellin'. So, y'know, I went out and he was standin' in the doorway cryin' about some monster under his bed.'

'That asshole Duke had told him that.'

'What's the accent?' he asked by way of conversation that didn't involve the kid.

'Asshole is something I picked up down here.' Her language was becoming riper, the rhythm of her speech stretched into the local drawl.

'Leaving that aside.'

'Minnesota. My folks were Scandinavian stock – their grand-parents came over still speaking in that sing-song way. They still have some of it. I've got the residue. My sister—' She felt a sudden jolt. Yeah, her sister probably wasn't in any kind of shit like this. She certainly got the best deal from a bad deck. Damn, more South West homilies. 'My sister sounds like she left Stockholm last week sometimes. We have, had, a catering business up there. Dad imported meats and fish, Mom, she could lay on the best smorgasbord this side of the Atlantic. I—' She stopped herself saying any more. She was certain he didn't want the Blatand family saga right now. 'Anyway, I am really grateful.'

Coogan nodded. He suddenly felt tired, wished she would just take the boy and go, but the adrenaline shock to her system had left her with something to burn off. He'd just go with it. Where was the harm? 'He seems a nice kid. Went asleep real fast.'

'Just like that?'

'Ten, fifteen minutes, no more.'

'He doesn't normally take to strangers . . . no offence.'

He shrugged. 'I carried him through and put him in my bed. Don't worry – sheets are clean – only changed today. Rosita? Works in the office? Does the place once a week.'

She smiled, hoping to reassure him that cleanliness wasn't high on her list of concerns for the moment. She pointed at the guitars. 'I hear you play.'

'Yeah. Sorry 'bout that. Must get some headphones.'

She could feel a slight edge of resentment in there somewhere. What had she done? 'No, no. I like it.'

'You like jazz?'

She couldn't lie. 'Is that what you play?' before she realised how that sounded. 'Oh, I—'

'Nope. It's OK. It's a bit of this, bit of that. Some jazz.' In fact he was heading backwards in his musical tastes. At one time it had been Stevie Ray Vaughan and Duane Allman. Now it had become more Grant Green than Peter Green.

'I don't really know much about jazz. My folks were more into classical – Nielsen, Sibelius'n'Grieg'n'stuff. Me, I'm more a TLC kinda girl – soul and R'n'B. But you play a lot. You must be good. I mean – you sound good.'

He shook his head. 'I'm OK. I can do most styles. They want some Schofield, some Frisell, maybe a bit of Pat Metheny – you know these guys? – or even a bit of Hendrix or Cobain. George can do it.'

In fact he sometimes felt like one of those records you saw in thrift stores – hits of the day played by a pick-up band that could approximate the real recording artist's sound. That was him. Play any style you liked. Except his own.

She stifled a yawn.

'You must be beat. I'll carry the boy over.'

'Pete. He's called Pete.'

He gave a thin smile. 'He said. Yeah. Pete.' He stood up, again keeping his back artificially straight.

She couldn't help herself, she suddenly blurted: 'What do the red dots mean?'

79

He swivelled and looked at the map of the USA on the wall. 'Oh, just places I've been. Everywhere I've had a gig or a recording date.' Everywhere I failed to get a real job, a real woman, a real life is what he really meant.

Wendy could see that the rash of circles covered almost every state from Montana down to New Mexico, California to New Hampshire. 'All those places? Jesus, you get around. You moving on from here?'

'I will, I guess. I kinda got stalled.'

She stood up and walked over, and realised the scribbles next to the dots were dates and initials and locations – recording studios, theatres, clubs. The time frame was all within the last ten years. 'You fly to all these places? I mean, that's expensive.' And you don't look like you got money to burn, she thought, otherwise you wouldn't be in a short-let rental trailer park.

He shook his head. 'I don't like flyin'. I prefer to drive. You get more of a feel for the country, you get time to think.'

'You drove?' She waved her arm across the country before her. 'All this? Shoot, you must have done thousands of miles. What do you drive?'

He had a feeling she wouldn't understand about classic muscle cars. He wasn't sure he could pinpoint their brutal, gas-guzzling appeal himself. Just a nostalgic throwback to another era, when cars were big and masculine instead of rounded and touchy-feely. Just like his choice of guitar. 'It's under the tarp round the side. It's a Trans Am.'

'I don't know much about cars.'

''S nice. I'll get . . . Pete.'

'Yeah.' She hesitated and felt she had to offer. 'I didn't leave him, you know. I mean I did, I went to work, but Duke was with him.'

'The monster-under-the-bed guy? You said.'

'Yeah. He's my . . . my boyfriend. Ex-boyfriend after this.'

'He the young guy? Buff body, tattoo on his arm here?'

She nodded.

'I seen him around, playing catch. Good-looking guy.'

'And nice, if you got beer in the fridge and your legs permanently akimbo. Sorry. I'm just . . . Duke is a fuck-up. He used to fly helicopters over the Grand Canyon, but one day this guy turns up and offers him two thousand dollars if he'll go outside designated space and fly below the rim. Man tells him he's a photographer, wants to get a shot of a particular formation.'

The mention of helicopters caused a little, lost muscle buried deep in Coogan's neck to spasm. He reached up and rubbed it. 'And?'

'And Duke, Duke loves all that dah-dah-dah-dah-dah stuff. Y'know, Ride of the Valkyries? So he sees it as a bit of harmless fun and it turns out the guy's an FAA inspector and Duke does it and gets a six-month suspension and a ten-thousand-dollar fine.'

'Isn't that entrapment?'

'Well, maybe, but they got a tip-off that Duke was the kinda guy who would bend the rules if the price was right. They weren't wrong. In the meantime they switch to these NOTARs. Choppers with no tail rotors, so Duke says – quieter. But he isn't rated on them, so they use it as the excuse to can him when his suspension is done. He moved down here because he has got a friend who runs one of those plane parks?'

He knew them. Out in the desert, rows and rows of military and commercial aircraft, glinting in the sun, mothballed in clean, dry air, just in case anyone ever needs a fleet of 707s, a brace of Tristars or a couple of Grumman Intruders. Spooky as hell they were. 'But helicopter pilots . . . gotta be work there.'

'Not with an FAA suspension on your card. Much like getting insurance with a DUI. Shoot,' she spat as her stupidity came back to her. She explained how she came to be over the limit. 'And if that ain't enough, they're going to contact Child Welfare in Tucson. They can take my child.' She felt a sudden constriction in her throat.

Coogan felt awkward, didn't know what to say. This wasn't

his area of expertise. Far from it. Eventually he muttered: 'I don't think . . . y'know I don't think that'll happen.' Then he fetched the kid, lifting him gingerly, distributing the weight across his torso, as if there were still stitches in his back. Pete hardly stirred as he lifted him into his arms, and hauled him across to her trailer, momentarily embarrassed at how much more like a home hers looked than his. He put the boy into his bed and Wendy pecked him on the cheek to say thank you and he tried not to recoil.

A while back he might have got loaded and thought of ways to hit on this woman, but not now. And not with the boy around. Trouble. Being sober, it kind of altered your perspective, he found. And Coogan felt like he had been sober a long time.

Some bonus, thought The Creep. Bitch had fought like a wildcat. They had put a gag on her, warning that she had a bite straight out of *Jurassic Park*. He had ended up roping her, face down on the bed, noting as he did so just how much better condition she was in than the others. Sleek hair, nice skin, decent amount of flesh on her bones. And tattoos. In one sense what he did to her gave him no pleasure this time, but he had to do it. He had taken two of those blue tablets that he had got from Brazil on the internet, the ones they said put a firecracker in your dick. Firecracker was understating it. It was like riding a a Scud missile, or driving an Italian sports car with the governor removed, red-lining his hormones until he was screaming to come, forcing him to pump away until he came in a big, heaving shudder, feeling great gushes of it force down his urethra and burst into her body.

He got dressed and untied her, and she crawled into the corner, whimpering. He had asked her name but she wouldn't answer. Then he remembered the gag. As gently as could he undid it, and said slowly. 'I am sorry if that hurt. Now, what is your name?'

'Fuck off. Just fuck *off*, you bastard.' And she spat at him. A big, slippery parcel of mucus straight into his eye. He slapped her across the face and put the gag back on, holding a handful of hair to keep her compliant, before grabbing his case and the sheet and walking out. Tarr was on the landing and winked at him, before turning to Mr Moustache and saying: 'London? Why the fook we goin' to London? I like it here.'

'The fook knows.'

They were unusually animated tonight.

He stepped outside and took a breath of the thick, warm evening air and looked up at the window of the room he had just left. The first little hit of nausea and disgust flared up and he smacked it down. Not yet. Strange, he thought. He couldn't be absolutely sure, but this one had sounded almost American.

NINE

Federal Plaza, NYC

They phoned him at work. Schmee again. But he just gave
him a number, a long distance one this time. He waited an
hour and went out to grab a sandwich, before ducking into
one of the cheap call shops that had sprung up everywhere,
run by Bangladeshi and Indians who served their homesick
countrymen.

He was given a booth, dialled the number, hung up and
re-dialled. 'Yeah,' he said when it was picked up. 'It's me.'

'Yes. We need some more.'

He swallowed hard. Payback time. The part of the deal he
always buried in some dark recess of his mind, but which they
always came and shone their flashlights into. 'How many?'

'Thirty.'

'Thirty?' He felt his voice screech up to castrato. He gave a
little cough. 'Are you fuckin' mad? I've never done more than
five. Someone'll notice.'

'Thirty over a period of two months. That shouldn't be
too bad.'

'You're pushing too hard, Schmee.'

'No names please.'

Thirty? He kept asking himself with increasing despair. Why
hadn't they just asked him to stand on Federal Plaza, pour gas
over his head and light up a Camel? That would get everyone's
attention just about as fast. 'This will fuck up everything.'

'No, it won't. We trust you. By the way, do you have any
dealings with Canada or Mexico?'

'Dealings?'

'Can you do the same sort of thing?'

'No. Absolutely not. No. Negative.' He tried to sound really firm on this.

'OK, OK. Thirty, we will give you the names at the next appointment. Right?'

'I'll give it a shot.'

'As always. Don't sound so glum. How does twins sound for this one?'

'Twins?'

'Two for the price of one.'

Despite the enormity of what they were asking, he felt his penis stir lazily against his trousers. 'Really?'

'At The Club. We'll be in touch.'

The line went dead, and his throat felt scratchy and dry. Not because of the request to risk his job and freedom again, but at the prospect of taking two of them next time. At The Club. They always kept the special ones out there. He let the images play in his mind, enjoyed the squirming in the base of his belly. Damn, he suddenly realised, he hadn't had the chance to ask if they were identical or not.

Jim Barry watched as Dick lined them up for fungo practice. The kids were in a semi-circle across the dusty, parched field. Raub was throwing easy pitches and Dick was knocking them in the air for the boys to practise their fielding skills. Tommy was standing under a ball, squinting at the darkening sky, taking tiny steps as he tried to position himself, the oversized gloves reaching up, like some kind of leather flower, and then the satisfying thunk as the cowhide sphere rammed home and was trapped.

'Attaboy, Tommy. Good catch.' Tommy beamed a wobbly-toothed smile over at him.

He also watched the kid Petyr stumble over his own feet as he tried to catch one, the white-and-red projectile falling three feet from him and bouncing away. Useless. Still, he knew that he would have to become more inclusive – some of the parents were even angling to get their daughters in. Saying no would open a pretty big can of gender-exclusion worms, but if he was more egalitarian with the boys, that might defuse things for a while. Like he always said, there was nothing to stop them setting up a league of their own for the girls.

Jim got himself a soda while they continued the practice, the diamond gradually filling up with missed and dropped balls; Tommy and Mike, Dick's kid, the star performers as far as he could make out. While he drank, he thought for a minute about the rather formal letter from Hooper that had been in his tray that morning, asking him to come to a meeting with Max Silverstein, the new Editorial Director over at Condé Nast next week. This was going to be it. A counter-offer to his proposal, no doubt.

Funny, he always reckoned he'd make forty with the magazine. Didn't figure it would make him rich, but it would see him onto the next stage of his life. Now, he was going to have to make decisions about his future sooner than he would have liked. Such as the novel he had talked about for ten years. Usually sometime after midnight, with a few beers under his belt, he would lay out the basic plot. A story of murder, mayhem and Major League baseball. Over the years he had created a pool of characters, from a Kevin Brown-like big-bucks guy, down to the sleazeball who deals steroids from the back of his truck, all the plot points, the back story of the players' strike after a rash of salary dumps, the renegade league, the death-threats from aggrieved agents and players, the gruesome demise in the locker room . . . just that he hadn't written one word as yet. Well, maybe with a few million bucks in the bank . . .

'What you say we try some of them as catchers?'

It was Dick, asking timidly, still feeling guilty about his boy going off to camp, but nevertheless trying to push his idea of more frequent rotation.

Jim nodded. 'OK, you do some pitchin' to me, let's see how they go.'

'You wanna pad them up?'

'Just the mitt, chest pad and face guard. Keep it gentle, OK?'

Dick positioned himself on the mound with a basket of balls, while Jim got himself a bat. He selected a wooden one, far too big for these boys, thirty-three ounces, but he loved the feel of it. He gave a few swings. He took the first kid, a tall lanky boy by the name of Harrison aside and wriggled a mitt onto him. 'Look, it isn't all about catching, understand?' The boy nodded. 'See, the catcher is the second most important player on the field. Think about it – look at me, not over there – the second key player after the pitcher. He not only has to pull down every pitch, he has to call each one. So the catcher must know about the strengths and weaknesses of every pitcher on the other side. OK? You understand? Now Dick is going to throw some balls. I'll hit a couple of them, but I want you to catch the ones that come by. Also, I need you to tell me all about his style. Got that?'

Harrison nodded gravely.

Dick pitched two dozens balls. Jim slugged at six of them, connecting perfectly with one, his hands well down at the knob, a perfect step as Dick launched at him, his front shoulder locked in, and the grunt of pleasure as wood hit animal hide, and he watched the ball fly in a long, lazy arc, bouncing off the perimeter fence. The kid managed to catch all but two of the other balls.

'Let Petyr have a go?' asked Dick.

Jim looked at his watch. This was taking too long, he wanted to do some base tactics work. 'OK. Just a half-dozen balls, though.'

Jim did a few more swings while the kid fumbled with his helmet and slipped the big ridged chest protection over his head. He could hear Dick encouraging him. While he waited he let his mind idle over the book.

OK, so the main character would be some real big hitter, someone like Mark McGwire or Sammy Sosa, up there at the top of the league table with maybe 69 or 70 homeruns, chasing Joe Bauman's 1954 totals, and hitting .390. But this guy is expensive, and the owner wants to dump him, get some cheaper new players . . . no, no. Maybe he should have a problem, like a drug habit or a mistress, something he would want to keep under wraps. Then the owner could blackmail him into taking a wage cut.

He saw Dick take his position on the mound and, without thinking, he kicked at the rear box line, obscuring it. It was an old trick to enable the batter to step back without the umpire being able to say he was out of his area. It was tolerated in the Major Leagues as a piece of tradition, the kind of chivvying at the rules without breaking them that might make all the difference between a hit and a strike. He gave it one last kick for luck as Dick started to wind himself up.

No, no, not the Bauman record, maybe he is chasing the perfect .400, and coming in at .390, like Brett in 1980. He had once thought of a name for him, Stan Williams, that was it, because real fans would recognise the reference to Ted Williams, who hit .406 in 1941. He was looking forward to describing the Williams style, trying to get some of the poetry down on paper. A big lugger, graceful, yet powerful. He imagined the pitcher opposite Williams, not Dick who was strolling into position as if they had all the time in the world, but some big wind-up merchant, who can do four-seamers, two-seamers, change-ups, knuckleballs and curveballs in quick succession, able to run the sinkers in and locate the fastball away. This would be . . . he struggled for a name . . . for this guy. Rollie Maddux would do, in honour of Rollie Fingers of Oakland and Greg Maddux of the Braves. Of course his Maddux was not too nice a guy. Let's say he's poking Williams' wife. And the hitter just found out. How would that make him feel? Mad. But the best way to get even would be to knock every one of Maddux's balls out of the ground. He breathed hard to try and imagine the combination of anguish and rage. He stepped back, imaging Maddux's ball coming straight at him, and, feeding on Williams's seething hatred for the lowlife, swung back with all the force his upper body could muster.

He felt the vibration from the blow judder down the bat and into his arms, heard the faint gristly cracking sound, and the gasp from Dick. He turned round and saw the folded form of the Sebastyen boy hit the ground, sending up a fine film of dust around himself, the catcher's mask in his hand, the darkening mark on his temple where the bat had made contact. Someone was pulling him aside, and the kids were crowding in. A voice hammered in his ear – Dick's, he realised, but muffled, the upper register wiped by the frantic humming in his own brain. Raub was there with a first-aid kit, and there were more shouts and barks, and Raub's face was in his own, the mouth moving, but his words weren't registering.

Then the scene became hyper-real in its clarity, he could see the sweat glistening on Raub's upper lip, could hear Dick's fast, frantic breathing mingling with his own, could understand what was being said, distinguish the worried noises from each kid.

'F'Chrissake, Barry make the call, 911, get an ambulance,' yelled Raub, spit dappling Jim's face as he worked hard to emphasise the gravity of his message. The next phrase rang out sonorously, as if someone had generated the words from the finest crystal flute. It was from Dick, kneeling in the dirt next to the small, shrunken figure. 'I can't get a pulse.'

The woman turned up at Wendy's trailer park two days after the DUI incident. She introduced herself as 'Margaret', showed the ID from Tucson Child Welfare and Care Department and said she would be her case officer.

'What case?' Wendy asked, but Margaret ignored her, offering only what she clearly thought was a warm, ingratiating smile.

Margaret sat down and looked around, scribbling notes as she did so. 'And where is Pete now?'

'Across the way with George. Coogan. Wanted to look at his guitars.' And Coogan had let him, a tad begrudgingly Wendy had thought. Precious about his toys, no doubt. Thank Christ Pete didn't ask for a ride in that precious car Coogan kept covered up to protect it from the sun.

Margaret sat very correct, knees together, straight back, khaki skirt pulled to her knees, her white blouse still crisp and unwrinkled, despite the heat. Wendy wished she had something on other than sweat pants and a Hard Rock T-shirt. A bra, perhaps, because she could see Margaret checking her breasts. Maybe not wearing underwear was grounds for losing your kid too.

'And how long have you known this George Coogan?' she said it in the same way you might hold up a soiled cloth, with two fingers, minimum pressure, not wanting to get too close in case it infected her.

'Not long.'

'And he is a musician.'

'Yeah. He's the one who took Pete in that night.' She tried to sound relaxed about this. 'He, y'know. He saved my ass.'

'And you let him play over there unsupervised?'

'Well, George's not a pervert if that's what you're sayin'—'

'Not at all,' she said in a way that suggested that it was exactly what she was saying. 'I just want to get the full picture.'

'What case were you talking about earlier?' she asked again.

'Well, when we get a complaint—'

'Whoa, whoa.' Wendy jumped in, startling the woman. 'Complaint? Who complained? The Sheriff passed you a report.'

'And at least a dozen readers of the *Gazette* complained.'

'It was in the *Gazette*?'

'Yes. You didn't see? I have it here—' She reached for her case.

'No. No. I know what happened, I don't need to see what they made up about it. So what case?'

'I have to file a report to see if there should be further action. A formal interview perhaps.'

Wendy felt her blood starting to boil and spit and tried to turn the heat down. 'Coffee?' she blurted. 'Sorry, I should've asked ... I'm a bit – on edge. It was kinda sudden, you turning up.'

'I know it would have been polite to have phoned, made an appointment, but it is our policy to call without prior notice. We find that given advanced warning many parents ... well, they tutor the kids, make a special effort with their home ... their clothes.' Margaret looked at her chest again. Christ, it was not like she had huge tits flapping around under there. They looked pretty good. Maybe the bitch was jealous. God, mustn't think like that. Remember the old, polite Wendy. Minnesota Miss, not Tucson Toughie.

'No coffee, thanks. Some water perhaps?'

'Sure. Coming right up.'

When she came back Margaret didn't drink from the glass, just held it up to the light, as if examining for smears or lipstick stains. 'So, tell me, this Duke ...'

'Dexter Fleming. That's his real name. Duke because he does a good John Wayne impression. So he tells me.'

'Mr Fleming was in charge of the child?'

'Supposed to be. I mean, he'd done it before. I've known him for five months.' Give or take a couple, she thought. She mustn't exaggerate, they'd catch her out, they were bound to check with Duke. 'Been, like, perfect every other time.'

'While you work at ... ?'

'Nunca. It's a restaurant out on 10.'

'Uh-huh. Listen, I would like to talk to Pete if I may.'

'I'll go and get him.'

'I'd like to talk to him alone.'

'He's five.'

'I know. The beauty of being five is, you tend to only know the truth. I'll need about thirty minutes, Miss Blatand.'

Wendy stepped out into the Sonoran furnace and pulled her T-shirt way from her body. Had it been her imagination, or had Margaret put an uncalled for emphasis on the word 'Miss'?

Duke turned up that evening, a couple of beers down the line. He knocked at about seven-thirty and Pete ran to open the door. She scooped him up before he reached the handle, in case it was Margaret or one of her kind. She could just hear the preachy voice: 'And you always let him answer the door without knowing who's there, do you?'

In the end that interview had probably gone well. While the woman was talking to Pete, she had grabbed some clothes and make-up and gone over to Coogan's, where she had changed, even putting on underwear, and Coogan had helped get her composure back, and given her a fistful of questions to ask. Most pertinent was – could I lose my kid? No, Margaret had said, almost with regret, the worst that could happen would be a supervision order, which meant a visit every week, just to check on Pete's welfare. However, that decision lay with 'higher authorities' who may require a follow-up visit and interview before a final ruling.

Wendy pulled open the door, and he was there slumped on the frame, dressed in blue jeans, cowboy boots and a cream Ralph Lauren short-sleeved shirt. He had a sheepish grin playing about his face. 'Hi.'

She went to close the door when Pete stuck his head round. 'Duke? Hey Duke, you wanna play Galactic Three Thousand?'

After the ordeal of Margaret she had bought him a new Playstation game, and he was keen to test out his planetary destruction skill with a worthy opponent, which meant a guy, not mom.

'Duke isn't staying, honey.'

'Aw, come on. I only went out for five minutes,' Duke whined.

'Five minutes? You lyin'—'

'OK, OK. I only intended to go out for five minutes. Honest, darlin'. God's truth. I swear. He was asleep. I checked. All I wanted was a cold brew. You never have enough beer in the house. So I barrelled out to get some. And I got this.' He gave a wide grin and she could see one of his front teeth had gone. 'Got into a fight with some guy said I owed him money. I called you at the bar, from the hospital. They said you'd gone home, so I knew Pete would be OK.'

'Yeah? They never mentioned.'

'I did, darlin', honest injun. Ask that woman who likes all that faggot English music. Can I come in?' She ignored him. 'Now I got cops and Child Welfare coming round. Seems they can prosecute me for child abandonment. I mean, fuck. I never seen this guy before and he starts hittin' on me for fifty bucks. Next thing I know I'm on my back. I only went to get a six-pack. Can I come in?' He smiled again, this time with his lips together, his eyes hooded. She never should have told him he reminded her of Matthew McConaughey.

Finally, she said: 'You wanna beer?'

'Oooh, darlin', now you're talking.'

He stepped in as she went out back and got a cold one. Pete was in his room, getting the Playstation ready. As she strode back she shook up the can, popped the ring pull and let it spray all over Duke's face, pouring the rest over his head, plastering his hair down, till he looked more like Jerry Lewis than some pretty boy film star.

He just stood there, scowling. 'You—'

'Just get lost, Duke. We don't need you no more. Thanks all the same.'

He spun on his heel and walked out, shaking his head like a mangy dog as he did so, creating a fine rain of Miller, slamming the door so hard the trailer shook, and the air conditioner fan squealed in protest.

His one consolation was he heard a long wail of disappointment as Pete realised his sparring partner had been sent packing. Bitch. Wait till he talked to Child Welfare next time. He'd tell them a thing or two.

PART TWO

TEN

New York State

Morgan Starkey was just embracing the first, slightly delirious moments of sleep, letting his brain slide off into neutral, where it chugged over, spinning out a kaleidoscope of unrelated images and scenes, when the crying started again.

At first it incorporated itself into the dreamscape, a sound that made everyone round the odd-shaped dinner table stop and stare. At the window was a large black bird, a raven, looking at them, first with one eye, then the other, and from its beak came the gulping yells of a colicky baby. Then the tableau faded, and he was back in his darkened room, and wide awake.

Well, not quite wide awake, he hadn't been that for six or seven weeks. At least. Not really since the kid came along. His brain was now full of some kind of fug, like those smogs they used to get in LA, blurring his thought process, rolling around suffocating his neurones, which seemed to be firing at half speed. He was two days late with a piece for *Men's Journal*, something he used to pride himself would never happen. No deadline surfing for him – always in well before the due delivery date, exact length, spell- and fact-checked, with all relevant sources annotated and transcribed. A sub-editor's dream.

Not this time. His editor had been understanding, but they needed it soon for the October issue. Even in his befuddled state – with critical faculties so blunted he had laughed himself stupid at the Austin Powers movie on TV the previous night – Morgan knew the copy he had so far wasn't working. It was shapeless and rambling, whereas he was once incisive and clarifying, and the words juddered and moved on the screen, swapping letters at random, apparently creating strange neologisms before his eyes. It was sleep deprivation, he knew. He was in some strange hypnogogic state, of this world but not quite in it.

He reached over and touched Mamie, but she snorted and moved away. He wasn't sure whether she was asleep or faking it, or her exhausted mind had gone into total filter mode and even the increasingly desperate tone in the pumping cycle of bawling from the nursery failed to penetrate the defences.

Stiffly he swung out of bed and rubbed his face. He hadn't felt like this since he got bad jet lag flying back from Europe. Weak and confused, with an immune system so compromised he went from one snivelling cold to another. Thank God they had managed to put on a good show for Jim and Belle the other day. It would be mortifying if, after all their moaning about wanting kids, they had betrayed the fact that the whole thing had turned into a nightmare. He had to face it, that's what it was, a total fuckin' nightmare. And to add insult to injury, he had just received another payment demand from that Paladin guy, over a thousand dollars 'incidental expenses'. Well he could go fuck himself – they had already paid well over the odds.

Morgan went into the nursery, bent over the cot, picked the little bundle up roughly and put her on his shoulder, patting her back with a little too much enthusiasm, then went downstairs to make yet another feed, hoping that would do the trick. If it didn't, he had no idea what he would do.

They followed the ambulance in Dick's car, keeping right on its tail as it drove the eight miles to St Ormond's. They had wanted to ride with the boy, but the medics had said they needed to administer CPR, and they didn't want any extra bodies around.

'It's a good hospital,' Jim said vacantly. 'St Ormond's. Good place. Be in good hands.'

Dick glanced at him and said with feeling. '*If* they get him pumping again. If not, all the good hands can do is zip up the body bag. What the fuck were you thinking?'

'I . . . I didn't know he was—' He felt it again, that vibration as the bat made contact, punching its way through the thin bone of the skull at the temple, wreaking God knew what havoc in the tissues underneath. But he's a kid, he kept thinking, they get knocks all the time, so resilient, so tough, like rubber balls. Why hadn't this one bounced back up?

'You'd kicked up dust rubbing out the back line – the very thing you balled Raub out about. The dust got in his eyes. He took off his helmet . . . Jesus Christ. This could finish us. You.' Dick was growling, an anger fizzing in his voice he had never heard before, and something else, too.

'I think we're insured. I think the coaching policy covers it. Ten million dollars. Sure of it.' Jim was still dazed, the enormity hadn't hit home. 'I'm sure he'll be all right.'

'Yeah?' There it was again, something close to hysteria in the voice, some unsettling undertone Jim couldn't pin down. 'The boy went down like he was poleaxed, Jim. He didn't look all right to me. And no pulse. Is that all right? Huh?'

'What do you want me to say?' Jim bit back. 'Sorry? OK, I'm sorry, I was a jerk. But shit, Dick, I never wanted the kid in the team for a start, I told you he was weedy.'

'Yeah, well you can forget the team altogether now.'

'What? What do you mean? Nah. Come on. Listen. Listen to me, Dick. It'll be OK. And insurance'll cover any medical bills.' Dick humphed in disbelief. 'What? Dick, come on, we don't know he's dead. For fuck's sake . . .'

Dick faced him again, a slight sneer on his face. He looked pale, worried, and clearly not just about the kid. 'I was forgetting, Jim. You still think he's a Hungarian investment banker, don't you?'

'Who—? Look out.'

Dick was forced to brake as the ambulance swung into the emergency admissions gate. After that it was all chaos, and Jim never did get to ask Dick what he meant.

* * *

Marion Volker of Solutions Inc looked at the couple in front of her and tried to arrange her face into a semblance of concern. The truth was they were all blurring into each other these couples, these faces lined with a perpetual anxiety, pain even, generated from their long journey to this room in Scottsdale. It had been the usual relentless descent from young optimism to premature disillusionment, in both nature and science, for these folks. For all of them, in fact. It was what people didn't understand. That this strange longing they all shared, everyone who came before her, this desire to procreate, eventually manifested itself as a constant physical pain, a gnawing, which left its track mark across their faces. Plus, of course, they all shared one other attribute: an intense hope that Solutions Inc would live up to its name.

She could imagine this couple ten years before, newly married, thinking they had all the time in the world, not worried that kids didn't come at first – they were enjoying sex without having to worry about contraception. Then twelve regular menstrual cycles later, the first doubts would have started. Maybe, after eighteen months he'd go and get a fertility check, and then so would she. Or maybe the other way round, depending on just how badly he took any slur on his manhood.

They might then have had nutritional and lifestyle advice, maybe they heard that stress was bad for fertility and she gave up her job, and he didn't take that promotion because it would mean longer hours. And all the time the humiliation of their friends' growing bellies, pregnant within days of announcing they were trying for a baby, and the anguish of watching all those documentaries on TV about unwanted and abused children, when they had a home where they could give so much love.

The path sometimes took some diversions, but basically the road to Solutions Inc was worn smooth by hundreds of pairs of leaden, weary feet. This was the last-chance saloon, and these people were willing to run up a bar tab of many thousands of dollars.

Of the pair before her the man looked the worst. Dark lines under his eyes, skin that would disgrace a walrus, the early appearance of middle-aged jowls. Volker looked at the medical notes and at the couple. They looked healthy enough, but her egg production was erratic, and his sperm count was borderline. They were seeing more and more of the latter now, but at least this case was equal non-opportunity – neither could really blame the other. They were both reproductively dysfunctional. No, she thought, not dysfunctional, 'discordant', that was the word she must use, as if their tubes and cycles were just hitting a few bum notes.

'You specified blonde-haired and blue-eyed.'

'Well, my father was both of those things,' the woman said.

Maybe, she thought, but the dominant gene right now was mousy. With brown eyes. Still, if they wanted Aryan, they could have Aryan. If they could find one. 'You know we are not a great state for blue-eyed blondes. We didn't get that many of the northern Europeans coming into Arizona.'

'No, we realise,' the man said. 'We were prepared to wait . . . a little.'

She nodded and made a show of turning pages. 'The thing is I do have a candidate. Tall, good-looking, blue-eyed, blonde, higher than average IQ, twenty-nine—'

'I thought we said under twenty-five.'

'Which means mostly students, and I'm afraid that many of the universities are actively discouraging their faculties from donating.'

'Oh.'

'Twenty-nine, one child—'

'Married?'

'Widowed,' she lied. Wendy was as good as widowed, her fiancé killed days before he was due to make an honest woman of her.

'And is she of good character?' asked the woman, suspiciously, as if she thought twenty-nine-year-olds had no business being widowed.

'Yes.'

'No criminal record?'

She toyed with lying again, but she had a sudden flash of lawsuit when their kid reached eighteen and got a DUI and all the pieces fell into place. 'Noooooo.'

'What? What's wrong?' asked the woman, sensing hesitation.

'She had an unfortunate incident recently. She was stopped for drunk driving—'

'My family has a history of alcoholism. We were hoping to lose that particular gene,' he said. Ah, that explained his dark eyes and puffy face – after a couple of years of ascetic food fascism he had slid into seeking solace rather than spermatozoa. That might also explain the increasingly depressed sperm count she could see on the reports before her.

'—and may be up before Child Welfare. I have to tell you this, but if you look at the facts—'

'Hold on. Wasn't she in the newspapers? They ran a picture of someone who had been booked at the Sheriff's office? I remember looking at her and thinking, my, she would do, blonde'n'all, if only she wasn't clearly a bad sort,' interrupted the woman.

A bad sort? Volker thought. How quaint. Like they could afford to be fussy. 'That account did not give all the facts. If you will just let me tell you the whole story. DUI is actually a misdemeanour, you know. Not a capital offence.'

'No, I'm sorry, I could never get that image out of my mind, of the mother with a number under her face, it would haunt me. That my baby might end up like that,' she said firmly. 'No, absolutely not. Next, please. We can compromise on the blue eyes, after all.'

Volker sighed. She knew she was going to get this every time now, but she dare not conceal it from any potential couple, because the clinic would be open to litigation for non-disclosure of all pertinent facts. Even the widowed white lie was risky. She would have to tell Wendy Blatand that the deal was off. They wouldn't be needing her eggs after all.

ELEVEN

New York State

Morgan splashed cold water on his face and shook it, trying to identify the source of the burning, irrational hate that had welled up inside him. He was shaking as he went to the refrigerator and took out a 7-Up, fumbling with the ring pull, before he got a welcome cold slug down his throat.

How did he let that happen? He was a nice man, one of the good guys, concerned about the planet, never cheated on his wife, didn't jack off over porn, never raised a finger to her. Didn't complain when she went through all that fertility shit, with the sprays and the obsessive calendar-watching and the faddish diets and the vitamin and mineral supplements – twenty pills a day – to the increasingly desperate, passionless couplings dictated by circulating synthetic chemicals, not by love or lust or need of any kind.

He could hear Mamie upstairs comforting the baby, uttering her soothing words. He wondered what would have happened if she hadn't been woken up by his tirade, his pouring forth of bile, and come to find him shaking the child, its head snapping back and forth like a glove puppet, the screaming becoming louder, shriller, not lessening at all. She had shouldered him aside and sent him downstairs, still dazed from his actions.

He finished the soda and made a fresh pot of coffee, sitting in the kitchen in the darkness, feeling the warmth creep through the cup into his hands, relishing the skin temperature rising to the edge of pain. It was nice to feel anything so clearly. Everything else was somehow muted, muffled, like sound in snow, every sensation, it seemed, except the tight band of pain that traversed his head, each day the circumference shrinking a little more, crushing his skull.

The door opened, the light went on and Mamie entered, her hair a tumbleweed tangle, a large stain on her nightdress where Ariel had thrown up. 'She's asleep.'

He nodded, blinking in the sudden glare. 'There's coffee.'

She joined him at the table and they sat there in silence. Laying there, between them, ignored, was the bill from Paladin. One thousand, two hundred dollars and thirty-four cents. Final demand. They were paying for their stupidity in more ways than one.

Eventually he said in a cracked voice. 'I don't know . . .'

'Ssshhh. It's OK.'

'I could've . . . hurt her. No, no, I mean part of me wanted to hurt her. It was . . .'

'Frightening?'

More than that, to feel what he was capable of at that moment. It was a glimpse into the void, that part of the soul that doesn't flinch from the most evil of deeds. It was that place where people must arrive when they commit war crimes, exterminate their friends, rape their neighbours, maim their children. Words seemed inadequate. He knew at that moment he had been capable of horror. He didn't want to go back to that dark corner. 'Terrifying. Yes.'

'I know. I've felt it too.'

'You?'

'I pinched her face together last week with my hands, so hard it marked her cheeks.'

'Jesus. I don't recall that.'

'I told you it was a milk rash, remember?'

'Yes. Actually, no, I don't recall too much any more. Oh Christ, Mamie. You think we should get help?'

'What kind of help? I called Doctor Wallis for advice. He said some babies are just criers. We got a howler I guess.'

'Counselling? Support group?'

'I don't know. I'd feel . . . like a fraud.'

'Oh come on,' he said, 'You didn't sign up for this. We just didn't expect it.'

'I . . . I . . .'

He could see something welling up inside of her and went over and wrapped his arms round her neck, nuzzling his face into her hair. 'It'll be OK,' he said, almost daring to believe it.

The words had only just left his mouth when they heard the sound again, the hopeless, helpless, heart-stopping cry of a baby bellowing for reasons unknown to God and man.

The call came just before Wendy was leaving to go to Nunca to work. Babysitter couldn't make it. Wendy felt panic rise in her. Who could she get now? She ran across and banged on Coogan's door, wringing her hands in embarrassment. From the other side she heard some lazy guitar picking stop abruptly.

'George. Look – I hate to ask. Could you . . . could you babysit for me? Tonight? I've just been let down.'

Coogan furrowed his brow. 'I . . . I dunno. I got some . . .' What did he have? He had some practice, that was all. It didn't sound important enough. She was chewing her lip so hard it was going to bleed, hopping from leg to leg like she needed to go to the bathroom. 'I . . . oh hell, OK.'

'Great. Great. George, thanks. I'll make it up to you. Pete really likes you. Likes the guitars.'

Terrific, Coogan thought. A fan. He said slowly: 'I ain't had much experience with kids. I'm not sure what to do.'

'Do? You don't do nothing. You call me if there is a problem.'

'Right.'

'Can you come now?'

'Uh. I guess. I'll be right over. Just gotta put this away.'

He could feel her staring as he laid the guitar back in its case, no doubt startled by the lurid mauve lining, long and shaggy, as if it was made of Muppets. It was a Gibson thing.

'Is it a good one?'

'This?' He couldn't keep the pride from his voice. 'Gibson 335.' A 335N he wanted to add. One of the rare blonds with the extended scratchplate made between 1958 and 1960. Only 209 known to have been produced. It was the sound of this guitar, as opposed to the Strat which sat increasingly neglected in the other case, that turned him onto jazz when he found it for sale in upstate New York. Broke the guy's heart to sell it, but arthritis in his hands meant his playing days were all but over. When he sat there and showed Coogan what it could do, first with clean, pure picking from a few simple runs, then, as he grimaced with the pain of making the chord shapes to 'Stardust', demonstrating the fat, gorgeous, generous sound of the 335, Coogan knew he had to have it.

It cost him most of his disability award, but it was worth it. Every guitar was different in small unpredictable ways, every 335N would be different, some of them would be clunkers, even though the same factory and craftsmen turned them out with the same care and attention. His one, though, felt and sounded just right, as long as you loved it. And played jazz. Rock music sounded all wrong, flat-footed and enervated, the Strat was much better than that. But give the 335 a piece of Mancini-Mercer or Coots-Gillespie, a Sammy Cahn or a Jerome Kern, and it made your heart sing along with it. 'Yeah, it's real nice,' he said finally. 'Better'n I am at playing it anyways.'

He flipped the catches shut and stood up, wondering why he had said yes to this. He knew what happened around kids. Boys. Been through this one before. Some of those dots on the wall, they involved the same sort of set-up. Shit, he'd done it now. They walked over across the dusty lot together.

'I only got four or five beers? That gonna be a problem?' she explained as she quickly re-touched her make-up in the living room mirror while Pete coloured in a *Son of Digimon* book.

He tried to be lighthearted. 'Not a problem with me. A

Dr Pepper shortage, well maybe. A Pepsi crisis, I'll have to reconsider. But booze, not an issue.'

'You're dry?'

'Clean and sober. Six months nearly.'

'Do you get clean and sober jazz musicians?'

'I would guess Wynton doesn't tie one on too often. Anyways, I ain't really a jazz musician. Not a real one. Besides, I still, y'know ...' Behind Pete's back he mimed taking a toke on a joint. 'Now and then. But it was the booze that was killing me.'

'What made you stop?'

'I did something stupid when I was drunk. Real stupid. I swore that was it. I don't like who I am when I drink. I can't expect other people to.'

Pete finished off his colouring with an excessive amount of scribbling and said: 'Can George play some games?'

Coogan looked at her for guidance.

'OK. Twenty minutes.' To him she said. 'Then he's in bed. TV remote here, music there. All set?'

There was the honk of the cab's horn outside. She hadn't actually lost her licence yet, she was going to appeal, call Cecco as a witness, but she wasn't going to take any more chances. She finished the last of her lips and turned to him.

'How do I look?'

'Fine.'

'Fine? Fine is the best you can do?'

Coogan managed another noncommittal shrug. He didn't want to play these games. Not now, not with the boy in the room.

The phone rang and she hesitated before picking it up.

'Miss Blatand? It's Margaret.'

'Oh. Hi. Hold on, can you? George, can you tell the cab I'll be one minute? Thanks. Sorry, go ahead Margaret.'

'Listen, I am afraid there has been a development.'

'What kind of development?'

'Mr Fleming has been in touch to say he remembered some other times when you left Pete alone.'

'What? Duke? He *what*? That . . . Margaret, that is not *true*.' She felt a mixture of anger and hysteria well up, and tears stung her eyes. How could she convince this woman? 'Margaret, please you've got to believe, me, on Pete's life—'

'There's no need to go that far. I did get the impression that he was . . .'

'Drunk?' she jumped in.

'Possibly.'

'Listen he came round and I threw him out after what he did. I didn't think he'd be so . . . so vicious. Margaret, please.'

'OK, I am going to re-interview him and ask him dates, time, corroborating evidence, that kind of thing. If he can't give chapter and verse, I'll consider it inadmissible.'

Wendy wanted to kiss her, right there and then, to give her a big hug. Maybe she wasn't so bad after all. 'Oh, Margaret, I mean, I don't know how to th—'

'Hold on, hold on. I haven't heard his side yet. I'll be in touch. Take care, Wendy.'

'Yes. You too. And thanks.'

She explained to Coogan and he nodded a couple of times. Shit. First he was meant to be some kind of fashion judge, now she was appealing to his protective side. He didn't think he had a protective side left till he muttered awkwardly: 'Want me to have a word with him?'

She almost laughed at the thought of anyone going up against big, brawny Duke, even someone of reasonable bulk like Coogan, but she stifled the smile. The offer was nice. And maybe Duke was all bluster. After all, someone had managed to loosen his teeth the other night. The real question she wanted to ask was 'Could you?' Instead it came out as: 'Would you?'

'Be my pleasure.'

'He's at the Mermaid Airplane Park. 'Bout ten miles from here? Usually rooms there, too.'

'I can't promise anything. Just maybe, coming from another guy.'

'George, you are a wonder.' And she kissed him on the cheek before bolting out of the door. He turned and looked at the kid in the doorway, wiped the spot where his mom's lips had been and gave him what he hoped was a reassuring smile. 'Now, how you play these games?'

The doctor came out from the theatre forty minutes after they had arrived at St Ormond's. He was ridiculously young, not yet thirty, but he looked bushed and haunted. Maybe they gave the new kids on the block all the shit work, thought Dick. Like breaking the bad news. NODER, they called it. Notification of Death to Relatives. He had seen it on TV shows a thousand times, the anxious patients and relatives being told the sad news by some handsome hunk of a doctor.

But they had never captured the weight of the air around them, as if they were encased in a transparent quick-drying concrete, dragging them down, making every movement painful and slow, smothering time so it crawled along. Nor did they convey the twisted, burning insides you felt, the horrible, terrible certainty of the words you were going to hear, words that the doctor and you both knew were worthless, empty platitudes, phrases so well worn and chewed over they had no power left in them at all.

'I'm sorry—' the intern began.

Jim's head snapped up, his eyes bulging with horror and disbelief. He didn't have to hear the rest. He, too, knew where it went. He started to rise, his mouth working, trying to form something appropriate to say, reaching out as if he wanted to grab the intern, shake the truth out of him, that they'd made a mistake, the kid would live.

And from Jim's mouth Dick heard a terrible, unfamiliar voice, deep and thick, guttural and crazed.

It was only after a second he realised it wasn't Jim's voice at all. Dick looked along the corridor, and under the hard, merciless lights he saw Sebastyen, Petyr's father, running towards them. He too must have seen this little piece of theatre played out in dramas as well, realised what the body language, the almost imperceptible shake of the head meant. Two men were trying to hold him back but he wriggled free and sprinted. Fast, for a man of his size. The quick-setting concrete of grief and guilt clearly hadn't got to him yet.

Jim reached his full height, as if he was going to face this like a man, but took a step back when he realised the guy wasn't going to stop. Sebastyen hit him at full speed, like a fleshy runaway loco, sending the pair of them tumbling over the bench, across the floor and into the soda machines. The front of one of the steel rectangles shimmied for a second, then a big crack appeared, unzipping the glass from corner to corner.

'Jesus Christ,' yelled the doctor. 'Get me some security here.'

Voices filled the air, cascading over each other in an incoherent babble. Jim's could be heard pleading it was an accident, but the loudest was Sebastyen's, barking and animal-like, unintelligible. Then Dick realised he was speaking in his native tongue. They didn't make it in time to stop him landing two hard punches on Jim's face, and even in the chaos they heard a bone break, saw Jim go limp. Sebastyen's hand was raised for a third when a scrum of doctors, nurses and security landed on him, dragging him to his feet. A nurse bent over Jim, holding his head.

Sebastyen was still yelling, while his two companions looked on impassively, unwilling to help restrain him as he thrashed wildly, kicking out at all and sundry. Eventually, three burly security guards managed to push him against a wall, pinning his limbs, enabling the doctor, his hair now pointing in every direction and his gown ripped, to step back and organise Jim being led away to a treatment room. Dick went over to Sebastyen, whose chest was heaving, his face still so contorted it looked barely human, more like some wild beast. Dick wouldn't have been surprised if he breathed fire.

Instead he spat, aiming for Dick's face, but only succeeding in splattering his shoulder. 'Stefan. It was an accident.'

But the eyes didn't register that he'd heard or taken it in. He shrugged off one arm and put it round Dick's neck, but didn't squeeze, just let the fingers flutter over the skin. One of the guards pulled his arm back and Sebastyen said something in another language, what sounded like a long stream of invective, spewing out in a hot torrent. Finally he switched to English in a softer, matter-of-fact, far scarier tone: 'Tell your friend. He is dead. Tell him. From me.'

'Take him to Room Seven,' said the doctor, shakily, clearly hoping that every breaking of news to the bereaved wasn't going to be like this. 'I'll talk to him there.' He looked at Dick. 'He'll be OK after a while. I'll give him something.'

But as they peeled him from the wall and marched him away, Sebastyen shouted over his shoulder. 'Don't forget to tell him. You hear? Dead. Jim Barry. He's a dead man.'

TWELVE

Tucson, Arizona

Coogan borrowed Wendy's Saturn to drive out to the aircraft park. It was the other side of I–10, a catholic assemblage of metal, civilian and military, seemingly parked up ready to take-off at any moment. Until you noticed the dust covers over the engine nacelles, the tyres that had been deflated to cope with the see-sawing ambient temperatures. It was just gone eight a.m., but already he could see a heat haze forming above the massed aluminium of the planes, distorting the mountains in the far distance, as each fuselage was stoked into an airless mini-oven. He pulled in at the office and asked for Duke.

The guy looked him up and down, didn't make him for any kind of law enforcement agency, and said: 'Duke? He'll be working on a DC-9. Go down here past the 727s, straight on past the BAC 1–11s, right at the DC-10s, then it'll be on your left. If you hit the military transports, you gone too far.'

Coogan drove in among the rows of mostly white planes, blasted over with a protective coat of paint, designed to help reflect the desert heat and slough off any rainfall. It was bizarre and he couldn't figure out why – he'd been around massed aircraft before. Then it hit him. Silence. Normally when you got this many planes together you had noise – take offs and landings, ground generators thrumming, engines warming up, tractors buzzing around. Here they sat in mute rows, muzzled like dogs, the same sort of unsettling peace you got in military graveyards.

Every one of these planes had worked its passage for years, thousands of rotations, millions of miles, but now, outmoded and outdated, yet needed for spares, they had been put out to grass. Or, more accurately, sand, retired to the Arizona desert where the climate ensured they would stay in perpetual middle age. Some were laid up because of their accumulated air miles, others because of changing fashions, or because they were just too noisy to meet twenty-first-century demands. A hefty proportion of the commercials were doomed because of concerns over their old, possibly inflammable wiring, and it wasn't viable to strip them down and re-loom them.

Now and then, he knew, a whole bunch got resurrected, when a shaky Third World airline needed planes and fast, or maybe a country's new military rulers wanted some ground attack planes or bombers and weren't too worried about state of the art, just as long as they could kill and maim.

For the most part though, these metal retirees just sat here in the sun like their human counterparts in the adult communities who came to Arizona to see out their days in clean hot air in an orderly, contained manner.

Coogan wasn't sure why he had volunteered to do this. Ulterior motives, for sure. He just wasn't certain which ones. He found Duke at the base of a set of ladders, staring up at the nose of a DC-9, a tangle of wires spewing out at him, while he supped on a soda. He was wearing just shorts, and Coogan could see he was a well-muscled young man. He probably went one-seventy, one-eighty. Duke barely glanced at him when he got out of the car, just carried on examining the front of the jet. Coogan's heart jumped when he looked down the row and saw the familiar shape of a Black Hawk, pushed into early retirement. Just like him. He went and stood behind Duke. 'We need to talk.'

Duke looked over his shoulder. 'We do? You are?'

'Coogan. George Coogan.'

'Do I know you?'

'I live near Wendy.'

He turned to face him fully and finished off the drink, meeting Coogan's gaze. 'The guitar player?'

'That's me.'

'You play every day?'

This threw him. 'Excuse me?'

'The guitar? You play every day? You always seem to be messin' with that thing.'

'There's an old saying. You miss a day, and you know it. You miss two days, and the band knows it. You miss three, and the audience'll know it. Gotta keep playing. Keep your chops.'

'Sonofabitch, eh? Like slavery.' He crumpled the can and launched it in the direction of some old droop-nosed Phantoms, sitting there in a real sorry-for-themselves pose. 'Look, I gotta get a transponder system out of this. You wanna tell me what you want?'

'Wendy is a little—'

'You hittin' on her?'

'No—'

'I mean, be my guest, pal—'

'I'm *not*. Just a . . . just a friend.'

He turned on his heel. 'Right. I don't need no words with "just friends", George. See ya. 'Bye.'

Duke made to climb the hot steel ladder and Coogan put a hand on his shoulder, slipping on the sheen of sweat.

'Exc—'

'Hey, old man, don't you fuckin' touch me.'

Coogan took two steps back and raised his palms to show no offence was meant. Duke had two inches and maybe a good few pounds on him he figured. And maybe ten years. But old? That was pushing it. He let it ride. 'Duke. You are causing her big, big shit. That's all I am here to say. Drop it—'

'Fuck that. My folks left me alone in the house when I was three. I bet yours did too. Now it's all Child Welfare and psychology and wrapping them in cotton wool. Too soft. Pete's not dumb – he phoned her f'Chrissakes.'

'It's not that, it's what you said later. About her doin' it regular. Know what I'm sayin'? Looks bad.'

'Like I should give a fuck. Listen, old man—' Duke approached and launched a stiff finger at Coogan's chest. In one smooth movement Coogan reached up and dislocated it with a loud pop.

The colour suddenly drained from Duke's face as he looked at the crazy angle of his digit and Coogan thought he was going to faint. All he could say was: 'Ah. Ah. Ah. Fuck. Ah. Ah. Ah.' His breathing was shallow, as if that could keep the pain at bay.

'Old, maybe. Mean, too. Don't forget that.' He suddenly felt good. It was a long time since he had squared up to anyone, had used old skills. You just had to be prepared to hurt. If he still had the knack, Coogan knew he could pop it back into place when he was good and ready. Been a while, though. He used the palm of his hand to push Duke into the shade of the DC-9, where they could chat without melting. 'Now,' Coogan said, enjoying himself. 'Do I have your full attention, cowboy?'

Jim Barry sipped at his tenth coffee of the night, watching dawn softening the shadows of the town through the window of his study, the Mac humming impotently on the desk. It was dawn coming up over the same green, picket-fenced prosperous Bloomsberry that the sun had risen over yesterday, the same bunch of media and money folk he had mentally sneered at.

And now it was all changed.

Every five minutes he was forced to run through the tragedy again, pinpointing those little What-if? moments where fate could have taken another road, depositing him at the end of the evening unscarred and unchanged, his team packing up and going home, the parents arriving to pick up their kids, the usual hasty hellos and goodbyes from people whose lives are dominated by a thousand little routines like this. If only he hadn't had the letter from Hooper, he wouldn't have thought about the book, got caught up in that moment, have swung the bat too hard. If only he hadn't scrubbed at the batter's box. If only the stupid kid hadn't taken off the mask and stepped forward. If only he hadn't said yes to getting the kid involved in the first place. Dick and Belle, sweet voices of reason, give everyone an equal chance. An equal chance to get killed perhaps.

He wondered how many times he had been at these junctions in his life, where if he took the left fork, someone died, the right, they all went on in sweet oblivion. Maybe you missed death by seconds dozens of times a day – unplugging the toaster with wet hands you are a millimetre away from electrocuting yourself, deciding to miss a flight you miss a freeway smash too, making one last call in the office you avoid a fruitcake pushing guys under a subway train on the platform where you usually stand. You just never know.

But what he did know, there and then, was that he could never pick up a baseball bat again, go to another ball game, that he would have to sell his Ty Cobb pennant and signed ball, the albums of chewing gum cards he had hoarded from eight to eighteen, the collection of bats. Everything to do with the game, every artefact and reference would revive that feeling of bone collapsing under the bat, smashing into blood vessels, generating a massive haemorrhage and then a clot. 'He must have had very thin bone there. It happens in some people,' the doctor had said. 'You weren't to know.' And he felt that judder through his arm again.

Carefully he went over and took down the signed, framed Mike Piazza poster and laid it against the wall. Would they have to move, to get away from the shame and pity and guilt and unspoken accusations that would swirl around them for months or years? Possibly.

One thing was for sure, he couldn't face the father. Couldn't see him in the street or the supermarket, at the liquor store or the movies, certainly not with Tommy, because every time it would drive home to both of them the lost son, plucked away by a careless father who was blessed to still have a fine, healthy kid. Mind you, there would be an inquest, so the police who turned up after the fracas said. Blame would be apportioned. He would have to face the father then, have to suffer his withering stare for the long hours or perhaps days it would take to reconstruct that night . . . last night he reminded himself.

He sat down and rubbed his stinging, gritty eyes, careful to avoid his damaged cheek-bone, and stared at the screen-saver, a repeating image of a pitcher feeding a ball to a hitter, who sets the red-and-white sphere spinning to fill the entire tube, freezing for a second on the ball so you could read the writing: Official American League Ball, William Harridge, Pres. and The Cushioned Cork Centre, before it shattered into pieces and the cycle began again. He quickly reset the control and display settings so it would now show the old flying toasters number, flapping in formation in eternal migration.

Surely there must be something he could do? Something for the family? Not money – someone who drives a top spec imported SUV and keeps a helipad is not going to take an offer of mere cash as any kind of recompense or restitution. There must be some way of repaying snatching a life like that? He thought about Marta, the mother. How old was she? Not too old, he had seen her once or twice, surely they still had time to have more kids? Shit, that wouldn't do. Sorry pal, never mind, just have to get humpin' and make another.

One thing was certain, he and Dick would have to get their stories straight. They hadn't had time before the cops took their statements, but hell, any discrepancy would be easy to blame on the heightened emotional state of the moment. Now he touched his cheek, purple and angry where the punches had landed. The nurse had reckoned there might be a cracked bone, but there was little they could do except let the swelling go down and let it heal. They could hardly splint his cheek now, could they?

A letter, he had eventually settled upon. That was the least he could do. Sincere – really sincere – condolences. Maybe, like in an auto smash, he shouldn't express responsibility, but the very least he could do was indicate that he was hurting, too. That the loss of the boy was going to scar his soul. Not in the same way as it was theirs – how could it? – but deep and livid all the same. The Mike Piazza poster, for instance. He'd won it at a *GQ* Man of The Year Function. Giving that away – even selling it – was going to hurt like hell.

He clicked into the Mac's letter file and started a new document. His letter-headed paper came up, and he winced at the little baseball bats crossed in the corner. He deleted them. How to begin? Mr and Mrs Sebastyen? Stefan and Marta? No, too informal. Mr and Mrs.

It was then he remembered what Dick had said. About him not being a banker. He looked up from the screen and out through the window again, where the sky had turned a delicate pink colour, and the town looked like it was blushing, a soft, maidenly hue. Perhaps it was – in shame.

He saw the black or blue – later it would be hard to recall – car draw up to the sidewalk outside his home at the end of the lawn. He looked at his watch. Five forty-eight. Cops?

The front window of the vehicle rolled down a fraction and Jim stood up, leaning closer to the window. Maybe people wanted to gawp at the home of the murderer, maybe he was going to end up on one of those ghoulish tours. See Where The Baseball Murderer Lived! And they'd take pictures, just like the jerk out there was going to.

It took him an extra second to realise that the tube being extruded from the crack in the window was no lens, but a gun barrel.

He hit the floor the instant the Mac disintegrated over him, bits of glass and chips and disc flying about the room as the tube imploded with a whump. He was aware of the thud of rounds in the wall opposite the window, of a pane of glass falling loose and smashing, papers dancing in the air as they were plucked from the desk, the smell of burning as something flared up in the computer. But no gunshots. Just the disintegration of the world around his into a whirling dervish of debris, as if a silent twister had sucked into the house.

Then it stopped. He heard the car drive away, and the room slowly calmed, as if an epileptic fit had just ended and a few fading twitches were all that was left of the neural storm. Sheaves of paper sucked into the air by the wind of high velocity ordnance began to swing slowly down to earth.

He knelt up and was instantly sick on the floor, a big gush, mainly liquid, dark brown coffee, splashing all across the polished wood, soaking the papers, his stomach knotting and squeezing and ringing, until it had evacuated everything right down to the sliver of bile that ran down his chin. He wiped his eyes, blurred with involuntary tears, and looked around the devastated, defiled study. He could hear movement upstairs, the thud of Belle's feet as she came to see what had happened. He groaned when his eyes alighted on the shredded form of Mike Piazza, great gaping holes in his physique where bullets had atomised the glossy image.

And even while his senses screamed incoherently, a cool voice in the corner of his mind realised this was what Dick had meant.

THIRTEEN

Tucson, Arizona

Wendy put the phone down and sighed. She was aware that Pete was saying something to her, but couldn't quite make it out. In the end she just snapped: 'Be quiet, Mommy's trying to *think.*'

He ran over to the couch and buried his face in a cushion, sobbing melodramatically. But she wasn't in the mood to be manipulated right now. So, no deal with the fertility clinic, the DUI had blown that one out of the water. Ah well, she thought bitterly, that'll teach her to put all her eggs in one basket.

The Volker woman had been nice, sympathetic even, and she said she would keep offering her as a donor, but the prevailing thought – you might call it a fad – she said, was for environmental and social considerations to be given as much weight as genetic ones. Apparently some woman had sued a clinic in LA when she discovered that her delinquent kid had also had a delinquent egg-donor mother, although that information had been fudged. She had won. So full disclosure was the norm.

'It's a drink-driving f'Chrissake,' she said to herself. 'Not Satanism or drug-dealing.' Jesus she felt like saying that to Margaret – why was she being hounded when she was sure there were women out there selling their kids' bodies to fund their crack cocaine habit.

She went over and gave Pete a cuddle and he clamped onto her like a koala. ''S OK, baby. You just gotta give me a little room to breathe. Time to think.'

There was a soft knock at the door. Who could this be? The CIA to accuse her of passing nuclear secrets to China?

It was Coogan, a dark silhouette in front of the noon sun, cradling a six-pack of sodas. He was streaked with sweat, and his clothes were dirty with patches of grease. He passed her a soda and the car keys. 'What happened? You have a wreck? Or a breakdown?'

He shook his head. 'I ended up helping Duke.'

'Helping him?' Guys, you leave them alone for two minutes and they start palling up. Probably talked about her ass or something.

'Yeah. He's none too good on electrics.'

'Is Duke coming over?' asked Pete.

'Nah, he's busy. Gotta work, kid,' said Coogan. What was that twinge he just felt?

'Oh. Cause he's the best at IndyBlast and I wanna play IndyBlast. Can I play IndyBlast, Mom?'

'No, Pete – you got one hour a day on that. You had your quota.'

He put his thumb in his mouth and guiltily she lifted him up. The boy snuggled down onto her chest. Not a bad place to be, Coogan thought for a moment, then squashed the thought. That wasn't the ulterior motive, he reminded himself. Get real.

'You OK?' Coogan asked, catching a look of something flit across her face. Despair it looked like.

'Oh, I got . . . actually I got nothing, that's what I got.'

'And what would you like?'

She laughed and kicked the door shut. Still hugging the boy she sat down on the couch. 'The usual. Money. A good man who might stay a while after the beer in the icebox has run out. A decent home, not something built out of old cereal packets. Clothes that didn't come from factory outlets or Wal-Mart—'

'Whoa. Whoa. Enough. I get the picture.'

'A Playstation Series Three console,' added Pete.

'OK, go on,' she said. 'Thirty minutes on IndyBlast. Then no more for the rest of the day. Not even a mention, or it goes away for a whole week. Deal?'

'Deal. George, you wanna play with me?'

No, I should walk away from here Coogan thought. Cross to my trailer, plug in, and play some tunes till you all go away. I am trouble. You are trouble. 'Yeah, you set it up, I'll be right in.'

Pete disappeared into his room, where the games were played through a TV Wendy had picked up at a garage sale.

'Stop beatin' yourself up. You get guys like Duke all over. I'd say you should raise your sights.'

'Thanks. Y'know it's easier to raise your sights when you got a coupla hundred thousand dollars in the bank. Wouldn't you say?'

'I wouldn't know.'

'Nor me. But I keep figurin' the time is right.'

'Any time is the right time for that.'

'You make money playin'?'

'Some. Never pays big time. I tried being in rock bands – I mean, I can do that stuff. I'm from Seattle originally, but I kinda missed that boat. Too young for Hendrix, probably too old for Nirvana. Anyway, by the time the city was coming onto the musical map, I was in the army.'

'The army?'

'Yeah, the army. Don't look surprised.'

'They have guitarists in the army?'

'They have men in the army. My old man was. I learned to play guitar with other service kids around the bases, here and Europe, got a power trio together, thinking all the time the service wasn't for me. I didn't realise it was . . . inevitable. That I'd enlist I mean.'

'So you ain't an eccentric millionaire livin' in a trailer park lookin' for a mother and child to dump your riches on?'

''Fraid not, lady.'

'Fat lot of use you are.'

'Now that's true. I better go and see Pete, before I screw that up, too.'

'So what about Duke?' she reminded him.

'Oh, yeah. Duke. No, Duke saw reason. He's gonna phone that woman and tell her he was just shootin' off. Don't you worry none about Duke.'

'Coogan, you're a genius.'

If only, he thought. If only.

Lower and lower he was going. Hitting rock bottom now. Twins. Poor fuckin' girls. Eighteen, nineteen. Scared out of their wits. He could see the look in their hollow eyes. But he'd taken three of those pills. Three. Too many. They set something in the metabolism far too high. Even coming the first time didn't help. He'd waited fifteen minutes and done it again. Then again. His balls ached and the end of his penis was glowing red from friction. At least, he hoped it was friction. Maybe he picked something up. He should go back to using rubbers, just to be on the safe side. He insisted the girls he took hadn't been turned out yet, but he knew those guys on the landings, Tarr, Mr Moustache, they would all have had a sampling. He looked at the Sig in his hand again, put the barrel against his forehead, but didn't bother with the safety. After today he knew there were no depths he wouldn't plumb. No good kidding himself. He wasn't going to kill himself. He was going to wait until the nasty, infected wound that was his life burst all around him and swept him away in its pus. The way things were going, he wouldn't have to wait too long.

FOURTEEN

Bloomsberry, New Jersey

The house was in semi-darkness, like it was in mourning, he thought. All the drapes were pulled, the blinds down, shutting out the daylight, preventing them being seduced into thinking it was another normal day in town, where the sun shone and the trees waved softly in the breeze, and there was the seductive buzz of lawnmowers, the occasional yelp of kids. But, for Jim, normality was no longer an option.

His hands shook as he lifted the coffee cup. He held onto the wrist and guided it to his lips, taking a long slurp, feeling the inner skin of his mouth crisp and curl it was so hot. But right now Jim needed sensation. He felt he was becoming numb, desensitised, shutting down in the face of mounting horror.

The joke was he had recognised the two cops. Donkey Schlong and Officer Stud. Despite the gravity of the situation, he had had an irresistible urge to laugh every time they opened their mouths. The previous year, in an attempt to win over the clumps of kids that had started to congregate on the street corners, the Bloomsberry PD had produced baseball-style collectors cards of each officer, with a short biog on the back. Some nerd had taken them, scanned them into a computer, relocated the facial images onto the male or female partner in some triple-X sex scenes downloaded from the internet, and produced a set of shadow-cards, each one of which had a highly imaginative sexual profile of the officer on the back. No prizes for guessing which of the two card series became the most sought after.

Yet even while seeing these guys in the flesh, as it were, tickled some sick part of his subconscious, their words were thudding home. No, Mr Sebastyen had been under sedation at the hospital all night, there was no way he could be involved. It could be a sympathiser, they accepted. They would question him the moment he was able to talk sensibly. 'You realise things may get worse,' said Officer Stud.

'Worse than someone trying to murder me in my home? OK, I'd like to hear this. What is it? Killing of all the first-born?'

'If there is a trial,' said Donkey Schlong.

He felt it detonate inside his head. His face must have shown a reaction. 'They didn't tell you?' asked Stud.

'I-I don't recall. The . . . it's a bit of a blur . . .'

'Maybe they thought you'd had enough for one night,' Schlong had said.

'It was an accident.'

Schlong raised an eyebrow: 'You know, Mr Barry, funny thing is, accidents are pretty much extinct in America.'

'Along with acts of God,' added Stud.

'There is always a guilty party. What we got here could be negligence, could be failure to exercise a sufficient level of care—'

'The kid took his helmet off.'

Schlong stood up. 'The body is at the State Medical Examiner's Office in Newark. The autopsy report will be passed to Homicide and the Prosecutor's Office over there. They will put the case before a Grand Jury to see if there is a case to answer.'

'A Grand Jury?' Like he was a mobster or something. 'How long?'

'Till Grand Jury? Two months, maybe more. Look, if it wasn't so obviously an accident of some sorts – we're talking maybe criminal negligence, tops – you'd be in custody right now. We're assuming there was nothing personal here. Are we right? OK. Take what comfort you can from that.'

Stud said glumly: 'Even if they don't move on it, there is always the chance of a civil action. From Mr Sebastyen.'

Jim couldn't help himself, he blurted: 'Who, as an interim settlement, is trying to kill me.'

'We don't know that. His alibi is an arm full of sedative. Not bad as alibis go. And as I said, it could be a frightener.'

'Can we go into some sort of protective custody? Witness Protection Programme?'

Schlong shook his head: 'You been watchin' "The Sopranos" re-runs, Mr Barry? For one, you are not a witness, two this is not a federal offence, so there are no funds for relocation and three . . . we can put an officer on the house for a few days.'

'A few days?'

'And after that you will be on the high priority call-by roster, so a cruiser always comes by. Every ten, twelve minutes.'

'Just in time to call the ambulance?'

'You pay your taxes, Mr Barry. You read the town's financial bulletin you get with each demand? You do? Then you know that there isn't much slack in the budget. We can't do it. Look, a kid is dead, feelings are gonna run high for a while, then settle down,' said Stud.

'Then they'll go back up for the Grand Jury. You gotta face it.'

'There's press outside now,' Stud warned.

Jim nodded. He had seen the vans. Belle had answered the door and been bombarded with questions, microphones and tape recorders. For the moment the cops had moved them back, but like in some late night zombie movie, the ghouls would eventually find a way through.

He sipped his coffee and shut the two cops out of his mind. They had had one positive suggestion. After the next interview, scheduled for later that day, leave town. As long as they knew where he was, then there would be no problem. He could check in with the local PD in whatever place he chose. They would prefer he stayed in New Jersey or New York, though, just to be on the safe side.

Belle came in. She was tired and drawn, the smudges under her eyes looked like misplaced make-up, but he knew it was exhaustion. She took a coffee from the pot and pulled it away from her lips as it scalded them. 'Why don't you take a pill and try and get some sleep?' she said.

'That bad, huh?'

'You've looked better. Jesus, Freddy Krueger has looked better.'

She tried to laugh but it quickly metamorphosed into sobbing. He went to put an arm round her. 'Belle, Belle. Come on. We'll be OK.'

She pulled away. 'We'll be OK? I wasn't thinking about us. I was thinking about that poor boy. About that poor woman. You killed her only son, Jim. With baseball. You killed him with baseball.'

'I didn't mean to sound . . . callous. I just . . . how do you think I feel, huh?'

She sniffed loudly. 'I dunno. Wanna tell me?'

Just then the phone rang and the doorbell went. Jim looked up to see a lens being shoved against the window, trying to film in the crack between the drapes. He threw his coffee, unconcerned about the fabric it would ruin, and saw the apparition instinctively pull back as it sloshed against the glass.

'Hunted,' he suddenly said. 'I feel hunted. As if they are coming for me.' The doorbell and phone went again, and a persistent knocking started at the rear door. He found himself shouting to drown out the noise. 'We gotta get out of here. I gotta think.'

Coogan crossed the bridge over the wash and walked out to the desert at six-thirty, just as the sun was rising over the mountains. He took the familiar path through the scrub, once a cattle trail, before the farmers over-grazed the land and turned it to dust. Within ten minutes he was leaving behind the tough grass and berry-heavy hackberry, and skirting the barrel cacti and some stands of low-lying junipers, stepping over the faturas and sacred cherries, pausing to take in the yellow flowers of the coyote melon, and most of all, to suck in that dry air, to let the silence envelope him, something that, he had heard, was becoming increasingly precious, as cars and bikes and aircraft encroached on the desert. But at six-thirty? The quiet was there to be taken in a large draught.

There was one particular spot he was after, where the rocks were piled high in an impossible formation, balancing as if some giant child had made them, and been called away by mom before finishing, leaving a frighteningly precarious confection of boulders. In reality the jumble was the resilient remnant of when the Santa Catalinas were much, much higher, before the upper part simply slid off towards Mexico, leaving the sharpened stumps of the present range behind.

The butterflies were out already, big bruising swallowtails muscling their way around, followed by the more delicate actions of the charmingly named dogfaces, ochre splashed with a Rorschach of black, and the untainted pure yellow of the sulphurs and dozens of others he hadn't yet learned the names of.

He found the rock he was after, a naturally hollowed-out chair, a formation that enabled him to sit at an angle to the sun, not being blinded, but feeling its growing warmth toast the left side of his face. And in front of him was Clint.

Nobody knew how old he was, but he had eight big, fat arms, and he knew that they didn't get their first appendage until they were seventy. Maybe three hundred years was a decent guess. Three hundred years since he and his like had this place all to themselves.

He'd heard the name from a hiker he had met, someone who had been walking these trails for ten years or more. Clint was a saguaro, a fine, multi-armed specimen, dominating this corner like an alpha male.

He was full of holes, of course. Woodpeckers, flickers, owls and rodents all used Clint for shelter and shade. But it wasn't the lodgers that were killing Clint, it was something else, something invisible, a bacterial necrosis slowly eating away at his flesh, turning it to string, like a cactus version of cancer.

Coogan sat himself down, and nodded to Clint, and watched a cardinal flit around between the arms. Five years it took for a saguaro to die. Which is why, of course, those landscapers who made a business of transplanting them could give a one-year guarantee with impunity. The hiker he had met reckoned Clint had three years left. Coogan reckoned he wouldn't stick around to see the end. Not now.

Because they were there behind his eyes again, the little stick people, scurrying at the edge of his vision. It wouldn't be long now before one of them detached and took up residence in his dreams, then in his waking moments. Always the way.

He took out a thin joint, rolled so that just a few strands of grass ran the length of the tube, fired up and took a hit. This was where he liked to think, away from everything, with just a mild stimulation. He had spent a decade trying to get his life together in bars, mumbling stupid plans to strangers, joining second-rate bands whose drummers really sucked, falling in love with whoever was left behind at closing time. He wondered how he could have been so . . . dumb. He had always laughed at those people who talked about places getting them grounded and focused, but whatever he wanted to call it, the desert was pretty good at blowing the dust from between his ears. Even dust as old and as orange as the stuff lodged in the crevices of his brain.

OK, so here was the deal, he summarised to himself. He guessed he had the hots for Wendy. He might have gone into denial on it, big time, but it kept creeping up on him unawares, like a sucker punch. Coogan and his will of jell-o. And with the woman comes the boy and with the boy comes . . .

He thought of Toots.

Toots had a plan, the kind of plan that would help Wendy. Get rich quick. He had shared it with him, with Flint and Nash and Jones and the others and they had all let Toots down. It was what they had done back in their army days. They had ribbed him. Got drunk, and started in on him, ridiculing him: What was he thinking, calling them in from all across America, just to tell them this bullshit idea that would get them all banged up? Except that now Coogan knew it wasn't bullshit. Too late for Toots now, though. He had gone over the top in every sense of the word.

He took a hit of the Mexican weed again and the truth stared him in the face. Clint over there, the big swinging dick of the cactus world. That's what he wanted to be. There in front of Wendy beating his chest, displaying his tail feathers, rubbing his over-sized antlers on the ground, telling her he could solve all her problems. He had told Toots it was dumb then, and it was dumb now. Except Wendy had inadvertently provided him with a missing link that Toots never had. Even if the thought made him want to vomit.

Shit, start thinking like this and he'll be just like Toots. Dead. Best move on, get out of this place. Get away from temptation, in all its forms. Get out of Arizona. Then he looked at his watch and realised what the date was. Shit, maybe it was worth one last look. For Toots.

FIFTEEN

New York State

Morgan finished the piece, spell-checked, copied and e-mailed it to his editor. Three days late. They had said if it didn't make it this month, there would be no slot later and it would wither and die. That might mean he couldn't even claim a kill-fee he thought. After all, it was his fault, and his alone, that it was late.

He leant back in his chair and felt the room spin a little. He had developed this strange lightheadedness that hit him whenever he moved suddenly, like a sudden sickening lurch of a boat, except, of course, he was on dry land. It might just last for a fraction of a second, enough to stop him in his tracks. Or it could go for the full carousel effect, and start hot sweat coming out on him, his stomach cramping, ready to empty before the world stabilised.

Exhaustion. That's all it was. Ariel was asleep right now, but at three in the afternoon she always was. Whereas at three in the morning she was busy going for the Ripley Believe It Or Not Longest Wail Known To Man. It was as if she had been born on Australian time, completely out of whack by half a day.

Mamie came into the study. 'Finished?'

'Uh-huh.'

She put a coffee down next to him. 'She's asleep.'

'I guessed.'

She put her arms round his neck, the first real, intimate physical contact they had had for weeks. 'I'm sorry.'

'What about?'

'You know . . .'

'It's not your fault.'

She sighed. That wasn't what he implied in the small hours,

when they were at the lowest ebb. 'You were ready to give up on us having any baby at all.'

That was true.

'I made you.'

That was true also. But he didn't hold the whole escapade against her. She was willing to try anything, even if it was technically illegal, to get a child. And now they had one . . .

She let go of his neck and he swivelled round to face her. 'Shall we go to bed?'

'To sleep?'

She reached out and touched his cheek: 'What would you rather have right now. Sex or sleep?'

What a choice. Two primal instincts battling it out for each other. He was saved from giving the wrong answer by the phone ringing.

'Hi, hi. How are you? No, great. Heard what? No, I've been busy . . . no shit. *No shit*. Jeez. I mean . . . is there anything I can do? No, no, of course. Of course. Look, it is not a problem. No, Mamie'll be fine. Be glad of the company. OK, see you then.'

He put the phone down and bit his lower lip, unable to quite grasp what he had heard.

'Well?' asked Mamie.

'It was Jim Barry. He's in trouble. He wants to stay here for a few days.'

'Here? With what we're going through? Are you out of your mind?'

'I couldn't say no. He sounds desperate.'

'What sort of trouble? IRS?'

Morgan shook his head. 'I think he said he killed somebody.'

Mamie went pale and left the room, trying to fight back another sobbing panic attack. This couldn't be happening.

Jim listened to Hooper's very reasonable voice telling him that, of course he had read about what he kept calling this 'tragedy' in the *Post*, saw the snatched pictures through the window.

Disgusting. Not fit to be called journalism. He had hesitated and then come out with it. Condé Nast still wanted to go ahead. But with a reduced offer. Six million over four years. Six million? Six? This was just coincidence, Jim, Hooper insisted, nothing to do with kicking him when he was down. They have some new predictions for the men's magazine market, and they have the word saturation written all over them. It wasn't like it was a strong e-title, after all. They could easily have pulled out, decided that print was about to go the way of morse code. But they had decided they could take a chance, but not a double-figures kind of chance. Six million? Was that enough to live his dreams on? He had to think about it.

But first of all he had another interview to face with some sour-voiced detective who had called, who sounded as if he wanted to shoot for Murder One, no matter what the circumstances. Dick had called and said he'd just been through the wringer with him, but he hadn't shaken the story. Kid's own fault, moved just as Jim did, right into the line of the swing. Just a shame. So get that over with, then they would all go to Morgan's, maybe get some peace and quiet and a good night's rest. That was what he needed. Sleep.

Wendy was lying in bed, thinking about maybe turning over and going back to sleep, when she heard the tap on the door and knew it was Coogan. She wondered for a minute if he was coming on to her and she was missing the signals, but he had been the perfect gentleman. In fact, if anything he was positively reticent sometimes. Which was just as well, 'cause the last thing she needed was more guy trouble.

She looked at her watch. Seven-thirty. Jesus, these ex-drunks liked to live life to the full. She pulled on a robe and flipped the locks, locks that were a waste of time when you could poke a finger through the walls of the trailer.

'Hi.' She could smell the sweet smoke on him. So, as he had suggested, not entirely vice-free then.

'Hi. Kinda early, isn't it? Even Pete isn't awake.'

Buzzing slightly from the grass, he lolled against the frame and relaxed. 'I wondered if you would like a trip. Both of yous.'

'To where?'

'The Canyon.'

'Which Canyon?'

'Which Canyon? There is only one Canyon in Arizona. The Grand Canyon.'

'The . . . Jesus, George. It must be seven hours' drive.'

'Six.'

'I gotta work tonight.'

'Call in sick.'

'I need the money.'

'I'll stand you it. You been there before? The Canyon?'

'The Grand Canyon?' she repeated unnecessarily. 'No. Duke said he'd take us when . . . if he got his job back. Anyway, isn't it really crowded this time of year?'

'Teddy Roosevelt said every American should see it.'

'But not all at once. I dunno . . .'

'I got a cabin. By the rim.'

'When? When did you do this?'

'Friend of mine had the booking. Months ago. He can't take it. I just realised it was tonight. Seems a shame to let it go.' And he added so she was clear about this: 'It's got two rooms.'

Wendy rubbed her eyes. 'And it's a long drive.'

'Don't worry,' said Coogan, sensing victory and indicating the tarped shape over his right shoulder. 'We'll take the Trans Am.'

He met Schmee at Lagoon, a bar in Chelsea, which rammed home a South Pacific kitsch theme as if it was in any way original, full of grotesque carvings and replica war canoes hanging from the ceiling. Still, the various Asian and Polynesian girls serving the drinks were easy on the eye.

Schmee was always the contact. A compact guy, his blond hair shaved close to his skull, he always wore suits that made him look uncomfortable. Or maybe any suit made him look uncomfortable. Maybe some kind of uniform would fit him better.

'You're a lucky man.' Schmee blinked those eyes with eyebrows so fair they almost made him look albino.

He nodded. 'I know.'

'He must have been feeling . . . indulgent.'

The Creep agreed that he wasn't entirely sure why he was still drawing breath. 'Maybe it's just expedient. He needed something done. I was the best man for the job. Difficult to replace.'

'Sure.' Schmee handed over a package. 'I'd've wasted you myself,' and he laughed. 'The last of those names.'

'Good.'

'And seven more.'

'Listen—'

Schmee's hand shot out and grabbed his wrist hard, his fingers scrabbling for and then finding a nerve point that sent arrows of fire up to The Creep's shoulder. It was all he could do to stop himself crying out.

'One of those twins, you know, is not much good to us for a week or two. I have noticed this. You're getting . . . more enthusiastic. I suggest you calm down a little.' He let the pressure off.

'Every time I go into a computer there is a footprint, every time I make a request from files, I have to justify it. Do you know how many forms there are, random checks?'

'Between nine and eleven. You told me. This is not our problem. This is your problem. Now, Hoek is moving his base of operations.'

'To where?'

'To where you won't find him if you came looking.'

'Why? Is it—'

'No concern of yours? That's right.' Schmee tried to put the pressure on again and The Creep managed to pull his arm away, but it was floppy, as if the bones had been filleted from it. 'We want a cold trail. A clean break. What we need to know is are there any other movements? Is anyone else taking an interest in him?'

'No.'

'How can you be sure?'

'I mean, no, I can't do it.'

Schmee ignored the man's protest, dismissing it by not acknowledging its existence. 'How close. And who. If anyone else is being flown in. All it will take is a little socialising, I'm sure.'

'I don't do much of that.'

'You should get out more. I tell you what, just as an encourage-ment. No more girls until you check back with that information. How's that?' Schmee flashed him a nasty, crooked smile.

The life came back into his arm, tingling as it revived. He sipped at his drink, swilling the rum-tinged concoction around his mouth. That would suit him just fine. He was going to give all this sex business up anyway.

Tommy walked into Jim's ruined study, now swept clear of glass, the carcass of the computer dumped, the window boarded, and watched his father take down the last posters and pennants, some of them tattered where bullets had penetrated. Damaged or not, they were going into a big black garden garbage sack.

'You taking those with us, Dad? Can I take mine?'

Jim looked at the little fella, seeing a shrunken version of himself, just a little stronger, brighter, more worldly-wise than he had been, but he guessed all kids were. He still remembered the little phrases Tommy had started uttering just a few short years ago. Starting, as all of them do, with 'No', then progressing onto 'Oh dear', which could be used to cover any calamity, and 'I've fibished' whenever a task, be it pooping or eating was done. And then the inquisitions – 'Why don't I have hair there?' or 'Where's Mommy's then?' or 'What was I like when I was in her tummy?' or 'Why does Daddy have a spider up his nose?' a question which made him invest in a nasal trimmer.

'No, Tommy. I just—' I just want to burn them, burn them all, cleanse by fire. 'Some of them are damaged, that's all.'

'From the bullets?'

He nodded. They had tried to explain it as a drive-by shooting, an act of random violence, and that they were leaving to give the builders and decorators time to repair the study and window.

'Can I have that one? I haven't got an Orioles.' Jim handed it over. 'We havin' practice next week?'

'No, Tommy. The rest of the season has been cancelled, as a mark of respect.'

'Noooooo,' he petulantly stamped his foot. 'It's not fair. It was that stupid kid's own fault. I saw it, Dad. It's not fair. Just because someone died. People die all the time, you said so. Gran'ma died, we still played baseball. We played catch at the funeral, didn't we? Please, Dad. Please?'

'We played *after* the funeral, not during. And I can't, Son. Can't change it. It's got to stay like that. We announced it.'

''S not *fair*.' Tommy turned to storm out. 'He wasn't even American. He shouldn't have been playing in the first place.' The door slammed and the sheeting in the window vibrated loudly.

Amen to that, Jim thought. Amen.

SIXTEEN

Tucson, Arizona

'That's it? Jesus fuckin' Christ.' She must stop cursing so much. She knew she was coarsening from the little Minnesota girl who ran away from the family business to get some space, to live down the shame, the stories of the guy who fucked two sisters in one night and got them both banged up. Yeah, then chose the prettier one. 'I mean, George, it ain't quite what I expected.'

Pete obviously felt the same, because he ran out of the trailer and stopped dead when he saw the car. Coogan seemed unfazed, he just shrugged. The once-red paint had faded to a pink, mottled with brown spots here and there. On the side she was looking at the wheel rims didn't match, and the door appeared to be held on with some kind of chicken wire. He'd picked it up in Oregon, and one day he would turn it back into what it once was, give it a second chance, another bite at the cherry.

'You crossed America in that?' she finally asked.

Coogan grinned. He no longer saw the defects, in his mind's eye it was already re-painted and re-chromed. 'Hey, this is the car that made the Kessel run in under twelve parsecs.'

'What? George, what the fu— hell are you talking about?'

'*Star Wars.* You must know, Pete. Han Solo.'

Pete furrowed his brow. 'Is he in *Star Wars*?'

Coogan sighed. 'Well, he was in my day. Don't look like that, the mechanics are A1 and the air conditioning works and it'll get us there.'

'And back?' she asked dubiously.

145

'And back, princess. We goin' or what?'

'OK. C'mon Pete.' She went to open the door and Coogan cleared his throat, embarrassed.

'Bit of a snafu with the lock, there. You all gotta come in my side.'

Morgan came out to help with the bags the Barrys had brought with them, but Jim waved him away. They could wait until later. It was, Morgan thought, hard to know which family looked the worst – his, red-eyed and tetchy from lack of sleep, or the pale, ghostly figures before him, drained of all life spirit. He ushered them in, took the coats and forced them into the kitchen where he made a pot of coffee. 'Mamie is lying down with the baby. Both bushed. Had a bad night.'

'Is she feedin' her OK?' asked Belle, automatically. It was what you said to new mothers, found out if they had cracked nipples or mastitis or blocked ducts.

'We told you,' snapped Morgan. 'She can't do that. She's using formula milk.'

Belle shook her head to clear it. She remembered something about it. Her distraction, her inability to focus, meant she had been forced to cancel all her ICE sessions. Couldn't bring herself to counsel kids on whether they should train for tennis at Boca Ratan or San Diego in the midst of this. A kid died – she would end up blurting: 'Who gives a fuck about your child's backhand?' Why was she so upset? Because, she realised, it could have been Tommy. Change a few key incidentals and it could have been Tommy lying there, the blood slowly pooling beneath his inert body.

Morgan gave the adults coffee, made Tommy a juice and took him up to the study, where he let him loose on a baseball computer game. Tommy looked at him: 'I don't think my dad would like me playing this. He's got kinda . . .'

'Sensitive?'

'Stupid.'

Morgan suppressed a laugh and said. 'I'll say it's something else. Galactica Three Thousand.'

'Wow, you got that?'

'No.' The boy looked disappointed. 'But I know it's number one in the charts. Let's just pretend, eh? When your dad asks what you been playing?'

The young brow furrowed. 'Oh, yeah. I get it. Lie to him.'

'No, just . . . yeah. We'll lie to him, Tommy.'

'Cool.'

In the event Jim just accepted that Tommy was being distracted. So Morgan sat down, pulled up a chair and asked him: 'Wanna tell me? I mean, I got bits and pieces from what you said on the phone.' He pointed to a newspaper lying discarded in the trash bin. 'And from that.'

Jim nodded and delivered the story in a flat, uninvolved monotone. Belle just looked at him, slack-jawed and with dead eyes, as if he were describing some horrible, traumatic event long, long ago, which happened to another family, not hers.

When he had brought Morgan up to date with the last, aggressive interview with the homicide detective, Morgan asked: 'You got a lawyer?'

'Yeah, Dale, one of the kids' dads. He was there.' Better than using Hooper, who couldn't even get a good price for his mag.

'What does he think?'

'He thinks I'm in for a few uncomfortable weeks, probably a Grand Jury, and then it'll be a case of what we all say – a tragic accident.'

'It was, wasn't it?'

Jim nodded with a conviction he didn't feel. Every accident starts with a stupid decision, a piece of bravado, an ignoring of the little voice in the corner of the head, warning this is a foolish thing to do. The accident may not happen directly or immediately as a result of that snubbing of the voice, but somewhere down the line, the check comes in and has to be settled. Only thing was, he couldn't decide which of his actions had started the inexorable slide towards calamity – accepting the kid for practice, putting him into catch, not doing up the helmet properly, rubbing the box line or pretending he was going for a .400 average.

The kitchen phone rang and Morgan looked puzzled then held it out to Jim. 'It's for you.'

Police or lawyers, they were the only ones who had the number. It was Donkey Schlong. 'Mr Barry, I'm putting my neck on the line for you here, so I'd appreciate it if you would keep this one quiet. OK? Good. Listen, I saw a fax of the coroner's preliminary findings. It seems like the kid had a tissue-thin skull. Not all over, just two or three places. He thinks the force of the blow in any normal kid would normally have caused bruising, maybe concussion, but not death.'

Jim thanked him as profusely as he could and hung up. He was shaking as he sat down, and Morgan gave him a whisky which he downed in one. Belle leant forward, fearing more bad news. 'What? Jim? What is it?'

He finally, nervously, cracked a grin, hoping he wasn't counting his chickens, but he said it anyway. 'I think we might be in the clear.'

'Really?'

'Really,' he said. He let out a big, heartfelt sigh. 'I'll go and get the bags.'

Coogan made good time north on I-10, through the scrubby flat country that was the Gila River Reservation, probably some of the dullest landscape in the whole of the state of Arizona. Wendy sat up front, riding the rhythm of the big, lazy engine, with Pete stretched out along the back, listening to story tapes, and occasionally singing along in a flat, wayward voice.

Neither of them spoke for the first few miles, both wondering, for different reasons, if this was a good idea. As they passed the airplane park on the left, Coogan said: 'You hear from Duke?'

She shook her head. 'No. That one's on the junk list.' Which, she realised, was getting far too long. One jerk after another.

'Maybe you should just do that.' He pointed at the intense white of the plane fuselages. 'Park him in the desert, in case you need him later.'

'No thanks.'

'Wendy, how did you end up here? If you don't mind me askin'?'

'I really, really wonder that every day. One minute I'm gonna take over the family caterin' business in the good old cold North, the next I'm in the desert with a kid, tendin' bar, keepin' losers in beer, wonderin' where the next few dollars gonna come from . . .'

'Heading to the Grand Canyon with a crazy old man.'

'Crazy, maybe. You ain't so old, Coogan.'

'Duke thinks I am. I went out and looked at a big old saguaro this mornin'. Locals call him Clint. He's dyin' y'know. Bacteria eating him all up. Thing is, it takes five years for them to die. So they just carry on, not knowing they're wastin' away.'

Wendy pulled down the sun visor and examined herself in the mirror. She dug in her purse for some lipstick. 'You think we're dyin' and we don't know it?'

'No, I guess it's worse that that. We're dyin' and we *do* know it.'

She blew out her cheeks. Wasn't easy following this guy's line of thought sometimes. 'So?'

'I just get the feelin' we're not makin' the best use of what time is left. You know what I mean? You and me both. We wastin' our lives, maybe through no fault of our own, who knows? But we got derailed. A trailer park in Arizona? Shoot. I think we ought to aim higher.'

'You got any suggestions, Coogan?'

He shrugged. He just might have after tonight, he thought. Hell of a suggestion.

They passed through the gridded sprawl of Phoenix at nine forty-five and Coogan stopped for gas on a stretch of highway adopted by the local Hooters. Well, she wasn't quite down to a job there yet. Not that she really had the tits for it.

Wendy could feel other drivers looking at the car, whether out of pity or curiosity she couldn't tell, but their eyes were certainly drawn by something. 'Because it's a classic,' Coogan assured her. Because it's still running at all, she suspected.

It was at Cordes Junction that they got the first hint of what was to come, after they had climbed the passes ('Turn off Air Conditioning. Avoid Overheating' warned the signs) and started the descent. Wendy turned around and made Pete take off his phones and look at the fossilised stone waves before them, breaking on some distant shore, as if whipped up by a primeval wind, powerful enough to eddy the rocks, and then freeze them, peak and trough after peak and trough.

'You won't see much more,' said Coogan. 'The Canyon and stuff kinda creeps up on you.'

Lunch was in Flagstaff, under the dark gaze of the San Francisco mountains, in one of the student coffee bars in the old town, pizzas and salads. They bought Pete some more story tapes before setting off on the last leg, the calm before the geological storm that is the Kaibab Plateau.

After they reached the park and queued to pay their twenty dollars – having accommodation meant they could go right on in, skipping the park-and-ride number – Coogan said something odd. 'I don't want you to look for the Canyon. You'll see it between the trees. Just don't look. OK, Pete? The first look is the one you'll remember. I'm gonna take you somewhere special. Got that? No peeking? Like when you get a Christmas present?'

Wendy found it a difficult request to comply with. She kept getting tantalising glimpses of a deep russet colour, and had to avert her eyes. Even so, just the masses of people, the videos, the binoculars, their peculiar stasis as they stood immobile and stared straight ahead, told her there was something pretty damn freaky out there.

Coogan took them out on the East Rim, past the crowded

viewing points, until he came to a scruffy pull-off, a pot-holed clearing in the trees that had closed in on them. 'Shoshone Point,' he announced.

Wendy pointed at the yellow sign and read: 'This facility cannot be used without permission. Apply at the Ranger Station.'

'It means barbecues. But the good thing is, most people just think it means going down that path, passed the locked gate. It don't though. OK, we gotta walk.'

It was a mile, through a spooky stand of blackened Ponderosa Pine, much of it with Pete on Coogan's reluctant shoulders because his legs were 'worn off', until they reached the barbecue area. It was, as Coogan had predicted, deserted. They were going to have that all-important first glimpse all to themselves, something that was, she suspected, a rare treat. Coogan led the way through a stand of thin, scrubby bushes, and suddenly it was there.

Wendy felt her head swim at the sight. In front of them a finger of white-ish rock, a promontory, topped by a couple of precariously balanced rocks, big one on top of smaller, led out over the sheer walls of the canyon. Ahead of them lay one of the most famous views in the world, the multi-coloured stratifications, the towering buttes and the cruelly slashed plateaux, cut by the river to the most awesome of cross-sections in a mere five million years – a watery knife through stony butter in geological terms. 'Wow. Look at this, Pete. Wow.' She held onto his shoulders, frightened that this big gaping hole might somehow grab him.

'Just relax now,' said Coogan, reverting to an old authoritarian army mode. 'Thing is, your brain can't take it all in. It's like one of those fancy cameras – you know, the ones that focus themselves? Well, you can always fool those suckers, so they can't quite get anything to latch on to. Same here. Your brain is goin' "whoa, that can't be right" and playing havoc with your eyes. Follow me.'

Cautious but confidently, he stepped out onto the finger of Shoshone Point, leading them so Pete never got too near the edge, and, as it narrowed and they passed the balancing rocks, to which someone had tied a now-withered bunch of flowers, Coogan scooped him up and held him tight against his body, ignoring the throbbing in his back. His spine was no longer designed for hauling small kids, he reckoned.

'Sit down. Look, dangle your feet, there is a ledge six feet down, stops you feeling quite so giddy if you know that's there. Here, Pete, you stay with me. OK, let's see.' He shaded his eyes. The worst of the heat had gone, but the sun was still high enough to cause them to sweat. Wendy put on a pair of sunglasses, and the colours became deeper, stronger, the fine etchings in the rocks more apparent.

'Over yonder, you can just see the rapids. That's the river. The Colorado. That's what made all this, Pete. That's Cremation Creek, and that big mother there is Vishnu Temple. Look, that line there is South Kaibab trail, the way to the river.'

'There are trails? I never knew,' said Wendy.

'Dozens of them. Old Indian trails, miners' paths. Amazing.' He pointed to the distant rim and then swept the scene with his hand. 'Ten miles to the other side. And thanks to those trails you can walk from one side to the other. Incredible.'

'Yeah,' said Wendy, feeling her focus shift, along with her stomach.

When Coogan stopped talking the only sound was a raven's wingbeat, a soft whoosh, almost like those wire brushes old jazzmen play on drums in hotel lounges, she thought. It was hard to believe that somewhere out there thousands of other people were enjoying the same view.

'You OK?'

'Yeah, I was just thinkin' about all the people we can't see. Looking at the same thing.'

'Not this view. Every view's different. We're pretty high up here, gives a different perspective.'

'We're lucky we got it all to ourselves.'

'Sometimes they do weddings'n'shit here, but if that gate is locked, you can be sure you got it pretty much to yourself. Look, condor.'

A big, black bird came circling their way, taking itself lower and lower as it traversed the canyon, checking for carrion as it went.

'What do you think, Pete?' she asked.

'Yeah. Way cool.'

'How you know all this, George? About the temples and gorges?'

'Friend of mine used to come up here. While the day away, just looking, shooting the breeze with anyone who would come along.'

'And?'

'He used to look at those condors, and say he wished he could do it. Just float on the thermals. I used to tell him they weren't as free as they looked. They all numbered, tagged, been released into the wild after breeding in captivity. It's an illusion. Shit, the Canyon condor people put out dead animals for them to find, just in case nature don't provide.'

'They're still beautiful, though.'

'For vultures, I guess.'

'Where's your friend?'

He lowered his voice. 'One day he decided to prove his point. He went off the edge.'

Wendy looked at him open-mouthed. 'What? Here?'

'Well, they found him under here. Nine hundred feet down.'

And he had brought them to the same spot? Jesus, maybe he was crazy after all. Maybe he had something similar planned for them. After all, there was something odd about Coogan, something disconcerting in the mood swings, as if he kept having to check himself. She shuffled her butt back, trying to get a better purchase. 'Was this an accident?'

'Wouldn't be the first. You get eleven, twelve, fifteen people die a year here. Some of thirst on those trails.' He pointed down at the delicate gossamer line, traced in the rocks by feet and the hooves of mules. 'About six accidentally fall over. Maybe one or two survive, you know, get a soft landing in a branch. Then there are suicides, without a doubt. They leave notes or people see 'em jump, y'know what I mean? Nobody saw Toots go, though.'

'Did you put the flowers there?' She pointed to the sad, dessicated bundle on the rock.

He nodded, a tad awkward. 'One of these days I should bring fresh ones.'

'Is this why you got stalled here?'

'Come on, let's get Pete into some shade.' He ruffled his hair. 'Sun'll still burn him, this time of day. You too, blondie.'

They made it back to the barbecue area and Pete ran off to climb on the tables.

'Is it?' she continued. 'Why you're here? Because your friend might have killed himself?'

'That. And the fact that I can't shake the feeling that, if he did do it deliberately, then it was my fault.'

SEVENTEEN

New York State

It was dark by the time Jim went outside to get the bags, but for the first time since the horror at the hospital he was allowing a little light to creep into his soul. As he stepped off the front porch and turned left to where they had parked the Lexus, he turned over the idea of the wafer-thin skull in his mind. No Grand Jury would send him to trial now, surely. He might not be home and dry, but he could certainly see the sunshine, feel the first warm rays.

'Are you running away, Mr Barry?'

The voice from the bushes next to the driveway made him start. It was more measured, less mad than the last time he heard it, but there was no mistaking the accent. He froze, wondering what to do, while gnarled fingers squeezed his heart.

'I . . . who's there? Mr Sebastyen? Uh, Stefan? Is that you?'

Sebastyen stepped forward so a little of the external garage light fell onto his face, but mostly it remained in deep shadows. Jim wondered if he had a gun. 'I suppose you heard already,' Sebastyen said calmly. 'What they are going to say. That he had a thin skull. That he was sick, weak, didn't deserve to live. Have you heard that? Do you believe it?'

'It was what the medical examiner—'

The anger flared. 'Fook the medical examiner. Fook him. Fook you, Barry. I know what that boy was like, I know what it cost him to be born, what it cost my wife. No more children for her. Petyr was the end of my line. I know what that means, not some, some quack with a scalpel and a fat bribe in his pocket.'

'That's not how it works, Mr Seb—'

155

Sebastyen laughed, a bitter, sardonic sound and edged closer. Now Jim could see that odd face, with the strange nose, and the eyes. But Jim didn't want to look into the eyes. He took a step back. At what point would the others wonder what was taking him so long? From the back of the house, would they be able to hear any of this?

'Not how it works? Not how what works? This country? Don't give me that bullshit. Land of the Free? Nothing is free here, Barry, nothing. Everything has its price. I could buy the medical examiner tomorrow. Except I've got a funny accent, haven't I? So I'm at a disadvantage. But you, Mr All-American, I bet they would take your money. No, don't deny it. But I am lucky in one way. There are plenty of others who will take my money. How do you really think I found you? Directory Services?'

'Look, Mr Sebastyen. I – I know I did a terrible thing—'

'You did a worse thing than you will ever know, Barry. Far worse. Far stupider. No, no, no – what am I saying? You will know. You are about to find out. You will have evidence for yourself, of just how imbecilic you have been. You chose the wrong child to kill.'

'I didn't choose him. I didn't mean to kill him. Doesn't the word accident mean anything where you come from?'

Jim moved further into the pool of light, but Sebastyen stayed where he was. 'You were careless with my boy. Careless. As in, you couldn't care less about him, because he wasn't a player, didn't fit in with Mr All American's plans. Couldn't care less. Think about that phrase. Where I come from, that means you murdered him.'

Jim felt a flash of anger of his own, grabbed it and rode with it. He may just be a magazine guy, but this, this bullying was intolerable. 'Look, Sebastyen, this isn't getting us anywhere. First you shoot at me in my home – don't deny it, I know it was you. The police know you were behind it, and they'll find whoever you hired. And now, now you come here, threatening me—'

'I haven't come to the threats yet.'

The voice was calm, with an authority that made Jim feel as if he was screeching like an adolescent. He backed off a little. 'Look. There is nothing I can do. How many times can I say sorry?'

'Never enough. But there is something you can do. You can ease my pain.'

'Ease your . . . ease your pain? How?'

'You can replace my son.'

The possibilities in this statement tumbled through his mind. Did he mean surrogate parenthood? Did he mean he and Belle should have another child and hand it over, like some Grimm's fairytale? 'I don't see how.'

'You have a boy. About the same age. Tommy.'

Jim was guarded now, treading gently, reining his thoughts in, trying not to second-guess the guy. The poor grieving guy, he reminded himself. Don't be too hard on him. Standing there in the shadows with his pain. He was almost like a ghost. 'Yeah? So?'

'I want him.'

'What?' He found himself blurting. 'Are you out of your fucking mind?'

The voice carried on steady, level, as if he was laying out conditions of a loan. 'The deal is simple. We call it recompense. Restitution. Like an eye for an eye. A life for a life. So, you will make me his legal guardian. Don't worry too much about the official papers. As I said, everything is for sale. I can do that sort of thing.'

Jim's lips stopped working for a second, and all that came out was an odd blubbing noise as ill-formed words collided with each other, trying to shoulder their way through. He wiped his mouth and started over: 'I don't know what to say. Where to start. Except to say you should see a doctor, soon.'

And now he finally came into the light, two quick paces, the body tense with coiled aggression. Jim found his back to the garage door. 'The last doctor I saw took me in to show me my boy's body. I put my fingers into the hole in his head, the one you made.'

'All the same—'

'All the same?' It was like a wave of venom. 'What a cute phrase. Nothing is the same for either of us, Barry. Or should I call you, Jim, now you are to give me your first-born?'

Jim reeled at the recognition of the phrase he had used. It was exactly what he had said to the cop. Was his house bugged now? Was that how he knew everything? He put some steel into his voice: 'In your dreams.'

'Ha. Tough guy. OK. Time to lay it on the line, as you say. I want your boy. Not now, once the fuss has died down. I will not contest the Grand Jury's findings, in fact I will push for a no-trial, and I will not undertake any civil action.'

'I am not scared of any civil action.'

'No. I imagine not. But there are things you should be scared of, Mr Barry. I know you probably got some big-shot lawyer friends, eh? Dale, perhaps? Dale's good, I hear. But the deal I am proposing, Dale will be of limited use.'

'And why is that?'

'If you do not hand over your son, then I will kill you all.'

'What?' He genuinely wasn't sure what he had heard. He looked at the man's face for a sign it was a joke, but it was dark and unknowable. 'What was that?'

'The boy. The fragrant Mrs Barry. You. Maybe even the friends in there giving you sanctuary, who knows? Dead. I cannot do this thing without your cooperation. I need you to give me the boy voluntarily. No kidnapping. Just a private adoption. So should you choose to refuse my offer—'

'Refuse? Don't be so stupid. Of course I refuse. What would you do in my situation?'

'Oh, that's very simple,' he said, sounding hearty, as if he had just been asked what he wanted for his birthday. 'If I were you I would probably kill *me*.' He poked his chest hard and Jim heard the hollow sound, as if it were empty within. 'But I suspect that isn't on the agenda. Eh, Mr Barry?' Now the finger was stabbing at him.

'You're fuckin' crazy.'

'You don't think I would do it, do you? I know what you are thinking. It is bluff. But, no, it isn't. You think you were meant to die in the house shooting? No, no, no. Please believe me. Had I intended you to be killed, then you would be in a casket right now. Then, you think, I could run. I can hide. No you can't. I found you here, I can find you anywhere.' He waved his arm in a large arc, as if to indicate the whole of America. 'Sure, it's a big country. But you would give yourself away – give out your SSN, use a Visa card, there are a million ways for you to pop up on a computer, Mr Barry, and I'd be waiting.'

'If I tell the police—'

He snorted. 'Now you really are being pathetic. The only way to get things done in this country is to do it yourself, Mr Barry. You should remember that. Police, courts, government, they'll let you down. Every fookin' time. Don't rely on others. My way is the only way.'

There was a long pause while Jim marshalled his thoughts, tried to calm his heart, to suppress the impulse just to rant at this poor guy, to spill out every vile phrase he had ever heard and then ram his fist into his face. But he wasn't a ram-the-fist-into-your-face kind of guy much as, at this moment, he desperately wanted to be. He was, though, astonished by the temerity of Sebastyen. As if he were going to take his son and hand him over to be raised by some demented stranger, just because the guy made a couple of threats.

'Is it money you want? I have money. How much do you want?'

'I don't want your money. I told you – I want your son.' He hissed the next bit, as if trying to invest a chilly emphasis. 'Or you all die.'

Jim shook his head in what he hoped was a pitying yet

159

understanding manner and kept his voice level. 'Listen, we will talk when you start behaving in a rational, civilised manner.'

Sebastyen sniffed. 'I was afraid of this. You don't believe me do you? Don't think I could possibly carry out such a callous, cold-blooded threat?' Now there was a smile, and it was more frightening than the fury it replaced. 'I expected that might be the case, that you might use the This-Is-America defence. You know: It Can't Happen Here. OK, let me tell you this – go and look in your trunk. All the evidence you might wish for is in there. Goodnight, Mr Barry.'

He stepped back into the darkness and there was an urgent rustling as he left. Jim stood frozen to the spot, as if he had just had a visitation from the spirit world and couldn't comprehend it. He looked across at the Lexus, silent and mute witness to all that had gone on. His eyes focused on the trunk. He suddenly knew why he hadn't heard from Dick.

There was an electrical storm on the North Rim of the Grand Canyon that night, and Coogan and Wendy stood outside the cabin where Pete was sleeping and watched it. It was like a miniature school-physics experiment. From ten miles away there was no sound, just the sudden flash of clouds being illuminated from within, like electric cotton candy, the vast discharges sending jagged fingers of lightning down onto the opposite plateau. This vast natural Duracell moved inexorably towards the tiny glow that was the lodge on the far side, slowly engulfing it in rain and hail.

In front of them no lights shone in the Canyon, apart from a weak flicker from one of the camp grounds. Yet still you could feel the chasm's vertiginous pull, even in the bible blackness of its cloak, as if some kind of spiritual magnet out there was tugging at your body, trying to draw it in. At least, that was how Coogan felt.

They had eaten an indifferent meal, and he had watched her drink half a bottle of wine while he nursed an Evian, and now it was time to turn in. He had the feeling she read his mind when she said: 'George . . .'

'Yeah?'

'You know I like you, don't you?'

'Uh?'

'And I'm grateful for what you did. With Pete. Taking him in that night.'

'Uh.'

'It's just that . . .' Her inhibitions started to creep up, but she batted them aside. 'That's as far as it goes.'

Coogan smiled at her. He could see her reddening even under the feeble lighting. In a strange way it was a relief, because he wouldn't feel compelled to start the dance, so he said as sincerely as he could: 'That's OK.'

'I mean, you might think I'm some stuck-up, unattractive bitch for all I know.' There was a pause where he was clearly meant to leap in feet first, but he ignored it. 'And I may be talking out of turn. But we gotta share that cabin. I just don't want a misunderstanding. Not with Pete around. I mean, I got enough trouble as it is. I'm sorry if I sound—'

'No, that's OK. I can imagine circumstances where my hormones'd be howling like one of those coyotes out there. But there'll be no . . . misunderstandings.'

She breathed a sigh of relief, and reached over and kissed his cheek. 'I didn't think there would be.'

He wished she would stop doing that.

'Hoo-ah.'

The noise, the old familiar Ranger grunt of a greeting, made him jump back, peering into the gloom.

'Shit, your night vision gone? I remember a time when you could've given lessons to a bat.'

He knew the voice. 'Nash?'

The guy stepped into the light, square-jawed, thick-necked, taller than Coogan, a little fitter maybe, hair barely longer than a barrack's buzz-cut. Nash, whoever he was, had piercing eyes

Wendy could tell would see through any defensive shield you tried to put up. He just stood there, looking at the pair of them and finally had to prompt. 'Coogan. You gonna introduce us?'

'Yeah. Uh. This is Nash. Skip Nash. But Nash'll do. He's an old friend.'

'Army buddy,' said Nash.

Coogan said, 'I didn't think I'd see anyone else here. The others?'

Nash shrugged. 'I don't think so. I came for Toots. I don't think the others will be making it.'

Coogan said, 'I figured.' He held up his left arm.

'Want a beer. Got some more in the trunk if you want some.'

'Sure.' It was Wendy.

They gathered around the table in the cabin, Wendy and Nash cradling a Michelob each, Coogan with a Coke he had fetched from the machine.

'How's Honey?' Coogan asked. When they last met Nash had told him things weren't looking too good with his woman.

Nash rolled the beer in his hand for a few seconds then looked up at Coogan. Wendy had known him for ten minutes, but she could see it was difficult for him, sense a pain. 'We didn't make it.'

'Shit, I'm sorry to hear it.'

'Anyone else?'

'Nah. You?'

'Me?' Coogan was pissed that Nash assumed Wendy wasn't his, but there was no point in pretending. 'Uh-uh.'

Wendy said: 'How far do you two—' and wagged her finger between them.

'Twelve years,' said Nash.

'Where did you serve?'

'All over.' Nash paused and they looked at each other before he added: 'Somalia.'

She looked blank. 'Where's that?'

Nash was used to the incomprehension by now. Either people knew exactly what it meant, or they couldn't find it on the map.

'Horn of Africa,' said Coogan. 'And we got impaled on it.'

She looked at their faces to see if they were joshing her. Nope. 'No shit?'

'Well, plenty of that,' said Nash. 'Too much. Shit and dust. Most goddamn place you ever saw.'

'And this guy, Toots?' she asked.

'Yeah, he was there too.'

'And so this is like, an anniversary. Of his death?' Despite himself Coogan did not like the way all her questions were being directed at Nash.

'No. Toots booked this a year ago. You gotta rent these rim-edge cabins that much in advance. We was all meant to meet here,' said Coogan, trying to get her head round to his direction. 'In the meantime he died.'

'All? Who was the "all"?'

'Six of us,' said Nash.

'Why?'

Nash looked at Coogan and Coogan gave him a nod, indicating she was cool.

He took a hit of beer, swilled in around his mouth and swallowed noisily before he admitted: 'Toots had this crazy idea about stealing the Grand Canyon.'

Morgan and Belle looked up at him expectantly when he came into the kitchen. First, they noticed Jim was empty-handed. Then they saw that there was no blood in his face, it had turned the colour of old parchment.

'He's . . . he's here,' Jim croaked.

Belle said: 'Who?'

His throat closed up with a mixture of fear and anger, he managed to spit out: 'Sebastyen.'

'What here?' asked Morgan, half rising. 'In the hall?'

'No, he was outside . . . can I get a drink of water?' Morgan gave him a glass and he took a long glug and told them verbatim, as best he could, the conversation.

He felt the incomprehension and confusion in them, all swirling together like an emotional maelstrom, building up to a great towering wall of hysteria. And he hadn't even mentioned the fact that the hosts, too, were possibly under threat,

It was Jim, the first to experience the sudden confusing rush of responses, who hit calm water first. 'Morgan. We gotta go look in the Lexus. OK?'

They looked up as Mamie burst into the room. 'Hey what the hell is going on here guys? I just got her to sleep and you start yellin', listen.' She held open the door and they heard the pumping sobs of the baby.

'Sorry, Mamie. Let me try,' offered Belle.

Mamie looked at her from under hooded eyes and said: 'Be my guest.' She took Belle's stool and heaved herself wearily onto it. 'What's happening?'

'We'll fill you in later,' said Morgan. He added nervously to Jim, 'Are you thinking what I think you're thinking?'

'Yeah,' confirmed Jim. Except he was realising it didn't have to be a whole body in the trunk. Just a body part. That'd do it every time. Then they'd sit up and pay attention.

'You gonna tell me more?' asked Wendy after the two of them had stopped laughing.

'Nah,' said Coogan.

But Nash continued: 'Toots had an idea that there was a way to get money out of this place. He booked this cabin for now and for Labor Day. Invited a bunch of guys to come and look it over. Me and Coogan, we told him we thought he was crazy. We said, count us out. Wouldn't listen. You'll be here, he said.'

'And?'

But she knew. Coogan said, slowly, steadily. 'We told him he could book this cabin for a year solid. We still wouldn't turn up.

We told him why. We got drunk and we rode the guy a little hard, I guess. The next day he did his world-famous condor impression. Now we're here. Too late. I guess we're payin' our respects.'

'Oh.'

The other two nodded. Both took a hit on their drinks, as if that was the end of the matter. Sensing she wasn't going to get anywhere further along that road – and not so sure she wanted to, she suddenly said: 'Look, guys, I'm gonna turn in with Pete. You two can bed down out here, I guess. Yeah? Goodnight.'

After she had gone, and they heard the toilet flush and saw the light go out under the door, Nash finally said. 'I'm sorry if I screwed anything up.'

'Nothin' to screw up. I'm goin' celibate as well as sober.'

'Still got the old problem.'

'Sometimes. Yeah.'

'This time?'

Coogan screwed up his mouth. 'I dunno. A few days ago. Nothing since.'

'No heebie-jeebies?'

'Not yet.'

'You sure you won't have a beer?'

'I haven't since . . . since Toots. And I kinda got used to being clear headed.'

'That must be good.'

'Has its pros and cons. Why did you really come here, Nash? I mean, now that Toots is dead?'

'Truth? I dunno. To touch . . . something. I mean, it's all fading now, isn't it? Just becoming harder to grasp, like smoke. Every time I try and make it concrete, it slips through my fingers. Is that where my life went? That was it? Ten fuckin' years since we went down—'

'Eleven, remember?'

'See what I mean? Twelve months gone just like that. I feel like those old Vets who think that maybe, maybe that was the one time in their lives when they was really alive. When everyone else was dyin' around them.'

'Dangerous way of thinking, Nash. You can't go runnin' around with guns'n'shit just to keep it real. Anyways, I'm here. If you wanna talk, I mean. Not the runnin' around bit, please. My spine ain't what it was before that big bump, so I gotta be careful. What did you have in mind? You wanna talk about old times?'

'Hell, yes,' said Nash.

'In which case,' Coogan stood up, 'I am gonna get myself another can of this damn fine Coca Cola.'

Morgan and Jim stood looking at the Lexus like it had transformed itself into an evil talisman, as if some aura was bleeding from the body shell, staining the ground. Now both had dry throats, afraid of what might be in there.

'You pop it. I'll have a look,' said Jim. 'Only fair.'

'No, I'll do it. I'm a lot less involved than you.'

'It's my call, Morgan. It's my fuck-up. Come on, pull it. You know where it is, you used to have one of these babies.'

Morgan leant inside and there was a soft click and the trunk lid gaped open like a lazy mouth, as if the car was some kind of filter feeder. Jim edged it up and the internal light came on. Slowly he raised the lid, bending down to peak underneath and sniffing. If there was any chunk of a human in there, surely he'd smell it. Nothing.

He raised it fully open and lifted out the two soft bags they had brought, then moved the blanket that was always in there. Nothing gristly or lumpy in there, no human head rolling around.

Morgan came to his shoulder and they both looked down. It was a minute before Morgan realised they had been looking in the wrong place. It was taped to the underside of the trunk lid. 'There,' he said.

Jim ripped it off and weighed it in his hands, laughing out of a sense of relief. No matter what this was, it couldn't have been worse than the movie his mind had been playing these last ten minutes. 'You got a video player, I hope?'

Wendy lay there in the dark, listening to their low voices, the rhythms of old, worn tales, with vocal impersonations offering a sudden, squeaky counterpoint, and low rumble of laughter. It was, no doubt, a guy thing. Old army buddies. It was just like her father and her older brother, the way they would talk after the annual hunting trip, spinning yarns of leaping salmon and spooked deer, filling her with envy at the camaraderie and the blood brotherhood they had shared. From the age of sixteen she had petitioned to be allowed to go, something her father resisted, but her mother championed. Her sister was simply indifferent. Girls didn't hunt. Not in the Blatand family, leastways. But she wore them down, and they let her come twice and they schooled her in using the rifles and they let her shoot at a deer and she missed – probably deliberately – and all the time she was out there she sensed their resentment, the feeling that she had intruded upon something precious. So after the second time and the deer incident she never asked again. The next year, her father bought her a car when they went away for the hunt. A little kiss-off.

She had no doubt that what was occurring next door was much the same as those post-camping BS sessions. But she liked the sound, the easy talk, the catch-up that Coogan and Nash were indulging in. They seemed like nice men, on the surface, but she knew you could never tell. She kept thinking she had really cracked it, and yet all she ever got were . . . what did that song call them? Scrubs. The young guys who were clearly going nowhere, not very fast. Even Duke, she had hooked up with him after the one thing he ever wanted to do – fly helicopters – had been taken from him. And Coogan and Nash? She suspected these were the kind of guys who had this one hot spot in their lives, burning bright – most men had some golden years, maybe the army, college, when they played ball, football, whatever – bleaching everything else into insignificance. They would spend the rest of their lives picking at the scabs.

She snuggled down next to Pete, and let the warmth of his little body bleed through, and rubbed her nose over his smooth skin. It was one of life's great joys, doing this, she thought. One day Pete would grow up to be a big, hairy, farting, fucked-up guy like every other, but for the moment he was hers. While she had Pete, she knew, everything would ultimately be OK.

EIGHTEEN

New York State

The film started with jumpy, jerky images, the light all wrong, one minute too dark to make out what was happening, the next so bright it was like staring at the sun, with a rolling gait that made you feel sea-sick, but eventually it settled down. The camera was clearly small, hard to hold steady, and the zoom was far from smooth, but eventually they could see a road leading into a ramshackle village and some far from familiar signs. The cameraman was in a vehicle of some kind, and part of the problem came from the road surface, which had that diseased, flaky look of neglected asphalt that had seen too many hard winters, and not enough road gangs.

There were skinny, whip-like telegraph poles to the side, many leaning at a drunken angle, supported only by their wires it seemed, some foreign-looking cars of dubious pedigree, mostly burned out and blackened, the odd Beemer standing out as a bit of class, and a series of low, simple buildings, mostly of cinderblock. One thing they were all certain of: this wasn't America.

The sound spluttered on, crackly and uneven, and the camera pointed skyward as a jet raced low across the sky, a rumble trailing in its wake. Again, no chance of identifying when or where this was.

There was a sudden jump cut. The vehicle had stopped, and now people were moving around. They could hear the crunch of boots on the road, and occasionally a shoulder or a head obscured the field of vision, a hand reaching out to push them out of the way. The cameraman clearly intended to document what was going on, but was considered excess baggage by the soldiers – if that was what they were – around him.

Over to the left side a chicken came clucking into view, looked up, and scuttled away. Even a birdbrain had enough sense to be alarmed. The old man came next, about thirty yards ahead, big, baggy pinstriped trousers, a cap and a rough wool jacket. He raised a hand, in greeting or as a halt gesture, wasn't clear. The sound suddenly distorted badly, and the camera shook again. The old man simply crumpled as the bullets hit him.

'My God,' Morgan hissed.

The first shots were like a starting signal and the men – they could see now they had some kind of dark green uniform on – started running, the soundtrack full of heavy breathing and shouts they couldn't interpret. A door was kicked open and a long burst of fire followed, but they couldn't see who, if anyone, it was aimed at, or whether this was just some Lethal Weapon-style acting for the camera.

The second room they could. Two children and a woman in a corner. A figure came into view, one of the green uniforms, and pulled the mother to her feet. He took her head and turned it to face the children as obscenely large rounds punctured the small, ill-fed bodies, flinging them around the room. He pushed her away and shot her in the stomach. She fell back close to her children and the camera zoomed in on the neat holes in her stomach leaking. She had been pregnant.

'Turn it off,' said Belle, a burning sensation in her throat . . .

Jim couldn't speak for a second. He croaked, 'I . . . there might be a message.'

'*Turn it off.*'

He hit the remote. There was only the sound of breathing, harsh and forced, as if they all had to remember to draw in oxygen. Jim went over to Belle. 'We've got to watch the rest.'

Belle stood up and grabbed Mamie's hand. 'You watch it. On fast forward. There is no reason why we should all watch this . . . depravity.'

After the women had left, Morgan fetched them a large bourbon each, which they slammed back before sitting in front of the darkened screen. 'Ready?' asked Jim.

'No. But then I'll never be ready. Go ahead.'

The image of the punctured stomach came back on and the scanning of the room continued, and then they were outside again, and they could see figures trying to flee. More rifle shots, and people fell down, almost comically, as if they had stumbled and would get up again, brushing themselves down and laughing at their clumsiness. But they all lay still except when further shots slammed into them, just to be certain. Smoke was starting to drift into view and the cameraman panned round to show the flames beginning to climb up the side of a building, the intensity burning the tube into a blurred orange/white supernova.

Jim fast-forwarded, stopping just now and then on images he couldn't believe he was seeing. More children slaughtered with an incomprehensible casualness. An execution through the head and, over at the far end of a courtyard, what looked to be a rape, a second soldier casually waiting his turn. It was like a compendium of horror, as if the perpetrators were trying to condense the whole of a century of brutal inhumanity into twenty, thirty minutes.

At last it was over, and the survivors – what looked like a whole family, from grandad down to kids – battered, bruised, were loosely roped together sitting on the floor of a big barn-like building, with a large opening at one side. From the shadows of the inside and into daylight came a figure with a cigarette in his mouth, a man with the bearing of a leader, one who has earned a post-operational smoke. Blood was splashed up his front, dirt smeared his face, and over one shoulder was a small, snub-nosed machine pistol.

The grandad struggled to his feet and slid a watch off his wrist and offered it to the man, who snatched it, examined it, held it to his ear, then casually threw it out of the door. Worthless. He pushed the old man back down again. It looked like the last bargaining chip had gone.

The man stepped outside and signalled one of his men over, who put a large piece of metal against the whitewashed wall of the barn. The leader sprayed a can of paint over it, and when the stencil was removed, they could see a crude, dripping skull and crossbones. The leader took out the cigarette, turned and proudly winked at the camera. Younger, thinner, nastier, with a very oddly shaped nose, but there was no mistaking Mr Sebastyen.

There was the sound of an explosion, and a startled look crossed his face, before he swung the machine pistol from his shoulder and cocked it. There was the sound of ricochets and, in the far distance, a dancing line of dust. The man gave another, less sure, smile at the camera, and pointed at the barn. Men appeared with cans full of what was clearly gasoline, and started splashing it around. Sebastyen looked down at his feet, bent out of view and came up with the old man's watch. He had trodden on it. He began to laugh, and the image faded to black.

Sleep would not come to Jim that night, nor, it seemed to the baby, howling and grizzling through the small hours. Belle had taken a sleeping pill from Mamie, but Jim loathed the fuzziness they left him with. Still, the lack of sleep would probably have the same outcome. The images from the tape kept flitting into his mind, causing him to shudder and toss and turn, as if there would be a position in the bed which would make him immune, make them go away. That last section had been intriguing, the one after Sebastyen had looked at the camera. The attackers had clearly come under fire themselves, and had decided to torch the evidence of their atrocities.

Where was it? He and Morgan had spent half an hour discussing it. But they had still come up with nothing more precise than somewhere in the Balkans. There was no date and time stamp on the film, so it wasn't easy to pinpoint. Bosnia, probably, judging by how young the guy looked. But they agreed on one thing – Mr Sebastyen was probably a Serb. It had all the hallmarks of the kind of atrocity those guys had come to specialise in.

Had Dick known this? That was the next priority, get to Dick. Ask about getting the cops and the Feds involved. Jesus, though, the content. If Sebastyen was capable of that . . . but surely that was a different time, a different place, other hatreds, ethnic, political, personal. Yet that was why he had sent the tape. To show them what he could stoop to if needs be. But surely something like that, some kind of genocide, couldn't happen in America. Then he remembered what Sebastyen had said. This was intended to convey to him that it could. It would.

But then again, it was possible that this was just a hustle, that behind it all, there was a sane, old-fashioned motive. Money. Scare the shit out of them, refuse to take any cash at first, and get them all so frightened they wouldn't balk at a multi-million-dollar pay-out. Maybe that was it.

It was as close as he was going to get to a comforting thought and he hung onto it as he felt himself starting to fold into sleep, just as the baby raised its game and began a full-on bellowing.

NINETEEN

Grand Canyon South Rim, Arizona

Coogan woke Nash with a coffee from the Bright Angel restaurant, and he rolled over, rubbing his bloodshot eyes. 'Oh. Mornin'. Thanks. What time is it?'

'Six-thirty.'

'Six— What's your goddamn hurry?'

'Just curious.'

'Curious about what? Oh, for fuck's sake. We went through it last night. Let it go, Coogan.'

'Like I said, the bird changes things.'

Nash stood up and pulled on his pants. 'I think I'll just head back.'

'Where to? Where are you now?'

'Albuquerque. Here.' He fished a crumpled card from his pocket and handed it over.

'Still snapping away?'

'Gone over to digital video. Corporate. Weddings. It's a living. I think it's a living, anyway. You?'

Coogan sipped his coffee. 'I play here and there. Got semi-regular gig at the university. Pick-up with some kids. It's a life. I think.'

'Coogan . . . I got something I wanted to say.'

'It ain't mushy, is it? I can't do mushy on an empty stomach.'

'No, it ain't mushy. Well, not too mushy. It's just that . . . you and me. I feel like we are the last ones left of the Chalk. Now the others haven't shown. You got the card, if you ever need anything.'

'Like a wedding video?'

'Yeah. That kind of thing. You're right.' He feigned punching him in the stomach. 'You gonna make this difficult?'

'Im-fuckin'-possible. I know what you mean, Nash. Thanks.'

'Yeah.' He held out his hand and Coogan took it, clenching hard, and Nash mumbled. 'See you around, Ranger,' he said with mock solemnity.

Coogan had them up by seven, on the road by eight, as if he were anxious to get back, even though Pete had wanted to watch the mule trains depart for Phantom Ranch. Breakfast was a rushed, buffet affair, but then Coogan spent ages dawdling around at the Ranger Station, and then drove out of the park at ten miles an hour.

'We'll get a real breakfast in Flagstaff.'

'It'll be dinner time at this rate,' said Wendy. 'Look I gotta work tonight. I can't afford to miss two slots on the trot. And I ain't takin' your money.'

'I'll just let this truck by . . .' said Coogan, and veered across onto the shoulder. He patted the dash. 'It's just I like to start the old girl real gentle in the mornings. Know what I mean?'

''Well, I like to be treated real gentle in the mornings.'

'I'll remember that,' he found himself saying, and started to blush. 'I mean . . . shit. That was a joke.'

She just grinned at his discomfort and settled down to stare at the back of a white Ford truck for the next seventy miles, listening to the lazy boom of the big car's engine, getting itself the equivalent of woken with a gentle shake and a cup of coffee.

Pete was plugged into the Native American story tapes they had got at the El Tovar gift shop on his Walkman, watching the pine forests of the plateau slip by. They passed Tusayan, and already the fleets of helicopters were ferrying the sightseers in and out, zipping around with an urgency that reminded her of bees returning to the hive with important information. Except the honeypot was already inside these flying creatures, passengers paying a hundred bucks or more to feel their stomach drop as the choppers powered over the edge of the greatest hole in the world. Poor Duke, he'd love to still be doing that. Coogan just looked at them and scowled, as if they were hornets disturbing his picnic. After a while she said, 'Thanks.'

'For what?'

'Bringin' us up here. I had a good time.'

He wriggled in the seat, trying to get his back comfortable. Helicopters. Always made it hurt. 'You don't have to keep thankin' me.'

'What did you and Nash talk about?'

'Old times. Where it all went wrong. Usual bullshit.'

'Did it go wrong?'

He nodded. 'I lost ten years in a bottle. Nash, he had trouble settlin' too.'

'And now?'

'He's cool. He just feels there must be more to life than this. Like us. Like I was sayin'.'

'He seems OK.'

'He's a good guy.'

She felt a long shared history close her out. 'We got six hours, Coogan. I'd like to hear the story.'

'What story?'

'Where was it? Somalia.'

He sighed and felt acid settle in his stomach. 'We don't all come out of it in a good light.'

'Hey, I came to the conclusion last night that the only men I like are ones who fuck up.'

'There you go again, running yourself down. Don't tut at me. Hold on.' Coogan suddenly floored the gas pedal, and the Trans Am leapt forward, causing Pete to almost roll off the back seat, swerving round the truck and eating up the open road in front of it. 'You deserve better than that,' he finally said, knowing he included himself in the reject pile. Then he began to tell the story.

❖   ❖   ❖

This one was different. The Creep knew it straight away when he walked in and put down the attaché case. Usually they were cowering or almost comatose, subdued, beaten, malleable. This one was sitting on the edge of the bed, smoking a cigarette with an insouciance that made him want to strike it from her mouth. He was in charge here, there was no room for any kind of insolence. He could feel his dick hard against his trousers, the drug pumping up the blood pressure, red-lining it, so it felt like his balls would explode unless he got down to business soon. He had taken just two this time. Four seemed to tip him over the edge, make him want to go even further, and there was only one place that road led to.

She was wearing a red shift dress, torn and stained in places, but gathered around her as neatly as she could. Her hair dark, jet black it seemed in the gloom, was cut short and severe, shaved up the back. Her eyes glowered with each pull on the cigarette, as if the lit end were attached to her optic nerve.

There was a sink in the corner, and he washed his hands, drying them on his shirt rather than risk the plague-infected towel that hung on a hook nearby.

'Get up,' he said.

To his surprise she obeyed him, unfolding herself to her full height. She must have been five nine or ten even with no shoes on, he thought. He could see she had a streamlined figure, small breasts, flat bottom. But then she probably hadn't had a proper diet for a few years.

He laid the sheet over the bed as usual, and tucked it down. When he leant back up he could see her looking in the case, and her eyes flicked back to him. There was nothing in there. No fear, no curiosity, and the glowering had gone. Just a level, uninvolved gaze.

'Get undressed.'

She let the dress fall to the floor and stepped out of it. He could see the harsh outline of each rib, the bones of her hips looking as if they were about to burst through. She needed another few pounds of flesh on there.

She walked past him and stubbed the cigarette out into the sink. Then she went down and sat on the bed. 'On my front or back?'

The English wasn't bad. He didn't want those eyes staring at him the entire time. 'Front.'

She pointed at the case. 'I would like you to know, there is nothing you can do to me that is any worse than I have had done already. Don't waste your time trying.' And she spread herself out on the bed.

He suddenly felt very angry. She was messing with the whole scene. His dick seemed to drop back a notch in hardness. No, this wouldn't do. This wouldn't do at all. He took out the first roll of tape. She would pay for trying to out-psyche him. It was a challenge, that's what it was. She'd thrown down a challenge.

TWENTY

Newburgh, NJ

'You thought *what* was in the trunk?'

'Your head.'

Jim met Dick in a diner just outside Newburgh, an old unreconstituted truckers' stop that they both knew. Jim had already drunk half a dozen cups of coffee, trying to keep sharp, and he was twitchy. He ought to switch to decaff. Dick looked tired too. He told Jim he had instructed Mike to stay on at summer camp for an extra week, keep him away from the nastiness. His catching skills were no longer a requirement, that was for sure.

'My head?'

'Dick, I thought he was going to get both of us. You did the pitchin'.'

'Oh thanks, pal.'

'No, I mean, I don't blame you . . .'

'How's Belle?' Dick interrupted.

'Belle? She's . . .' He ran a hand through his hair, noticing with disgust a small shower of dandruff. Stress, he always got it when he got stressed out. He brushed his shoulder. 'Ever seen those people in the aftermath of a train or car smash. The ones who survived, unscathed, but they wander round, like something knocked their brain out of gear?'

'Seen them? I am one. More coffee?'

They both got a refill from a waitress who was as unreconstituted as her diner, with make-up and hair from thirty years before, and still squeezed into the uniform she wore back then when, no doubt, it was a somewhat looser fit. 'Anything to eat, or you just gonna get yourself stoked on caffeine?'

They ordered some bagels and Jim picked up the thread: 'Not like Belle you ain't. She's not making a lot of sense. And she's supposed to be the head doctor. You know? Full of sage advice. Not now. And me? I'm just a guy with a shitty little magazine. I am not used to . . . to people shooting at me and threatening me. Why doesn't he just take the money and fuck off? That's what he wants, isn't it? Bottom line? Christ, the deal goes through with Condé Nast, I can give him a million or two to get out of our lives and let us be.'

'The tape. What was on it?'

Jim told him, the abbreviated version, the acid eating at his stomach walls as he did so. 'Dick, you said that I still thought he was a Hungarian investment banker. Remember that?'

He shook his head.

'On the way to the hospital? I can't remember what you said exactly. What I mean is . . . did you know about any of this?'

'Oh Lord. That I knew the kind of thing that was on the tape? No. Jim, how can you suggest that? You saying I knew a mass-murderer was in our midst? Jesus—'

'OK, OK. Well what did you mean?'

'I don't even remember saying it. I was pretty . . . you know, out of it. Panicked.' He took a deep breath. 'Look, I knew there were some rumours that he wasn't above board, y'know, maybe some money-laundering. Shit – you know the number of banks been hit by that. So I thought maybe he had some heavy friends. OK, truth is I figured he might have some contacts in the Russian Mafia. You know, Hungarian, old Commie country. I didn't reckon on him being some kind of . . . some kind of holocaust merchant.'

'OK, well I think we got him anyway. I been thinking, we could go to the police with it. After all, it is something that will interest the Department of Immigration and Naturalization.'

'How come?'

'We have the tape. The evidence. The International Criminal Tribunal for the former Yugoslavia in Brussels?'

'It's in The Hague,' said Dick. 'ICTY is in The Hague.'

'Wherever. Those guys were going to try and get Arkan there before he got whacked. In the story we are running? This guy is clearly like him. We got enough to get some kind of extradition. Must have. Here.' He took the tape from his jacket and handed it to Dick. 'OK, I'm sure the cops, the FBI and your guys, in the State department, would be interested.'

Dick considered for a moment. 'Christ, you're dealing with bureaucracy on an international scale. It's slow, slow, slow, Jim, but – uh-oh.'

'What?' asked Jim warily.

Dick spun the tape in his hands, examining it from each side. 'You rewind this? Play it again?'

'What? You think it's like "Friends"? We watch the same episode over and over again. It's sick, Dick. Horrible.'

He said solemnly: 'Jim. It's a OUO.'

'Uh?'

'Look here. OUO. One Use Only tape. It wipes as it plays.'

'You're shittin' me?'

'Nah.'

'Who the fuck would want a one-use tape?'

'Record companies, movie companies. To stop piracy. You send a critic a video, a movie or whatever, it wipes after one play. So they don't get to copy it or sell it down the video exchange.'

'I don't believe it.'

'Hey, go home, try it.'

'I don't mean I don't believe it ...' The bagels arrived and he nibbled at one out of sense of duty rather than hunger. 'I mean ... I just don't believe it. Of course, it makes some kind of twisted sense. He wouldn't give us the evidence to lynch him with, I guess. Damn. Dick, what can we do? What next?'

Dick shrugged. 'Cops?'

'We could try. He didn't seem all that frightened by the thought of the cops. My hunch is it's still money.'

'Could be. Look, I can do some digging on him. Off the meter at the office. Find out if we can nail him on anything. Put a name check through the Feds.'

'Yeah. Yeah, I'd appreciate it. Then I'll call the Bloomsberry PD, tell them what our friend and neighbour is up to. And what he has done. Yeah, good.' He paused and took a bigger bite of bagel. 'One thing bothers me, though.'

'What?'

'If this guy wants a replacement kid so bad . . . well it can't be that hard. He says his wife ain't gonna give him no more, but he could bang up some broad, he could go to Guatemala and get himself one for five grand, so I hear. We ran that piece two years ago. So maybe six by now. Why doesn't he do that?'

Dick stirred a heap of sugar into his coffee and licked the spoon. 'This is just a guess.'

'Yeah?'

'If what was on the tape is true. Not a fake.'

'I'd say it was real.'

'If he did what you suggest? Gets another kid, either biologically or financially? There is one big element missing.'

'What?'

Dick pointed the spoon at him. 'Making you suffer.'

It was October 3, 1993, over a decade ago. 'Just one awfully big fuckin' adventure,' the lieutenant had said. In, out, home for a cold beer. An hour tops. It must have been the shortest combat hop in the history of warfare. Three minutes, door to door, from US-controlled airstrip to target building in downtown Mog.

Chalk Five consisted of twelve men, Rangers all, fearsome and bulky – desert fatigues, Kevlar vests, heavy fire-power, from H&K subs to big, vicious 60-calibre guns, debilitating flashbangs charges to maiming fragmentation grenades.

They loaded into the choppers quickly – after all they had done this four, five, six times a day, kitted and armed up, only to be stood down at the last moment. This time as the

Black Hawk swallowed them they cast furtive glances at the four other Chalks, feeling conflicting messages explode around their bodies, fear mixed with relief that it was going down at last, after dozens of false starts, a real mission. OK, it might only be a fifty-minute mission, but it was in the real heart of darkness, the Bakara market of Mogadishu, bandit country.

Twelve Rangers, pilot, co-pilot, two crew chiefs with mini-guns, all in a stripped-out Black Hawk, ready to take them into this hostile environment, where they would rope down, and set up PS for the D-boys. Perimeter Security. Sounded so simple. But Coogan had already seen the Somalian mobs, the way they emerged from nowhere, stupidly ready and willing to take on the elite of the US army. Shit, hadn't these guys seen what had happened to the Iraqis on the Basra Road? Didn't seem to stop them, they kept coming in wave after wave. Maybe they thought they could grind down the Yankees like the Vietcong. But Vietnam was a long time ago, a lot had been learned. No attempt to win hearts and minds of the populace here. Chalks One through Five were going in to snatch a couple of the warlords who were grinding this country into its red dust. Chop off the head, make sure it doesn't re-grow, that was what they were sitting in the sweat, fume-filled belly of a Black Hawk for.

There was a squawk in Coogan's ear. It took a second for him to pick out the crucial word in the sudden, excited babble.

Lucy.

It *was* going down. Coogan ran through the men. Men. Ha. Boys. Eighteen, nineteen, most of whom had barely completed Ranger training at Fort Benning before being shipped out here. Still, the D-boys, the Delta force, they were the ones at the sticky end, they'd do the hard part. All he had to do was deploy his Chalk as PS one block north of Chalk Two, to stop the technicals – the trucks with big .50s bolted on the back – coming anywhere near the target building.

The rotors thudded at full volume now, a deep bass, chest-thumping rhythm, and the Black Hawk lifted off into the afternoon sun, chased by a posse of dust devils. In his head-phones he heard the pilots check that they were all away, no problems and confirm that the ground convoy was in position, ready to roll within five minutes.

Eleven men under him. The ever-reliable Nash, a couple of years his senior, who had been through Benning with him and should have made sergeant by now, Rollins, Caruso, the radio operator, machine-gunners Flint and Jones, Mab, his fellow sergeant, a year older at twenty-five, but showing no resentment that maybe this should have been his call, his squad. Then there was Toots, the only black guy in the Chalk. The rest were the real boys – O'Brien, Riley, Russell, half a dozen zit-faced, white-bread youths artificially inflated with the name Specialists and Private First Class, kids who shrunk down to nothing when they shucked off the Kevlar and the ammo belts, almost as skinny as the locals when stripped, but the Somalis didn't know that. At the moment they looked like Imperial Storm Troopers, ready to kick ass.

Low and fast, fast and low. The SOAR chopper boys knew how to fly. They could go down Mog's alleys with the rotors skimming the windows, drop you in a courtyard that you would swear was ten feet narrower than the blade circum-ference, scrape the Hawk's underbelly on top of the traffic down Hawlwadig Road. Then go back and do it again at night. Nevertheless, Coogan felt his stomach lurch as they banked hard, with little regard for their passengers strung out on ammo boxes and crude benches, some half out the door. Still, by this stage even the greenest Ranger appreciated that when you flew with these boys, you better hang on.

Mogadishu came up below them, a pox-ridden, diseased vestige of a town. It reminded Coogan of one of those faces you see in magazines eaten away by bacteria, only the vaguest human feature recognisable. Here and there you could see a hotel, a mosque tower, an apartment block. Apart from that, he could only think of a tropical version of post-bomb Nagasaki, or Berlin or Hamburg, circa 1945.

He heard more chattering voices in his ears. Super Six Seven in place, ready to rope drop. Chalk Four, which would be to his west.

Coogan peered ahead through the plexiglass, he could see the leading Black Hawks manoeuvring into position, circling for the kill, with the Little Birds, the smaller rocket-carrying choppers flitting around like angry symbionts.

There was fire below. Smoke. And dust, lots of dust, the red earth billowing up like cumulus at sunset. The white target building was fading, losing focus, disappearing into the whirlwind.

A jabber in his ear. A hint of . . . not panic but a deviation from the script.

The smoke was obscuring too much. Chalk Four were going to rope down from higher up. Seventy-odd feet. High. Coogan looked at Mab who, hearing none of this, gave him the thumbs up. Coogan smiled back then pointed at the red kerchief he had insisted they all wear. He pulled his own up over his nose. Mab frowned and passed the word. Now they looked like Imperial Troopers who planned to rob a stagecoach. Still, better than donning the full, claustrophobic rubber cups of anti-chemical breathing masks.

They were circling over the drop zone, the note from the blades rising and falling as the pilot altered the angle of attack. Below was a boiling cauldron, it was like looking into the cone of an active volcano, one spewing earth instead of smoke.

The pilot couldn't see. They would have to go in blind.

Coogan looked down.

His call. He could say no. No blind entry. No coming down on top of a technical or a bunch of itchy-triggered D-boys or just a wild, swirling mass of locals.

But was he going to risk aborting his first action as squad leader?

No.

OK, he found himself agreeing, we go.

Russell first. Good point man. Knew not to stop and admire the view from the bottom and to get the hell away before a pair of boots crashed onto him. The thick nylon rope curled down, and Coogan watched it disappear into the mist.

The Crew Chief hustled Russell into position and, as he grasped the thick nylon rope, Coogan saw it below. Just a flash in the clouds. A glimpse.

'There's another chopper down there!' he shouted.

Russell carried on moving and Coogan grabbed the Crew Chief's arm. 'I see blades.'

The Chief looked at him, then peered down. Then he, too, saw a glint of what he was about to feed the Chalk into, 'Jesus Christ get us up!'

They felt the sudden strain on the fuselage as power kicked in, pulling them up, another bank.

Someone, somewhere had got confused.

They started a circle, still low, over the courtyards and tin roofs of the city, the streets suddenly full of crowds running, running towards the action, as if the circus has come to town, banking back round towards the seething, boiling cloud, making sure they had the right intersection. Then they all felt it at once,

The days and nights in the machine meant they all knew what a Black Hawk should feel and smell and react like, what was a normal creak and groan and strain, and what wasn't. The sudden metallic screech and the lurch were definitely extra-ordinary.

The engine note changed. Harsher, more desperate, they felt the body of the machine start to edge out of alignment beneath the blades. Auto-rotation. Something had hit the tail rotor.

That couldn't be, a small voice said in Coogan's head.

The pilot yelled an instruction that was lost in a sudden wash of static.

The rotors' noise slackened as the pilot cut power back, trying to control the revolution. Something must still be running back there, Coogan figured, otherwise they would have gone into full laundromat-spin mode. There was a sudden grinding noise and the Black Hawk bucked, as if it was going to vomit. 'Super Six R going down. Repeat—' Was all Coogan caught of the last transmission.

'Brace!' barked Coogan as loud as he could, feeling something tear in his throat. The helicopter lurched up again, and Coogan could see the pilot's anguished face, worried and panicking but determined all the same. His machine. The earth shall not have it. But it started sinking again.

This wasn't happening, thought Coogan, not to a Black Hawk. Not to Rangers. Not against this, this rabble. They had dropped thirty feet, were still a couple of hundred yards shy of the dust zone, where the D-boys might save their asses, and level with the top of one of the remaining apartment blocks.

From up there Coogan saw the muzzle flashes. The Crew Chief on that side was leaning over to the pilot, hadn't noticed the shooting up there.

'Nash. Nash. Three o'clock,' Coogan bellowed, his voice now rasping.

Nash had his back to the roof, but at least he was on the right side of the machine to get a clear shot. Coogan didn't want to be firing over heads when the Hawk was bucking and banking. Nash edged round, cocked his weapon and let out a burst. The thudding noise filled the cabin, spent cases bounced off the floor. The Crew Chief, jolted into realisation of the situation, joined in with a minigun, vaporising the concrete parapet.

Then the machine tipped, like a boat caught by a sudden, unexpected wave. They watched as Riley, who had let go to raise his weapons to join in the fusillade, pitched forward and went flailing down towards the earth, bounding off a parked car, leaving a huge indentation in the roof.

Coogan found himself yelling in defiance of what he had seen.

He looked at the pilot, saw the great splashes of red over him and the co-pilot, could see the strength ebbing from his arms as he reached up to kill the main engines completely. The auto-rotation began again, slowly, as the helicopter fell. Nobody needed to be told not to brace or get spread-eagled as the machine came down on top of the alley with a fearsome speed, snapping in half as its rotors twisted and buckled and flew off, filling the air with the terrible shriek of mangling metal as the body of the stricken beast twitched and thrashed as if trying to break free of invisible chains. There was a sudden eye-blackening spin and an enormous impact and Coogan felt himself punched into the darkness.

He had been staring straight ahead while he was telling the story, not wanting to look at Wendy. He paused and flicked his head, then went back to watching the road. Eighty miles to go. Time enough to finish it. Get it all out. Make her realise why he liked to keep his distance. Why Pete scared him.

'Jesus, Coogan.'

'Yeah. Jesus.'

'So?'

'What?'

'What the fuck happened next?'

'We got a visit from Hell, that's what happened.'

It was raining. Coogan could hear it. Pitter patter. Raining in Mogadishu. That was what they needed to flatten the dust. He opened his eyes, tasted blood, lots of blood, felt a jackhammer trying to open up his skull. Then reality snapped in. Leader. His squad. Failed. First time out. Against a Third World country.

Get them out. Stop the self-pity. It isn't over. Get them out.

The cabin was filling with smoke. Both pilots were slumped in their straps, everyone else was a tangle of desert fatigues, Kevlar and weaponry.

And it wasn't rain. It was gunfire.

He heard a louder rattle. Mab returning fire. He spun round and pointed at his nose and grimaced and pointed up.

Coogan felt it burn his sinuses too. Aviation fuel or oil or both. He could see fluids of various hues bleeding out of the quilted soundproofing on the ceiling.

Coogan suppressed the desire to just close his eyes again and scream, to roll up in a ball. Leader. His squad. Get them out. He ripped off the headphones, pulling the jack out of the roof as he did so.

'OK, let's move it,' he shouted to anyone who could hear. 'We need to re-group.'

He tried to shift, realised his legs were pinned. Russell was slumped across them, and when he pushed at him he was suddenly aware that young Russell wouldn't be re-grouping. Russell had lost a chunk of his throat. Coogan touched his own face and felt the stickiness. It wasn't his blood he could taste after all. It was Russell's. He rubbed it off with his sleeve as best he could.

'Out, out, out, this side, away from the fire.' As Coogan moved he felt a jagged stab of pain up his spine. Something was crushed in there from the impact. Ignore.

Nine of them climbed out, eight of his and one Crew Chief, all running to flatten themselves against the crudely whitewashed, badly mortared wall that delineated the alley. The floor was thick with garbage and bits of mangled US Army helicopter, the air still filled with millions of dust motes and flies. Lots of flies.

As he left, Flint fired the big M-60 gun through the gaping side of the downed machine, raking from side to side, into the smoke and dust on the far side and the firing stopped.

Coogan looked back inside to see if anyone was still alive. Hard to tell. Just bodies. Russell had been the Chalk medic.

Caruso tried to raise HQ on his set and shrugged. 'Fucked.'

'Dump it,' said Coogan and pulled out his walkie-talkie handset. Try and stay calm, he told himself. This was no time to become panicky or incomprehensible. *Losing men, losing men,* a jittery little voice kept saying and he slapped it down, hard. 'This is Chalk Five on Super Six R. Have . . .' He found this hard to say. 'Have been downed by enemy fire. Do you co—'

The firing started again from the far side of the chopper, the odd round flying through the cabin and out their side with a deceptively flat crack. He swore he felt the lethal breath of one kiss his forehead, like a deadly lover.

He looked at Flint who stepped past him and set up another curtain of fire before scrambling back into the chopper. He felt for a pulse in each neck in turn, including the pilots, between the two-second burps he let off, trying to keep the hot barrel away from the unknown liquids dripping all around him

Flint emerged and shook his head. 'We should take them with us.'

Ranger creed. Always take a fallen comrade. But the air was starting to hiss and zing, and Coogan could feel his brain slowly seizing up. He needed time to think, to take this in. Life, and death, was happening too fast.

'Later. We gotta pull back,' Coogan said, and started down the alley. 'Let's put some distance between us and the bird.'

He looked to the sky. Somewhere up there was a big old spy plane. The cameras trained on the action were so good he knew they could see them, if they could only penetrate the cloud of filth climbing heavenwards – from the streets all around them evil-looking columns of black smoke spiralled up. Tyres being burnt, the traditional way of summoning armed help in these parts.

His walkie-talkie crackled. The lieutenant. What was their status?

'We have casualties, we have casualties. Men down. Repeat, men down. We need to be pulled out. Over,' said Coogan as calmly as he could.

'Don't shout. The land convoy knows your position. There are half a dozen technicals between you and them. Can you fight your way out to the intersection south of you? Over.'

There was a sudden clatter as a helicopter went overhead, another Black Hawk. Several people waved from the open doorway, but it was gone in a flash.

South was the far side of the chopper. Fire had re-started from that direction. Rounds smacked into the wall near them. There were several long blasts in reply from his Chalk. Both sides firing blind into a settling cloud of dust and smoke. 'Maybe. I haven't had time to assess—'

Another five-second exchange. This time he felt skin crackle on his cheek as a hot one zinged by. 'Shit.'

'Secure your area,' said the lieutenant firmly. 'We'll come and get you. Over and out.'

Secure your area. They were in a long alley, twelve-, thirteen-feet wide, with white walls perhaps seven feet high on either side. On the far side of the chopper, armed Somalis. If the Sammies capped the open end, which was maybe three hundred yards away, they'd be pinned in. This was a death trap. They had to get out.

'Sarge.' It was Flint. A big southern boy, Bible Belt raised with a strong sense of righteousness, he didn't spook easily. It was like having Elmer Gantry with heavy firepower on your side. But now there was fear in his voice. 'Look at this.'

At the far, northern, end of the alley was a row of women and children advancing slowly, maybe eight abreast. You had to look hard to see it, behind them were the muzzles of AK-47s, held by men crouched between the human shield. The mob was too distant to be able to be certain of the expressions on the faces of the women and children clearly. Were they scared, doing this under duress? Or did they know the rules of engagement the Rangers were under? Shoot only if you see who is shooting at you. Avoid civilian casualties.

Jones raised his M-60 towards the crowd.

'They're kids,' yelled Caruso. 'Jones, they're kids.'

Jones didn't have time to answer. A line of bullets stitched across the wall and floor in front of them, drawn as if by magnetism to O'Brien's leg, which convulsed as his knee cap was pulverised. He screamed and went over. 'I'm hit I'm hit I'm hit,' spewed out of his mouth.

In the micro-window between action and reaction, those milliseconds before Jones scythed down half the local populace, Coogan could taste the fear and panic pouring out of pores around him, knew they were a breath away from becoming a mindless, dangerous rabble themselves. Coogan's mind spun like slot-machine tumblers. What was the response? What was it? Think. Click. The tumblers stopped.

'Over their heads,' he said emphatically and fired a burst of his M-16. The others joined in, a ragged chorus of different muzzle signatures, the big baritone of the .60 occasionally drowning them all out.

They stopped and looked. The wall of flesh hesitated, a ripple ran through it, a backward step maybe, no more. A check that none had fallen perhaps. Then it came on, like a multi-headed bulldozer blade of human flesh.

'Sonofabitch,' said Jones. 'What is it with these mother-fuckers?'

Coogan remembered this question from the Ethics and Responses unit at Fort Benning. There was a next step. The answer took its own sweet time popping into his head. 'Grenades!' Coogan shouted.

He unclipped and threw his two flashbangs, and turned away as they detonated, searing eyeballs and burning throats in the mêlée. As the smoke cleared the crowd had gone. Non-lethal but effective. For a while.

Lying there in the dirt was a single AK. From the shadows a spindly figure appeared, edging along the wall, coughing and spluttering from the gas, but not deterred. Six years old, seven maybe, hard to tell with these undernourished kids in their baggy thrift-store clothes. The Rangers all watched in amazement as this shadow stepped into the open, edging towards the fallen weapon, eyes down as if not looking would make the Rangers disappear.

'Shit,' said Caruso, part in admiration, part in the terror of facing an adversary who seemed not to know rules or logic. Or even fear. He shouldered his M-16.

'Hold it,' said Coogan, grimacing as his spine sent more diamond-hard needles of pain up his back.

The boy made it to the rifle, bent down and picked it up. They waited for the triumphant sprint away. Just one more AK in a city that probably had a million of them, Coogan thought. Let it be.

The boy raised, cocked and fired in one smooth practised movement.

Coogan felt grit sting his eye as the wall exploded near him. A low grunt of pain. Mab. The Sergeant. Hit.

Still the boy fired.

Ethics and Responses says, what?

No contest. Protect your men.

Coogan raised his M-16 and let off a long burst, watching the tiny emaciated figure jerk back as if pulled on a cord, roll over in the orange earth two or three times and lay still. 'Damn,' he said to himself. It was the first time he had killed something that wasn't cardboard or plywood. 'Shit.'

As he blinked he saw an image of the boy, a snapshot from the arc of death as the bullets tore through what little flesh there was. It was as if some sportscaster had said, 'Let's see that again, Bob.' Except this was real slow, with each blink of his eyes the frame advanced just one fraction of a moment, like those sequential shots of a horse galloping the old photographers took. 'Shit.'

He felt something at his side. Nash. Calm. A hand on his shoulder. He knew. Could sense the paralysis that was about to hit. 'The trick, Ranger, is to stay alive long enough to let them become nightmares.'

Coogan looked at the older man. Why wasn't he cool like

that? Nash said: 'Mab's bleeding hard. He'd taken the plate out of his vest.'

'Shit.' Coogan realised he would have to widen his vocabulary. Fast.

He blinked hard and the boy died again and faded.

'OK,' shouted Coogan with what he hoped was a firm voice. 'Up the alley, first courtyard we can get in is our fire base. Go, go, go. Nash, give me a hand with Mab.

They ran as fast as their bulky equipment would allow them, Flint and Jones dragging O'Brien between them, Nash and Coogan with Mab, crouched low, hearing sporadic fire coming their way, all wondering when they were going to feel the blow in the back, catapulting them forward, parting the Kevlar, then skin, then fat, then organ and blood vessel.

Toots made it first, diving left through a door made of flattened metal drums of some kind, the others piled afterwards. It was the dusty, crap-filled yard of one of the tin-roofed huts that made up most of the city, twenty feet square at most. They laid O'Brien up against the wall of the shack. He was shaking, his skin grey. But that was just the pain. He'd live. Mab's eyes rolled in his sockets and disappeared, just the whites showing. There was a gurgling noise. Coogan looked down as he died and swore to himself. On his watch. Why the fuck on his watch?

Flint popped a head over the wall and scoped the alley. 'They'll be back,' he said. 'Any of you guys ever see that movie *The Alamo*?'

'Check the building,' said Coogan irritably, fighting the aching in his back. He looked around at the boxes and trash in the yard. He kicked at a couple of the more substantial containers, ones that could take a man's weight. 'Flint, in the absence of John fuckin' Wayne bein' here I suggest you and Jones take a corner each – one 60 looking down the alley, the other up—'

'What about the chopper?' It was Flint.

'What about it?'

'You know what they do to the crew. The Sammies. They'll chop them to bits.'

Coogan nodded. He'd heard those stories. He thought about Riley who had fallen out. They would have reached him by now. He hoped the impact had killed him. But those guys in the mangled Black Hawk. He'd assumed some of the ground forces would come for the bodies sooner or later. It was part of the Ranger mindset. Don't leave them behind. But this time . . . what was best – having them in bits or not at all?

The thought of them being sliced and diced was bad for morale he figured. 'OK. Flint, you, me, Chief, let's see if we can make it back, grab one each. The rest of you . . .' He almost laughed at the comical sound of the next bit, but it died in his throat. 'Cover us.'

Coogan stepped out into the alley, the view obscured in one direction by the broken-backed bird, the other by dust and residual smoke from the grenades. The boy was still there, now just a hump of lifeless tissue. 'Good to go,' he said.

It was as if that was the signal for the AKs to open up. The entire alley started to hum, as if it were a resonating pipe, bullets exploded down it from both directions. Coogan felt one crease his helmet and pushed the others back in, slamming the door and breathing hard. 'There are people out there . . .' he gasped ' . . . who want us dead.'

'What about the guys?' asked the Chief forlornly.

'No good adding to the total,' Nash said, jerking a thumb in the chopper's direction. 'They'll understand.'

'I can ignite it. I got a mag of tracers.' Flint said it quietly, seriously as if he were offering to perform a sacrament.

Coogan felt his throat go dry. His call. Burn them up. Ashes. But they'd get the dogtags, they'd get a burial. Wouldn't be the first time there was less in a coffin than a family knew. Unable to actually speak the order he nodded and stepped away from the wall, listened to Flint reloading and then the deep rattle of the gun.

There was a heavy whump of air as the chopper's fuel detonated, shaking the ground and sending a shower of debris up into the sky. Coogan felt the blast singe one side of his face, causing an eye to start watering. He thought of the men instantly incinerated, before he caught sight of the Crew Chief whose slick it had been. He was shaking his head in disbelief.

'I'm sorry, Chief. It was better . . . Let's hope they took a few of the Sammies with them, too,' Coogan managed to say. The Chief inclined his head slightly, and Coogan took it for understanding.

As the wreckage settled down to smoulder and ignite and pop sporadically, the air was becoming unbreathable, as vaporised plastic and people joined the noxious swirl of tyre rubber and dung that was the regular olfactory signature of the city.

Coogan pulled up his kerchief again and shouted through it. 'Caruso, I want an i/r and radio-homing beacon activated so they can locate us with no delay. You got them? Good, and check ammo status.'

'House is empty,' said Nash, emerging through a tattered beaded curtain, then ducked as the wall behind him vapourised. 'Heads up. Sniper.' He looked up at the roof of a three-storey building one block across and let rip. 'One o'clock guys.'

Flint joined in with a heavier burst.

'Whoa, whoa,' said Coogan. 'We don't know how long we gonna be stuck here.' He motioned to one of the Rangers. 'Toots. You kneel here. You see anything move on that roof, blow it all to fuck. Man, woman or child. OK?'

Coogan felt Nash's arm on his shoulder. He allowed himself a deep breath and winced at the spasm in his spine. 'How am I doin'?' he asked.

Nash curled his lower lip. 'Take a while to pay for the Black Hawk, even with combat bonuses.' They both laughed at that. There were no combat bonuses. These were guys who would *pay* to go into action. Well, before this, anyhow. Fucked up by dust, pondered Coogan. Who would've believed it? 'How 'bout I take the house and monitor the street with Caruso and the Chief?' Nash pointed at the burly helicopter crewman who nodded a 'whatever' affirmation. 'You keep the alley clear. We move men as required between the two positions, depending on strength of Sammy's numbers?'

Coogan nodded. He was really thirsty, but like all the others he had left his canteen behind in an attempt to keep the weight down. They were only going to be an hour after all. He smiled at the thought. He felt the air sizzle with more stray rounds and instinctively crouched. This was going to be one hell of a long hour.

Nash helped a sweaty, pale O'Brien into the house and fed him some painkillers, then laid him down in the shit where at least he could point his rifle out into the street. It was chaos out there, people running like the proverbial headless chickens. Except the road was full of genuine headless chickens, caught by a stray blast of .50 fire, and they weren't going anywhere.

Coogan had just allowed himself a moment leaning against the shack, fantasising about a cigarette and beer, then it started again.

'I got Skinnies!'

It was Jones, looking up past the wrecked Black Hawk, where figures were emerging through the fumes, gingerly picking their way between fires and razor-sharp shrapnel and debris.

'Me too,' said Flint.

Coogan kicked a crate over to the wall and climbed up. No human shield this time. Instead, on Flint's side, there was a pair of cows and a donkey with men crouched behind them.

'Jesus,' said Coogan.

'Amen,' replied Flint and pulled his trigger.

Jones did likewise and both of Coogan's inner ears spasmed under the twin onslaught. He looked to his right to where the Somalis were streaming over the Black Hawk wreckage, raising their AKs and firing wildly; to the left the cows seemed to be soaking up high-velocity rounds like sandbags.

Coogan suddenly felt the hopelessness. There was nothing that would stop these guys. They could kill five hundred and another thousand would come, with guns, clubs, machetes. He could feel the wave of hatred from the mob hitting him like a solid object, pounding his ribs, tightening his chest. He felt as if his heart had swelled to five times its normal size.

The air suddenly thickened into a buzzing soup and Coogan looked up, luxuriating in the warm rotor-wash, taking a deep breath. A Little Bird gun-and-rocket-platform chopper moved overhead, describing a long lazy arc. It came back round and started in from the right, a low, nose-down run. Coogan grabbed his two .60 men and pulled them backwards, along the yard to the scant shelter of the house, pushing Chief and the others with them.

The chopper opened fire, its multi-barrels sending a chainsaw of bullets along the length of the alley, churning everything in its path. Coogan watched the strip of dirt turn into an abattoir, arcs of blood and bits of limbs and hunks of flesh, human, equine and bovine, spurting high into the air above the wall. He was suddenly glad the cinder-blocks had been stacked so high.

As the Little Bird banked away, its human-shredding work done, Coogan heard Nash shout: 'There's a Humvee coming up the street.'

Don't relax, Coogan. This is when you get careless. And get killed. 'Keep on that roof,' he told Toots as the boy stood up. Then he looked at Flint and dared to say: 'Looks like it won't be the Alamo after all.'

Flint raised an eyebrow. He scanned the smoke-filled sky, listened to the increasing number of machine-gun volleys from both sides and the flat thud of RPG rounds and drawled, 'Yeah. Ain't the Battle of New Orleans, either, Sarge.'

Coogan blinked, and the boy was there again.

Pete was asleep by the time they got back, late in the afternoon, and she lifted him gently out of the car, leaving Coogan to put his precious junker away under the tarp, and laid the boy down in bed. Rosita, one of the office staff at the park, would look after him tonight. She couldn't ask Coogan again, she was coming to rely on him too much.

He came in for a soda, and she said to him: 'That is a helluva story. I never knew. I never heard that.'

'It was like Vietnam in one day, that's why. A foreign country, soldiers who didn't understand why they were fighting, an army not sure of its objectives, a local populace who showed big ballsy machines aren't everything.' And, he could have added, a bunch of Rangers who realised they were scared little boys. 'Toots, you know, he always said it was a victory. The Deltas got the warlords they went in for, and we survived. Shit – some of the Rangers made a whole night out there, with Sammie crawling up their asses. We was lucky.'

'You got back OK?'

No, he wanted to say, it was a bloody firefight every inch, the air full – absolutely full – of bullets and RPG rounds, men screaming and dying every few minutes, all of them reduced to firing indiscriminately, the rules of engagement not only broken but trampled underfoot. There were other kids, mothers, babies . . . but he had told enough.

'Yeah, my spine was jarred by the crash, so I was out of the army.' There was a beat while he decided whether to tell her. Gone this far. 'The boy . . . the kid I shot—'

'That must've been rough.'

'He comes back.'

'What?' she asked, finding it hard to imagine Coogan believed in ghosts.

'I see him. It's like he represents all the others who . . . I mean, shit there were hundreds of them. He's like the elected representative. He comes back and reminds me every so often. I see a little crowd of them and he detaches himself, like their agent. Hey – you kill people like me. Especially if . . . especially if I am around kids. Boys. When I get to be near them, he comes,

I see him in my dreams, behind my lids. Like a warning to me. Don't get too close.'

'What shit,' she said impatiently.

He blew his cheeks out. She'd never get a job in therapy, that was for sure.

Her voice softened. 'Come on, you know it ain't real.'

'You don't see him.'

'You ever get any help?'

'Post-traumatic counselling?'

She nodded.

'Nah.'

'Why?'

'Because most of the time I know when it's coming and ride it out or move on. I get counselling they gonna want to open up my head, and I am real happy it stays closed most of the time.'

'Is Nash the same?'

Another negative. That day had different effects on each survivor. Some felt more alive than ever, bloodied by combat. While facing off death with a diminishing supply of ammo, watching their buddies turn into raw slabs of meat hamburgered by AKs and RPGs, they had skipped to that higher plane, the one where every fibre in the body screams out to stay intact, to celebrate its sentient status, like a big hit of the most potent endorphins in the world. Real life seemed flat after that. Nash had a taste of it, that edge-of-the-world feeling that no high in the world would ever take him there again. He had also rationalised it to himself. They had to kill those people, or they would have torn them limb from limb. Nash never had nightmares, never saw the Skinnies scuttling around the periphery of his world.

'You didn't get round to Toots. His part in all this.'

'Such as?'

'Such as telling me what the big deal was. The one that made him go play condor off the Canyon.'

'No. I'm not sure you're ready.'

'What? After what you just told me?'

He stood up and rubbed his back. 'Ha. Now it gets really crazy.'

Jim Barry pulled the Lexus back in front of Morgan's house and rubbed his already raw eyes. So it all came down to calling Donkey Schlong and filling him in, trying to convince him that the cops needed to hide them properly. But could he get them to take it seriously without a tape? Dick had taken it to ask the lab if they could recover any residual images, but he didn't hold out much hope.

From inside the house he could hear the insistent yell of Ariel, and he almost got back in the car and drove away. The kid was turning the house into a pressure cooker. Sooner or later someone, or all of them, was going to ignite.

He got out, locked the door, and had just turned away when the side window crazed and shattered. He stood for a second staring at it, wondering if he had slammed the door too hard when the sound of the rifle reached him. He took a step back and watched two holes punch their way through the metal of the door skin, and the leather seat jerked twice. He flung himself onto the driveway, ignoring the cuts and rips to his clothes and scrabbled across the gravel towards the door. Another shot hit the hood, zinging off into the distance, leaving a large crease indicating its path.

He risked a glance back. Across the road was a wooden hillock topped by some shrubs and a couple of trees. Bound to be in there.

His heart pumping he made the doorway, curled himself into a ball and hammered on it, unable to make anything like a decent sound that could be heard over the damned kid. He jumped up, stabbed the bell, and crouched down again, rolling into the hallway at the feet of Morgan when the door finally opened.

'What the—?'

'Get down, get down, shut the fuckin' door,' he managed to bark. 'They're shootin' at me again.'

203

Morgan dropped to one knee. 'You sure?'

'Take a look at the Lexus. Full o' holes. Jesus. Call the cops.'

Just then the phone rang. Morgan picked it up, listened and put it down.

'Who was that?'

Morgan's voice was shaking, with a mixture of fear and astonishment. 'It was him. Your guy. He says to tell you if you call the cops or anyone else, he'll know. And next time, they won't shoot wide.'

Suddenly, Jim wanted to curl up in a ball, right where he was, and cry.

Toots paced up and down in front of the table where they sat. Nash. Jones. Flint. Caruso. Coogan. He was nervous, palms sweaty. Behind him was a big map of Grand Canyon Village and the road to Flagstaff and he kept glancing at it, as if to reassure himself.

'I know I already said it but thanks for comin', guys. I know it was hard for some of you but . . . listen, you gotta bear with me, OK? I ain't no speaker. I just work here, tending bar. Three years now. But it's gnawing me. I gotta get it off my chest. I don't know about you guys, but I can't shuck the feeling that we got the bum's rush. After the Vietnam and Gulf vets, what do we get? Ignored. All this time, I keep thinkin' the country owes me. Owes me for sending us into a shit-storm we shouldn't have gone into. Owes me what? A reward, that's what. Due restitution. I'll get to it, cut to the chase. Imagine this – five million people, paying twenty dollars a time. What's that? Right, a hundred million. OK, so not all at once, but divide that down, three hundred and sixty-five days a year, it's a quarter of a mil a day – and listen, some days are just real, real better than others. Memorial Weekend. Labor Day. So you can figure half, three-quarters of a mil, maybe more. I would guess more. Now whether yous in or out, this is for your ears only, you know what I'm sayin'? No further than this room. I gotta trust you, I'm takin' a chance here. So pretend we're Rangers again. Got some kind of code, honour. Yeah? You with me? It stays here? Good.

'Look, the money comes out in one truck, one truck, and it has to go down 180. Here. Now sometimes it goes 64 to Williams, this way, other times it carries on on 180. That's the only variation. You hit it in the first thirty miles, you got the entire takings of the weekend. I think it is real poetic. After what this country did to us, it's fair restitution. They took the best of our lives, we steal from the biggest fuckin' icon they got. Short of liftin' the Statue of Liberty, what better than takin' the Grand Canyon?'

When Coogan paused for a sip of soda Wendy said, 'I'll be damned.'

'I reckon Toots might be.'

'Was he serious?'

'Hell, yes. Guy had that cabin booked, another over Labor Day. He was going to come in and check the situation over, make sure the run was still at the same time, then on the day after Labor Day take the armoured car . . . but I gotta say, his masterplan was full of holes.'

'And you told him that?'

'Me and Nash. And the others. But mostly me and Nash.'

'So he killed himself.'

'You sure you wanna put it quite like that? We told him no way. He killed himself. I felt real bad. We both did.'

'I didn't mean it was your fault, exactly. Come on, his mind must have been disturbed.'

'Maybe.' He gave a bitter little laugh.

'What?' asked Wendy. 'What's funny?'

'Those holes? The ones in Toots' plan? One night, me'n'Nash, we sat down and we figured out how to plug those holes. How to do it. After two hours we knew how to rob the Grand Canyon.

We just never got a chance to tell him before he went off, is all.' Coogan leant forward and there was a frightening intensity in his eyes she hadn't noticed before. 'What you was talkin' about the other day? 'Bout wantin' money? To be rich? How about it? Nash'd do it now, I know he would. Nash wants that combat high again. And he'd do it for me. What you say? You'n'me'n'Nash? We rob the fuckin' Grand Canyon?'

TWENTY-ONE

New York State

It was like a council of war. They had dispatched Tommy to play in the rear garden, where they could see him through the big French doors, and now Jim, Belle, Mamie and Morgan were seated around the table in the kitchen, sandwiches and coffee arranged in the middle. None of them looked at their best, but Jim had had the wind knocked out of him by those shots. Like anyone who missed Vietnam and the other conflicts of recent memory, he had always wondered how he would be under fire. Now he knew. Fuckin' useless.

Well, he tried to console himself, maybe it was different if you had a uniform and your own gun. Yeah, being able to shoot back. That would make a difference.

'I have a rifle in the basement,' said Morgan, telepathically. 'And a handgun.'

'A handgun?' asked Jim. 'You?'

'We're pretty isolated here. Just a couple other houses up the road. I keep it just in case. In a child-proof safe.'

'I don't think they'll be coming in the window just yet,' said Belle. As Jim faded, so she seemed to be drawing strength from somewhere, her thoughts clearing, something akin to steely determination rising in her, a fearsome clarity. 'It's not like we're surrounded by Indians.'

Jim, not so sure, said: 'So we're agreed? We don't think it's money after all.'

Morgan shook his head. 'He's playing the hand out too long if it is. I mean ... I hate to say this, but I think he's serious.

About Tommy. I know, I can't believe it either, but it is the only possibility.'

'Shit. And if we go to the police . . .' Jim let his voice trail off. He knew the others thought he had crumpled under the threats, but they hadn't felt hot lead slice the air inches from their head, hadn't stood face to face with a madman out on the drive, listened to his twisted threats.

Mamie spoke up in a tremulous, weak voice. 'Morgan and I have been talking.'

'I know,' said Jim. 'We'll leave as soon as we can.'

'No, not that. We wondered if . . . if he might take Ariel in Tommy's place?' And she burst into tears, Morgan put a hand on her shoulder.

'What?' Jim tried to get a handle on what she was saying. 'Ariel? Your kid? The one you tried for for ten years? Are you fuckin' nuts? It's a great gesture, Mamie, but . . . Jesus, as if we could do that.'

There was silence around the table. It was a rare commodity in the house, and they all savoured it. Ariel slept, unaware of how she was being offered up as a bartering pawn.

Belle said: 'Jim's right. It's very noble—'

'No, it isn't,' said Mamie with some undertow of venom. 'She's driving us crazy. I can't stand the thought of being tied to her for the next twenty years, of always having to think about someone else. I . . . I didn't think it would be this hard. We have no life, we don't see anyone, we don't go to the cinema, we don't have sex—'

Belle snapped: 'Hey, f'Chrissake join the club. It's called having a kid. Pull yourselves—'

There was the now familiar sound of a baby emptying its tiny lungs in a rising scream. Mamie stood stiffly and went out, still snuffling. Belle said to Morgan: 'I'm sorry—'

'No, no. I just . . . we didn't expect the impact to be . . . so great. Or maybe we thought we'd handle it better.'

Belle remembered what she did for a living when life was

normal, she helped people like this. It came as a shock. Who was going to advise *her*? 'Look she's polyphasic right now. Means she sleeps in lots of little units, doesn't care whether it's day or night. You, you're monophasic. Used to one big lump. You'll adapt. You have a kid – you never sleep again, not the way you used to, not that deep nourishing near-death of your twenties. Look, it don't mean she's some kind of monster, it isn't personal, it just feels like it . . . it's what they always ask a new parent. Everyone. Does it sleep and does it feed? If it doesn't, then it's a bad baby. That is such crap. She isn't bad. She's just a baby.' There was a particularly loud wail. 'One with good lungs, I will grant you. Look, there's lots to try. You know the Ferber let-her-yell method? OK, it isn't infallible, didn't work with Tommy. But giving her away? How could you? How could you even think of it?'

Morgan looked down at the floor; he had no answer he wanted to give.

'Giving her as a subst—' Belle trailed off, as if the long diatribe had exhausted her breath, before turning to Jim. That pin-sharp focus was suddenly there again. 'Sebastyen. How many times has he seen Tommy?' she asked suddenly.

Jim shuddered at the very name, the way it conjured up the image of the man's face in the hospital, like a malevolent jack-in-the-box, waiting to uncurl right at him. 'I dunno. Three. Four. Why?'

'So you wouldn't say he was entirely familiar with him. Couldn't pick him out in a line-up?'

Jim shook his head. 'No, Tommy wouldn't know him. Not really.'

'Not Tommy, you idiot.' Impatient now. Why couldn't the others get on her wavelength? They were wasting time. 'Sebastyen. Would he know Tommy, for sure?'

'I guess one blond five-year-old boy looks much like' – then he realised what he was saying – 'another.'

'You're right,' Belle said forcefully. 'Cute, blond, lively little kid. Ten a penny. I see them coming into ICE every week, and I get confused. Is this the tennis player? Oh, no, sorry, the new Bobby Fischer, my mistake. What was it the Jesuits used to say? About getting a kid before the age of five, or six, or whatever? And being theirs for life?'

Morgan looked up and caught their expressions, at once both furtive, guilty yet oddly hopeful. 'What?'

'We throw him a substitute,' said Jim.

'Right,' said Belle, relieved someone had caught on. 'Not Ariel. Another boy.'

'We haven't got another boy,' said Morgan, puzzled.

'Not yet we haven't,' muttered Belle. Once a week, at Davies hospital, she looked into the dark corners of the mind, the ones that you wouldn't want to walk into alone, or without a powerful flashlight. But she knew what was in there, if you wanted to face up to it. This was the real bogeyman. And it was very simple: anything is possible. There is nothing in your sickest imaginings that human beings won't do to each other. She knew, she'd heard it all, either directly or indirectly – from the woman who'd castrated her own son because she'd really wanted a little girl, to the teenager who killed his mother when his father had a heart attack, so he could get a two-for-one funeral deal. In the context of the human sediment she shifted through at Davies what she was thinking was almost sane. 'Get me a kid, I can make him ours to do with as we please.'

The two men tried to absorb the enormity of what she had just said, and slowly each one faced up to the fact that, yes, it was an avenue they could explore. A dark, spooky, evil-smelling avenue, but all the same, they had to go down it, see if it contained any kind of salvation.

Mamie returned with little Ariel in her arms, sucking hungrily on a bottle of formula milk, still managing to get the occasional gasping sob from the side of her mouth.

Belle suddenly decided she'd had enough beating about the bush. This was not the time for social niceties. Mamie and

Morgan were their oldest friends, the ones who said they'd always be there for them, yet she knew they had been lying to her. Had sensed it straight away. They'd broken the rules. All bets were off. It was time to get real. She turned and said to Mamie: 'Now. You want to tell me where you really got that kid from?'

Burt leaned his sweaty bulk across the bar and hissed at Wendy. 'Listen, you may have a cute butt, but I can't have you missin' shifts. You know what I mean? Any more sudden disappearances, I gotta re-think. There's dozens of girls who'd jump at a chance of getting into those shorts.'

'And guys, too,' said Cecco.

They both shot him a look. She still hadn't forgiven the barman for plying her with so many drinks. 'You know what I mean,' said the boss.

'OK, Burt. I get the picture.'

'And stop worrying about fly-boy over there.'

He was right. She couldn't keep her eyes off the booth where Duke was talking animatedly to a washed-out blonde with hair that looked like it had been knitted. Duke's hands were swooping around, carving arcs though the air, and she guessed he was telling combat stories about bloody dogfights with those damned ravens over the Canyon.

The Canyon. She had to laugh. The thought of a bunch of washed-up Rangers fantasising about committing armed robbery – she guessed they would have to be armed – for a few thousand lousy dollars. Coogan had been offended when she had said this. Said he half agreed with Toots's idea of restitution.

'From the government, maybe,' she had said. 'But Wells Fargo?'

'It ain't Wells Fargo. Don't know who it is. Those trucks don't have nothing on the side. Didn't you notice?'

The realisation had dawned on her then. 'That truck we

followed from the gates, down to Flintstone Village. That was it, wasn't it? That's why you hung around at the Ranger's Office after all but force-feeding us breakfast. That was the takings, wasn't it?'

'Mmm.'

'Wasn't it?'

'Yeah.'

Her mouth hung open in astonishment. This was no longer some party game they were playing. 'Coogan, you ain't serious?'

'I'm not if you're not. As you said, it ain't much money, Not enough to make it worth risking thirty, forty years in a State prison. Maybe a Fed penitentiary if the bank got Federal Insurance. Maybe I'm just dreamin'.' But the arched eyebrow suggested he wanted someone to tell him otherwise.

Yeah, well, she supposed fantasising wasn't against the law. Yet. She heard a peal of laughter from the booth where Duke sat. The girl had a laugh like a prize steer who'd swallowed its tongue, a sort of snorting, choking sound. Not pretty.

Cindy came by with a tray and Wendy clamped her arm on hers. 'That for Booth Six?'

'Yeah. Why?'

She looked at the slop on the plates, standard issue ersatz Mexican. She thought for a minute about spitting on it, adding extra chillis, but in the end she thought Carlos's cooking was punishment enough. After all, Duke deserved it – he had probably come in just to parade his grow-your-own girlfriend.

As the food arrived the girl got up to go to the bathroom, sashaying by in her too-tight jeans, her little tits swinging free under a vest top. Wendy thought about her own body, the subtle hints here and there that at one time this had been stretched and blown. Although miraculously it had come back, the odd little silvery line, the smile of a pucker in the skin under her navel, a fractional lowering of her breasts, all testified that she had borne Pete.

She went over and said hi.

'Hi,' said Duke, with a grin.

Smug bastard, she thought. 'Nice-looking girl.'

'Yeah, thanks.'

'Thanks? What did you have to do with it?'

'She blossoms when she's with me, darlin'. Just like you did.'

She was about to tell him that if he was going to eat Carlos's fajitas, the first time he farted she'd wilt, but thought better of it. She saw her coming back and said, 'Enjoy.'

'Thanks. Hey, Wendy, don't drink too much, eh?'

She gave him the finger, sorry she had taken the trouble to try and be polite. Scrub.

Mamie gave Morgan a panicky look. 'What have you been sayin'?' he blurted.

'She hasn't said anything, Morgan.' Which was true, and it was the absence of gushy child-centred motherhood that had confirmed Belle's suspicions. You don't have normal conversations with new moms. Yet it had been her who had had to keep dragging Mamie back to the subject of Ariel whenever they were alone. 'But I'm not stupid. Look at you. You're torn apart by that kid, so much so that you offer to give it away? I tell you, you go through all that pushin' and shovin' and screamin', you don't want to get rid of the baby like some used tissue. Also – how'd you end up with one so dark? I said to Jim when we came and saw you – kid looks like a Mexican. I mean, I might be wrong, here, you might have relatives that took the Alamo, but I don't think so.'

Morgan rubbed his forehead. 'They only do three IVF cycles, and that's it. They all failed.'

'I was past the age date.'

'And, shit, you know about the adoption rules now? With the natural birth rate fallin'? We offer to take a retarded, brain-damaged kid with no limbs from some Third World country, then maybe we'd be in with a chance. Unless your name is Mia Farrow, that is.'

Jim was about to say that Mia Farrow deliberately targeted such kids, but figured Belle wouldn't appreciate the interruption. She seemed to be on a roll, let her speak.

'So you went to one of the grey agencies, the ones that'll get you a kid from over the border for a price. No questions asked.'

'Except this one, Ariel, she was already on this side. Illegal immigrants. They couldn't register the kid. We found this outfit in Florida who put it all together.'

'How much?'

'Fifteen thousand.'

Suckers, Jim thought. Too much. He couldn't help himself saying: 'They're only five in Guatemala. Maybe six.'

Belle punched his leg.

'Fifteen,' she said. 'So what would these guys want for a five-year-old?'

'They won't do that,' said Mamie indignantly. 'That's . . . kidnapping. It's illegal.'

'What you did is also against the law. I bet if the money is right they would get you anything. It is only a matter of degree.'

'We signed a confidentiality clause,' said Morgan. Jim was looking at him in a new light, wondering if this was the same guy talking, Mr Ecology.

'Like that's binding?' said Belle incredulously. 'Like you're in the FBI or the Secret Service?'

'Well, it was more like one your Mr Sebastyen might draft,' said Morgan sarcastically. 'The gist of it was: tell a soul and we'll cut your fucking hands off.'

Belle said: 'If you don't tell me I'll cut your fucking heads off.'

'Belle,' protested Mamie. 'Really.'

'Either that or turn you in.'

'You wouldn't.'

'Wouldn't I? You may want to dump your kid, but I'm not about to hand mine over to some insane Nazi just because of a few threats. You think that?' She stood up and started to pace, trying to burn off some of the anger, both at the predicament and her so-called friends. There was no room for sentimentality at this juncture. If they were in the way . . . 'Who the hell do these people think they are dealing with?' she finally spat. 'Someone who just rolls over and sticks their ass in the air and spreads their cheeks? OK, so we're soft, spoilt New Yorkers, but we've got to have some moves left in us. Or have we evolved into useless lumps of ectoplasm that anyone can fuck over with a few threats?'

Jim, feeling his manhood being called into question, protested: 'It wasn't a few threats. They *shot* at me.'

Belle found it hard to keep the sneer from her voice. 'Well, maybe it's time we shot back. Metaphorically speaking.'

'But another kid,' said Morgan, 'Jesus. What about what you'll be doin' to someone else? You'll be doin' the same as this guy – bustin' up a family, causin' pain. That ain't right, Belle.'

'*That ain't right, Belle,*' she mimicked. There ought to be a sign on Morgan: Danger Bleeding Heart Liberal At Work. When it suits him that is. How politically correct was keeping handguns? Or buying your kid? Maybe he thought fifteen grand was enough over the odds to make a difference to the mother's life. Belle would give good odds that only a fraction of that money made it to the madre, though, the rest was sure to have lined Mr Middle-Man's pocket.

'I thought of that,' she said eventually. 'I see families. I see dozens a week. And half of them deserve to be broken up. You think – get the kid away from these monsters. And I don't just mean in Newark. You get scary ones at ICE, too. People who should never be allowed near impressionable minds, not with their hang-ups. And just think how many people there are who see their kids as an inconvenience.' Mamie and Morgan had the good grace to look uneasy. 'Girls who got banged up when they were thirteen, and regret every minute. Who mistreat their kids. Who let their boyfriends knock the kid around. Or the stepfathers abuse them. It's a big country out there, Morgan. Somewhere, in the whole of America there must be someone with a five-year-old blond kid with a mother who doesn't deserve him. Am I right? Of course I am. All we've got to do is find them. Now, are you going to tell me who got your kid for you, or do I go to Child Welfare and Immigration in the morning and tell them about Ariel?'

TWENTY-TWO

Miami, Florida

Richard Paladin walked the two blocks to Hoya, his favourite Cuban restaurant. Just a few hundred feet from the faggot madness of Ocean Drive, Hoya had remained much the same since the days when all the local hotels were flea-ridden low-rent long-term efficiencies, before it got all glammed up, like some overdressed whore. Like some overdressed faggot whore, he reminded himself.

His eyes took a second to adjust to the relative gloom inside the simple room, with its plastic tables and chairs, and pick out Mig, the owner. Paladin sat down at his normal table, ordered the shredded beef, beans and rice and looked at a book of photographs by Diane Arbus, a cheap re-issue he didn't mind getting the odd splash of gravy on.

It was a good life, he thought. He had a woman, no spring chicken, it was true, but she was good to him, didn't ask too many questions, and a decent business. Who would've thought it? After years of dealing in the most despicable of human acts, now he was in the reproduction business. Bringing a little sunshine into miserable, deprived, empty lives.

His company, LifeForce, apparently acted as a clearing house for information on latest fertility treatments, which hospitals and clinics had the best results, what the local rules and regulations were, who was banning or regulating donors, capping fees, limiting number of cycles, that kind of thing. It also dealt in illegal eggs, those that had been harvested and, ostensibly, destroyed rather than re-implanted. But anything that has a monetary value will always find its way onto the market,

Paladin reckoned, and it wasn't hard to get a steady supply of unfertilised, or even fertilised, ovums for implanting. And for those who couldn't go down that route, well, there was a range of alternatives.

As always when he was reading he played with the little notch in his left ear, the one where a shotgun had punched a triangular pattern out of the lobe, the event that made him get out of front-line action and into brokerage – selling others' illegal expertise to the American underworld – before he re-located from the cold north down to the sunnier climes of Florida.

The food arrived just as his cellphone rang. Impatiently he punched the button. 'Yeah?'

'Mr Paladin?' It was a woman's voice, tight and businesslike.

'Who's this?'

'I got your name from a friend.'

'Yeah? Yours or mine?'

'Mine.'

Paladin hesitated. 'You wanna tell me the name?'

'No.'

'I see.' That was a good sign.

'They just said you could help.'

'Did they.'

'They said you were a specialist.'

'What part of the country are you in?' he asked her.

'Florida.'

'Close then.'

'I am now. I flew in this morning.'

'To call me? What if I won't see you? You was takin' a chance.'

'I came determined not to take no for an answer.'

Something told him she wasn't just spinning him a line. You got to know these things. He looked down at his plate and felt his stomach contract with hunger. 'I'm having lunch. You wanna call by the office? It's on—'

'I know where it is. I can see it from my car window.'

That was determined. He pondered whether this was a sting. But he'd be able to smell that, too, he always had, which is why he was still in business, and so far the scent was sweet. 'I'll be thirty minutes.'

She was a New Yorker, he figured. The smart, sharply cut suit in a linen mix looked like this season's. The haircut was expensive. She had good nails, a nice urban smile, and an identifiable twang. Someone on the East Coast had given his name out without asking his permission. He would find out who, remind them what the word confidentiality actually meant.

'Mrs Barry?'

'Belle.'

'Belle, I don't normally do this. Without an appointment. Or a background check. Just in case.'

She looked at him, kept her gaze fixed on his eyes. Mr Paladin was far from pretty, with thinning hair and a bulbous nose, and emanated a slight feeling of menace, as if crossing him would be trouble. She could see why Mamie had been so unwilling to give up the name and number. But menace, that was what she wanted right now. Needs must.

'I appreciate that.'

His offices were two rooms, both fairly spartan, with some very stylish black-and-white photos on the wall, but nothing that shouted money, money, money. Richard Paladin was never going to be in *The Good Office Guide*, which suited him just fine.

'OK. So I hope you don't mind this. Can you empty your purse?'

She took the small clutch bag and tipped the contents on the table. He sorted through, picking out a cinema stub. A multiplex in New York State. The purse itself was Prada. Probably genuine rather than street-corner bought. A receipt from a restaurant, this time New Jersey. He was narrowing down the list fast.

'Mrs . . . Belle. Would you kindly take your jacket off?'

Her composure slipped down a notch. 'I only have my underwear on.'

'Please. This is not any kind of voyeuristic pleasure.' Nevertheless he looked long and hard at the bra. It was one of those thin, see-through ones, no room to hide a tape or wire on there. She did a quick pirouette. 'OK, you can put that back on. If you would raise the skirt.'

She did as she was told, thinking that if the man in front of her wasn't quite so toad-like this could be an erotic experience.

'Thank you. I gotta be real careful. Entrapment.'

'You could've asked,' she smiled.

'You could've lied,' he said. 'But y'know you gotta rely on this sooner or later.' He tapped his nose, 'To tell you how something smells.'

'How do I smell?'

He sniffed. 'L'Occitane. Madison. Madagascan Vanilla.'

'Very good.'

'Yeah, not going to help me if they got a big umbrella mike trained on the window, is it?'

'Can they do that?'

'Well, not with these windows, they are acoustically reflective. But theoretically, yes.'

'So what does your nose tell you? Apart from where I shop?'

'That you are a pretty tenacious woman. Not poor. You live somewhere outside the city. Maybe New Jersey. One of those commuter towns. You got at least one kid – the tissue, the cream for cuts and bruises in your purse – but you still like to go to the right movies and restaurants, wear some famous brands. You probably got some pretty hot-hot job. And you are serious.'

'Yes, I am. Very. Absolutely.'

'How serious?'

She thought of her book royalties. 'A hundred thousand dollars.'

Paladin nodded appreciatively. 'You can get a lot for a hundred thou. But not all of it through me. There are certain services I no longer perform. If you are having husband trouble, I can suggest a few operatives—'

'It isn't that. It's right in your line of work. It is just highly specific.'

'How specific?'

'A boy, between four and six, blond, blue eyes, around four foot two, three. Looking as much as possible like this.' She pushed a picture across the table. 'American, of course.'

Paladin didn't pick up the photo. He just looked at the woman, and she met his gaze. 'Kidnapping?'

'Possibly.'

'With a ransom?'

'No.'

'Abduction, then. Still a Federal offence.'

'You're picky are you?'

'A hundred grand doesn't seem enough suddenly.'

'I can go one-fifty.'

'Really.' He scratched the back of his neck, then went over to turn up the air conditioning. He was suddenly very hot. She seemed unaffected. 'Anything else I should know?'

'Yes, there is another very, very specific requirement.'

'What's that?'

'We must be doing the kid a favour by taking him away.'

He narrowed his already piggy eyes, and they disappeared into fleshy folds. 'I don't get it.'

'It's simple, Mr Paladin.'

'Richard.'

'Richard. I need a child. He will go to a good home, be well looked after, and I just want to make sure he will benefit from this. You never heard of bad parents?'

Now he knew this wasn't any kind of sting. No law enforcement agency would dream up anything so out of whack. 'Oh sure. We get some in here looking to have kids, and I think, Jesus, pity the poor saps who get you as mom and pop.'

'What do you do?'

'I take the money. Look, the real thing is a pretty big lottery. I'm just a little side bet. You don't choose your parents no matter how they came about you. I gotta tell you, this worries me.'

'Which part?'

'Which part? The fuckin' kidnappin' part, that's which part.' He sat back down. 'I can get you the kid. Find a suitable case, I mean. Bit of digging. We can go through LEGEX, it's a database, contains court cases, newspaper clippings, every detail you wanna sift through to find out who's been doin' what to who. Costs fifty bucks an hour, plus I got an operative, so a hundred bucks. She's worth it though – she can burn through that thing and get you a top-six candidate list in half a day. Take you or me a week.'

Every misdemeanour, child-abuse case, court hearing, they all went onto computer file somewhere, complete with documentation and pictures. Plus there were newspaper archives and search engines. If a kid like she described was out there – and statistically Paladin knew he would be – then they could find him within twenty-four hours. 'So it'll be close to a thousand dollars to get you the candidates.'

'OK.'

'But I ain't doin' a snatch. Y'know, bundlin' some screamin' kid in the back of a car and takin' off. Feds up our ass. It's gotta be better, cleaner than that.'

'I agree.' She liked the sound of this.

'And whatever we do, we need one thing to be worked into the scenario.'

'What's that?'

Insurance, he almost said, for his sake. We got to make you dirty as well, just in case you get cold feet down the line. But he actually said: 'A woman. Kids trust women. Everyone trusts a woman more than a middle-aged man like me. So thing is, Belle . . . you say you're serious. You'll need to be, lady. We go to get this kid' – he tapped the photo of Tommy – 'you're comin' with me.'

Belle felt her confident smile slowly fading.

TWENTY-THREE

The Landing Strip, La Guardia, NYC

Hoek glanced up from his desk in the office above the club as Schmee entered, and then down again at the list of figures. Business was good. It was a calculated risk to move the base of operations, but if he had been good at one thing in his life, it was knowing when to move on. Like when the old country suddenly became too hot for comfort after the Arkan hit. And now was a very good time to skip again. He looked at Schmee, who fanned out a bunch of blue passports.

'What's that?'

'Your new identities. Blank one for the new boy. Till you get his picture.'

'Ah.' The new boy. 'Petyr. We will still call him Petyr. Only the surnames will change.'

'You'll be forgetting who you are soon.'

Hoek shrugged. 'Names never meant much to us in the old days, even. Marta will answer to Sevdije, Zahide, Myzafere, Merita – she has used them all at one time or another.'

Schmee looked uncomfortable. Hoek rarely mentioned his wife. He liked to keep the life in Bloomsberry well away from the kind of things that went on out here. But you couldn't compartmentalise like that. He knew it, Hoek knew it. So when Sebastyen's kid was killed, it wasn't Sebastyen the Hungarian banker who reacted, it was Hoek, the trader in human lives. To that man, asking someone to hand over their son was no great leap to make: families were made to be broken, after all. Schmee knew what he had to ask: 'Is Marta OK? After . . . the boy thing.'

'My son being murdered you mean? Marta? Did I ever tell you about Ciret? No? Ciret was just a village, a few hundred people. But they marched us there. Two days. There was a big cowshed. Huge. Owned by old man Ibishaga, who has the good sense to leave as soon as it all started. I got caught visiting Zah . . . Marta, she was Zahide then. They caught me, made me join this march to the shed, along with all the other men. The women, they forced them to take their best clothes. Their hairbrushes. Their make-up. They told them to make themselves as beautiful as possible. Those that didn't, they'd shoot the husbands there and then. Then, when they had finished, when the women looked like they were going to a wedding or a dance . . . they tied them to steel troughs where the animals used to feed . . . you know the rest. Marta says she lost count, but I know, because I had to watch each one. Nine. One after another.' Schmee wondered how he kept any trace of emotion out of his voice. It was five, six years ago at most, the scars could hardly have healed. 'She is covered in bite marks, because they bit them as they did it, like vampires tearing out great chunks of flesh. Nine. She was lucky. Some got more. Still, we know eight of them are dead, which is something. You know why I still go down to see the containers being opened? One day number nine is going to walk out of there.' He reached into his pocket and brought out a wooden handled clasp knife and pulled the blade out, showing how the end had been sharpened and shaped to a vicious curve. 'My only dilemma then will be – which bit do I cut off first? So Marta, Marta knows how to suffer. Petyr wasn't mine, you see. He came out of one of the nine. But Marta wouldn't have an abortion.'

Schmee felt his jaw drop, knowing what that meant to these people. Another man's child? Another *race's* child? He couldn't keep the astonishment from his voice. 'And you raised him?'

'He was just a boy. What did he know of how he came into this world, so sick, so weak? All those illnesses. Ach, he wouldn't have made seven, even if that idiot hadn't killed him.' He paused for a minute, thought about the stupid, feeble man. No idea of fighting back, he could see. Too scared to go to the cops. He must watch this – obviously living in America filleted your backbone after a while. 'You know a lot of men had trouble with their wives after Ciret and the other places. Couldn't see them the same way – as if they had encouraged the bastards. Not me. No abortion she said. OK, I said. She was a brave woman.' He stared off into the distance. 'Is a brave woman.'

Schmee scratched his head, hardly daring to disturb him, then said: 'But the fact you survived—'

'Is another miracle. A bombing raid began. They pulled out. They shot six, maybe seven of the men. The rest of us, this one guy went along the line and slit both our nostrils up the side, flapping the skin open. One after another. A little souvenir. See here? I had it fixed, but not too much. You can still see the lines. Why? Because, yes I do want the little souvenir. To remind me of him.'

'That was number nine?'

'Lazar Glogvijc. Number nine. We knew them all, you see. They had served us bread, made our suits, delivered our letters. Of course we knew them. That was why it was so easy to find them. All but Lazar. So—' He shook his head, locking the memories away again for another time, and pointed at the passports. 'What names do you have for me this time?'

TWENTY-FOUR

Tucson, Arizona

Wendy clutched the lab results in her hands and gave Pete a hug. So, it was set then. Soon she would lose her licence. The lawyer had said, even with Cecco, Cindy and Burt to back her up, she needed Duke. And Duke wasn't playing ball. He thought it was some kind of trap to get him in trouble with the Crimes Against Children Unit.

'Duke,' she had pleaded. 'I'll get a ban for sure.'

'There's a good cab service just down the highway.'

Mr Sensitive. Still, she had time to work on him, the hearing wasn't for another two weeks. Lots of things could change in that time. She told Pete he could have another Playstation session, and went to try and quieten the air conditioner down. It had started to squeal now whenever it was on maximum, as it had to be at the peak of the day, and she was worried something was going to burn out. She should mention it to the old Indian who passed as a Super.

The phone rang. 'Yeah?'

'Miss Blatand.' A woman, precise, clipped.

'Yes . . .' She sounded the word correctly, stressing the end syllable. This sounded official.

'This is Agent Tinker. Federal Bureau of Child Welfare and Protection.'

Her heart sank. More. 'Yes?'

'As you will have read, we are the new agency empowered with looking after the welfare of the nation's children.'

She did remember something about that, the President pledging

227

to tackle the epidemic of abused and missing children. 'I think so.'

The voice softened. 'This is just a formality, Miss Blatand. Our charter means we have to follow up each State case with a visit and a report. This report is logged onto a computer—'

'What, I get a record?'

'—to which only we have access. No, you don't get a record. It is kept on there for one year and wiped. It is just in case . . . look, you understand, we have to keep a check.'

'I understand,' she said bitterly.

'All it means is I have an interview with Peter.'

'Pete?'

'Pete. Yes. Alone. You will be able to accompany him, of course.'

What again? The kid was going to get a complex she felt like saying. 'I can't sit in?'

'A parent's presence often influences the answers a child will give. But we will show you a list of the questions, and his answers. You will then have an opportunity to comment on them.'

'Fuck,' she mumbled.

'Excuse me?'

'I mean – is all this necessary?'

'Well, yes. Our charter specifies comprehensive follow up.'

'When? I mean – when do you want to do this?'

'We'll be in touch.'

'Can you give me an idea? A day? A week? I got work I can't miss.'

'Sooner rather than later, Miss Blatand, is all I can say right now.'

'OK. I didn't get your name.'

'Agent Tinker.'

'OK. Thanks.'

Wendy sat down and fought back the urge to cry. It simply couldn't get any worse, she thought.

❖   ❖   ❖

Jim Barry downed his sixth beer and turned to Morgan, his elbows on the sticky bar of the scruffy roadhouse where they intended to get marinated in booze. Both looked bleary-eyed, they were going to regret this in the morning. But in one sense they both needed it, to go and get ripped, to let the emotions pour out, freed by the copious quantities of alcohol.

'Sonofabitch,' said Jim.

Morgan nodded vigorous agreement. 'Fuckin' right. That it should come to this.'

'I don't get it. Belle. She's like . . . I don't know her. She socked me one yesterday. Here. Look.' He turned his cheek to show the inky bruise. 'I got two matching now. One from Sebastyen and one from the wife.'

'Sonofabitch. What did you say to make her hit you?'

'That maybe we should hand Tommy over.'

'What? You serious?'

'I was only exploring the possibilities. She wouldn't let me go to the cops, said Dick was a piece of shit, trying to save his own skin. Her idea was the only one she'd consider, period. No contest.'

'What do you think?'

'Dick's a good guy,' he slurred. 'Mike's a great catcher.'

'No, about what she is doing.'

Jim shook his head. 'I dunno. Would you do it? Someone has come up and said, we want your son. What would you do?'

'I ain't got a son. And Ariel . . . well you know about her.'

'Yeah. But he will, he'll kill us all. Won't he? You saw that tape. At least Tommy would be alive if we gave him up.'

'There's that.'

'Belle won't . . . listen.'

'I guess it's that mother's instinct you hear about.'

'I guess it is. Don't come between a mother and her child. You know what she said to me? She said if she had to choose between me and Tommy, she'd choose Tommy. Just to let me know where we stood, she said.'

'Wow. You know what she was threatening to do? Tell Immigration and Child Welfare 'bout what me and Mamie did. Ariel'n'all. You think she meant that? You think she would've? If we hadn't given her this guy Paladin?'

Jim rubbed his cheek where she had hit him. 'I reckon she would.'

Morgan looked at the bottom of his empty glass. 'Sonofabitch.'

TWENTY-FIVE

Tucson, Arizona

Coogan opened the case and lifted out the Gibson, mentally offering apologies for being away so long. He fetched a new set of strings, taking the old ones off and carefully winding them and bagging them. The last thing he needed was a sharp edge to scratch the maple of the 335. While the strings were off he cleaned the fingerboard, polished the body, checked the neck for warps, before fitting the new set, tensioning them with a string-winder, then using the electronic tuner, a device he both loved and loathed. It still felt like cheating. He dutifully checked the action and the intonation, again keeping the little screwdriver away from the polished wood, and gave a preliminary strum.

Awful.

It felt different, as if a ballerina had been forced into a pair of Timberland boots. It was part him, part the new strings. He checked the tuning again, then took them both through a clunky rendition of 'Misty', followed by 'Stella By Starlight', played around with 'Red House' and 'Crossroads' before admitting it was the wrong guitar for such things and came out the other end with something that approximated 'Round Midnight'.

He smiled to himself. Getting there, he thought. He picked idly at some single-note runs. There was, he decided, nothing better than this. Well, maybe being rich, he thought, but he had no idea how that particular tune went.

They came real early. Wendy heard the knock on the door, grabbed a robe and opened the screen. In front of her was a smartly dressed woman with expensive shades. From over her shoulder she could hear Coogan, playing some cheesy old showtune, but toying with it, slapping it around, obviously having fun, like a kitten chasing a ball of wool.

She squinted against the sun and managed to ask: 'Yes?'

'Agent Tinker, Miss Blatand. We spoke on the phone? About the interview? Federal Bureau of Child Welfare and Protection?' She handed over a card which she managed to focus on. FBCWP, with a Washington address and then the Field Office on E. Benson in Tucson.

'I thought you were going to call—'

'Ah. I did say we were wary about parents prepping kids. Is Peter here?'

'Pete? Yeah, sure. Er . . . I'll get him. I mean, this is a bit like the Nazis, isn't it? The unexpected knock.'

The woman removed her glasses. 'Miss Blatand, please. This is just a follow-up visitation and interview. No need to be unpleasant.'

'Yeah. Well.'

She looked beyond her to the stocky guy in the black sedan, the window down, toying with his ear. He too had a pair of shades on, so she couldn't see his face clearly. He raised his hand in what was meant to be a friendly greeting, then went back to worrying his ear.

'Could you get him dressed? We have to interview him in Tucson. At the Field Office? As a new Bureau we are sharing the Sheriff's premises until we get something permanent. Pete can ride with us, you can follow. Is that your car?'

'Yeah. Can't he come with me?'

'Departmental guidelines, Miss Blatand. Last month one mother panicked, took off, we never saw her, or the kid, again. You can follow right behind, no problem. Tailgate us if you want.'

'Er . . . yeah, OK,' she said, trying hard to snap her brain in gear. 'Look, Agent . . . uh . . . , can I get a cup of coffee? I was working late last night.'

'No Federal Office has a shortage of coffee, Miss Blatand. But you go ahead if you need one that bad. Can I come in?'

She stepped aside then suddenly asked: 'Listen, I shoulda . . . you got any ID? Besides this card?'

Agent Tinker pulled out a wallet and flipped it open. Wendy squinted at it, checked the photo and the badge and nodded. 'OK. You wanna cup? No? Pete. PETE. Come on, we gotta get going. Pete?' She opened his bedroom door. 'Pete.' The boy grunted and snuggled down further into the hot, humid womb made by his blankets. 'Come on, we gotta get going. Look, there's a policewoman here, just wants to ask you some questions. OK, up in ten, soldier. One—'

She poured herself the coffee, went to the bathroom and shoved her head under a tap, towelled her hair dry. 'Four.'

She slipped on some jeans and a sweatshirt. 'Eight.' And combed her hair into shape, changed the jeans for a skirt and the sweatshirt for a blouse and put on a quick film of make-up, sipping coffee as she went. 'Ten.'

She went in, lifted Pete out of bed, dragged him to the bathroom, splashed some water on his face, cleaned his teeth and then dressed him in cargo pants, a checked shirt and boots. He looked cute. She grabbed a drink for him, a snack, and put it in his Futurama rucksack, found her purse and finally said: 'Right.'

She flicked the grumpy air conditioning unit to low as she left, watched as her little boy slid into the back of the sedan and felt something cause her heart to jolt. It was only when you got to stand back, to see them in context – a rare event as kids were rarely far from your side – that you realised just how small and vulnerable they really were.

She jumped behind the wheel of her car and got ready to follow.

Jim Barry woke early, ears straining, wondering what had disturbed him, what had slid its oily tentacles into his chest cavity and squeezed. Some dream, some ball game ending in catastrophe. They were getting weirder. The other night he had wiped out half the Hall of Fame. Cy Young had been pitching to him, and he had hit the man's curve ball straight and true, right into Cy's face. The pitcher had collapsed, holding his hands up to his nose, blood squeezing between his fingers like it was coming from a fire hydrant, drenching all of them, the white turning to deep crimson. He had stepped back and elbowed Berra, caught Barry Bonds with a wildly swinging bat . . . it was like an in-field massacre.

He looked at the clock. Just gone five. The next interview with Homicide – just to go over some facts about exact positioning – wasn't until ten. He mustn't let on he knew about the skull thing with the kid, but it gave him hope that the Grand Jury would find no case to answer. Dale agreed.

Jim had come back to Bloomsberry, leaving Tommy up with Morgan and Mamie – the boy didn't seem to hear their screaming kid, no matter what vocal gymnastics she performed. Since he had been gone the ambulance chasers had moved into town. Several of the parents had got together to begin a class action for the psychological damage done to their boys during the incident – trauma that meant they would be deprived of their enjoyment of the All-American game for the rest of their lives. Jesus, what did they think that was worth?

He slumped back down on the pillow and wondered what Belle was up to. He had tried to reason with her, tell her she was being crazy, irresponsible. People just didn't do such things, but she had dismissed him. People do whatever they have to do, she had said. I have seen it. While you read about people in your galleys and proofs, I live real life and I hear it from the horse's mouth. In case you haven't noticed, it is a shitty world out there. I will do whatever I have to do to make it less shitty. You just stay here. There was a dismissive tone in her voice, as if really he should be doing this, risking his life and freedom, but was too weak.

Maybe she had a point. But how did these roles get reversed so quickly? He was left at home, fretting, and she was mixing with dubious characters who made their living exploiting human misery. Maybe he should've gone. But he knew that Belle was going to be better than him. Belle was focused, Belle was prepared to blow her royalties and the whole Condé Nast offer that Hooper had on the table if necessary, whereas he hoped to save some of the money, keep it back. And maybe a woman, with less to prove, might just be better at dealing with those testosterone-rich characters.

He'd give the money one last try, he decided to tell Sebastyen he could go to one and a half, two million. But something told him Dick was right, this guy meant to make him suffer. So the real problem was: how could they get a kid to Sebastyen and convince him he was their own? Belle was sure she could pull it off. They had stalled for time. Asked for two weeks to get the boy used to the idea of changing homes. 'I'm a goddamn shrink in everything but name,' Belle had said. 'If I can't screw with a kid's mind, who can?'

So for the two week period of grace Belle was going to work on the new kid. If she got one. His stomach flipped at the thought. Right now, she was planning a kidnap, maybe even carrying out one of the most heinous crimes imaginable, one that would bring the full might of the FBI to bear on her. He was suddenly sweating, a sickly, dirty oozing from his pores, like there was a poison coursing through his veins and his body was trying to purge it. He got up to take a shower. He wouldn't be sleeping again this morning.

Coogan smiled as he put the guitar down and turned off the Mesa-Boogie combo. He'd switched to the Strat and played some straight-ahead rock and boogie, plundering everything from the Bob Dylan to the Green on Red songbooks with some Neil Young thrown in for good measure. The urgent hammering on his door cracked the mood and resentfully he walked over and flung it back. It was Wendy, her face twisted with something, anger, frustration—

'Coogan, Coogan, you gotta,' she was gasping, hyperventilating. He grabbed her shoulders and squeezed. 'The car. Can I borrow – they're not waiting – can I borrow the car?'

'My car? Sure. I'll drive you. Calm down.'

He grabbed the keys, locked his trailer, pulled the tarp off and let her climb inside, spun the wheels and reversed most of the way up Quality Street before spinning round and turning onto Mango Road. He looked anxiously at her. 'Which way?'

'Tucson. East Benson. You know it?'

'Uh-huh.'

'Sheriff's office.'

'Where's Pete? He OK? He's not by himself, is he?'

She gulped. 'They said to follow, but my car . . . it wouldn't start . . . wouldn't catch. I yelled at them to wait. Ran after them. But they just took off.'

'Who?'

'The Feds.'

'The *Feds*? What the fuck you done now?'

'It's . . . here.' She handed over the card.

'Federal Bureau of Child Welfare and Protection? Holy shit, who are these guys?'

'They follow all potential child-abuse or neglect cases. They've got Pete for interview. They wouldn't stop.'

'Hey, don't worry. Benson's not that far.' He winced as the muffler scraped on the apex of one of the hillocks. The low-slung Trans Am wasn't built for these roads. Not at speed, anyway. He glanced at Wendy who was chewing the inside of her lip, hard enough, he was sure, to draw blood. 'I shoulda gone with them.'

It took them fifteen minutes to find the address, and Wendy was out of the vehicle almost before Coogan pulled to a halt. The low white building had a series of steps up to it and he watched her take them in two bounds and fling open the door.

He risked parking on the lines directly outside, and kept an eye out for anyone who might ticket him. Still too early even for those guys, he figured.

She was out within two minutes, looking around with a baffled expression on her face, staring hard at the card in her hand and at the number on the building. In a daze she walked over to the car and he lowered the passenger's window.

'OK?'

'No. Not OK. They say they never heard of these guys.' She waved the card. 'They say they're not here.' Her forehead was deeply furrowed, and he could feel her mind trying to make the jump, to connect the strands, to put together what this all meant, yet swerving away from the only conclusion as if scalded. 'In fact, they say they're pretty sure there is no such agency. They checked the Federal listings.' Tears started to stream from her eyes. 'Coogan, what the hell's goin' on?'

He didn't answer. They were there again. The stick figures scuttling at the edge of his vision. Taunting him. Moving in for the kill. He suddenly had a very bad feeling about this.

TWENTY-SIX

New York City

Schmee pushed the last of his fruit salad round the plate. It was early morning, the diner at 65th and Madison had yet to experience its full morning rush. The Creep watched Schmee wipe a dribble from his chin and felt repulsed. The man's blondness, those impenetrable blue eyes, they made him feel sick to his stomach. Or was it what he had done for this man, all the lies and distortions, that really made him want to throw up?

The Creep reached down and pulled the thick brown envelope from his case and pushed it across. 'Everything you asked for.'

'Good. Hoek will be pleased. Now, tell me about the other matter.'

'Total disarray since Krok. He was the one pushing it forward. There is, was, talk of flying others over, but nobody credible. And now there is no Krok, it looks as if the unit will be disbanded even sooner.'

'Ha. Excellent. By which time we will be gone.'

'Gone?' He felt some kind of hope come into his heart. If they weren't there to tempt him, then maybe all this could change, he could go back to something close to a normal life, with a regular woman. Take it away, he willed them, please take it away, make it easy for me.

'I told you, Hoek has a place outside London. Very comfortable.'

'London?'

'More coffee?' They both accepted a top up from the waitress.

ROB RYAN

'Don't worry, the operation will still be here. Our contracts still have three months to run. I will be coming in on a regular basis to make sure there is a plentiful supply of fresh faces.' He grinned. 'Just for you.'

'Schmee . . . I don't want to do anything else. Like this.' He pointed at the envelope. He hoped the weariness in his voice was convincing. It was certainly genuine. 'I can't.'

Schmee sighed. How many times had he had this conversation with all the informers he used to run throughout the Seventies and Eighties? Just one more bit of information, and that is it. But it was never over. In the case of all those Germans, the little mark on their files damned them as informers, ruined their lives forever. This man was the same. A weakness that would never go away, an opportunity for exploitation. Whenever he was needed, he would be there. 'Don't worry, there is nothing for the time being. As I say, Hoek will be pleased. Well, as pleased as he can be at the moment.'

The Creep took a last sip of his coffee and got up to leave. 'I'm thrilled for him.'

'You should be. But what I know of Hoek of old . . . as I said before, you'd be dead after what happened to the boy. He must be going soft.'

The Creep threw down the check and tip. 'Sometimes, I think life would be a lot easier if I were dead.'

Schmee grinned at the illogicality of it. He took a folded piece of paper and held it out. 'Just to remind you why you continue to draw breath.'

The other man looked at it, a paper siren calling to him.

Schmee, puzzled by the hesitation, explained: 'This week's phone number.'

Another six heartbeats, in which The Creep toyed with the idea of not taking it. On the seventh he snatched the sheet and walked out without looking back, his face burning with shame at his spinelessness.

✵   ✵   ✵

The deputy finished writing and looked at the card. 'So you didn't see the guy?'

'No, he had sunglasses on. He looked like a fuckin' Blues Brother. All I remember was this nick out of his ear. Here.' She grabbed her left lobe. Wendy was pacing the floor of her trailer, where they had retreated, hoping somehow the Feds had come back for her after she hadn't followed. They had waited twenty minutes and called the Sheriff's department.

Now Coogan sat in a corner, watching her shake herself to pieces as wave after wave of emotion hit her hard, coming from all directions, although the big one that crashed through her every now and then was guilt. She was beginning to realise, just as he was, that maybe she was the victim of some kind of con. She pushed it away, screaming and sobbing. But each time it came back stronger, sharper, able to stay and inflict its pain for longer.

Coogan kept thinking he should've done what his gut told him that first night he took the kid in. Hand him back and don't get involved. Maybe that way this would never have happened.

Deputy Davies closed his notebook. He was in his late twenties, a big fair-haired farm boy, sympathetic, but ultimately as puzzled as they were. The door opened and a blast of heat entered along with Deputy Kidd, older, more lined, and more suspicious. 'I just spoke to Washington,' he said. 'And the guys at Benson were right. No such agency.'

'There has to be. I have the card. Here.'

'We'll take this,' said Kidd. 'See if anyone round here ran it up. It's a fake, Miss Blatand. You realise that?'

'It can't be. And they had badges.'

'You ever see an FBI or an ATF badge, ma'am?'

She shook her head. 'Then how you know what a real one looks like?' Kidd asked.

'I . . . Oh God.' She sat down on the sofa, sobs racking her body. 'Pete . . . why?'

The two deputies looked at each other. This wasn't the time to speculate. 'Let's worry about why later—'

'Let's worry about how,' said Coogan sharply. 'Let's worry about an APB, maybe roadblocks. It's an hour now. More. What about airports? Tucson? Phoenix?' He tried not to sound too pushy. Cops hated being told their jobs. Sure way to get all the systems to shut down.

Kidd said, 'We looking for two people and one child? You know how big a job that is?'

'Too big for a coupla deputies,' Coogan said, standing up. There was clearly no point in pussyfooting. 'State Police. FBI. This looks more and more like a kidnapping.'

'It looks more and more like something. Abduction, maybe. It ain't kidnapping until we get a ransom demand.'

'What?' asked Wendy. 'You don't do anything till then?'

'The FBI only come in when State lines have been crossed. What we got at the moment, ma'am, is a missing child, but also a story that doesn't make sense.'

Coogan said quietly. 'If you don't call the FBI, I will.'

Kidd looked at him and tutted, like he was a child who had committed some indiscretion. 'I already put the call in. The Field Office is in Phoenix, not Tucson. But there's an RA in Tucson.'

'RA?'

'Residential Agency. Coupla overworked guys. So it'll take some time. And they are here because of this—' he waved a card. 'Impersonating a Federal Officer. But it gets them in the picture. I have also contacted the CACU – Crimes Against Children Unit – and State Police. Both have asked for some recent photos of Pete they can scan in and disseminate. So don't start giving me bullshit about not doing anything.'

Coogan had the grace to say: 'Yeah. OK, pardon me. We're just—'

'Anxious, yeah. So am I. To get to the bottom of this. You

know we normally wait twelve, maybe twenty-four hours to put out a full alert—'

'They could be anywhere in the country by then,' protested Wendy.

Kidd turned and looked at her. 'I know. So we'll kick things up a gear. I would like you to go into Tucson with Deputy Davies here. Tucson PD got some good computer ID programs, stuff we ain't got. We can get some faces to put with that of Pete's . . . well, it's gonna double our chances.'

'What are you gonna do?' she asked. 'While I am gone I mean?'

'I'm gonna question the neighbours see if anyone saw anything. Take a look around here.'

Coogan said flatly: 'In case they dropped anything.'

Kidd caught his gaze and saw Coogan incline his head momentarily towards Wendy. 'Yeah, tyre tracks, things the tech boys can look at.'

But Coogan knew what Kidd was thinking, what he had to rule out as a possibility: she could always have done something to the boy herself.

Belle gave the kid another Coke and watched his eyes droop and his limbs become floppy. At the first gas station to the east of Tucson, they switched his clothes, putting a pair of Osh Kosh dungarees on him, and pulled the booster seat out of the trunk and strapped him in. Just another snoozing five-year-old. Now she had done it, her hands were shaking, knowing what could come down on her. 'I'm going to change,' she said.

She was back in three minutes from the washroom, out of the Fed-like suit and into jeans and a hooded top. She had splashed cold water on her face, too, Paladin noted. He took off his jacket and rolled up his sleeves. Somewhere down the road they would unclip the Arizona plates and put Texas ones on, but that could wait. They could also dye the boy's hair if things looked like going against them, but for the moment they had put an oversized Disney World baseball cap on him.

'How long?' she asked, once they were underway again. 'Before the hunt starts?'

'Two, three hours. Thing is, the story is so crazy, y'know what I mean? 'Phony Feds Kidnapped My Chilld'. It's one step down from 'Aliens Stole My Baby'. *National Enquirer* stuff. So they'll check and double check before the truth hits 'em.'

'Won't they notify the airports?'

'Arizona first. Y'see part of the beauty of our cops, is they think in borders. State Police'll think local airports first. By the time the Feds get there, we'll be out of El Paso on our way to Denver. Then it's up to you to get the kid to New York. You gotta give him enough stuff to keep him sleepy, disoriented. Too little and he'll start screaming, too much and someone'll remember you carrying some rubbery kid and they'll pick up the trail.'

'Is that likely?'

'Not if you do like you're told. And if the kid co-operates.'

'Oh don't worry about that,' she said, turning up the air conditioning as the sun climbed higher and the scrubland began to glow, as if incandescent with the heat, 'he'll co-operate.'

She glanced over her shoulder and wondered at what a close likeness Paladin had found. But then, it was a well remunerated job, she supposed. Just remember, she said to herself over and over again, that woman back there in the trailer park didn't deserve him anyway.

Coogan and Kidd watched the deputy drive off with Wendy, both squinting into the sun. Kidd took out a pair of sunglasses and slipped them on, before looking at the hard-packed ground across the trailer park.

'Tyre tracks?' said Coogan.

'I know. Excuse me, but I'm kinda curious. Just what is your relationship with the . . .' he fished for a word.

'Accused?' finished Coogan.

'Complainant.'

'Friend. I look after the boy now and then. She wouldn't—'

'Do anything to harm him?'

'We gonna spend the day finishin' each other's sentences? You wanna coffee? My trailer's just there. Ain't as nice as Wendy's, but my coffee's better.'

'Sure.'

Coogan brewed some fresh and they sat outside on his steps, feeling themselves starting to steam in the building heat of the morning, as the bleaching sun slowly drained the colour out of the surroundings.

'You a Vet, Mr Coogan?'

'A Vet? I was in the army, yeah. How you guess?'

'You got a dozen books in there,' he pointed over his shoulder. 'Half of them are about guitars, the other half about the military. Where did you serve?'

Coogan hesitated. 'Somalia.'

'Rangers?'

'Yup.'

'Rough, I was in the Gulf.'

Coogan nodded and said quickly: 'She didn't do anything to that boy, Kidd.'

The officer looked at him. Coogan could see he was running a number on him too. He was pretty sure that computer print-outs on George Coogan would be on Kidd's desk before long, pored over for signs of aberrant behaviour. Hey, he was full of that – restless and fucked up. If he was Kidd, he'd probably lock him up right now just to be on the safe side.

'Is that your word as an old soldier, or you got proof?' the cop finally asked.

'What the fuck could she have done?'

'Listen, here's a statistic for you. Two-thirds of adults who report something has happened to their children had something to do with that something. Two-thirds. Which is why the first person you check and double check is that parent sobbin' and cryin' on TV appealing for their child back. Good odds they know where their kid is, and why he ain't gonna come back. Let's see what we got here.'

Kidd took his time. Coogan kind of liked him, the easy professionalism, even if he despised the way the man's mind was working.

'OK, she gets pissed at him, hits him, doesn't know her own strength, he falls down dead. She decides to make up this story, gets you in as a bit of corroboration. You know, the hysterical bit. You didn't actually hear anything.'

'I was playin'. Guitar. You get kinda absorbed.'

'Well, there you go. She waits till she hears you, gives it ten, fifteen minutes and then drops this pile of dog turds on your stoop.'

'Or I'm part of it. You think of that?'

'Yeah, I did consider that. Don't see you as the kind of guy who could win Oscars, though.' He took a slug and swilled some coffee around his mouth.

'And she is? An actor? You think all that was a performance?'

'Women, Coogan, are more talented than us. They have depths of survival instincts that Standard Oil couldn't explore.'

Coogan made an effort to keep a sneer from his voice. 'So she kills the kid, accidentally, makes up this story and runs down the print shop to get some of those fake Fed cards made up.'

Kidd nodded. 'There's that. The card worries me.'

A grey panel truck pulled into the lot, and Kidd stood up. He handed the cup to Coogan. 'Thanks for the coffee. You ain't goin' anywhere, are you?'

'Got a gig at the University of Arizona. Tonight.'

'I meant further than that.'

'I might get a stand-in anyways. Might not be able to concentrate. Who are these guys?' He pointed at the men emerging from the van.

246

Kidd started to walk over to them and turned back, apologetically. 'Scene of Crime, Coogan. Scene of Crime.'

'OK. I got one for ya.'

'What?'

'Check out why Wendy's car wouldn't start.'

Kidd scratched under his hat brim, releasing a small rivulet of sweat down his forehead. He nodded. 'If it fires first time . . .'

'Then I'll have some questions of my own.'

Coogan must have drunk two gallons of water by the time Wendy returned, looking pale and twitchy. Her usually pale face was blotchy, ugly red patches having broken out on her skin, and round her eyes. She had been crying. She must, Coogan thought, feel like shit.

The SoC boys had already combed through her trailer, and were scruffing about in the areas immediately in front and behind. There were four of them, dressed in overalls, carrying an assortment of plastic bags and tools and probes. As she got out of the cruiser she looked at Coogan who said: 'Clues. Looking for clues. How you doin'?'

She nodded, but too enthusiastically and felt queasy. 'I been sick. Threw up. I . . . I couldn't get a clear picture of them. I don't know whether it looks like them or not. Fuck it, Coogan, I was half asleep. I did a voluntary polygraph test.'

'A lie detector?'

'U-huh.'

'I think you're meant to have a lawyer when you do that.'

'I offered. I ain't lyin', Coogan. Don't you doubt me too,' she pleaded, 'I couldn't stand that.'

Coogan said: 'Shit, Wendy, I just, I don't trust machines, is all.'

Deputy Davies got out of the driver's side and said: 'She did OK. Got a description of the people and the car, eight good pics of the boy. They goin' Statewide. We went through the story with the State Police.'

'Again,' said Wendy wearily.

'Well, ma'am, there's the FBI yet. And CACU.'

Wendy turned to him. 'Here's a novel idea, Deputy. Why don't you give them a copy of your report?'

'Well the FBI got two crimes here – abduction and impersonation—'

Kidd emerged from the trailer just in time to hear this. 'First one bad enough, second pisses 'em off mightily. Someone else strutting around in those suits with those haircuts? Gets their goat every time. Sorry, ma'am, didn't mean to be flippant. But when they get here,' he checked his watch, 'we gonna be tossed aside like cigarette butts.'

The SoC guy came round the corner of the trailer and said quietly. 'Deputy, they cut the fuel line, and blocked both ends of the cut, so gas didn't spill on the ground.'

Without giving Wendy another look, Kidd followed the forensic to the rear of her home. She walked over to Coogan, who offered her a slug from his water bottle. She took a long hit.

'Does that deputy in charge believe me now? Or do they think I cut it? I feel like they all think I'm lying. I passed the polygraph for Christ's sake.'

'From what I hear, cops only trust those machines when they say you're lying. Otherwise it's a false positive.'

But the next voice she heard was Davies, the previous friendliness replaced by a steely distance: 'They found a body, ma'am. You wanna come with me?'

TWENTY-SEVEN

Texas

The boy started stirring just outside El Paso and they stopped to give him some breakfast. They got a take-out from a Denny's and sat in the parking lot. Belle slid in the back seat and fed him pieces of egg-and-bacon burger and fries, brushing his hair back from his eyes, talking to him softly, spinning a long, involved tale about how they had come to take him to his real parents. The eyes looked back uncomprehendingly, only once did he kick and struggle against the seat straps but the drug residue in his bloodstream made this hugely ineffectual. She slipped another quarter of a tab into the Coke carton and watched him slurp greedily.

She had fourteen days, possibly less, to rearrange this young mind. It went against everything she had been trained in, every instinct she had developed to protect anyone who came for help. Then again, maybe it didn't. She was going to give the kid a lifeline, something to hold on to, a set of reasons for why his world was changing in ways he couldn't comprehend. And if she knew anything about young minds, she knew they would grasp whatever ropes were thrown to them. The real mother would be sidelined, isolated, compartmentalised, locked away until all memories of her faded.

Paladin kept checking his watch to make sure they didn't miss the flight to Denver. He was fairly sure they were going to make it all the way now. Belle had been pretty cool, after all, pulling off the impersonation shit like a pro. It never failed to amaze him how far these people went to get kids, and to hang onto them. Dangerous drugs, intrusive medical procedures, shady deals, bribery and corruption and kidnapping. This wasn't his first. Since he'd switched from old-time felony stuff to being an arm – albeit a strong-arm – of the reproductive industry, he had done four abductions, and countless purchases of children. It was all the same to him. Generally speaking, he figured, the kids were going to a good home. If the people wanted 'em so bad, usually they doted on the child when they finally got one. This woman was a little strange, but he figured he knew what was going on.

The boy they had to match was no doubt dead, and the grieving parents were trying to replace him with a clone. He looked in the mirror and saw Belle's concerned face as the kid's head slumped again. Yeah, that was motherly love all right, or his dick was a doughnut.

They were waiting for him when he got into the office from the meeting with Schmee. Big fuck-off steel-balled Internal Inspection Unit guys, men who had forgotten how to smile. They were in the little cubicle, at his computer, files open, memos piled high, going through the pocket of his bright blue raid jacket that always hung on the peg. A raid jacket he hadn't used in three years. He should have looked outraged, have shouted and screamed and objected, but there was something about them that suggested histrionics would bounce off them like bullets off Superman. Whether their gaze was a professional nuance, honed by hours in front of a mirror, he wasn't sure, but both sets of eyes gave out a simple, heart-piercing message: 'We know everything. Come quietly.'

Strangely his first reaction was relief, the knowledge he could tell Schmee that it really was all over. This had been inevitable all along, he could see that now, a headlong rush to destruction, to pulling the pit props from under his life and waiting for the collapse. It was entirely possible, he realised that he had done it deliberately, left his footprints all over the last set of falsifications, a muddy trail that led all the way back to this office.

They took him down to the supervisor's office, cautioned him, took away his gun, badge and accreditation, then told him they would expect him to remain contactable. He gave them his word, which caused at least one raised eyebrow. He knew he was lucky – no on-the-spot interrogation, no being taken into custody. They warned him that his home was being searched as they spoke. That charges were expected within a week, two at most. Would he like to sit down and make a confession? He declined, making a half-hearted protest about his innocence, and looking forward to the chance to clear his name. Get a good lawyer, one of them suggested. Get one of OJ's, the other said. Maybe Von Bulow's.

Outside he considered his options. He didn't want to go home, be sitting there while his house was turned upside down, his garbage ransacked, his computer files printed off. He caught a cab to Midtown and went to his security box, where he removed a spare badge and an S&W auto. He wouldn't be using either, but he felt naked without them. Then he dialled the number Schmee had given him. Best go out with a bang, he figured.

Coogan followed two paces behind Wendy, who seemed to be slumping in the heat. He knew what was going on in her mind, because a version of it was going down in his. It was as if there was a short circuit in the brain, flashing off and on, cutting reality in and out. She would be switching from a narcoticised, fuzzy version of the world, to one bathed in a hideous clarity, where she knew she would never see her son again. Except, in his case, there was the feeling it was all his fault.

The rear of the trailer was a kind of minimalist garden, rows of stones placed in wiggly lines by young Pete delineating it from the rest of the desert, the dusty floor covered with scrappy ground cover and the odd cactus, with a number of thorny bushes dotted around. The Scene of Crime Team and Kidd were standing by one of the bushes, over a freshly dug hole, with three long-handled spades wedged into the earth. Coogan held back not daring to see what was in it, not wanting to believe what they were suggesting. Wendy slowed and so did he, she looked up at the red, sweat-drenched faces staring at here, and into the hole. Coogan could see a cheap Indian-style blanket and, from one end of it, a tuft of hair.

There was the click of a camera as one of the SoCs took a few photographs. Coogan couldn't believe this. They were going to unwrap the body in full view of the prime suspect and him, her friend. He tried to catch Kidd's eye, but he had a grim set to his face, glaring at Wendy. Now Coogan saw, this was some kind of punishment, a ritual humiliation, intended to make it impossible for her to deny what she had done.

Deputy Davies put a hand on Wendy's upper arm, but not in a friendly gesture, gripping her bicep as if she were going to run away. Already he was playing with the handcuffs on his belt, as if he couldn't wait to get her wrists in there.

Coogan should have seen it coming. He had been expecting something, but nothing so fast. He had forgotten just what a big girl she was. That Swedish stock. Wendy raised up to her full height, straightened her shoulders and in a seamless, fluid movement that Michael Jordan would envy, shrugged off Davies's hand and reached for an SoC spade. She took a step back to make sure she had the right distance, and swung it, luckily with the blade flat, or she might have taken his head off. There was a cartoon-ish clang as it made contact with the deputy's face, and he folded down, his hat flying off, all thoughts of handcuffing gone. All thoughts of anything gone.

Kidd was going for his gun when she dropped the spade, shouldered aside the nearest SoC and yanked at the blanket.

They watched in horror as the corpse tumbled out, its eyeless head testimony to weeks in the ground, the flesh mushy and decomposing, the fur coming away in clumps. A cloud of dust and mites and organic particles rose into the sunshine as the carcass flopped down with an unsavoury wet-fish noise.

'It's a fuckin' dog, assholes,' she shouted. 'It's Duke's dog.

Name of Noodler.' And she started to cry, the sobs coming from deep within.

One of the SoCs was bending over the fallen deputy, checking his purple cheek, when the big booming voice filled the yard. 'Hullo?'

Coogan spun round to see a large bullet-headed black man, dressed in a dark suit and shirt and tie, seemingly oblivious to the heat. 'Senior Special Agent George Slight, Tucson RA,' he said in a voice like summer thunder. Slight – by name, but certainly not by nature, thought Coogan – took in the chaos around the excavation, the groaning, prostrate Davies, Kidd with his gun half out of the holster, and a near-hysterical woman and said: 'Anything I can help with here?'

The address they gave him was high in the 70s on the East Side, a decent address for once, the top floor of a chi-chi apartment block, more likely to be home to women with poodles than women forced to give their bodies in return for an immigration visa of dubious validity. After the call he took three of the little blue pills, and instantly felt as if someone had attached electrodes to his balls and was giving him mild electric shocks, all tingly and nice.

The doorman nodded him through when he gave the address and he rode the elevator to the top floor. It was the only apartment up there, and he stepped out into a lobby with a long corridor running off it and maybe half a dozen doors. Sitting in the lobby were two of the regulars, Tarr and Mr Moustache, both smoking, playing cards across a small table. They barely registered him.

'What, you mean I got to learn to like hockey?' Mr Moustache said. 'And snow.'

'Fuck that. I like it here,' Tarr grunted. He looked up. 'Ah. The Creep. You're early.'

'I'm not.'

'I mean, it's early in the day for . . . this kind of thing.'

'Fuck you. Which room?'

'Fuck me? Fuck me?' Tarr stood up. 'I have a message for you from Schmee. He said just in case you was gettin' even colder feet, to remind you that we have enough film of you to keep the Cineplex on Times Square busy for a week. On all screens.'

Film? They'd been filming it? He tried hard to stop his face reddening, but with anger or embarrassment he wasn't sure. 'Which door?'

Tarr sneered. 'Third on the left. And don't worry – no filming today. We're all a bit bored with the sight of your pimply ass—'

Tarr was against the wall, the S&W almost up a nostril before he had a chance to finish the sentence. The Creep could feel over-compressed blood pumping through his brain, making it throb, causing an eyelid to twitch, and suddenly he wanted to pull the trigger, to blame this piece of slime for all that had gone wrong, all that would come tumbling down over the next few days and weeks, wanted to make sure they were swept away with it. He could see Tarr's wall-eyed hirsute friend reaching for something. 'Don't do anything stupid here. I can open up the back of his head like a cantaloupe. I'd like an apology. Now.' He pressed the gun harder, threatening to split the nasal septum.

Tarr looked at the guy's dilated pupils, at the sweat on his upper lip, felt the tension in the quivering hand, as if only an enormous concentration of willpower was stopping that index finger squeezing the trigger. There were times to fight and times to walk away. He managed to grunt. 'Sure. Just playing about. Leetle fun.' His accent was coming back now he was scared.

The Creep let Tarr go and put the gun away. Well, what did you know. He had needed it after all. He tried to casually readjust his trousers, aware of the big erection that was still in there, picked up the attaché case he had dropped and waited for them both to resume card playing, before he strode off, with as much dignity as he could muster, to have a leetle fun of his own.

❊   ❊   ❊

It was dusk by the time Agent Slight and his team had left. Coogan got them both a soda and they watched the sky darken, and the bats come out, looking as if they were chasing their own tails. There were nectar-feeding bats too, flitting from cactus to cactus, stocking up for the imminent journey south to Mexico, following the agave blooms. He felt like joining them.

A few other residents of the site were wandering around, mostly avoiding their eyes after all the excitement. Nobody here wanted cops around too often. They were being branded as trouble. But one of them had come good, had verified Wendy's story, had seen the couple drive off with Pete, saw Wendy trying to start her car. Slowly the cynicism, the 'two-thirds-of-all-parents-actually-did-it' demeanour softened, as they began to believe what had happened.

'The Fed seemed OK,' she finally said, her voice small and crackly, like a badly tuned radio.

Slight had been all business-like, but didn't seem to doubt her version of the abduction and had dissuaded them from any assault charges for playing spank-the-deputy-with-a-spade. And he had helped with one exchange. 'Did you see the car's plates?' he had asked.

Wendy had shaken her head. She had been through this. Through everything. There wasn't a fresh question left.

'But not Arizona, right?'

'I didn't see them.'

'New Mexico, you think.'

She was puzzled now. 'No, I didn't see them.'

'New Mexico means they are probably heading out of State,' Slight continued as if he hadn't heard. 'Means we can issue a UFAP.'

'UFAB?'

'UFAP. Unlawful Flight to Avoid Prosecution. Full airports alerts, trace requests on suspects . . .' His voice had trailed off. 'Did you see the plates?'

'New Mexico,' said Wendy weakly. 'I think.'

'OK, "I think" is close enough – I'll get a UFAP issued immediately. I will also speak to the Justice Department and telephone company about putting a tap'n'trace on the phone. In case it does become kidnapping.'

'I thought you guys stayed on the spot trying to trace calls?' Coogan had said to him.

'We always do. Every time. Six or seven of us. Especially if it's Mel Gibson's kid who's been snatched. Sorry, but there ain't enough manpower to spend days here.' He had taken Coogan aside. 'Look, you get a feel for these things. I ain't judgin' you folks, but exactly what would they expect you to use for a ransom? She lives in a trailer park. She's a cocktail waitress—'

'Barkeep,' he said.

'Whatever. If you were going to risk a Federal crime like kidnapping, would you snatch a kid from here? No.'

'Then why would you?'

He hadn't answered, but had slipped him a card. 'You will find some answers here. I shouldn't be givin' you that – NCMC and the rest fine, this one the Bureau thinks is trouble. Persona non grata. Know what that means?'

'Yeah. It's Latin for you shouldn't be givin' it to me. Thanks.' Coogan slipped it in his shirt pocket.

'My guess? They wanted the kid, not money. Whole set-up was designed to confuse, and it sure did that. Might've lost us a lot of time. You should thank Kidd. Most deputies would've held off before inviting us in.'

'So it's your case now?'

Slight demurred. 'Always a local case. We just do the rest of the country for them. Trans America Corporation, that's us.'

Wendy brought him back from thinking about Slight when she said: 'My mind won't stop working. It's like seeing the same few scenes over and over again, pinpointing where I could've done something different.'

Coogan nodded. 'I told you about the kid. When I got back he was there all the time, all the time. I daren't go to sleep, little skinny fucker would show up. In the end . . . What I'm tryin' to say is . . . it's gonna keep playin', that show. Twenty-four seven. You gotta take somethin', 'cause you won't be sleepin' otherwise.'

'I don't want to sleep.' Wendy looked at him with her big blue eyes, now suffused with pink. 'I'm frightened.'

'You gotta sleep. You gotta stay sharp, Wendy, we to do anything.'

'What can we do? What can we do?' There was a note of hysteria, and he tried to keep his own voice calm.

'Like Slight said, lots of people to contact.'

'What, get Pete on the side of a milk carton?'

'Slight's already got it on the internet. It's on the National Center for Missing and Exploited Children in Virginia, and the Missing Children Help Center in Florida. They pass it on to other organisations nationwide. They can age adjust, too.'

'What?'

Coogan realised he had said the wrong thing. Slight had explained to him that when a kid was missing for a long time, the various charities used an age-progression programme to update the picture, to guess at what that little twelve-year-old would look like now she was a vivacious nineteen-year-old. If she had made it that far. But, Slight had warned him, Wendy shouldn't be told just how many kids were still unaccounted for after two, three, five years. So Coogan changed the subject. 'Plus he said the Feds have a new Child Recovery Unit almost operational in Washington. Coordinating everything across the country. Oh, then there is this one. He was kinda secretive about this.' He handed her the card.

Dusk was sliding into true night. There was no moon, just the dense cytoplasm of stars emerging in the ink-blue sky. Somewhere, probably further away than it seemed, a coyote howled and he felt Wendy shiver. He stood up and peered at the road. He could just make out the shape of a Sheriff's department cruiser, put there to keep any prying press away. Missing kid. Heartbroken mother. Always good copy. Both Slight and Kidd wanted some breathing space before that happened. They had a few options before it was tearful TV-appeal time. 'Come on, let's get you inside and to bed.'

She just sat there staring at the card, the desolate words biting deep into her, causing the shake Coogan had seen. 'Missing Kid? Dial 1–800-The-Lost-Ones' it said. Lost. Not missing. Pete was lost. What must he be feeling right now? Confused, abandoned and lonely. So lonely. And lost. She started to cry again, and the sound hurt Coogan more than he had thought possible.

Jim Barry was watching re-runs of *Mission: Impossible* when he heard the noise. He put down his beer and tensed himself. There had been some nasty incidents of late – kids throwing rocks at the house, chanting things he made sure he closed his ears to. Just young punks, he rationalised. Even so, there was a coldness in the way the adults were treating him, a distance, and it was more than just a dead foreign kid at stake here. His actions had divided Bloomsberry, created a tension over exactly who should pay whom and for what. The ambulance chasers, drawn by the scent of blood, had found the raw wound in the community, put their hands in, rummaged around, and were now hoping to pull out sacks of money, with complete disregard to what happened to the bleeding animal.

He was standing up as Belle walked into the room, threw her bag down, and went straight over to fix herself a drink.

'Belle?'

She took a big slug of gin that had been merely threatened with some tonic, and gagged slightly. 'Yeah. Hi.'

He almost daren't ask. 'How . . . how'd it go? I mean . . . did you? I thought you'd call. Why the hell didn't you call? I've been worried.'

She nodded wearily. How could she convey that she felt like

the lowest form of scum on earth, as if she had slit open a pregnant woman's belly and snatched the child out. She was no different from those animals they had watched on the tape. She needed to scour herself.

'So you found one?' Jim repeated, stunned that it had worked.

'Yup.' She reduced it down to a staccato explanation, too beat to string the sentences together that would explain how Paladin had come up with a list of potentials and little Pete had leapt out of the list. 'Newspaper clipping service. Arizona. Drunk mother. Left him home alone. Like in the movie. Didn't deserve him.'

'And? Where is he?'

Belle said, slowly, so he would understand. 'What? You think I would bring him here? Parade him round the town and say – look, this is our decoy. We are going to give him away instead of our son. Great plan, eh? And we only had to kidnap him from his unfit mother.'

'Belle.' She had been shouting.

'Yeah. Yeah. I dropped him at Mamie and Morgan's—'

'Morgan's?'

'Yeah, Morgan's. What did you want me to do? Leave him at the local Motel 6? I just came to pick up some things. I'm staying up there with him. I've got a lot of work to do on him.'

'Work on him how?'

'If I keep giving him those drugs he's gonna have the IQ of a chimp by the time we hand him over. I always tell the folks who come to see me that kids are very adaptable, well, for once I am going to find out just how true that is. You know my pet theory? The one that got me on the *New York Times* bestseller list? Compartmentalising? Well that is where his old life is going. Into the cupboard.'

'Jesus.'

Belle strode over and Jim stepped back, thinking she was going to strike him. 'Don't Jesus me. If it wasn't for me, we'd have waved bye-bye to Tommy by now. You would've just handed him over. It was me who had to go swimming with scuzzballs to get this kid. He's goddamn perfect, but we got a lot to do to make sure this works. *I've* got a lot to do. As usual. You just stick with your cable channel, eh? You put this place on the market yet?'

'What?'

'You had a realtor in? For God's sake, Jim, am I the only one thinking here?'

The venom wrong-footed him. 'Did we talk about this?'

'We can't stay here with Tommy, can we? Think, think, think. We hand over the kid, and say, here's our boy. Meanwhile our Tommy is playing in the yard? We'll have to split, Jim.'

'Shit.'

She suddenly spat fire at him, a quick, scorching blast that took him aback. 'OK, big boy, gimme a better option. Come on. Let's hear it, Jim, because I would quite like to be able to sit back again and let you do the running around while I watch *Days of Our Lives*. Come on, anything. Show me the light, I am just dying to see it. Nothing? Then get this house sold.'

'Where will we go?'

'Canada.'

'Canada?'

'I figure it gives us one extra hurdle for this guy to clear if it all goes belly-up. It's another country, he might not have friends and influence there, he might not even think about it. Most people don't.'

'And you get a lot for your dollar,' he said, repeating a familiar mantra by rote.

'There you go, sport. Now you're thinkin'. We can stay with Morgan and Mamie while the deal is going through. Just remember to pack the earplugs. That lungfish of a kid isn't any better. I'm going to grab a shower.'

Jim sat down again, feeling the maelstrom thicken and quicken around him, making him nauseous, until his eyes finally focused on the television. The usual suspects in a white panel van in overalls with Acme Electrics written on the back, about to pull the government's ass out of the fire once again. Where was Mr Phelps, he wondered, when you really needed him?

TWENTY-EIGHT

Phoenix, Arizona

The Lost Ones occupied a former retail unit in a depressing windblown mall on the outskirts of Phoenix. It had once housed outlet stores for big-brand names, and their ghostly logos were still scattered across the frontage – Nike, Levi, Timberland, Pottery Barn. Now only the Barnes & Noble looked like it was thriving, the rest of the stores were the second-league brands – the kind of stuff, Coogan thought, you wouldn't be too keen on at any price.

He pulled up outside the address on the card, but the blinds were pulled, and he couldn't see in. He looked at Wendy. 'You OK?'

She nodded. Her eyes had shrunk, and were peering out through black rings. She looked awful, as if she was slowly folding into herself. It was becoming difficult to see the real Wendy. The snatched shots that a few of the press guys now hanging around the trailer site took would show a haunted woman. The kind of face that you could say to yourself over your cereal – yeah, I bet that bitch did it. Look at those eyes.

'We gotta get you some proper sleeping pills,' he said. 'I think you gotta be strong for this. There's other people, their kids never came back. It won't be easy to hear.'

'I know.' There was little she could be told that her imagination hadn't already supplied throughout the long night. Images of Pete battered and bruised and raped and thrown in a ditch, of him locked in a filthy room, fed scraps, and, strangely the most horrifying of all, him in a warm, comfortable home, slowly forgetting who she was.

'And you must eat. We'll get something after this.'

'I can't.' Her stomach heaved at the thought, empty and acidic.

'You must. Soon you'll be runnin' on protein, burning up your muscles. If not for you, do it for Pete.' She mumbled something that could have been an affirmative. 'OK. Three deep breaths and we go. Ready? One . . . two . . . three.'

Mercy Haystead apologised for the state of the office, which was, indeed, nothing short of chaotic. 'I only just moved in. Well, two months ago. Got a good deal on the place. I hope to get those boxes unpacked soon. Sit down, sit down. Coffee? Sally Ann? Can you get me a couple of coffees here?'

Sally Ann and Mercy looked like a double act. Whereas Mercy was a big woman, with the kind of breasts that are vaguely threatening, even hidden under a voluminous Grand Canyon sweatshirt that could, Coogan figured, be ironic, but probably wasn't, Sally Ann was a thin, withered vine.

'So,' said Mercy, matter-of-factly, 'I'm sorry to hear about your boy. You been onto the National Center? Good. They'll assign you a case officer, who will take care of all the internet stuff. Word of advice – keep callin' them. Lest they forget. Know what I'm saying? It's our watchword here. Ain't it, Sally Ann? Lest they forget. You have a picture?'

Wendy handed over one of the dupes Coogan had made and felt a catch in her throat again as she saw the image of Pete standing outside the trailer, an oversized catcher's mitt in his hand, looking small and helpless.

'Good-looking boy. And you got other details?' She took the sheets containing all that Coogan had managed to coax from Wendy on the minutiae of Pete's short life. Mercy cast an eye over them. 'You looked up the listing on the internet?'

'No. Neither of us has a computer.' Wendy's voice was soft and ethereal.

Mercy logged on, waited for a page to load and spun the

screen around. It was full of lines of type, mostly names, ages and dates, each one underlined so you could jump to further information on the case. She scrolled down, and while the names were blurring into each other, she said; 'The As . . . the Bs, lots of Bs . . . the Cs.'

'Jesus,' said Coogan. 'How many are there?'

'How many on the list? Or how many missing kids? I gotta tell you, there are a whole range of categories shown here. Most are under twenty-five. Some older. When I started this place, it didn't take me long to learn one truth. You can be eighty, with a fifty-year-old kid, but something unexplained happens to him, hurts just as much as if you were thirty and he was five. That mother-love thing? It's a bitch.'

Wendy looked at Coogan. This wasn't quite what she expected.

Mercy carried on: 'Figures are not easy to come by. Last year we estimate there were a hundred and fifty thousand attempted abductions of children by non-family members. In 1990, it was a hundred and fifteen thousand. Around seven thousand successful abductions were reported to the police. 1990, four thousand six hundred. Now when it comes to family, the figure leaps up – half a million. Parents, grandparents, aunts, brothers, sisters, as often as not thinking they was acting in the kids' best interests. Now we also got about six hundred thousand per annum who run away – mostly teenagers, the majority of whom come back or call in. But then there were a hundred and fifty thousand children who were abandoned.'

'Abandoned?'

'Yup. Left at hospitals, police stations, in motel rooms, on the shoulder of freeways. Last year Highway Patrol found three kids wandering along the shoulder on Interstate 17. The parents had stopped, unloaded them, left them a drink and sandwich each and drove off.'

Coogan asked: 'You get them?'

Mercy shook her head. 'The parents? If there's any justice they died in an auto wreck two miles down the road.' She said it without a trace of rancour, which made it all the more chilling.

Coogan wanted to ask if there was any justice in any of this, but kept his mouth shut.

Wendy, however, had one burning question. 'Will I get him back?'

Mercy's face softened slightly, her jowly features sagging. 'I can't answer that. They do come back. They do. US Department of Justice found that around ninety-three per cent of children reported missing are recovered.'

'Seems good odds,' said Coogan.

'Yeah. Very good. If your child is playing in a neighbour's garden, or Granny took her out shopping and forgot to tell you. That's what distorts those odds. But once they are missing more than forty-eight hours . . .' She shuddered. 'Who referred you to me?'

'Agent name of Slight,' said Coogan, rubbing his hand across Wendy's shoulder, feeling the steel hawsers bunched under the skin. Funny, his own back had stopped hurting, as if it knew this wasn't the time.

'Oh, yeah. Slight. He's a good guy. We worked a case together. I mean I helped him back when the internet thing was just taking off. Got one back. It's a good feeling. A great feeling. A high-five feeling. A going out and getting blasted feeling. Which is what we did. But he knows I don't pussyfoot around with all this. The truth is more than five hundred kids a year don't come back. Doesn't mean to say they are murdered, although some are. Ten years ago it was three hundred. There are those who say we are out by a factor of two. I pray not, but they may be right.'

'Why did he say the FBI wouldn't like us to talk to you?' asked Coogan.

Mercy snorted. 'Because they are assholes. No, that's not true. We lobbied for a Crimes Against Children unit in every metropolitan area with a central coordinating bureau in Washington.

What we got was this CRU – you hear about that? Child Recovery Unit? Now the FBI, God bless 'em, are used to doing things in their own way. Slow. You know they only just gave agents computers? Before that, all reports were done on dictaphones and had to be typed up. By a secretary or stenographer? Which is great for Washington employment stats, less so for speed of investigation. It can take forever to get anything out of the Bureau. Which is why we wanted a *new* Federal Agency. Instead we got an offshoot of the existing one. So the director of the CRU has decided not to share information with what he calls "amateurs" like me. He wants all we can give him, oh yessir, but it's a one-way flow. So I am pursuing a FOI act case against him. Make him tell me what they doin'. Look, you know how most paedophiles communicate these days? E-mail. Now they tend to use code, you know, like that old one of "chickens" for under-age children, although it's more sophisticated than that. Now, the CRU has done a study into paedophile language, and is monitoring transmissions through ISPs. Do we get to know any of this? Not a goddamn. I don't want the transmissions – I just want to know what the current slang is. Then we can warn parents what to listen out for. You know? Some guy talking about "bloomers" at the school gate, we might just know he means early-teen pre-pubescents. Then there is the fact that the CRU is wilfully under-reporting the true missing figures. By any standards this is an epidemic – America's children are disappearing in ever-increasing numbers. Meanwhile, the CRU accuse us of being hysterical, of fomenting fear. I guess the FBI said the same thing to the MSHC.'

'Who?'

'The guys in Florida? Missing Children Help Center? Until they got going you couldn't declare a child missing until you had a ransom note or twenty-four or, in some cases, forty-eight hours had elapsed. In 1983 those folks got the Missing Children's Act passed, to eliminate the waiting period. Florida was the first state to mandate it. I tell you – they deserve all our thanks. More coffee? Sally Ann, I'll have one this time.'

Coogan looked around, taking in the wall of fresh faces, of kids from four months to late teens, mostly school photos, with a background of fake academia, a wall of leather-bound volumes, and over-groomed, scrubbed kids showing the stages of dental work all American youth goes through.

Wendy suddenly said. 'I need some air.'

When she was gone, Coogan said, 'You holdin' anything back?'

'Do I sound like I'm holding anything back? No. OK. But this is a weird one. This scenario, I mean. It took planning. I mean paedophiles are both deviants and devious, but there is something very cool about this. Something I ain't really seen before.'

'You think it's paedophiles?' He looked at the door, hoping Wendy couldn't hear.

'You heard of NAMBLA? North American Man/Boy Love Association? No? You are a lucky, lucky man. I wish I hadn't. They have a slogan – sex by eight is too late. So they have a kind of elite club, men who claim to have deflowered an under-eight kid. Course there is a female equivalent – the Loam Society. Not made up of women, don't get me wrong. Just sick fucks who prefer little . . . John Loam was a guy who molested young girls. He got caught in Texas with his hand up this guy's daughter's dress. The man coldcocked him and called the neighbours. It wasn't a pretty death by all accounts. Well, so these assholes have themselves a martyr. The Loam Society are a bit more flexible than NAMBLA – it's only after twelve they reckon sex with a female is a waste of time. You wanna watch the arm of that chair there?'

Coogan looked down and saw his white-knuckled grip was in danger of snapping the thin bit of wood. He relaxed and kneaded his hand.

'You see what we are up against?'

Wendy came back in, still hunched, moving quietly, gently as if she felt she might shatter at any moment. 'Miss Haystead.'

'Mercy.'

'Mercy. Can I ask you . . . how did you start all this, and . . .' She gulped. 'And how can you stand it?'

'Sally Ann? Can you go get us some donuts? You folks want some? No? OK. Just for me, then. I tell you I used to be as skinny as you. I started to overeat when my little girl went. You talk to a lot of other agencies, you'll find a similar story to mine at the core. My girl was called April. That's her over there. The blonde one with pigtails. That was about six months before she was taken. She went across the road to get some candy. We think she was grabbed on the way there, because the store owner don't remember her coming in. We had one confirmed sighting a day later on a convenience store camera, when she was sent in to get sodas. Same clothes. Dirty, now, though, and she looked . . .' Mercy suddenly wiped a tear away. 'Haunted, I guess. Sorry. Look, I'm fortunate. We found her body in the desert two years later when some animals turned over the grave. If you can call it that.'

'Fortunate?' asked Wendy. 'That's fortunate?'

'That's lucky. You gotta face up to it. Look, I don't want to sound like some shitty confessional daytime TV number, but, y'see, I've got closure. I got to bury my daughter proper. Most other people I know doin' this kind of work, they don't even know for sure they are dead. They live with the hope some swanky twenty-year-old gonna come through the door and apologise for all those missing years. If the grave hadn't been disturbed, I'd be one of them.'

Sally Ann returned with the donuts and Mercy polished off two immediately.

'So . . . so why do you keep doing it? Doing this? Now you know?'

Mercy opened her desk drawer and pulled out a large shiny automatic pistol which she slammed down, making Coogan jump. It was pointing at him. 'They never caught who did it. But, y'see, most of these people are serial offenders. So he – I know it is a he – is still out there. Still doin' it. I hope one day they get him, and in the plea-bargaining they let these scum do, that he tosses in a little girl he took near Phoenix, Arizona, and then I'm gonna wait on the steps of the courthouse with this, put it against his eye and pull the trigger. Hey, everyone's got to have an ambition. Ain't that right, Sally Ann? Anyway, I've been doing all the talking. You got any questions here?'

Wendy felt the power of hatred cross from this woman, the surge of energy that her thoughts of revenge gave her, negative thoughts maybe, but strangely also the first positive stirrings she had felt. She nodded at the gun on the desktop. 'Yeah. You got any more of those things?'

Belle unlocked the door and went in to see the boy. He was lying on the bed, staring at the ceiling, but blinking hard. The drug was moving out of his system. He was in the top of the house, under the roof eaves, and it was stifling. Belle opened the roof vents that Morgan had installed and turned on the ceiling fan.

Pete sat up, saw it was her and slumped back. 'I want to go home now,' he said.

Belle sat down. 'I brought you some things.' She tried to stroke his head but he rolled away.

'I want my mom.'

'I told you, she is . . . in trouble. She can't look after you any more. She asked me to find you a nice new home, with parents who can give you everything you need.'

'Why didn't she tell me?'

'She was too upset. Peter—'

'Not Peter. Pete. Pete.'

'Pete. It happens a lot. We all change parents, it's what happens when you are five or six. New folks, new house, new friends. It's nothing to worry about.'

'Can I talk to her?'

'One day, maybe. Not now. It would be too sad for both of you. Look I got you some clothes. Look. Gap. Great T-shirt, eh? Want to try it on. Oh, and this?'

From the corner of his eyes he saw the big box emerge from the box. A Nintendo 128. Not as fast as his Playstation 3, which came in at 256, but pretty neat. He bit his lower lip. He still wanted to cry, still wanted his mom, but found himself saying: 'You get any games?'

'Yup. I had to ask the assistant. One here called Galac . . . something.'

'Galactica Three Thousand?'

'That's the one.'

He sat up fast then slowed himself down, affecting a casualness his little heart didn't feel. Maybe this wasn't going to be so bad after all. 'I'll need a TV. To play it through,' he said, the unsaid word 'stupid' hanging there between them.

'Sure. I'll get one brought up.'

'And a drink.'

'And cookies?'

'I guess.'

'There you go.' He didn't pull back when she ruffled his hair this time.

'How long can I play? On the game?'

'How long do you want to play?'

'An hour?'

'Two if you want.'

As she turned she was sure she saw a little grin starting as he tore into the packaging.

Downstairs she told Morgan what he wanted and he went to sort a spare TV set out. She set about making milk and cookies, working around Mamie as if it were her own kitchen. Tommy came in from outside and said: 'Can I play with the new boy?'

'No . . . he's . . . he's not well. He's infectious. You know what that means?'

'He has something I can catch.'

271

'Good boy. He'll be gone soon. I bought you some new cars while I was at the mall. They're in the hall. Go on, go and have a look.'

When Tommy had gone Mamie said quietly, 'We've become monsters.'

'What? Don't you start. I've enough with Jim. One day I'm going to sit down and tell him why all this really happened. That because he gave Tommy a train set when he was one, construction kits at two, soccer lessons at three, baseball at four . . . all too soon, too soon. And because he couldn't wait and got everything for the boy too damn early, because he coached babies who couldn't understand why you wore headgear . . . because like all men he never grew up. That's why we are here. This kid? He'll be better off than where he was. It was a real shithole. His mom was a drunken slut. Cute. But a real screw-up. You know the type? White bread white trash. He will come out of all this ahead. Just like Ariel. You're going to give her a better life than she would have had. We'll all win. And I appreciate what you are doing—'

'We're thinking of giving up the baby.'

That stopped her dead.

'What?'

Mamie suddenly broke down, and put her head on Belle's shoulder, and she could feel the tears forming a damp patch through her blouse. 'Belle, we can't . . . stand it any more.'

'It won't be for much longer. Look, they grow out of it. They grow out of everything. You'll laugh at the sleepless nights in a couple of months' time.

'No, no, there's something . . . something not right. Maybe it's the genes. We didn't ask enough questions. We just said to that horrible man, get us a baby, something to love. We can love anything. That's what we said.' She looked up into Belle's face. 'Now I know you can't.'

Belle did not need this. She had enough problems of her own. 'Will Paladin take it back?'

'You kiddin'? It's not sale-or-return.'

Belle nodded. She could imagine trying to broach the topic with that toad of a guy. And the response. 'What can you do?'

'Leave her at a hospital. Lots of people do. There is no trace to us. Not like they can do DNA tests, huh? Or hospital records. We never even registered her yet.'

'What'll you tell people?'

'Who? We've only really showed you. We've got no close neighbours. Anyone asks, we'll say the baby died. Or it was fostered. I don't know. Belle, I just want my old life back.'

'Jesus, Mamie. So do I. So do I.' She swept up the tray of goodies and went back upstairs to see her hostage.

Mercy Haystead licked her lips as the sixth and last donut went down and asked Sally Ann for more coffee. 'There's another reason they don't like me. The Feds I mean. I'm afraid that I support affirmative action. What we're meant to do is sit at home and wait for the professionals to strut their stuff. Wait, wait, wait. Me? If I'm gonna wait I like to do it in someone's office, so that I get so annoying they drop whatever they are meant to be doing and give me their attention. And using people. I like that, too. Use whoever you can. Got a cop friend? Use him. Local Child Welfare? Use her. Newspaperman? Start writing columns now, do press releases, get their attention. Look, in my time I've had one FBI agent fired and two deputies reprimanded—'

'And that guy in Las Vegas,' interrupted Sally Ann, shocking them all into silence at the wispy nature of her voice.

'Oh yeah. Some counsellor got fired. Like I give a rat's ass. Guy was a pervert. Not the one we wanted, but a pervert all the same. See, I don't mind treadin' on toes. Anyway we can progress a case, legal or illegal, fine by me. You know the Martin Luther King phrase?'

'"I have a dream"?' suggested Coogan.

'Do I mean Martin Luther King? "By all means necessary"?'

'Malcolm X,' said Coogan.

'Yeah,' said Mercy. 'Malcolm was a bit more kick-ass, wasn't he? "By all means necessary". Now, they tell you about GM?'

'Genetically modified?'

'Geographical mapping. Using the the National Crime Information Computer, some people have developed a way of pinpointing crimes by modus operandi. It can work real well. Vancouver developed it. Seattle got a good programme, Miami, too. Now, they will do it for you. Once. Maybe twice. But the NCIC is FBI-controlled, so we can't get regular access just on the basis of seeing if anything new has come up. See what I mean? And the other problem is that your G-man may be all fired up, but if the leads go to Nebraska or LA or New York, he can't just fly out there. He has to get some other agent all fired up, too, and it's hard. 'Cause in the end, well, it's not unusual for an agent to be processing fifty, sixty cases at one time. Who wants an extra from out-of-town? So even your agent, the main case agent, he has to be kept under pressure. 'Cause he gotta pass that on to maybe two, three other guys. Oh, he'll be sympathetic. Caring. Concerned. Professional. But at some point during the day he'll go home and forget about it. You can't. Which means the only one who feels the fire in their belly like you do is . . . you.'

'I know someone on the Seattle PD,' said Coogan. 'Might be able to help with the mapping thing.'

Wendy looked at him oddly. 'You do?'

He shrugged. He'd been around.

'Great,' said Mercy, slamming the desktop. 'Great. Use him. But let me tell you what's gonna happen. Wendy, right now you're in shock. You'll be in shock for a week, maybe two, then you'll get angry. Real angry. Use that anger, focus it. Come to me and I'll tell you what to do with it. Just don't waste it punchin' walls and eatin' Twinkies like I did. But talkin' of Seattle, there is one other thing you'll find. This all takes time. It's a full-time occupation, a job, a calling. And money. It takes lots and lots of money. You guys got any?'

Wendy could suddenly feel Coogan's eyes boring into her. She didn't want to look at him. She was scared of what he was thinking.

TWENTY-NINE

Seattle, Downtown

John Tenniel walked into the bar and hesitated as he shook the Seattle rain from his coat, feeling himself slip back three or four years. He was fatter then, all those snatched carbo-rich meals and sitting in cars or behind desks for hours on end. Back then he would have found himself here when he had just finished a shift, coated with the felonious grime of Seattle, everything from convenience stores through to multiple homicide. What he would really have needed was a hot bath and a good dinner and bed, but as often as not he would be drawn here, to the Looking Glass, a bar not far from the Public Safety Building. It was dark brown, and heavily mirrored – hence the name – although the amount of smoke in the atmosphere in the early days meant you could rarely see yourself. Now, of course, the air was cleaner, sweeter and Tenniel kind of missed the fug.

He looked enviously around at the faces, a different generation from his, hardly anyone he recognised, but no doubt all with the same problems he'd had – long hours, low pay, disintegrating family life, temperamental computers, law suits, IA investigations. Every now and then one of them gave him a quizzical look. He remembered doing the same to retired officers who came down to the old haunts, wondering why they kept coming back like tortured spirits. Why couldn't they just cut the ties, get on with real life and forget about it? Because, he now realised, the longer you were in the job, the deeper the anchor points for those ties worked into your flesh, until you couldn't remove them without mortal damage.

He shouldered his way to the bar and he could see her

talking animatedly to a fellow officer, her arms splaying out wide as she described some explosion or trauma, then her head went back in a sudden burst of laughter. He touched her shoulder and Isa Bowman span round and his heart gave that once-familiar stutter.

She'd grown her hair, had better clothes on, a neat grey two-piece, and her face was just a tad more lined, but it was the Isa he remembered. 'John, John. You came. Great to see you. Uh, sorry, John, this is Mike. Mike Dreyfuss? John Tenniel? John taught me everything he knew,' she laughed.

'Yeah, and on the second day of the job, she started learning for herself,' he added.

They shook hands and Mike said he had to run and neither of them protested. He ordered a beer and got her a second whisky sour. All around him he could feel that old crackle, adrenaline burning off in drink and conversation, each individual slowly winding down until their metabolism was in sync with the rest of the population. Until tomorrow, when they would have to crank it up again.

'Been too long, John.'

'I don't get into town much. I had some tax shit to sort out.'

'Well, it's good to see you.'

'And you.'

They sipped, feeling the slight awkwardness, but not worrying too much. It'd pass. 'How's your wife . . . no, don't tell me. Catherine.'

'Good. I mean, life out there, on the islands, it's pretty relaxed.'

She punched his stomach. 'You lookin' good on it, John. Retirement suits you.'

No, it doesn't, he almost said, I want to be here, shooting the breeze, bitching about superior officers, telling of near misses, of fallen perps, cases closed and arguing over gun calibres. 'Yeah. Part of me misses it, though.'

'Which part?'

'Not my brain. That's for sure. It ain't a logical career for an old man. How you been?'

'Yeah, OK. Did I tell you? I'm thinking about moving over to the Office of Chief of Police. Public relations.'

'Off the street?'

'For a year or two. Recharge, you know what I mean? Nine-to-five job. A raise.'

'You always hated nine-to-five.'

'And you said you'd never retire.'

He finished off his beer, shocked at how quickly it had gone. 'So I did. How's it goin' with that sergeant?'

'It ain't. Hasn't been for eight months. Try and keep up, John.'

'So who's the lucky guy now?' he asked, feeling the contrived sentence almost stall in his mouth.

'I got a cat. I had this thing with one of the instructors on the gun course for a while. ATF. Nice guy. But same old, same old. He went east. Actually he got caught in a firefight. I ain't seen him in a while. I feel real guilty.' Was it the distance or the thought of the wheelchair that kept her away she wondered? Every time she e-mailed him she promised she would visit real soon. Best not dwell on that. 'You know what it's like on the job, you shack up with someone in it, it's all too claustrophobic. Anyone outside, shit, they don't last ten days. Remember I had that thing about musicians? Musicians and cops, what a mixture. You were lucky, with Catherine. That it lasted.'

'It was touch and go.' Mainly, they both knew, because of her, because they had never really defined their relationship. It was Tenniel who had decided. Platonic. And he was still glad he had. Because this way he didn't have to go through the crash and burn that would have been inevitable, given the difference in their ages.

Isa started to say something in low, conspiratorial tones. 'John, I may be right out of the ballpark but—'

Her cellphone rang and she cursed. 'Bet you don't miss this

bit. Yeah, Bowman. Who?' She felt herself redden and turned half away from Tenniel. 'It's noisy. Jesus, how are you? Where are you? No shit? Go on, run it by me.' There was a long pause while she listened and Tenniel played with his empty glass. Finally she said: 'Yeah. When was this? Shit. Fake? Well I don't know. Geographical mapping? Yeah. No, I am surrounded by cops at the moment – you got good timing, Coogan. I dunno. I'll ask. But it's not our, I mean, their jurisdiction. You tried that new Child Recovery Unit? Yeah, I guess. I don't know what to suggest. You wanna leave it with me? Give me a number where I can get back to you.' She took a pen and pad from her jacket and wrote down two numbers. 'Where did you say that was? Arizona. Really? Look, let me see what's what. Yeah. Good to hear from you.'

She clicked off the phone. 'Speak of the devil. You remember George Coogan? No? Might've been when I was over on the East Side. One of those musicians I was just talkin' about. Got a kidnapping case he's involved in.'

'Kidnapping? You serious? Don't go there, Isa. FBI.'

'I know, but someone has been telling him it'll just get lost in the cracks. Even with the CRU.'

He pursed his lips. No good denying it happens. 'Could be right. What was that about geographical mapping?'

'You know that? They use it a lot over at Child Centered Crimes. Don't think they'd let civvies swing by and start playing. Coogan could put a request in through Arizona State or local police. Take some time though. Hell of a backlog, so they say.' Then her face clouded and her brow dropped an inch.

Tenniel remembered the look of old. 'What? You got something?'

'Jesus, it's like, hey, meet all Isa's old boyfriends in one day.' She darted a glance in case he thought he was included in that roster, but there was no reaction. 'The *other* guy I was telling you about. This Fed. He ain't an agent any more, invalided out. But he does something similar. To GM. He subscribes to one of the big private crime databases. The ones insurance companies use? You know, for actuaries? So they can work out what are the chances of dying in an auto wreck while smoking and playing Flaming Lips CDs? It's not like the NCIC, but he was telling me it's pretty damn impressive. They pay PDs to file an annual summary of crimes under something like sixty headings.'

'So this is, like, his hobby?'

'He's one of those guys who can't let the job go—'

Tenniel laughed, recognising the little pulse of excitement Coogan's call had induced. 'Yeah, I know that one.'

'No. Not like you. He's big on using computers. He has to be. He can't walk now – the firefight I mentioned? – so he uses the internet. I could give him a call.' She checked her watch and said to herself: 'Or I can e-mail him.'

He could see he was losing her, her mind turning over whatever case this Coogan had outlined on the phone. And he didn't want to lose her. 'What were you saying?' he asked, trying to reel her back in. 'Before your cellphone rang? About the ballpark?'

But the moment had gone. Isa just said: 'Nothing. You got time for another?'

The realtor made appreciative grunting noises as she walked around, mapping the size of the rooms with her infrared tape, and scribbling notes on the fixtures and fittings. 'This cooker?'

'Staying,' said Jim. 'All staying. The buyers can have what-ever they want.'

'Fine. Shall we sit down?'

He led her through to the living room and they sat on the couch. 'Here is a copy of our terms and conditions. As you can see there is a substantial discount for exclusives. Now, subject to a full survey, I would say, given the current situation, we could hold out for nine hundred thousand dollars.'

'Really?'

'Yes. To the right buyer. Nice town, easy commute. I don't

have to tell you all this. All the reasons you bought into Bloomsberry still exist. But we need to wait for the right buyer—'

'No,' he said agitatedly.

'Excuse me? Are you OK?'

Jim was aware of the fact he had recently developed a whole repertoire of nervous ticks, including furiously rubbing his eyes. He stopped and said: 'Yeah. Fine. Just some allergy I guess. What if we said, sell it now. Ask, I dunno, eight.'

'Eight?' she said with dismay, feeling a small pile of commission slipping through her fingers. 'Eight is too cheap. Too cheap and people get suspicious. Believe me, they are happy paying near market value. Give them a bargain, by all means. But not a steal, Mr Barry.'

'Whatever. First decent offer over eight.'

'Well . . . I could sell it tomorrow. Tonight.'

'Do it.'

She sighed. 'What's the hurry in this town?'

'What do you mean?'

'Well, this is the third sale where the owners are acting like their pants are on fire. You got advance notice of a meteor strike?'

'Who else?'

'Excuse me?'

'Who else is moving?'

'Let's see. There's one in Conduit Avenue.' That would be Dick. Figures. 'And another in Kensington Gardens. The big house.'

'You sure?'

'Sure? Course I'm sure. You don't forget a million-eight valuation overnight. You know the house?'

Yes, he knew the house. The one with the huge grounds and the helipad out back. Of course he knew it. The Sebastyens' home had figured large in his nightmares for the past week.

THIRTY

Grand Canyon

The sun is just coming up as the security van pulls up to the Grand Canyon's only bank. It is Tuesday, the day after Labor Day, when the great slash in the earth has been seen by hundreds of thousands of pairs of eyes, at twenty dollars the pair. The gift shops run by the Fred Harvey Company have sold truckfuls of t-shirts with the logo 'I Hiked the Grand Canyon', mostly to people who, clearly, have not and could not. Coachloads of tourists have been shuttled into the giant car park just north of Tusayan and transferred to the natural gas buses which have taken them to the nearest viewpoint. There they emerged from the vehicles with their eyes glued to videocam viewfinders, where they remained for much of the duration. Many of them did not see the real Canyon at all, but an electronic version of it. They bought an indifferent lunch, and yet more souvenirs, before being coached out again.

The two guards who come to the Canyon's bank know little of this. They are glad to have been far from the madness, the kind of mass tourism that saps the will to live, to serve, to be pleasant, the reason why, almost uniquely in America, there is a tired, jaded atmosphere to the tourist industry round here. The numbers are just too great, the nationalities too varied, the Grand Canyon simply too famous.

The guards don the protective gear they must use when emerging from the van, and supervise the loading of the big square steel boxes into the rear of the truck. Over a million dollars in cash, much more in credit-card sales, from three days of constant spending, dawn to midnight. The pair keep an eye on the proceedings, hardly noticing the increasing orange-brown glow from the walls of the Canyon as the sun catches the sandstone layer and it begins to reflect its fabulous warm hues. The light isn't yet strong enough to bleach all those subtleties out, and the rim itself is crowded with those who are up early to witness the display at its finest.

Loaded up, the guards check all the locks on the truck, and climb into the cab. An hour to Flagstaff and to breakfast. Then a run down to Phoenix and back, and that's the day done. One of them gives a circled thumb and forefinger to the manager and they set off, back past the Visitors' Center, through the park gates, skirting the huge ugly patch of asphalt that is the car park, bristling with poles carrying identifying letters and numbers, although for the moment it is spookily deserted – the day visitors won't be along for another hour or two.

At Tusayan the helicopters are already starting their ferrying, buzzing in and out of the strip, the new NoTARS almost whispering giants in comparison with the old whiney turbines of the previous generation of choppers.

One of the guards, not the driver, contrary to company rules, risks a cigarette and turns up the air flow. They talk sports for a while, settling into the familiar level of non-essential conversation, as if their vocal chords just need to keep going in case they seize up.

They pass the signs telling them they are in the Kaibab National Forest, the long, straight featureless road through scenery that is surprisingly dull, considering what a great prize it holds in its midst. Down the road the driver can see that the road works they drove by earlier have started. No stop-go signs, though, these guys are using automatic traffic signals. They are still green, and the driver floors the accelerator to make sure he gets through the single file just as it sequences to red. There is a long, long run of cones, but it doesn't surprise them. This two-lane blacktop sees a lot of traffic, millions of cars a year, rain, shine, hail or snow. Most days there is some maintenance work being done.

The driver checks his mirror and sees there is nothing behind them. Up ahead, he can see the specks of the workmen bent over something, as if inspecting roadkill. They seem to be in his lane, so he slows. As they get closer he begins to get a strange, uneasy feeling, which he suppresses. Until, thirty yards away, he sees a guy step out with something hoisted to his shoulder. Now he has a very bad feeling indeed. He brakes hard, and reaches for the cellphone. He punches the emergency code, but the screen flashes up at him: No signal. The other guard tries his own cellphone. No signal. The driver pulls a handgun and focuses on the man in the road.

He realises that the guy has an RPG-7 rocket-launched grenade at his shoulder, the sort that was used in Vietnam, the missile capable of slicing through twelve inches of armour. It is pointing right at them. He tries the cellphone again. Nothing. He pulls the slide back on the pistol, when he notices there are now two of them in the road. The second man has a big square piece of card held at chest height. On the card is written a number. 'Ten'. The man looks the driver straight in the eye and inclines his head towards the rocket-launcher his pal is still holding rock steady. To the left is a third man, and to the right a fourth, both with automatic weapons.

The driver engages reverse and, as he starts to back up, there is a series of small explosions, rocking the truck, sending them both out of their seats as the truck slews slightly and stalls. He restarts and tries to reverse again, but there is only the sound of grinding metal as the truck judders impotently. The wheels have been blown to pieces by small impact charges.

The driver looks back at the man with the sign who now takes the top card away to reveal another underneath. This also has a number on it. 'Nine'. Then the next. 'Eight'. The guards look at each other. 'Seven'. They wouldn't dare. He sees the RPG man adjust the sights. 'Six'. They could stay put. 'Five'. The card man nods with a smile. He knows what they are thinking. Yes, we would, he seems to be saying. It is no bluff. Still no cellphone signal. 'Four'. The driver hands his pal the pistol and reaches for the shotgun, but the other just lets the pistol fall. No, he isn't going to die for the Fred Harvey Company. 'Three'. Without asking, the non-driver punches the security code that unlocks his door and dives free. 'Two'. The driver drops the shotgun and bowls out as well. 'One'.

The RPG flies on its erratic course, punches through the windshield and detonates, bowling the truck back down the road, scything open a huge section of the armoured body, starting sparking, spluttering fires, but leaving the steel money boxes inside tossed around, but unharmed.

A second rocket enlarges the hole, almost throwing the mangled beast on its side. The guards are wise enough to put their hands up, and the men tie them up and push them to the side of the road. Meanwhile, the RPG man dons thick gloves to protect his hands from the torn metal and climbs into the still-smoking truck to start removing the money boxes.

Coogan stopped the story there and took a hit of Coke. They were in a small diner halfway between The Lost Ones office in Phoenix and Tucson, and talking about ways to finance a trip to Seattle. Neither of them, it quickly transpired, had much in the way of money. But that wasn't hard to figure, as the Fed had pointed out – they wouldn't be in that trailer park if they were flush, would they?

'And then?' asked Wendy who, eyes closed, had managed to visualise every aspect of it.

'We'll come to "and then" in a minute.'

'OK, so what were the holes in Toots' plan?'

'They have cellphones in the truck. They could just sit tight and call it in.'

'So?'

'So Nash came up with a broad-band jammer – something that would screw up communication in a half-mile radius. We used them in the Rangers.'

'Really?'

'Yup.'

'What else? The getaway?'

'No, got that.'

'OK. I got one for you, Mr Ranger.'

'A what?'

'A problem with what you just told me.'

'Shoot.'

'OK, the non-verbal communication with the signs. Where is that from?'

'A Bob Dylan movie – *Don't Look Back*. Before you say it, it's before my time, too.'

'OK. It's cute. Now if you or I saw some mad fuckers with a missile pointing at us and a countdown, we know what we'd do. Right? We'd get the hell outta there. But these guys. They are company men. What if they won't get out?'

'I don't follow.'

'The driver and his pal. They stay put. Could you still fire?'

He thought of the red dust of Somalia, of skinny people running into his line of vision, the firefight as the Humvee shot its way back to base. More kids. Women. Stick men. 'By all means necessary'. 'Hell, yes,' he said.

'And you're the guy who gets nightmares about some little kid with an AK? Big macho Coogan? You'd do this – risk killin' some guy who might have a kid of his own? Look, Coogan, I got a feeling I need you, don't know why, don't know how. You're all I got for the moment. Do I want a partner who would do that? No, I don't, is the answer. I mean, thanks for the thought, and the money'd be real nice but—'

'Partner?' he interrupted.

'In the business sense.'

'Partner in what?'

'We get Pete back, you can name your price, Coogan.' There was a harsher edge to her voice now. He wondered if the soft mush inside her was starting to harden, if the hatred and despair was congealing into something solid she could work with. 'If I have to sell my ass on the Strip every night. But not this way, not the Canyon. Not murder. It damaged you once . . . this would be worse, much worse.'

Coogan thought about a widow and a fatherless child and mangled bodies lying under the Arizona sun. Killed for a payroll. Then flipped across to more fly-infested bodies lying in orange dust under a clear African sky. At least there had been something at the core of that action, something noble, something right, even if it did turn out to be misguided. The solid image of the Canyon road and the truck and the RPG he had carried with him for months now suddenly began to wobble and fade and break apart. 'You're right. I couldn't do it.'

'Nash?'

'I . . . suppose not. Something we overlooked, I guess.'

'I would've thought that after Mogadishu – was that the name? – that you'd know you can't script these things. Something always goes wrong. Someone always gets hurt.'

'Fuck,' he suddenly spat. 'It ain't easy tryin' to be Smith and Jones, is it?'

'Who?'

'*Alias Smith and Jones*? Robbed banks without killin' any . . . just how old are you?'

'Twenty-nine.'

'Well, I ain't that much older. You never watch the reruns?'

'We didn't have a TV as a kid.'

'Really?'

'Parents thought it was bad for us. Sixteen before I wore 'em down.'

'No TV as a kid? I ain't sure, but I think that's unconstitutional.'

She laughed, a proper deep laugh for the first time in what seemed like years, and had to catch herself.

'You can still do that, you know. I know it feels bad doin' it . . . like disrespectful—'

'He's not dead,' she suddenly yelled, causing other customers to throw furtive glances.

'I know, I know.'

'Well, don't talk like he is.'

'I didn't mean that. Just that while Pete might be . . . y'know, confused and lost, it doesn't seem right to laugh. But you gotta. I keep tellin' you – your best chance is to keep sharp. I remember in Somalia—'

'Coogan.' She wasn't in the mood for more Tales From Mog. 'Enough.'

'Yeah.'

'So you'd've got this big stack of money. What then? You said the beauty of this was there's only one road in and one road out. But the same applies to you.'

'That's right. A single roadblock and we're finished. What we needed was a bird. A helicopter.'

'A helicopter?'

'I know. It took me a while to get used to the idea. I still get a little sick when I see them. Makes the back go off like a motherfucker, too. But that's what it came down to. A bird. Yes. Lift us outta there. Fly north to Utah.'

'Aren't they kinda pricey?'

'What we always needed was someone who could walk into Tusayan airport and steal us one. Someone who had a grievance maybe, and would like the chance to poke them in the eye. Didn't get us one till recently.'

It took her a second to twig, and suddenly Coogan's generosity at the air park, his willingness to take on the domestic squabble, made perfect sense. He's been filling in a few more gaps in the plan. This time she laughed and didn't stop. And there she was thinking he was just trying to get in her pants. This was even more preposterous. 'Sonofabitch. Duke?'

'I knew you'd appreciate that part.'

THIRTY-ONE

New York State

Belle stopped at the doorway to the kid's room and listened. She could hear voices, soft, gentle voices and suppressed laughter. It made a change. The atmosphere in the rest of the house was dour, like some ultra-gloomy production of *Macbeth*. She couldn't believe Mamie and Morgan were going to go through with the baby dump. But part of her would be glad to see the back of the kid, too.

She hesitated a little longer then went in. Tommy and Pete were kneeling down, playing with a couple of GI Joe figures, one dressed in a spacesuit, the other in ninja garb. The smiles froze on their faces as they looked up.

'Tommy.'

'I was lonely.'

'Me too,' said Pete.

'How'd you get in?'

'The door wasn't locked. And he's not really ill, Mom. Just a bit homesick, I think. I don't think that's courageous.'

Shit, she must have forgotten to re-lock after delivering breakfast. 'Contagious,' she corrected.

'Do you really have to have new parents?' asked Tommy. 'Pete says you said that you have to change them. Will I have to change you?'

Belle looked at the pair of them side by side, the generic young Americans, fair-haired, healthy, cute and she felt herself sag. Jesus, maybe she should keep them both.

'Only sometimes, Tommy. Pete here is going to a good home. It'll just be strange for a while, that's all.'

'Can I ask you something?'

Why did kids always do this? Ask if they can ask a question when in the same space of time they could have gone ahead and asked it. 'Go ahead.'

'Can I still see him? With his new folks?'

'I . . . maybe.'

'Cool.'

'You wanna play with the Nintendo?' asked Pete

'Yeah—'

'Tommy, no. Pete and I have to talk.'

'Aw.'

'Tommy.'

'It's not fair.'

'Tommy. I will count to five. if you are not out of here by then, you can forget ever seeing Pete again. One. Two. Three—'

At that half-speed shuffle that all kids seem to master instinctively – the one that says: I'm going, but I don't like it one bit – Tommy shuffled past her and clomped noisily down the stairs. Belle looked at Pete and smiled. He smiled back nervously. Poor kid, she thought. Maybe Mamie was right. Maybe we have become monsters.

When they got back from The Lost Ones, there was a flurry of messages on the answerphone, from the Sheriff's department and the FBI and one from a caseworker with MCHC and two newspaper reporters. Coogan advised talking to the latter. Anything to get publicity, anything that might jog someone's memory. She replied to all the calls then went across to tell him. Just as she was at his door, it hit her, a great wave of clarity, pin-sharp and painful, the sheer scale of the undertaking. Finding her son in a vast, vast country.

Coogan recognised it as soon as he opened the door, and jerked her inside. He made some coffee, and sat down next to her. 'You know,' she said quietly, 'I prefer being numb. It's when the numbness goes that it hurts. The rest of the time . . .'

'It's your brain. Self-narcoticising. Until it thinks you're ready. I should know.'

She pointed at his map on the wall, the one covered with a rash of red dots. 'Look at it. Look. It's huge. My boy is out there somewhere. My poor little boy. He could be where any of those dots are. Anywhere.'

'You know that thing about three degrees of separation? Or is it six? That everyone really knows everyone else, but is just a few steps removed. Like the Kevin Bacon game? Look at those dots, you join 'em up and you have a network, like an airline map, covering the whole country. Well, there's a little gap in Nebraska there. If we can get enough people interested in Pete, if we can cover the country like that, a kind of national network, it won't be so . . . intimidating.'

'What are those dots?'

'I told you. Places where I . . . places where I fucked up.'

'That's a lot of fuck-ups.'

'I'm good at it,' he caught himself. He didn't want to hint that he was the jinx here, the one who caused the dark finger to point at Pete. He had to tell himself that wasn't it. It was *lucky* he was here. Not the opposite. Please, God, not the opposite.

'I'm sorry. I think I'll go lie down.'

'Yeah. Look, I'll cook up some food. Come over with it. Rice'n'beans. 'Bout all I can manage. And don't give me that "not hungry" shit. OK?'

He had to help, he felt like shouting, had to feel he had a positive role in this.

She looked at him funny. 'OK.'

Coogan opened his guitar case and took out the Gibson after she was gone. He plugged it into the Mesa-Boogie, set it low, played a few bars of 'Goodbye Pork Pie Hat', real slow, letting each note sound and hang in the air, like cigarette smoke in a jazz club. He was sorry he'd missed his gig now. He was just about to lay it down when he heard her knock again. 'Coogan.'

'Yeah?'

'I got a message.'

'Who from?'

'Them.' Her voice was wobbly, reedy.

'Them?'

'The kidnappers. Abductors, whatever.'

He dropped the guitar into the garish furry womb of its case and hurried out to listen.

Agent Slight took out his notebook and read the scribbled notes. 'OK. I think I got everything. I asked the office to run a check with the phone company.'

'Can you trace it?' Coogan pointed at the recording device they had put on the phone, nothing more than a high-quality answering-machine.

'Thing is, you see all that shit about traces in the movies? Now everything is computerised, you can always do a trace. Problem is, local calls, there's so much traffic they can take up to a week. Long distance is real fast.'

'So this was long distance?' asked Wendy.

'We'll see. If it's from a cellphone, well we might have some luck. If they didn't block the caller-number function, we can not only get a trace but a fix. Big city? We'll know from the relay stations, to within a few hundred yards, where they made the call.'

'And if it is blocked?'

'Well . . .' said Slight, 'I don't wanna get your hopes up, but remember this is the wonderful world of itemised billing.' He pointed at the phone. 'Somewhere out there that number is on a bill. You might get lucky.'

His own cellphone went and he answered, his face getting grimmer as the call proceeded. 'OK, they got it. Real quick – the phone company's apparently set it up to ID out all incoming numbers. The bad news is it's in New York City. A payphone.'

'New York? *New York?*' Wendy's voice went up an octave. 'Pete's in New York?'

'Not necessarily. The caller was in New York. It's also possible it was routed through New York by someone who knew about telecommunications. Or they could've got an accomplice to make the call, just to throw us off the scent. You see?'

What Coogan could see was that Wendy had made a small pile of Pete's clothes, freshly ironed and washed, as if he would be coming in. It was heartbreaking to him, God alone knew how it felt to Wendy.

'Can I hear it again? The message?' asked Slight.

She nodded and he hit the repeat button. There was a pause, a long one, where the caller seemed to be summoning up the courage to speak. When she did it was breathy, rushed, almost panted out. 'Your boy. He'll be fine. Don't worry. He'll be. Well looked after. You have my word. We're sorry.'

Slight looked at Wendy and he could see the new light in her eyes. And he smiled at her. He had to hope that it wasn't a hoax, some sick bastard of a woman who, ultimately, would make the suffering far, far worse by giving false hope.

'It means he's alive, doesn't it?'

Slight said: 'It probably does. Just don't . . . just don't let go of that word "probably". We get strange things happening. Someone reads about it in the newspapers—'

'It's not in the newspapers yet.'

'It's on the net,' he reminded her, and watched her deflate slightly. 'But it could be genuine. I'm gonna take the tape and get it voice analysed. So if anyone calls again, we'll know if it was the same person. But—' Jesus, there was no easy way to put this. He took a deep breath. 'Let's say it is genuine. It doesn't sound like a ransom demand is coming.'

'So?'

Slight sat down next to her. No easy way to say this. 'So . . . maybe they plan to keep Pete.'

Coogan stood staring at his map and started peeling off the dots. Time to wipe the slate clean. Start again. That was what the Canyon had been about. Another mission with the boys. Do it right this time. Show the world that Rangers are more than bumbling amateurs. It wasn't really about the money. Now he realised he had another task. She needed a partner. She said it. Someone to be there for her. Admit it, Coogan, go on. You like her. Yeah, I like her. And you can help. Yeah, I can help. Will help. How, he wasn't sure. Somehow that had yet to be written.

He thought about the phone call from Isa, and the information that she had some former agent on the case. He took the last spot off the map, rolled himself a joint and put on some Stevie Ray Vaughan. He and Isa had been a three-month red-hot tussle. He hadn't been back from the army that long, had gone to see what was happening in Seattle.

What was happening was that everyone and their dog had a band. So there were gigs, even if they didn't pay shit. Isa had come along to one at the OK Hotel and he had spotted her. Then again the next night at Colour Box. Then at Crocodile Cafe. So he had spoken to her and she told him she dug axemen. Great. It was two weeks before he found out what she did. Didn't matter, he told himself. Ex-army, he was establishment too. But it did matter. Cops were worse than army for sticking together, turned out. Like being at war every day. No room for civilians, especially not a stoned, drunk guitarist with a bad back.

He mapped out the drive to New York City. More than two and a half thousand miles. Four days. Back when he was putting dots on a map, when he had all the time in the world, it seemed like nothing. He'd drive for twenty-four hours just to sit in at a gig that wouldn't cover his gas money. But four days of crossing the country, counting telegraph poles, the rhythm of their passing mirroring the constant rap of thoughts about Pete. It was too long. He'd have to fly. Which meant money. And there was only one way he knew to get money. It was going to be difficult, gut-wrenching, but as the woman said: 'By all means necessary.'

THIRTY-TWO

The Margaret Henley Federal Recuperation Facility, Virginia

Ernie Shepard sat in the big recreation room, listening to the sound of ping-pong balls rattling across green tables, and the satisfying thunk of pool balls and thought, once again, that the Federal Recuperation Facility was, in many ways, cruelly located. From the picture window he could see the rolling hills of Virginia, covered with grass as soft as down, an almost English scene. In the distance a couple of horses pranced in a field, occasionally breaking into a lazy canter, their heads back, manes flying, a little display designed, he was sure to taunt him and some of his fellow inhabitants of the centre. Hey guys, they seemed to be saying, don't you wish your legs worked like this?

Two years previously on the third of July – probably because the building was closed on the fourth – some fruitcake who had a deportation order against him had driven a small imported Japanese van between the planters on Federal Plaza in New York City intending to crash the front of the centre and detonate the fertiliser bomb he had in the back. The planters, which had been put in place in the wake of Oklahoma City, jammed the vehicle tight. So he detonated it anyway. The blast shattered the front of the building, caving in the glass, causing surprisingly few deaths – the only Federal Agent who died was Margaret Henley – but a remarkable number of serious injuries. In the aftermath the money was raised for a new facility to treat any Federal employees – after all, there were a dozen different agencies in the building on Broadway – who suffered severe damage while on duty.

It was nice, but it was a bit too near Quantico for Shepard's liking – the FBI guys treated the place like it was their outfit, and the others were here on sufferance. Well, they always did have an elitist opinion of themselves, and a low one of other agencies, like his ATF.

He span his wheelchair round and looked at who else was in the room. There were about a dozen, half of them, like him, confined to chairs. One of the two pool tables had been cut down to facilitate the paraplegics. Those who could walk were damaged in a variety of other ways – blindness, missing limbs, impaired co-ordination. All human suffering was here. Shepard wondered how many of them had lost their partners, as he had in a bloody, pointless gunfight on the Jersey Shore and, along with their physical scars, had to tussle with the guilt of being the one who survived. His trauma counsellor had explained it all, made him read Primo Levi, but it hadn't really helped assuage the feeling of responsibility. Not when you read that little postscript about Levi topping himself. Some recommended text, guys.

There had been some new arrivals recently, he knew, but neither were in the day room. One guy was on crutches, waiting for his artificial limb, his scars still fresh and livid, both externally and, judging from his eyes, internally. That one could move around, but chose not to. And there was another case, down the hall from him, a DEA officer who had uncovered a trade in police weapons in Baltimore and been shot twenty-six times. Rumour was he was virtually hollow and nobody knew how he had survived. Maybe it was the will to tell the world that the perpetrators – if the rec room scuttlebutt was to be believed – had been police officers.

Shepard's own time here was nearly through, he knew. The counsellors had done all they could, physiotherapy had given him back the use of both hands, and one and a half arms. But the legs were gone forever. He had sold his apartment – stairs, no elevator, no use to him now – and had a place in Silver Lake converted so he could use his wheelchair. Say what you like about his employers – and plenty of people here lived solely to bitch about them – they looked after their fallen.

One of the staff, Miss Holmes, came over to him, a big solidly built woman. He wondered if they chose the personnel for maximum blandness – all the women seemed asexual, something he was grateful for. He didn't need reminding any further about his other impaired functions.

'Agent? You got a call. Want to take it next door?'

Agent. He liked that. Everybody here got to keep that title, just like ex-Presidents were always Mr President until their demise. It was a way of pretending they were still on the job, still had some use, when, in truth, none of them would see the field again. A few might make it back to a desk. A very lucky few. For most of them, their crime-busting days were over.

He wheeled himself out of the recreation room and into the small office that was adjacent. Miss Holmes closed the door behind him to give him some privacy. There was a small observation panel in the wall where he could still see the former agents trying hard to fill their days.

'Hello?'

'Ernie?'

'Yes?'

'It's Isa. Isa Bowman. Seattle?'

'Hey – it's just my legs not working, not my brain. Although my spleen's gone too. Although I find I haven't missed that. Make you wonder, huh? Did you really need it in the first place? Hey – how are you?'

'I'm great. Listen, I've got this problem. I'm gonna e-mail it to you. You mind?' He said he didn't and, as she explained everything on her mind, Shepard stared through the little window, watching a guy on crutches try to fight with another wheelchair-bound guy. They swung and poked at each other, but the metal and wood just kept getting in the way of what a manly fight should look like. By the time Miss Holmes got over they had collapsed in helpless laughter at their utter uselessness.

'So you know the father?'

'No. He's a friend.'

'Of yours?'

'No. Well, yes. Kinda. He's not the kid's father anyways. He's an old boyfriend if you really wanna know. Ernie? Ernie? You there?'

'Yeah.' Flat, disappointed. How old, he wondered? Pre- or post-him?

'Look . . . I'm sorry I never got down to see you.'

'Me too.'

'I . . . I'm changin' departments, going on the admin side for a while. So I can get some vacation squeezed in there. Would you wanna see me now?'

He pictured on the other end of the phone, an image that dissolved to the days spent with Isa in bed, a sheet wrapped around her, a cigarette in her mouth, laughing so hard the headboard was shaking. 'Yeah.'

She noticed the distraction, as if his mind was elsewhere. 'A little enthusiasm might just convince me.'

'What? No, Isa. Yes. Really. It'd be . . . it'd be great.' But not as great as what is happening down here, he thought. 'Please.'

'OK, I'll get some dates. And I'll e-mail you the full spec on the case.'

'And I'll try and fit it into my busy schedule. Thanks, Isa. I'll see ya.'

The whoop he made as he put the receiver down made everyone in the rec room stop dead. For the first time since the firefight, the one where his partner ended up impaled in a car wreck, Ernie Shepard had himself a genuine, full-on boner.

Hoek watched the diseased-looking yellow container descend slowly from the belly of the overhead gantry, wondering how the people inside felt. He turned to Mason and asked, 'How many?'

'We got payment for fifteen.'

'Men? Women?'

'Four women, eleven men.' He sniffed, a horrible pig-like sound. 'How you think they all get on banged up like that for a week? You think they share them around?'

Hoek ignored the question. 'Listen, Mason, as of next week I will not be here for the remainder of the contracted shipments. We are making other arrangements.'

'No?' Mason tried not to sound pleased.

'No. But here is what is going to happen. Schmee here will meet every shipment. Sort the women. The men – you listening to me?' The container had touched down now, and Mason's men were unclipping the shackles, ready for opening. 'The men, Schmee will photograph with a digital camera and send the images to me. Got it? They don't move on until I have seen all the faces on my computer. Is that clear?'

'Yes, Mr Hoek. Crystal.'

The doors opened and the expected blast of fetid air came out, although this time with a strong chemical component. Good, Hoek thought. They dealt with the sanitation. The usual assortment of pale, gaunt figures appeared, shuffling and blinking into the New World. He indicated to Szento to pull the women to one side, and take them in the shuttle bus over to the club. Hoek looked at Schmee who shook his head. No prime candidates for the stage there. Mason knew the drill. He pushed the compliant men into a single file, and indicated they march past Hoek one by one.

As they approached he looked at them hard. Some stared back, their sunken, dark-rimmed eyes defiant or confused, and many unbelieving, convinced that the journey was going to end in disaster. Well, in many ways it would for them, because they had entered the country at the very lowest level of the pecking order, to be exploited and abused, with the fear of exposure as illegals crushing down on them a little harder each day.

Hoek crossed them off one at a time. Too old. Too young. Too tall. Too blond. Too . . . too nothing. This one couldn't help himself. As he came level the face turned away, as casually as he could manage, as if the rusty brown metal boxes in the corner were suddenly the most interesting thing in the world. And as he did so Hoek could see that face in another place, on top of Marta, the mouth biting at what little flesh was left on her bones, like he was carrion stripping a carcass.

He bellowed at Schmee who stepped over and grabbed the man's arm, marching him out of line. Lazar was no longer the big, beefy soldier he once had been – after all he had been living on starvation rations for a week or more, and Hoek's forearm smash sent him down to the floor.

Schmee stepped back, frozen like all the others, wondering how the show was going to end. Hoek had the knife in his hand, flipped out the blade and grabbed the bristly, unshaven face. The wicked hook at the end of the blade was at the skin, already a globule of blood forming under its point. All he had to do was guide it in, hooking under the carotid artery, then pull out, popping both carotid and jugular, and watch that rich, thick, gush of blood spread itself over the stained concrete of the harbourside. He turned the face to get one last look at the eyes. The jolt hit him in the chest. It wasn't right. It wasn't him.

Whoever he was, this man was not Lazar Gllogvijc, had never violated his wife. Now Hoek would have to stand up and brush himself down and explain that he was beginning to have hallucinations. That he had made a mistake. But then, again, whoever this stinking creature was, the one now shitting himself beneath him, he was sure he had done something terrible in his life. They all had. Why else would they be here, like this? The decision made he pushed the blade home and pulled outwards, feeling the life-giving tubes rupture beneath the blade.

THIRTY-THREE

Bloomsberry, New Jersey

'You're leaving too?' Jim was standing on Dick's doorstep, a six-pack in his hand, waiting for the invitation to enter. Dick stepped aside and waved him through. The place was a mess. Books had been thrown on the floor, not in neat orderly piles, but as if an arm had swept along shelves, scattering them on the floor. CDs were similarly thrown at random, some of them cracked where they had been trodden underfoot. The drapes were still drawn, even though it was early afternoon. It was more like a burglary than packing.

Dick closed the door. He sniffed. He had a bad cold coming on, one of those bugs that come out to play whenever your body is run down and vulnerable. 'Leavin'? I feel like I'm a leper here. Don't you?'

Jim shrugged. 'It was me who . . . made contact with the kid. You think you got it bad?'

'Yeah, like these people bother to read the fine print as to who did what. We're both guilty in their eyes. I thought this was a nice, friendly liberal town. I suppose killin' their kids brings out the worst in people. Can I have one of those?'

'What?' Jim looked down at the six-pack. 'Oh sure.' He broke two off and they pulled the tabs and drank. 'What's on your mind?'

'Everything.'

'You called.'

'Yeah. Sebastyen. He's been in touch.'

'With you?'

Dick nodded. 'Said he wanted to speak to someone he didn't have the urge to strangle.'

'Oh great.' Jim involuntarily reached for his throat.

'I tried to tell him we had joint responsibility—'

'Forget that shit. He doesn't believe it, that's all that matters. I'm America's Most Wanted as far as he is concerned. Can I get some light in here?' He pulled the drapes across and saw Dick blink, as if unaccustomed to the light. Maybe the guy was turning vampire on him.

'Thing is. He wants the boy. He's leavin' this weekend. Friday night he said. Or . . . he said you know what will happen.'

Jim nodded.

Dick waited for the fireworks, the gnashing of teeth, but Jim just stood there calmly, as if Dick had told him a bowling date had changed. 'Jim. What are you going to do?'

'Exactly what he says, Dick. Exactly what he says.'

Ernie Shepard had a fantasy. It was a very simple one. It was a parking lot in Cotchford New Jersey. Behind him a burning truck and a diner sizzled in the rain. Two mangled cars were stacked together, and from the door of one of them hung Alice, his partner, impaled on the metal corner. Dead.

He was walking across the lot, his shattered legs still working then, blood coming from his nostrils and a big gash on his face, and ahead of him two men were getting out of a car. So far, so like real life.

But in the fantasy he raised the Colt SMG and took a bead on the two men and squeezed the trigger. They didn't have a chance. A stream of slugs tore into them, pulping flesh and bone, opening up arteries and capillaries and veins, dumping litres and litres of blood into the downpour, turning the sidewalks a lurid frothy pink.

Instead, on the actual night in question, he'd played it by the book. He'd told them he was an armed Federal Officer. He had tried to keep them there, covered, until help arrived. But he'd been betrayed. His treacherous, pitiful body had let him down, blacking out from the pain, and the two of them had pumped their own bullets into him, leaving him for dead in the puddles, slowly darkening with blood seeping from a body that, by rights, should have offered up its soul there and then.

The two men had disappeared from New Jersey after that. Well, not before they had carried out another double homicide down in Atlantic City. One of the pair, Brownie, he knew was dead. Heart attack. Fast exit. Too fast. When it came to retribution, there really was no God. Brownie should have died from something slow and nasty, haunted by the faces of his victims, something positively Shakespearian. Instead he dropped down dead when his horse came in 100-1 at Saratoga.

One down, one to go, and when he got out of here, the first thing he was going to do was organise the search for the other one. OK, it wouldn't be easy in a wheelchair. Which is why he had honed his computer skills, because there were databases out there the average Joe couldn't dream of. America was like a big thermal imaging pad now, wherever you went, whatever you did, you left a little blip, like a drop of sweat, glowing hot. Unless you unplugged from the rest of the society, there really was no hiding place, as long as the hunter knew where to look. And if that failed? Fuck it, he would get wheeling. If Raymond Burr could do it, so could he. For Vincent Wuzel – that was the name he dreamt of every night – there really would be no hiding place.

Richard Paladin sorted through the latest clippings while he slurped at a spicy bean soup in the Cuban restaurant, separating the news stories into three piles – no, interesting and yes. All concerned something to do with kids or reproductions. Stories of States banning egg donation or restricting the fees or clamping down on surrogate motherhood – stories which meant more business his way – others of abusive mothers, adoptions gone right or wrong, anything that might impinge on the child business. Or childless business to be precise.

It was number eight in the pile and he sent a spew of soup across the table, choking as he did so. It was big, page three. The story of Bethany, as the hospital had named her, a young baby abandoned along with a note saying the parents couldn't cope. But he knew Bethany. Bethany was one of his, and last he'd heard Bethany was Ariel and in New York State. Had to be. He hadn't handled that many Mexican babies. The same people who had put Belle onto him without permission had now decided to give up their kid. And they still owed him over a thousand dollars. What did that make them? That made them loose cannons. And there was only one way to deal with loose cannons. He had to de-commission them. Fast.

Shepard logged on with the Apple he kept in his bedroom and checked his e-mails. Nothing new. He had put an appeal out on G-Web, and also performed some geographical mapping on a number of sites that stored crime statistics. But what he really needed was access to some of the bigger players, government computers and files, stuff that was covered by data protection, and technically beyond his reach. Thing was, he didn't want to let Isa down. Not at this stage, not when they had made contact, might see each other.

He went out into the corridor and down into the main recreation area. It was still early, most of the other inhabitants were still tussling with their own sleep demons. He rinsed out the coffee pot in the specially lowered sink, and brewed up a fresh batch. That old habit of shooting the breeze around the pot, a staple of every Federal office, still survived even in here. OK, they no longer had a shared agenda, similar cases, because there were people here from every Federal outfit – DEA, Customs, Treasury, FBI, ATF, Immigration . . . everywhere – but it gave the place a focal point.

John Cohen, a tall, rangy FBI guy who had recently lost

an arm came in and nodded. He poured a cup, then, realising Shepard hadn't helped himself, did a second and handed it over. 'You OK?'

'Yeah. Fine.'

'You don't sound fine.'

Suddenly Shepard said, 'How'd you lose your arm?'

Cohen looked down at the stump, as if surprised to see the limb gone. 'Truck ran over it.'

'Accident then?'

Some guy had knocked me to the ground, out cold, then reversed over me. Accident? I guess not.'

'What were you working?'

'Robbery.'

'Oh.'

'Why?'

'I just wondered if there was a missing persons expert in here.'

'Oh, I did some time on that. Abduction. So did Lamarq I think. You lost someone?'

'Friend.'

Cohen raised his eyebrows, assuming that Shepard's lover or wife had left her man because of his disability.

'I mean a friend has lost someone. Little boy. Five. Snatched in Arizona by a coupla phony Feds. Been a call from New York City.'

'Ransom?'

'No. That's what is so weird. Just a message saying the kid would be fine.'

Cohen kicked a chair over and sat down to be on Shepard's level. He lowered his voice: 'You try G-Web?'

'Got a leads appeal out.'

'It can be slow. People don't log on every day. You know – you ever thought about this place?'

'What? Here? This facility?'

'Yeah,' Cohen leant forward, even more conspiratorially. 'You

307

ever thought about how many disciplines there are in here?
Almost every goddamn Federal agency.'

'Yeah, I was just thinkin'. DEA—'

'Treasury—'

'The Bureau.'

Cohen nodded vigorously. 'So what if you sat everyone down
and said: This is the case.'

'What?'

'Maybe even get your friend over here. The one who lost the
kid? Imagine if twenty, thirty Federal agents – bored Federal
agents – gave the case a work-out. And think how many favours
we'd be able to pull in. We all got two, three friends or partners
still doing their time, yeah? Some of whom feel real guilty about
us being here. So suddenly there's maybe eighty of us. It'll be
like that old film – *The League of Gentlemen.*'

' "The League of Cripples" more like.'

'Hey – you don't need your legs for this one. It's an idea I
been kickin' around. What do you think?'

Shepard let the idea bounce around his mind, thinking about
those two guys fighting out of sheer frustration in this very room.
He looked at his watch. Still the middle of the night in Seattle. He
could e-mail her though. 'So let me get this straight? You think
we should offer the services of a hospital to the mother?'

'Uh-huh.'

'It's the stupidest idea I heard in a long time,' he finally said.
'Let's do it.'

'He's not ready,' Belle barked down the line.

'He's gotta be ready.'

'Well, he's not. I need more time.'

'You ain't got more time,' Jim said as firmly as he could.

'Where is it going to happen?'

'Underneath the Interstate. Just outside town.'

'Jesus. He still . . . he still talks about his mom. Wendy.
Sebastyen'll know.'

'What can I say? You'll have to drug him.'

'Damn, Jim, I . . . I'm not sure about this.'

Jim furrowed his brow. After days of being Iron Jill, to hear her wavering was completely alien.

'OK, give Tommy over,' he suggested sarcastically. 'Keep the new one.'

'F'Christ's sake.'

'You've come this far. We only got two choices. Or have you started preferring this kid to our boy?'

'*No.* No. It's just they are so alike. It's like I'm really giving Tommy away.'

'In which case Sebastyen will be real happy. I gotta go. Dick says he's gonna get more information tonight.'

'Right. Jesus . . . if I had a week. He's a bright kid. Free associates all the time. But . . . yeah, OK.' She yawned.

'How you sleepin' with little Miss Lungs over there?'

There was a snort. And Belle shook her head in something that could have been disgust.

'What? Ariel? You gettin' any shut eye?'

'They dumped her yesterday.'

He felt his voice go croaky. 'Dumped her?'

'Well, they left her where she could be found. Warm and safe, they said. With a note. I tell you, you never saw two happier people. That's what I call ironic. Jim? You there?'

Coogan knocked on the door, and waited for Wendy to get it. When she appeared she had a robe wrapped around her, her hair had been quickly combed and there was some colour in her cheeks. She looked better than she had for a couple of days.

As he came inside he asked: 'You get some sleep?'

'A little. Just knowin' he's alive. It helps. I'd been thinkin' about . . . all these ditches and shallow graves . . .'

'Yeah. Like the man said, I hope it's not . . .' he hesitated.

Talk about raining on parades. 'I think it is. No, I do. Really. Any more calls?'

She shook her head.

'I got one.' He explained the Bowman conversation, and the idea that they should stop off at some kind of asylum in Virginia.

'Asylum?' she asked. 'What, like, for you know, loonies?'

'Asylum was the wrong word. Where you go to get better. Sanatorium?'

'Convalescence?'

'Yeah, kinda convalescence. Isa tells me her friend tells her they got all sorta hotshots banged up in there with nothing to do all day but wait to get better. The idea is we give them something to chew on.'

'What do you think?'

He shrugged. 'If we drive to New York, we could stop off.'

'Drive?'

'In the Trans Am.'

'Oh.' She couldn't help looking worried at the thought of the car.

'We could fly if you want.'

'I . . . you . . .' She said suddenly, 'Coogan, you don't have to come.'

'Oh I do. I'm the banker.' He took the money from his jeans pocket and threw it down on the couch. 'Six grand. Not much, but enough to start a war chest.'

'Six grand?'

'I know, it ain't quite the Grand Canyon payroll, but it's better than what we had.'

'No, I didn't mean that.' She looked at him long and hard, and he felt himself squirming. 'Where did you get . . . Ohmigod. You didn't . . . I won't let you. Coogan. I can't.'

'Too late. It's done.'

She came over and kissed him.

He nodded. 'Now we're both in the same boat. Now we both lost our babies.'

Except his was sitting gleaming and freshly polished in a pawnshop window with a price tag and a twenty-eight-day limit on it.

THIRTY-FOUR

Outskirts of Bloomsberry, New Jersey

The commuter traffic was rumbling thirty feet above their heads when they pulled up the car. They had driven exactly one point three miles down the old farm track that ran parallel to the freeway and come across the dark mouth of a tunnel that ran at right angles beneath the elevated road. Jim was puzzled as to its purpose until he stepped out and saw the churned-up ground. It was to allow a free flow of cattle between the two big fields the freeway had bisected in its haste to get the cars from Manhattan and into New Jersey as quickly as possible. There were no animals in evidence in the field today, just a patch of empty green sloping upwards to a small clump of trees.

He studied those for a minute, screwing up his eyes into the low sun, wondering if he was being observed from there. No matter. But now he regretted putting Morgan's pistol, the little Ruger, into the glove box. Fetching it might be a little too obvious. Mind you, he had to be honest, the thought of him getting into a gunfight was little short of ludicrous. Truth was, he really was a soft New Yorker. If he'd been a red-necked Texan or some Montana cowboy, then maybe he could turn into Dirty Harry. But then, maybe he wouldn't be in this shit in the first place if that had been the case.

The instructions were clear. Just the three of them. They were to drive out here, he and Belle and the boy, and park opposite the tunnel. It was a perfect spot, hidden from passing traffic, which was obviously raised up into the air, and anyone trying to follow – cops for instance – would have trouble hiding themselves in this open space.

The boy was listless. He had thrown a body-rolling feet-kicking tantrum when they had told him what was going to happen – or at least, a sanitised version of events. Jim had figured if you could get kids to believe in Santa Claus and the Tooth Fairy, then the concept of parent transference couldn't be hard to sell them. He was clearly wrong. They had resorted to a hefty dose of anti-histamines, the kind parents use to dope children for long flights. It kept him woozy and compliant. He was even answering to Tommy now and then, and Belle had a cover story – she would tell Sebastyen that they had tried to get him used to being called Petyr, hence the confusion. That should muddy the waters.

Mind you, Belle had done a good job of fucking things up their end as well. When she told him about the phone call he became incandescent. OK, it was payphone, not a cellphone or a domestic landline, and it was one sentence, and she had driven all the way into the city to make it, but if they could trace it, they'd know at least which coast they were on. Belle, it turned out, still believed that thing from the movies where you had to recite a Norman Mailer novel down a phone before they could get a fix.

He motioned for them to get out and join him, and she half dragged the kid over to his side, an achingly small suitcase in her other hand. All his worldly goods, and all new, no character even imprinted on them yet. The evening sun was warm on Jim's face, everything moving to a glorious happy orange glow, the kind that made you want to sit in a yard with a cold one and let the soft, fuzzy darkness fold around you. That was what they should be doing, he figured. Not this crap.

He thought about Tommy, safe back with Morgan and Mamie. It could be worse. He could be giving him up.

He heard a squawk, a quick stab of electronics. They looked at each other. It repeated, and Jim saw that hanging by a cord, maybe seven feet above the ground, was a small, black rubberised Motorola handset, one of those limited-range walkie-talkies that kids love. He walked over through the slimy surface, whipped up by a thousand bovine feet into a mud meringue, jumped up, and on the third attempt managed to unleash it from the nail.

He held it to his mouth and said, 'Hello?' then pressed the button with an ear on it.

'Ah, Mr Barry. Glad you could make it.'

The voice was unfamiliar, the accent different. 'Sebastyen?'

'No, Mr Barry. Mr Sebastyen couldn't be here himself. But do not worry, I have his full authority in all matters. Now, I hope that, as we demanded, you are all alone. Very good. However, if you could just open the trunk and all the doors of the car, just in case you have some extra baggage we cannot see.'

Again Jim looked around, wondering where the voice was coming from, where the prying eyes would be located. In the meantime he did as he was told, leaving the car looking like an automotive flasher, and kept listening.

'Good. Good. All clear, then. Now, Mr Barry, this exchange is very simple. Mrs Barry and the boy will walk through the tunnel. To the other side. You will stay where you are. We will take the boy, Mrs Barry will walk back. Does he understand what is going on?'

'We had to give him a sedative. He isn't crazy about this. He is likely to be confused.'

'Of course. We have every intention of treating him well, Mr Barry. Better than you ever could.'

Jim felt his anger start to bubble at the implied slight, but suppressed it. This wasn't his kid. It didn't matter. Don't rise to any bait.

A snapped 'Who the fuck are you?' was his way of relieving the pressure.

'Me? Not important. Now, if Mrs Barry will come. Kvickly.'

German, he thought. This one is German. He nodded at Belle, who took the boy's limp hand and started to lead him.

Pete tugged back, then started to lean his body at an angle of forty-five degrees. His feet dug into the mud, creating a sludgy wake as Belle tugged at him.

'Noooooooooo,' he shouted. 'I want my—'

Jim clipped him around the head, hard, cutting the giveaway sentence short, replacing it with a wild piercing scream. The radio crackled. 'What are you doing?'

'He doesn't want to come.'

'Make him, Mr Barry. We don't have all evening.'

He bent down and took the boy by the upper arms and shook him. 'Listen, listen. Unless you do this you will never see your mommy again. Never. Understand? We are going to leave you with some nice people, who will look after you, and, maybe, one day, your mommy will come visit with you. Would you like that?'

He started to sob, the corners of his mouth turned down like a clown's, but he also managed a nod and a little, long-drawn-out: 'Yeeesssss.'

'OK, Pete, Pete. I'm sorry I hit you. I didn't mean anything. Now I know this is strange, but it will be all right in the end. I promise. Look, I brought this.' He took out the model of a red 1955 Ferrari he had seen him pushing back and forth with Tommy. He'd get Tommy another. The boy grabbed it hungrily, and the sobbing reduced to a chest-wobbling sniff and hiccup combo. 'Good. There'll be lots more of those where you are going. OK?'

He watched the pair of them walk off towards the gloomy passageway, him shuffling behind, one hand in hers, the other clutching the car to his chest. Belle had packed new t-shirts, trousers and sweaters – the thought of giving him Tommy's cast-offs was just too cruel. He'd laughed at that. As if what they were doing was anything other than extreme torture, for the boy and his doubtless distraught mother. Still, if what Belle had said about her was true, maybe this really was a fresh start for the kid, a leg-up in the world. But what kind of world?

'Get back in the car Mr Barry and wait.' He shut the doors and trunk of the Lexus and sat in the passenger side.

They were twenty yards into the tunnel when they stopped and seemed to negotiate something, then continued, silhouettes now. And at the far end he could see some smaller figures moving, the reception committee. He hoped Belle had the sense to just hand over the kid and sprint back. He just wanted to be away, far away from all this.

She reached the two men in the other field, and the four shapes merged into one amorphous blob. He could see Belle move back, heading towards the tunnel and stop. There was a shout. He leaned his head out of the car so he could hear the voices, but he couldn't catch the words. But the tone was there. Someone was angry.

Shit, they'd guessed.

He shuffled over behind the wheel and had re-started the car when the Motorola on the passenger seat came to life. He pressed the ear symbol, the tone feigning regret and sadness. 'Mr Barry, Mr Barry. Counterfeit goods.'

He looked through the tunnel again, and there were now two groups of silhouettes, one with the boy, another more fluid, its black shape shifting, as arms and legs shot out. The struggle was brief, and he could see one form go limp.

'Don't worry, Mr Barry. How about we take Mrs Barry and call it quits? At least we know *she* is the genuine article.'

He had engaged drive on the shift, still staring at the shadow puppets down the tube, when he saw the flash. There was a metallic slap as the bullet careered along the Lexus's roof, and instinctively he ducked. By the time he came back up there was an empty stage, bright and clear at the far end of the underpass.

He felt the wheels spin as he reversed to face the tunnel, his mind racing, trying to figure out what he would do when he got to the other side. He managed to get the car turned, and reached across for the revolver in the glove compartment, but the front screeched onto the edge of the concrete wall as he lost a little control, buckling the metal. He let go and straightened, feeling the car fishtail on the churned, slippy surface of the passageway, catching the walls of the bore with the fender, sending up a spray of sparks like a cutting wheel. Fuck the car.

He accelerated towards daylight and the sudden, unexpected impact threw him forward. He banged his head on the windshield, blinking as lights exploded in his vision. The car stalled. It had skewed and wedged itself into the tunnel. Something had stopped it dead. He managed to open the door, hearing it ping as it did so, and looked at the low metal bar that had been cemented a foot from the floor. The bar he had seen them negotiate on their walk through.

Jim reached over, grabbed the Ruger, squeezed by the front of the car and started to run, aware of the chest-throbbing rumble of the traffic up above, chanting to himself, 'Dirty Harry, Dirty Harry,' like he was cheering on his favourite team. But then another sound cut in, and the air around him started to hum and whine, and he could feel something slapping against his face. The whole tube was suddenly filled with noise, assaulting his eardrums, screeching up towards the pain threshold. His pace was slowed down by the lack of grip underfoot, and from the smell he realised what it was, a mixture of mud and cow shit, slowly liquefying to a foul goo in the darkness.

Still the noise grew until he had to clench his jaw and squint to try to diminish the agony, but then he skidded into the open, blinking, and looking at the source of the noise as it lifted off, taking Belle and the boy with it.

He raised to fire the gun, but they were clearly expecting him and the hot line of fiery pain across his cheek sent him diving back inside, where he slipped and fell into the sludge, and the cold, foul wetness soaked straight through his shirt, the gun skidding off away from him. He cursed loudly, his voice amplifying impotently in the pipe. A helicopter. Of course, Sebastyen's house had a pad in the grounds.

The chopper was up now, he could see the grass slowly raising itself back up as the downthrust lessened. Awkwardly he got to his feet and stepped out as it backed over the freeway, out of his sight and took its whiny song with it.

He touched his cheek and regretted it, looking at the mix of filth and blood on his fingertips. This was no deliberate near-miss. They'd been trying to blow his head off. He'd have to get that wound cleaned, maybe get a jab. Then he leant back against the concrete and let the realisation of what had just happened hit him like one of the big Macks thundering above his head. Dirty Harry? Dirty Harry? He held up the gun and looked at it. Blow your head clean off? Which of them was in danger of being beheaded here? What was that old Western cliché? A gun is only as good or as bad as the man using it. Or, he added, as absolutely useless. Dirty Harry? Just a dumb, ineffectual magazine editor, that's what he was. He started to laugh, uncontrollably, at the absurdity of it all.

THIRTY-FIVE

Tucson, Arizona

'I got two tickets to Baltimore booked, plus a Budget Rent-a-Car, which we can then take up to New York. I got the out of state drop-off charges waived, long as we leave it at JFK or Newark depot.' Coogan had to shout over the sound of the vacuum as Wendy cleaned the room for what seemed like the third time in the hour. It was all he heard from her trailer these days. She was either doing that or washing clothes that Pete hadn't worn, to keep those drawers restocked and sweet smelling.

Wendy switched it off and looked at him disbelievingly. 'Coogan – why are you doing this?'

'You said it yourself. You needed a partner.'

'I know. But I can't ask . . . all this. It's too much.'

'I'm here. I got no job, no dependents and time on my hands. The perfect resumé. Anyway,' he continued, assuming the objection was dealt with, 'you'll have to tell Slight. I don't want UFAP flapping after us, know what I mean? I got us a cellphone, too. So the Sheriff, CACU or FBI can always get us.'

'My God. How much was that guitar worth?'

Everything, he almost said.

Ten grand easy. Even the pawnshop guy had realised that. Said if Coogan didn't come back, he'd give Eric or Nils a call. But he just said: 'Not as much as your boy.'

That shut her up. She rubbed her face thoughtfully. 'I'll have to pack . . . look, this idea your pal suggested. With Virginia?'

'Yeah?'

'It's nuts, isn't it?'

Coogan thought for a minute. It was true, it was not doing it by the book. As Mercy had said, what you were meant to do was sit back and wait. And wait. Wait for that phone to ring, while you developed a bad Hoovering habit or worse. 'Let's settle for unconventional, huh?'

'What'll we tell Agent Slight?'

Coogan unplugged the Hoover, retracted the cord and lugged the machine out of the way, he put the tickets and vouchers down on the table, and held her by her shoulders. 'Tell him we're going to find Pete.'

Jim had just dialled the first two digits of 911 when the hand slammed down on the receiver, cutting him off. He turned to face Morgan. 'What the fuck you doin'?'

'They called.'

'Who?'

'The people who have Belle.'

Jim looked over his shoulder and he could see Mamie's worried expression.

'What they say?'

'That they'd kill her if you called the police. That was an hour ago. Where you been?'

'I went back home. To see his place. See if the helicopter had been there. They took her in a chopper, you see. I should've guessed. I asked the neighbours. No sign. An hour?' He looked at his watch. Time had lost its usual even flow, it was flashing by in jerks. It must have been ninety minutes or more since she was taken. It seemed like ten. 'They said what? What else?'

He could see Morgan looking him up and down and he followed his gaze. His clothes were caked with a mixture of mud and shit, with some splatters of blood. Somewhere along the way he had cut himself and he looked at his hand, a jagged gash of metal. Now he remembered. Pulling the fender away from the wheel so he could drive the car. That had taken time, getting it out of the tunnel. There wasn't a straight panel left on it now. No wonder the neighbours had stared at him so hard, turning up in a wreck. He almost laughed. As Belle would say, now he really did look like an extra from a George A Romero movie. 'You think I'm bad, you wanna see the car,' he said. 'What else they say?'

'That you'll get her back if you just stay cool. That's what they said. Stay cool. I thought you should know that. You can call the police now if you want. It's your call. But they were pretty adamant – you'll get her back. Why did you come back here?'

'I thought . . . I thought they might have released her. She is more likely to come here than go back to Bloomsberry. Friends. Y'know. You guys. Our friends. Shit.' He suddenly realised he was blubbing self-pitying sobs, welling up from deep inside, like small earth tremors. It was embarrassing, but he couldn't stop them, and when Morgan led him upstairs to the bathroom, they got worse, and he cried all the time, even while they ran a deep, hot, soapy bath and Morgan peeled off the ruined clothes and lowered him in.

After ten minutes he managed to stop, and looked over at Morgan, sitting on the john. He told him the full story of the tunnel, in sequence, right up until the take-off, then he started again. He sniffed and composed himself. 'I . . . Jesus, I'm sorry – I wasn't cut out for all this. Running around with a gun, f'Chrissake. It's so stupid. I . . . I always thought it would come down to money. Y'know? That all this was a feint and then would come the sucker punch. But I guess I am just the sucker. God, how can I apologise—'

'Don't. Don't apologise. I used to weep with frustration when we had . . . her.' He couldn't bring himself to say the name any longer. She, it, was gone. Ariel was dead as far he was concerned, along with any desire to be a father ever again. 'What you goin' to do?'

'Do? Fuck . . . I dunno. Find Dick. I think we should come clean. With the police.'

'About the kidnapping?'

323

'I . . . I suppose I got to tell the cops. It's a little embarrassing, I guess. Ha. A little? Jeez, Morgan. They'll chew my balls off. I just . . . I just can't think of anything else.'

'Listen, Jim, no offence, but I don't want police round here. Not now. Not after Ariel and all that shit. You just never know. FBI? They'd be here, too. Jesus Christ, what a mess. You'll have to go back to Bloomsberry if you are going to tell them. And keep us out of it. As a friend. Do this for me.'

'Do you think . . . think they're harming her?'

'Belle?' Morgan knew what this question meant, he was stalling. Knew that lurid images were starting to play across the man's mind. 'No. I got the impression this is just a little payback for the fake boy.'

'Did they ask for Tommy?'

'No. Like you said, maybe it's any boy they want.'

'How did they know it was the wrong one?'

'I can't figure it either, Jim. You bring the gun back?'

'In the car. Didn't fire it. Don't know whether it will fire now it's full of cow shit. You think she's OK then?'

'Yeah, sure,' Morgan said with a positiveness he didn't feel. 'I mean, really.'

Her brain, or at least her consciousness, was detached from her body, hovering somewhere outside, way outside, cowering in a corner of the dark room, occasionally getting little packets of sensation from the body, but for the most part all systems had been switched down into a protective cocoon mode. She knew she had been drugged, knew that the cotton-wool, fluffy, floaty feeling was chemically induced, and that she had to fight not to succumb to it totally.

They had landed at a small airport, which was where they had made her and the boy swallow the pills. They had known. They knew all along he was a ringer, even before they set eyes on him. How did they . . . ? How did they what? The thought went, escaped, pinged off into the night, an orphaned question never finished, never to be answered.

They had done things to her, she could feel that. But she somehow knew that it had been perfunctory, like something that was expected of them, part of the ritual, no, not a ritual, a routine. Nothing personal, almost. But that was just a feeling, the details of what they had done and where, they were hazy.

She needed to clean her teeth, though, she knew that. There was a bitter, metallic taste in the back of her throat. And she was chained to a bed, she knew that, too. But she had no idea where she was. Or how long she had been there. But the mists were clearing. Soon it would come to her, soon she would have to face up to reality.

She felt the hands press on her, holding her body, then her head forced up, and the chemically-tinged water at her lips. When she spat, more from instinct than resistance, a hand slapped her face, so she gulped it down. They were going to do what they wanted anyway. Almost immediately she felt the clouds start to roll in again, nudging each lucid thought aside, enveloping it, isolating it, stripping it of meaning. Still, Jim would come soon. Who would come soon? Ji— Someone? No, probably not. Best sleep.

Wendy felt nervous as she walked down the corridor towards the room where they were waiting. She could tell Coogan was too. She had hardly noticed the drive south from Baltimore, skirting the sprawl of DC until they hit the gentle, delicate hills, the copses and fields and manicured villages and the countless signs indicating Civil War sites. She had only really started to take notice when they had reached this place, this hospital – no matter what fancy name they gave it, it was still a hospital – albeit one with heavy-duty security, with a barrier and a guard who had to be satisfied you had an invite. The complex was a series of interlinked low, modern buildings, which could easily be a light industrial unit manufacturing circuit boards or the offshoot of a drug company. The modernist, round-edged cubes were set in well-maintained, traditional grounds, with lawns and fountains and flower gardens, deserted save for the odd patient slowly traversing one of the red-topped rubberised pathways that snaked around the site.

They left their luggage at reception and a nurse led them to one of the corridors that linked the satellite units. At the far end she stopped to open the door, and they could hear low conversation. It shut off when they entered.

There were a dozen people in the room, which was clearly some kind of communal lounge, with a huge Panasonic projection TV dominating one wall. But the rows of chairs that would normally have been laid out in front of the screen had been pushed to one side and now the men were facing them, five of them in wheelchairs, the rest forming a half-circle at the back, one of them, she noticed, on crutches, another missing an arm. There was an awkward silence.

'Miss Blatand?' There was a whine as one of the motorised chairs jerked forward and she looked down at a blond man, somewhere in his thirties, who had the muscular overcompensated upper body of many chair users. 'Shepard. Let's say Agent Shepard, just for old time's sake. OK, Nurse Holmes, thanks.' The nurse nodded and retreated.

She took the proffered hand. 'This is George Coogan. A friend of mine.'

'And of Isa Bowman's, I hear. George.' They shook, the wariness of two ex-suitors crackling between them, each thinking, oh, *that*'s the kind of guy Isa likes. 'Here, sit down. I'll get some coffee in a while. But first I ought to introduce these guys.' He indicated around the room. 'These folks are the few people in this hospital, recuperation unit, whatever, whose brains are less mushy than the food.' He rattled off the names faster than she could follow and said. 'Don't worry, you'll get it. I'll be honest, I expected a bigger turn-out, but between them they got nearly all the Federal bases covered. More would've been nice, but . . .'

Coogan said: 'Twelve Feds?' A Chalk, that was a good omen, he figured. 'Sounds fine to me.'

'Yeah. We was thinking of calling ourselves the Clean Dozen,' said Nico, a Treasury Agent. It was a poor joke, but it broke the ice.

'And we got a real bonus in John Cohen here, from the FBI. John used to do some abduction work. Isn't that right, John?'

Cohen was the guy with the missing arm. 'Yup. Hope I can help. Hope we all can.'

Wendy cleared her throat. 'Shall I tell you what happened? From the top?'

'Yes, ma'am,' said Cohen.

She started from the DUI incidence and finished at their departure for Baltimore airport, leaving nothing out. To her amazement some of them took notes, and a few asked questions along the way. When she was done she asked for some of that coffee, and they buzzed the nurse for it.

John said slowly: 'FBI Tucson done everything right so far. UFAPS. Traces. Kids, you see, don't leave marks like adults. We big ones wade through society throwing off little markers, like clothes catching on branches, you know what I mean? We buy a house here, a car there, apply for a licence, car, or gun, or dog. We have a Social Security number, credit cards, loans, mortgages. Kids, they ain't got none of this.'

Shepard caught the look on Wendy's face. She hadn't travelled all this way to be told what they couldn't do by a bunch of mangled guys. He said, 'Hey, John. We're meant to be helping.'

'I know. But ya gotta be straight. We got a call from a payphone in New York. That's it?'

'John.' It was Lamarq, from the Department of Transportation, who had investigated disappearances from trains and planes and airports in his time. 'I don't have to tell you what it's like. You're in New York, you get a trace request from someone in Phoenix, pardon me, Tucson. You do what you can, but you know, you got your own cases.'

327

'Yeah, we all know that. What are you saying?' asked Cohen.

'I'm saying make this personal. Anyone know anyone on the New York Bureau? Maybe you can just express an interest. Not heavy. A mention. Description of the kid, a photo to pin up. Things like that, though, they make a difference. Even more important, it makes it stick in your mind, understand? Someone down the hall wants some info, you're more likely to pick up on things and go down to his cubicle and shoot the breeze or mention it over a cup of coffee. More than if it means makin' like a call to some stranger out west.'

'I know someone,' said Shacochis, ex-Customs Service. 'Ernie – that guy, Norwood, remember him? He was OK, wasn't he?'

Ernie was about to reply when a voice said: 'What about G-Web?'

It came from a door to their left. Wendy had not noticed someone standing there, was unaware of what point he had come in. Yet he must have made some noise, for the newcomer was another guy on metal crutches, who clearly had no leg below the knee on his left side. He looked paler than the others, gaunter, as if whatever brought him here was fresher.

Shepard looked at him, at Wendy and back again. 'Hi. I don't think we've been introduced.' This, he knew was one of the new arrivals who, like most people, had withdrawn into themselves. It usually took a couple of weeks to be able to face anyone round here, something old hands like himself sometimes forgot.

The guy shuffled forward and nodded at Coogan and Wendy, before turning to the room. 'Well, I guess I ain't been feeling myself. Least not down here.' He waved the stump. 'I'm not sure who I am now, but before I lost this I was Senior Special Agent Roy Krok, State Department. Pleased to meet you.'

THIRTY-SIX

The Landing Strip, La Guardia, NYC

She had soiled herself and the sheets. Her drug-addled body simply had no control, no concept of sphincters or nerves, and had just emptied where she lay. They had been furious, she knew that. She could pinpoint where they had hit her, could feel the throbbing of painful, broken skin, but at one step removed, almost as if it were someone else's pain.

They had washed her down with icy water, dried her with towels so hard they were closer to sheets of sandpaper, dressed her in a thin robe and now just one of her wrists was clasped in a metal embrace by a handcuff, attached by a chain to the bed, which gave her enough reach to make it to the plastic bucket.

As long as they kept her at this level, bobbing just below the surface of clear reality, like a waterlogged corpse, she would be OK. She had just enough sensation left to know when her bladder was full, and to know her stomach was empty. She was sure she needed to eat. How long had it been? But whenever she thought about time the world started to spin, a big, lazy, black circle and she began to feel nauseous. She had to hang onto something else.

At least Tommy was OK. She hadn't told them anything. Insisted it was her boy she had brought along. But they weren't fooled. Now they had stopped asking things. Now they didn't seem to care.

She heard the door open and a shuffling. The sound of something, a tray maybe, being put down on the wooden floor. She didn't bother to open her eyes. If they wanted something they would tell her soon enough. She could hear breathing, loud exhalations through a nose, almost a pant, fast, almost animal. She was tempted to open her eyes but didn't. The door closed, but she sensed that the person was still in the room. She could feel the heat of a superwarmed body, the fast, shallow breathing coming nearer. She could smell him now, smell the sweat, even above the other odours in the room, something sharp and prickly and acrid, part chemical, part musk.

She could feel her head swimming again, the effort of all this thought making the clouds come back, felt herself falling into that sludgy whirlpool, so she opened her eyes. She knew that face. She did, if only she could focus . . . it was a friend. She knew that much. Someone had come. She was saved now. Saved. Thank God. A tear squeezed from the corner of one eye.

Then she saw him reach down and unzip his trousers.

'Come on, guys, you know about G-Web.' Krok laughed at the puzzled faces. 'I don't believe you. It's the whining site. You know—' His voice took on the timbre of a spoiled child. '*We bust our balls every day out here, and for what?*'

Shepard lied. 'Must be after my time.' Of course he knew about it, but it was like that old Brad Pitt movie from a few years back. The first rule of G-Web is – you don't talk about G-Web. He wasn't going to acknowledge he had already punted a can-anyone-help message into cyberspace.

'What? OK, I know you ain't supposed to discuss it.' He looked at Coogan. 'Code words are only given word of mouth. Gotta be a good guy to get one. But, it could be useful. They got a help room, f'instance. Feds can go in and help each other anonymously. Like a chat room. You got computers here, we could do that. You got one,' he pointed a crutch accusingly at Shepard. 'I heard you tapping away. You on-line? Good. Also you could scan in the computakit images of the suspects. You did do a description and a FacCon – excuse me, a facial construct?' Krok nodded at Wendy.

'Yeah. Isn't very good, though.'

'They never are. Let me see.' Coogan took the photocopy from his pocket and handed it over. 'I see what you mean. The woman's better than the man, yeah?'

'I hardly saw him. I think she came in while he fixed the car. So it wouldn't start—'

'Yeah, I heard all that through the door. Now what we should—'

'Excuse me,' said Shepard, suppressing the irritation at having his thunder stolen by some stranger. 'Agent Krok. It's meant to be, like, a collective thing. A forum. You know what I mean? I think we should explore some other avenues.'

Krok nodded. 'Yeah. I just got carried . . . no, sure. I'll just . . .' he hobbled over to a chair and managed to slide awkwardly onto it, and continued studying the two faces.

Shepard said. 'OK, anyone else?'

There was lots of shrugging and tutting and shaking of heads.

'What, nothing?'

'We need a break,' said Nico. 'It's a big old world out there. The New York call. It ain't enough.'

'Neither are these,' said Krok regretfully.

Coogan could see Wendy was close to tears. Despite what she had said about this being a nuts idea, she had clearly expected, or hoped for more. But he saw her catch herself, pull herself up in the chair. They were no further along, but they hadn't slipped back. And maybe this G-Web could do something. She sniffled and pulled herself straight then said to Krok. 'Thing is, if I was going to do that now, I'd make the notch bigger.'

'What notch?'

'The one in the guy's ear. Look. There. I think it was more prominent.'

Shepard pressed the switch on his chair, rolled up to Krok, took the image, and expertly span himself round to face her. From his shirt pocket he took a pen. 'Show me.'

Wendy scribbled on the copy, marking in rough lines the

missing section of the lobe, the one he had been playing with that day outside the trailer, like a nervous tic.

As Shepard looked at it the rough approximation of features gelled. It was like the brain suddenly being able to make sense of those 3-D drawings that initially look like multi-coloured squiggles then turn out to be some Roman orgy. He looked at Krok and back at Wendy and then at the face, just to make sure it was still there, the visage he remembered. The one he could see, but the others couldn't, as if he had some kind of terrible gift. This was no clumsy construct, but a living, breathing head to him. A person.

'What?' asked Krok eventually.

'Son . . . of . . . a . . . bitch,' said Shepard slowly, relishing the words, turning them over as you might a piece of meat on a spit. Maybe, just maybe, there was a God after all. 'Wuzel. Vincent fuckin' Wuzel.'

The Creep stopped dead when he saw her. Felt the panic hit him. Knew he had been suckered. This was the man's final joke. Someone special, they said. At The Club. It was always special at The Club. Rooms cleaner. Girls more interesting. He didn't normally mind the cab ride out to La Guardia. On the way over he had taken a bunch of the pills – four? five? – and now they were in full effect pumping the kind of hydraulic pressure through his dick that you normally found behind the Hoover dam.

Well, he thought, maybe she was asleep, drugged, and wouldn't notice, but her head turned towards him and the eyes opened, half opened, true, but he could see the confused, trippy recognition in there, the mind trying to piece together what she was seeing, separate reality from hallucination. His dick stirred hungrily and he unzipped himself to give it some room.

Her eyes dropped to look, and was that interest he detected there? A spark of fascination? Maybe she had always wondered about him. Just the way he had about her. He was here now, why not find out? She wouldn't say anything. He could tell by her pupils she would never be sure. Never be certain it really was him.

Before he knew it he was naked in front of her. He undid her robe, and was pleased to see there was nothing underneath. He paused to examine her body, to gaze at the reddish curl of pubic hair and the fall of the breasts, the slightly puckered stomach, to memorise it all, before he turned her onto her front. She didn't resist, she just groaned. As he reached across for his case his face came down level with hers.

'Hello, Belle,' he whispered. 'It's Dick. Don't worry. You'll enjoy this.'

A spark had flown round the room of the recuperation facility, a little frisson of excitement leaping from agent to agent. They all knew the sound in Shepard's voice, all knew what it meant. They had heard it a thousand times, echoing around rooms from San Diego to Boston. It was the first domino. The first chink in the armour, the very first piece of the puzzle that nestled home with a satisfying – no, exhilarating, clunk. Gotcha.

'Who?' asked Krok.

'Vincent Wuzel. Anyone know him? John, you never came across him? I . . . Jesus. Sorry, I gotta get a breath here. I don't believe it. Wuzel is why I am here. Wuzel was a fuckin' gun for hire, until he started being a contractor. Finding people to do the job for him, for a percentage. Like a job agency, y'know? Motherfucker was one of the ones shot me. Excuse me, ma'am.'

'You go right ahead. If this guy's got my boy I can think of worse than motherfucker.'

Shepard looked again at the face before him, felt himself transported back to a wet, windy, squally night where he was left for dead on a parking lot. He had expected to feel something more than this. Something more elemental, a burning rage, perhaps. But all he got was a cold feeling that, sooner or later, he would see this man dead. He gave the people in the room a quick snapshot of that night of fire and carnage.

'We can put the name out on the internet, do a G-Web appeal,' Krok said when he had finished. 'He on NCIC?'

Shepard shrugged. 'I don't know. Yeah. I would guess. We're asking a lot for people to go onto NCIC.' Accessing the National Crime Information Computer for personal reasons was technically illegal, even though it went on. There were no less than nine safeguards built in where, sooner or later, you had to justify what you did. So you had to cover your tracks by inserting your request into another case, that was all. Hell, though, there were private eyes who boasted they could get in any time they wanted, he was sure they could.

'The government asked a lot of us in its time,' said Lamarq.

Shepard said: 'Amen to that. But we should save the National Crime records for when we're down to our last nickel. See, Atlantic City PD will probably have a card on him. I can get to that.' He looked at Wendy. 'But it's not where he's been. That's what those will tell us. Where he has been. It's where he is now we want.'

A sudden babble of voices threw out suggestions. Now they had a name they knew places to look – Department of Motor Vehicles, Land Registry, voter registration, county courts, credit-card companies, the assessor's office, credit agencies such as Equifax and TRW. Coogan had never known there were so many places they could find you.

'You figure him for still being in the North East?' asked Nico.

'Ye—' he began and then stopped, remembering the last small victory he had had, or at least the one before he got that boner the other day. 'Except his partner died down in Florida. Brownie. At an illegal off-track bookies. Horse came in at Saratoga, Brownie popped off from shock at Fort Lauderdale. He was another cocksucker.' He felt a stab in his chest, like a reminder of where the man's slugs had hit him, taking him to within a few centimetres and half a pint of blood away from the long, long darkness. 'Maybe we should try there.'

'Hey, I'm your man in Florida,' said Cohen. 'Guys in the Bureau there, they owe me one.' He held up the stump of his arm. 'Know what I mean?'

The conversation within the room split into small groups, as each former agent bounced ideas off his neighbours, trading stories of fugitives either tracked down or lost for ever. Shepard looked at Wendy and wheeled over. He put his hand on her knee. 'Don't get your hopes up. It ain't much.'

Wendy sniffed hard, realising tears had been coming down her face, but not the bitter ones of the last few days, but salty, fresh-tasting ones. She was more touched than she had thought possible by a room full of strangers – damaged strangers – applying themselves on her behalf. 'I know it isn't much,' she sniffed, 'but I'll take it.'

THIRTY-SEVEN

The Landing Strip, La Guardia, NYC

As she surfaced from that nightmare, the pains began, little flares of fire, exploding all over her body, every so-called erogenous zone complaining about its abuse, from her anus to her nipples. She managed to slide off the bed and make it to the bucket. She squatted over it, but yelped as the stream of urine started, burning like sulfuric acid as it came out, causing her eyes to sting.

She hobbled back to the bed, wondering when she would be fed. She was thirsty and hungry, and the drugs were wearing off and now she had to try to distinguish what was real from what was a chemically induced delusion, to try to make sense of voices and snatches of conversation, words and phrases, speeded up or slowed down, scrambled, some in English, others in a mixture of tongues, to give some kind of chronology to it. But time's arrow had been bent and snapped and stomped on. There was only one thing she could remember clearly, and it made her shiver and the tiny agonies start again. 'Hello, Belle. It's Dick. Don't worry, you'll enjoy this.'

She made it over to the bucket in time to spew up a thin stream of green bile. She wondered at what point she would decide to wrap the tether to the bed round her neck and end it all. An hour? A day? One more session like the last? She heard the key in the door and even as it opened she smelt hot food and her stomach contracted and her mouth filled with saliva, her poor violated body still getting on with the mechanics of living. Not yet, then.

❖ ❖ ❖

None of the group slept that night. Coogan and Wendy decamped to a motel in nearby Stanford. She spent the hours of darkness staring at the ceiling, watching an internal movie of Pete playing and replaying, a movie that had become faded over the past few days as Pete became more ethereal, his features increasingly indistinct. Now he was solid, real again, within reach.

Coogan sat on the bed, trying to piece together his feelings. He was being sidelined, he knew that. They had all the expertise, he was being filed under 'Companion'. That was not what he had had in mind. Why the fuck was he here if not to be in the thick of it? He lay down and closed his eyes, shuffling into a comfortable position for his back, waiting for the little stick figures to come. But they didn't. Hadn't for a while now. That, at least, was something to be grateful for.

A few miles away, Shepard and Krok each spent the time wrestling with their monsters, the faces that haunted them, except Krok's didn't have a face, just a blank canvas onto which several possibilities were superimposed. But he knew that one day he'd make that face real, just so he could have the pleasure of smashing a fist into it. Twice. One for his leg, and one for an Englishman who died on a miserable rooftop car park.

He thought about the day in Kosovo with poor Harry Darling, when they watched the lead vehicle take to the air, surrounded by smoke and flame, tossed aside like a bag of feathers, bouncing on the road, killing and maiming the State Department's men who had hitched a ride with a British KFOR contingent. His men. And the hideous aftermath they found in the village, and that leering, obscene skull-and-crossbones on the wall of the charred barn, announcing that Hoek and the Pristina Pirates had been there. That was the face he had to find, cut out and keep. If Shepard could get his, Krok was damned sure he would find his own.

❊   ❊   ❊

When Wendy and Coogan returned the rec room smelled of stale sweat and cigarette smoke, although nobody was actually smoking. Shepard was in front of a Dell computer, complaining about Windows not being as good as the Mac OS, and Krok was ignoring him and tapping into a Compaq laptop. Piles of paper surrounded them, some of them clearly printouts of e-mails and web pages. There were three new phones sitting on a side desk, their wires snaking out into the corridor. Nico and Lamarq were also there, scribbling notes or doodling, it was hard to tell.

A new figure was also in the room, standing over the agents, tall, grey haired, white-coated. A doctor. He glared at them as they came in.

'As director of this facility—' he was saying to Shepard.

'Your job is to help these men recuperate and readjust.'

'But not to use this as some kind of incident room—'

'Look upon it as therapy, Doc,' suggested Shepard.

'Like the smoking?'

'I'll stop that. Two in the morning, you're waiting for an e-mail from San Francisco—'

'No smoking in here under any circumstances.'

'OK. Deal.'

'And I want the phones during the day – you are clogging up the lines.' He pointed at the cables. 'Not to mention the corridors.'

'We got three extra coming in later today.'

'What?'

'Cellphones. On us, Doc. Our bill.'

He leant forward. 'There are some very sick men in this facility Agent Shepard. If I suspect for one minute your vigilante antics are harming any of them—'

'I know, I know, Doc. It's a one-off special. Trust me.'

The director raised up and swept by without acknowledging Wendy and Coogan, with a face that said trust was the last thing on his mind, and leaving a trail of invisible ice particles in his wake that made her shiver.

'Trouble?' asked Coogan.

'Only with the bureaucratic mind.'

Wendy said: 'I didn't mean to start anything. We could go.'

Shepard said, 'You kiddin'? You brought me Wuzel, which in my book makes you a fairy godmother. The Doc can go fuck himself.'

'What about harming some of the guys?'

'Bullshit. Everyone in here has a Wuzel they would love to get to. The Wuzels kept us alive, I reckon, most of us. You lyin' there leakin' all over the floor and you can feel that easy option – close your eyes. Let go. Drift off. And a little part of your brain is sayin', whoa you got unfinished business here. Ain't that right, Roy?'

Krok looked up. 'On the money.'

'Who's yours?' Wendy suddenly asked him.

'Pardon me?'

'Who you after?'

Shepard shot her a look. It was just possible that Krok's wounds were too fresh, too raw for this.

Wendy repeated softly, cautiously: 'I was wonderin' . . . who you after?'

Krok caught Shepard's warning glance and shrugged. 'It's no big deal. I was . . . I am with the State Department. I was in Kosovo after the Serbian withdrawal. We came across some things . . .'

'What? The Serbian atrocities?' asked Coogan. 'I heard about them.'

'Well, those. But you know, we had names to put to those – Arkan, Georgie's Boys, the First Eleven. This was afterwards. The Albanians, the KLA, started revenge tactics of their own. Serbians, gypsies. Got almost no media coverage here. But, shit, it was every bit as bad. There was this one guy, we knew he had a unit of irregulars, the Pristina Pirates they called themselves. Whenever they hit a village or a house they would stencil a skull and crossbones on a building. Their calling card. Now the leader, this guy, we knew he was in his thirties, knew he was funded by the drug guys over the border, knew he had several names – Anton, Hoek, Vogel, The Captain – but we couldn't get to him. Didn't even know what he looked like. The photographer who we are fairly certain got a shot of him, we found him decapitated. Look, I got to be honest, nobody was that interested here. The Serbs were the bad guys, they were the ones with the war-crimes warrants against them. It was a little embarrassing to admit that some of the guys we went in to save were just as fucked up as the enemy. Then the War Crimes Commission started finding the thousands of mass Kosovan graves NATO reported weren't thousands after all, and slowly the whole thing fell apart. Buried. Chechnya became news, then Sierra Leone, Morocco, Indonesia, Turkey, India and Pakistan . . . Always another war. So rumour began that it was a cover, the guy didn't exist, maybe it was a KFOR bogeyman, or it was a way for UCK and KLA to take revenge and blame it on the mythical Pirates. I didn't buy it. We saw the results of a visit. So we kept our ears to the ground and last year we hear he is here. In the US.'

'Doing what?'

'We didn't know. But we got ourselves a shortlist of possibles. And we had one ace. An English guy who had been in KFOR, he saw him. He saw him through binoculars.' While Krok had been trying to pull his dying friends out of a wrecked personnel carrier, but he decided not to go there. 'He swears, swore, he saw the guy.'

'So you home and dry?' asked Coogan.

'When we brought him in through . . .' Krok hesitated. He thought of Darling disintegrating under the hail of high-velocity rounds, the life torn from him in an instant. 'When I brought him in through JFK, they were waiting. Ambushed on the roof. That's how I got this.' He tapped his leg. 'Or lost it, I should say.'

'Jesus,' said Wendy.

'So it's this guy, this Albanian you want?' asked Coogan.

'Yeah. But more than that. I want the guy who told them we were going to be on the roof.'

They let that sink in for the moment.

Krok shook his head, as if he could fling off the thoughts by centrifugal force, cleared his throat and said in a voice with the merest hint of a tremor. 'That's for later. Right now, Vincent Wuzel. Not a common name, you would think. But we got three. Wisconsin, California, Carolina. All wrong age or wrong colour or wrong history.'

Wendy frowned. 'Is that it?'

Krok said. 'That's it for a quick search through the records we can access easily. Thing is, guy like Wuzel probably doesn't file IRS returns on a regular basis. He's in here somewhere,' he tapped the Compaq. 'But finding him. Could be days. Weeks. If the Doc gives us that long.'

Wendy said: 'What if he changed his name?'

Krok said: 'What? From Wuzel?'

'Like your Albanian. You said he had lots of names.'

Krok looked at Shepard, and he said quietly: 'Well, we're fucked then. I mean, yeah, it's not only possible, it's likely.'

Somewhere in the back of Krok's mind some class at Quantico many lifetimes ago stirred in his head. He said: 'But people don't change at random. No, they don't. Even subconsciously you pick something that you are happy with, that you'll remember. Something you feel comfortable with. You know when people change their date of birth, they always pick a sequence similar to the old one? Names, they often have something that makes them smile, a hero, mnemonic. But it has to feel comfortable, familiar. So you don't hesitate when asked and will turn around if you hear the name in a room – you know, if someone is calling you. What would Wuzel be happy with?'

Shepard thought. He had found out a few things about the man. Photographers, he knew he had a thing about them. Unlikely to call himself Henri Cartier Bresson, though. That was hardly sinking anonymously into the populace. Then he remembered. 'Paladin. His agency was called Paladin.'

'Paladin?' asked Wendy. 'What's that?'

'It's a TV show. Western. Have Gun, Will Travel. Wuzel called the agency Paladin as a joke. It was the name of the character. What was the guy? Face like a vegetable?'

Wendy said. 'It was—'

'Before her time,' finished Coogan. 'Boone. Richard Boone.'

Krok shook his head. 'So which you wanna try? Richard Boone's a common name. Well, common-ish.'

Shepard ran them through his mind, feeling each one, trying to imagine what this man would take as his new, given name. What would appeal to the guy, the kind of man who would name a murderous agency after an old western? Finally he said: 'Richard Boone. Start with that. No, no, hold on. I bet he liked the name of his outfit. I bet it made the fucker laugh, Paladin.'

'What was Paladin's first name?' asked Wendy.

'Far as I recall, he didn't have one,' said Shepard. 'He was like the missing link to the Man With No Name. He just had the one.'

Wendy hesitated, but she knew she was past caring about making a fool of herself. Let them laugh. 'How about trying Richard Paladin then?'

THIRTY-EIGHT

New York City

Richard Paladin took a cab from Newark into Manhattan, the first time he had been back to the city in over a year. Not that he would have chosen summer as an ideal time for a trip down Memory Lane. Humidity was off the scale, and the place was being sprayed again on a weekly basis to keep the mosquito population down, now that they were transmitting three different types of encephalitis.

He dropped his bags off at the cheap hotel on Broadway and continued down to Little Italy. Already his shirt was soaked, and his face burning red from the exertion. He looked at his watch. Five p.m. It had to get cooler soon. The cab deposited him a block away from Jimmy's Bar, one of the last bastions of old-school Little Italy, even though Jimmy now co-owned it with a Chinese guy, and most of the staff were Orientals. But the bare wooden floors, the chalked menu, the wobbly tables, still attracted some of the original inhabitants. Rollie was one of them.

Paladin found Rollie nursing a cold beer in the raised section at the back, reading the sports pages. Rollie had put on weight: he had a healthy belly straining over his trousers and jowls that gave him a lugubrious expression. All that beer and German sausage. Paladin sat down opposite, ordered a Bud.

'Vince,' said Rollie, as if the last time he had seen him had been the night before.

Paladin smiled at the old name, and slipped back into it, like an old sport's jacket. 'Rollie, how ya keepin'?'

'Yeah, OK. Things are quiet. Not much action in town. I miss you, Vince. From a business point of view.' When he was

ROB RYAN

Vincent Wuzel he would pass a variety of jobs to Rollie, from delivering packets of dubious contents to organising beatings.

'Hey, don't get all sloppy on me now. Cheers.' Paladin took a sip of beer, then a gulp. 'So fuckin' hot out there.'

'Yeah. Normally I'd be out at the Hamptons, this time a' year,' said Rollie sarcastically, 'doin' laps in the pool. What can I do for you, Vince?'

Paladin dropped his voice. 'I need a piece.'

'What, you ain't got your own? Vince Wuzel?'

'I flew in. Ain't worth the hassle trying to get it through metal detectors. And I ain't got any of those plastic numbers. Can you get me anything?'

He asked the Chinese girl who had come over to wipe down the table next to them for a refill, holding up his glass.

'Is it something special or a one-off?'

'It'll be going in the East River, so I don't want anything fancy. Suppressed, though.'

'Suppressed?' Rollie rolled some saliva round his mouth, the same way he did food, a habit that hadn't got any more appealing in his absence, Paladin noted. 'Listen, I got something might suit. Taurus? PT99 model? Chambered for nine mil. Full suppressor kit. Very popular with the death squads in South America. Browning type of thing. Cheap.'

'How cheap?'

'Three hundred. Fifty for the suppressor.'

Paladin didn't say anything as his beer arrived. When the waitress had gone he said. 'That's cheap up here now, is it? Ammo?'

'Hey, Vince, you know me, I always include the stuff. No good without ammo. Two fifteen-round mags. Or I can do you a Daewoo.'

'A Daewoo?'

'DP51. South Korean. Got them on special. No suppressor, though. I could get one made up, take a day.'

'I'll take the Taurus.'

346

'You gotta give me an hour.'

Paladin looked at his watch.

'What time it get dark?'

'Nine. Little after maybe.'

'OK. I'm gonna get a bite to eat. That good Vietnamese still on Mott? Great. See you back here in an hour.'

Jim Barry tried to read Tommy the story, the one about the dragon that couldn't fly, three times, but either his voice tailed off or he found himself fighting back tears. They were downstairs in Morgan and Mamie's living room. The couple were getting ready to go out, twittering to each other like this was *The Sound of Music* or *West Side Story*, only stopping when Jim's face reminded them they were in the midst of tragedy. They'd offered to cancel and stay with Jim, but he told them not to be stupid, and they'd looked relieved. They had a new life to get on with, after all.

He gave Tommy a hug, smelling his freshly shampooed hair and inhaling deeply. 'Daaad. Come ooooonnn,' the boy whined. 'You gotta finish it.'

'Just a minute,' he snapped, then felt bad. He gave Tommy another squeeze and tickled him through his pyjamas, causing him to wriggle and laugh.

'When's Mom coming back, Dad?' Tommy had a crumpled picture of her clutched in his hand, which he had refused to let go of. He would sleep with it under his pillow.

'Soon.' Jim had been within an ace of dialling the police again, but the thought of what would come down on him as the whole tawdry picture unravelled had stayed his hand. There had been no more communication, so all he could actually depend on was that one call, saying she would be released. Probably, he figured, before the Grand Jury hearing, now set for three weeks' time. So what were they doing to her?

'What you say we go swimming tomorrow? Maybe catch a movie?'

'*Star Wars Episode Three*?'

'If you want.'

'*Yes*. Coooool!' How come five-year-olds now sounded like the kids on that old *Melrose Place* show? he wondered. The whole life and growing-up thing seemed to be concertinaing – soon kids would be straight out of diapers and into dating.

Tommy flicked the book in his hand. 'Come on, Dad. Finish it.'

Maybe he should, he thought. Before it got any worse. Maybe he should finish it.

Richard Paladin drove past the driveway twice to make sure he had the right house. On the second run he managed to catch the name on the mailbox as confirmation. Excellent. Detached, no near-neighbours, the sort of house opportunist burglars might pick for a little robbery, which could go horribly wrong. He pulled up the hire car two hundred yards down the road and checked the gun Rollie had got for him. The Taurus was a nice piece, a Brazilian copy of the Italian Beretta M9. He checked the safety, then screwed on the suppressor, a big fat bulky number which badly affected the balance of the gun, meaning it would have to be fired two-handed to be accurate. No problem. He wasn't expecting any trouble on this one.

He changed his shoes to the new sneakers he would later discard along with the weapon, and walked back down the two-lane blacktop towards the house entrance. He had to admit to a strong sense of excitement as he listened to his body. It was like starting up a classic car that had laid in the garage for years, yet still fired on the first turn of the key. He'd been out of this a long time. He'd considered phoning it and delegating the action, but he decided there were just too many people involved already. He checked his heartbeat and his hands, both reassuringly steady. No, this was a job for the old school, for that guy Vincent Wuzel he used to know so well.

The lights were on in the house, so it was a good bet they

were home. He kept close to the shrubs and bushes that lined the driveway. It wasn't yet fully dark, but he guessed that nobody looking out of a window would spot him in the shadows and branches.

He made the porch and the front door, and pressed himself to the wall at one side, listening, but nothing came through. Would he have to go round the back? Or find a window? He tried the latch and the door gave. People are stupid, he thought. Complacent and stupid. Shit, he could be anyone. A burglar, even.

He felt his whole self prickle as he stepped inside, his senses, that radar for self-preservation, cranked up to the maximum. Now he could hear a voice, droning, but couldn't catch the words.

Ahead of him was a big staircase, wide and majestic, dark wood, with ornate balustrades. At the top a landing with fancy wall mouldings. Some decent artwork on the wall, although he didn't rate that shitty posed Herb Ritts working-men stuff. Nice house, he thought. Downstairs, to his left, opposite the bottom of the stairs, was a big, carved oak door, from behind which the rhythm of speech was coming. The darkened hallway at the side of the staircase led out back, probably to a kitchen and more rooms.

He took a step towards the living room when she appeared at the top of the stairs, the woman he remembered, the one who had been so thrilled with the kid a few months before, and had now dumped her like some strung-out fourteen-year-old would. She didn't see him, she was still looking over her shoulder and shouting. 'Don't worry, Hon, you finish your shower. I'll get Jim to hook me up. Can you hear me? Oh, shoot.'

Paladin did a quick calculation and head count. 'Hon' upstairs, that'd be the husband, Morgan, and someone called Jim down, and, unless the guy behind that door was talking to himself, he was speaking to another party, so maybe four. Double what he had expected. Any second now, he knew, he would have to act. Use the surprise.

He saw her head swivel and her eyes screw up as she caught sight of him, thinking it was her friend for a second, perhaps, wondering what Jim was playing at. Was he dressing up? Then would come the realisation, and the inevitable shout or scream.

She was still at the puzzled stage – didn't she recognise this guy from somewhere? – when he fired twice, satisfied at the soft hiss that came from the suppressor. She went straight back onto the stairs, and he thought she would stay put, but one dead arm lolled over, giving enough momentum for the body to roll down the steps, a great gallumping sound that everyone must have heard.

Jim Barry certainly did. He had just managed to make the part where the little dragon took its first tentative flaps, and paused, when he heard wood and flesh making contact in the unmistakable sound of a fall. Someone had slipped on the shiny floors of the landing, maybe. He scooped up Tommy under his arm, ran to the hall, pulled the door open and stopped dead. He could see Mamie lying at the foot of the stairs, twisted into a grotesque human pretzel. And someone else. With a gun. A Sebastyen hitman, his brain shouted. *Do something*.

Paladin swivelled the Taurus smoothly to face Jim. He registered the kid, and hesitated, thinking for a second it was the one they had taken from the trailer park. So alike.

Jim used the moment's pause to throw Tommy back into the room behind him, and turned to try and make the bureau, where he knew the Ruger was. Cleaned now, but he'd probably be no better with it. Still, had to try. There was an explosion of sound behind him, even as he rotated, and he felt the bullet tug at his shoulder. Instinctively, he went down, rolling into a little ball, his knees up to his chest, waiting for the pain that would precede the end, trying not to vomit in fear. He could hear Tommy crying, and he prayed that the little boy would live, otherwise this made no sense at all. No sense at all.

A few seconds later he felt Tommy's arms circle his neck, his hot breath on his cheek and the splash of tears. He unravelled himself and reached over to his back. There was nothing there. No hole. No sticky mess. Yet he had felt something punch into him. He laid Tommy aside, told him to stay put, and crawled out into the hall on hands and knees.

Mamie was still splayed out where she had landed. In front of her was the hitman, dressed rather warmly for the time of year, all in black, except for a pair of new, dark red Nikes. He was face down, or at least, if he'd had a face it would be down, for most of it seemed to have been sprayed across the hallway, and the rest was leaking into the big puddle where he lay, flowing around the confetti of glass that formed a halo around his shattered head. Jim realised that he hadn't been hit by a bullet at all, but by a chunk of skull, punched out at speed as a round passed through the man's cranium.

Jim tried to take all this in. Was it Sebastyen or one of his cronies lying there? And Mamie? Mamie couldn't be . . . ?

The shout from above made him realise she was, and a naked Morgan rushed down, screaming, pulling his wife up into his arms, propping the lolling head, not even noticing Jim or the corpse or even the two men who came through the entrance, weapons drawn.

Jim, still on his hands and knees looked pleadingly at them, as if begging for something that could piece all this together, that could put some kind of meaning into this crazy, surreal tableau. But two puzzled, apprehensive faces looked back at him. They had no more of a clue than he did, probably less. One of the pair bent at the knees to come near his level, his pistol still raised up, covering the hallway and stairs, and whispered: 'Federal Officers, sir. I'm Agent Shand. Edgar Shand. Is anyone else in the house?'

THIRTY-NINE

The Margaret Henley Federal Recuperation Facility, Virginia

Ernie Shepard put the phone down and told Roy Krok what he had just heard. Roy was sitting in a chair, idly massaging his truncated leg with one hand, sipping from a can of soda. It had gone eleven p.m., and most of the team had turned in. It had been a busy few days.

They had found Paladin through land registry in Miami, followed him through credit agencies and finally credit cards. Using some heavy-handed deception, claiming this was official business, they had got the flight he had paid for on MasterCard through the airline, and had his trail picked up in Manhattan by a couple of ATF guys that Shepard knew. A couple of off-duty ATF guys, who were just meant to see what he was up to.

Now, it turned out, he had been on a hit. But without a warrant the officers had been reluctant to act too soon, a reluctance which cost a woman her life.

'What do you think?' asked Shepard.

Krok shook his head. 'We're fucked.'

'We got extenuating circumstances.'

'Such as?'

'Such as if they hadn't been there, all three would probably have died. It's just a shame they killed Wuzel.'

'Why?'

'I was kinda hopin' to do that part,' Shepard said wistfully, as if he was regretting not getting World Series tickets. 'But you can't win them all.'

Krok suddenly started laughing, as much out of fatigue as

353

anything else, and Shepard joined in. 'So . . .' he said after a while. 'Are your boys in trouble? I mean, this was hardly official ATF business.'

'Edgar told Trenton – the ATF bureau? – they went into Little Italy for something to eat and saw what they believed to be an illegal weapons purchase. They couldn't call it in because of a faulty transmitter—'

'That old one—'

'Old ones are the best, Roy. They'll have the sense to make sure it isn't working. Don't forget they fired a weapon. Details in triplicate, tribunal, the works.' Nobody ever mentioned this bit of law enforcement. They give you a gun, but the moment you shoot it there are dozens of people asking: why the hell did you do that? Every detail would be dissected now, just to make sure they were justified. 'Of course the shooting him through the door part is tricky. But, like we said, their best defence is, if they hadn't been there at all, it would have been a bigger bloodbath. I mean, one out of four, it's one too many, but it's a result of sorts.'

'Four? You said three.'

'I did? I meant three adults and a kid.'

Krok said: 'A kid?'

Shepard suddenly realised how tired he had been, how the sleepless nights had caught up with what used to be a sharp analytical brain. Now, it was clearly porridge. 'Yeah.'

'What sex?'

'A boy. A five-year-old boy. Jesus, Roy,' he said, angry at himself. 'It didn't occur to me he'd be doing a hit on some family he helped in a kidnap. I just thought it was an unconnected job.'

'Nothing is unconnected,' said Krok enigmatically. 'You learn that in my field quicker than most.'

'Fuck. What an idiot.'

'Well, it might not be this boy Pete. On the other hand, maybe it was a bad debt and Wuzel decided to cancel it in the old-fashioned way. Can we get a photo?'

Shepard scratched his head, trying to get some blood moving in there. 'Get Wendy up there is better. If my guys don't get suspended they can get her into the home.'

Krok said: 'Let's fly them up first thing. Her and her lap dog.'

Shepard thought that unnecessarily hard, but he didn't have time to comment before the phone rang. He grabbed it and listened, grunting occasionally. His face looked dark when he put the receiver down. 'That was Pennsylvania Avenue,' he said, meaning the mammoth J Edgar Hoover Building in Washington.

'Working late.'

'It never closes, you know that. They are sending a team of agents down tomorrow to look at what we've been doing these past three or four days. They suggested we get ourselves lawyers. Guy sounded real pissed. We're being shut down, Roy.'

Dick Crichton read the report on the shooting in the paper the next day. In an uncharacteristic piece of soft-peddling by the press it was presented as a burglary gone awry, thwarted by brave Federal officers who arrived too late to save Mamie. He couldn't help himself, he started to cry, he lay down on the couch and let his body weep for a good ten minutes, until there was no more liquid to be squeezed out. He cried for all the terrible things he had done, for himself as much as his victims, for Jim and for poor, poor Belle.

After he had laid there a little longer, he got up and re-read the official letter from the Immigration and Naturalization Department Internal Investigations Unit, summoning him to a preliminary interview to ascertain 'which charges, if any' were to be filed. If any. There was a joke. They were simply going to decide how big the book they were going to throw at him should be.

He screwed up the letter and lobbed it towards the trash bin, scowling when it bounced off the side. Nothing would go right for him now, he knew. The markers were all being called in. Every debt had to be repaid, every one of those girls done penance for. He felt the tears of self-pity well up again, wondering how it came to this, as he chartered his path from stroke mags, through Internet porn, and on to lapdancing bars, encounter booths, prostitutes and into Hoek's sick little fucked-up fiefdom. Well, maybe there was one lazy way to make amends, maybe he could wipe the slate clean. Or at least leave it not so disgustingly grubby.

He went over to the desk and wrote out a long list of instructions, including who should look after Mike, should anything happen to him. He then detailed exactly what he had done, and what he was about to do. Then he signed all three sheets of paper, folded them in an envelope and propped it up on the coffee table in the middle of the living room.

Then he called Jim at Morgan's house. The phone was picked up by a voice he didn't recognise. 'Yes?'

'Morgan?'

'No, I am afraid Mr Starkey is under sedation. This is Deputy Sheriff Foggerty. Can I help?'

'Jim? Jim Barry? Is he out too?'

'No, hold on.' Then as an afterthought. 'Who is this?'

'Dick Crichton. Family friend.'

'OK, hold on.'

The voice on the other end was cracked and hoarse. 'Yes?'

'It's Dick.'

'Dick? Where the fuck have you been? There's been a terrible—'

'I know. I saw the paper. Listen, Jim. I know where she is.'

'What?'

'Belle. I know where she is.'

The hope flooded into Jim's throat like spring water, and the constant dryness suddenly vanished. 'Where? Is she OK? Dick, how do you know? Has he called? Did Sebastyen tell you?'

'I'll go and get her.'

'You'll what? Dick, don't hang up—'

'Goodbye, Jim. And I'm sorry. Really I am.'

The ATF man met them at JFK with a car. His name was Edgar Shand, he said, and Agent Shepard had been his mentor. As they went on to the roof, Wendy thought about the poor Englishman Krok had described being shot down in broad daylight. The concrete had been hosed down within the last half hour, but the early morning sun was so strong it was already steaming. Wendy shuddered anyway.

Shand took her and Coogan to the car. He apologised for driving himself, but he thought it best to keep this as tight as possible. 'Ernie told me a little bit of background.' He swivelled as they negotiated their way out of the airport and started moving north across Queens. 'We gotta play this real careful. Because I can't pretend you are agents or nothing. And I got no real jurisdiction in this case now. But the SoCs and homicide were all over the place last night. It might be clear today.'

Coogan cleared his throat, felt like he had to say something, so he managed an anodyne: 'We appreciate what you are doing.'

'I got kids, too.'

Coogan felt uncomfortable. He still hadn't been able to contribute much these last few days, and it didn't look like much was going to change now. There was no way he could pretend to be a Fed, not in black jeans and a T-shirt. Wendy had on a smart cotton two-piece in navy, that might just pass muster as some kind of official outfit. He zipped up his jacket, hoping it might make it look more authentic. After all, they only needed a glimpse of the kid and they could be on their way. Or otherwise. 'What's their story? The people who this guy went to wet?'

Edgar shrugged. 'The husband is pretty shook up. We haven't got much from him. The friend who was staying there with his kid says it beats the shit out of him. Listen, I got a picture of the dead woman here. Polaroid. It ain't pretty. You wanna see if she's familiar?' He looked in the rearview mirror at Wendy. She was sitting bolt upright. She saw him look and nodded.

He waited a while as he overtook a couple of trucks, trying to get them through the heavy traffic as fast as he could and onto 87, which would take them across the Hudson and into the southern part of New York State. They were already passing the old World's Fair ground and the Unisphere, and Shea was up ahead, so they were making good time.

He passed the photo over and Coogan felt Wendy stiffen. 'Is that blood?'

'Yes, ma'am.'

'All of it?'

''Fraid so. Two nine-millimetre slugs. One in the heart.'

She passed it back before Coogan could see. It didn't worry him. He'd seen enough real dead bodies, he didn't need the bright garish colours of a Polaroid to remind him. ''S not her,' she said.

'No?'

'Too much hair. Wrong colour. Mine had cropped, dark.' She sounded despondent. Coogan risked squeezing her thigh, hoping she would recognise it for what it was. Or, at least, what he hoped it was. Reassurance.

'Shouldn't you just tell the FBI what you're thinkin'?' asked Edgar. 'It might be simpler.'

Coogan had to be careful here. He was pretty certain that, even if there was rivalry between agencies, dissing one in front of another as an outsider would not be good policy.

'We're here now,' said Coogan. 'If it is the boy, then we'll get them in. Otherwise . . .' he let it tail off and looked over at Wendy's miserable face. She had gone from being pale to almost white, bleached, except for the dark lines under her eyes. Still pretty, though, he reminded himself. Except that was the last thing on her mind right now.

As she read that signal, she suddenly said: 'If it isn't him, I'm going home, Coogan. Maybe all this isn't such a good idea. I don't think I can take much more.'

They drove up through the grounds of the Recuperation Unit in two black sedans. There were five of them. Two were computer experts who confiscated the Dell and the Compaq – but missed the Mac in Shepard's room – and went off to unravel their secrets. That left three to do the interrogating. Everyone who had been involved would be interviewed separately said the SAIC, a gnarled old veteran of the Bureau called Cote.

At one point he sat down next to Shepard and said: 'You can save me a lot of time by telling me who the two civilians were.'

'What two civilians?'

'The ones the Doc told us about. The one this little game was played for. A man and a woman. A looker, he says. Blonde.'

'I can't tell you that.'

'You're in big trouble, you know. You think an ATF record or a citation are going to save you? Or your friend over there.' He indicated Krok, who was staring out of the window. 'Do you know how many careers you've blighted by calling in favours? How many privacy laws you've broken?'

Shepard said: 'I'm sure you will tell me.'

'You get that lawyer?'

'Not yet.'

'Make it your first call. Oh and Shepard,' Cote tapped the frame of the wheelchair, 'don't go too far, eh?'

There were two deputies on duty, mainly to prevent the little knot of reporters from getting too close to the house. Incident tape had been strung across the lane to keep them at a distance, and Wendy, Coogan and Edgar had to park the car a few hundred yards away and walk back. When they got out of the car Edgar pointed at the attaché case on the rear seat and said to Coogan, 'Bring that.'

One of the reporters went to take a photo and Edgar strode

over, flashed his badge and snarled. 'Do that and I will clear this area. You put lives at risk by taking photos of these people.' The man shrugged, bored, like he had only been killing time anyway.

The deputy at the tape looked at the badge and said, 'SoC's already pretty much hoovered the place.'

'Ballistics,' said Edgar.

The deputy looked quizzically at Coogan, who lifted the attaché case in a workmanlike way, and at Wendy, then raised the tape for them to duck under. Edgar whispered: 'We lost him when he came down here. This is a dead end – just two more houses down the track. It meant if we drove down, it would have alerted him. So we came on foot. Not quick enough, though.' He sighed, he knew he was lucky not to have been suspended over this foul-up.

They made the door, now boarded up where the glass had been shattered by Edgar's bullet, and rang the bell. Another deputy opened the door, and Edgar said: 'I just wanna show my friends here something about the trajectory of the rounds. Ballistics.' He was careful never to claim they were actually ATF staff, Coogan noticed.

The deputy let them in and they could see white taped outlines of where the bodies had lain. They skirted them carefully, as if the empty space still contained the bulky three-dimensional corpses. Edgar began to speak mumbo-jumbo in low tones to them, before he turned to the deputy and said: 'Is Mr Barry around? I just want to check what he saw.'

'He's pretty beat, Agent. He's made three statements already. He's lying down with his kid.'

'Look, we'll just go up and see him. Save him coming down. If he's asleep we will leave him be. OK? Which door?'

The deputy pointed up. 'Second on the left.'

Before he could think anything peculiar in it the three of them bounded up the stairs and Edgar knocked. 'Mr Barry? Agent Edgar Shand. From last night? Can I come in?'

There was a muffled 'Yes' and Edgar pushed the door open. Jim Barry was laying fully clothed with his kid, who was asleep next to him on top of the covers. Barry put a finger to his lips and tiptoed over.

Coogan could see enough to know it wasn't Pete lying on the bed. He looked at Wendy and shook his head.

Edgar said: 'Sorry to disturb you, sir. I just need to clarify how many shots you heard.'

Barry looked puzzled. 'Shots? I told you. One. Yours. The other . . . the dead man. He had a silencer.'

'Suppressor,' corrected Edgar automatically. 'How's the boy?'

'Tommy? He's fine. A bit . . . confused but, fine.'

'Daddy?' At the sound of his name he woke up.

'It's OK, son, I'll be right over.'

Coogan felt Wendy slump further. The voice was wrong. It wasn't Pete.

'I'm thirsty,' the boy said.

'OK. Look.' Jim indicated the three figures blocking his exit. 'Can I just get him a drink? From the bathroom?'

Coogan moved aside to let him pass. Wendy stepped forward into the room, staring at the boy, as if willing him to be Pete. She took three more paces and stood before him, and the child cowered. Coogan followed her, frightened of what she was going to do. He touched her on the shoulder. 'Wendy—'

She shrugged him off and bent down to the kid's level, indicating the photo he had clutched to his chest. 'Can I see that? Is it your mommy?' The viciousness of the snatch startled Coogan and as the kid started to wail, Edgar was pushed aside by Jim, slopping water from a glass everywhere.

'What the hell are you doing?' he asked, but already Wendy was in his face, her features twisted into an ugly mask of rage, the mouth working to spit out the words. Jim fell backwards, driven by the torrent of invective, but still she kept coming until his back was against the rail. In her hand Wendy had the photo of Belle that Tommy had been hugging, the unmistakable image of the woman she had thought of as Agent Tinker, and she shoved it up into Jim's face, ignoring the deputy coming up the stairs to see what the hell was going on. 'Where is she? Where is she? Where is this bitch? And where's my boy, you bastard?'

Jim felt a sudden jolt burn through his body, causing his heart to stutter, as if he had stepped on the third rail in the subway. It couldn't be. That trail was cold. Belle had said so. Yet it was her – the white-trash trailer-park mother. She was here for her son. The game was, he suddenly realised, very much up.

It did not surprise Dick that he had trouble getting a cab out to Queens. New York was melting, the streets glaring at anyone who dared to walk them, workmen stripped to the waist, cops in summer blues, stained all over with great splodges of sweat, every car humming with air conditioning on full. And here he was, on a street corner in a raincoat with a leather holdall. He looked like a loon.

But, sure enough, after ten minutes one stopped. As he climbed in, he gave the guy the address and asked him to turn up the a/c. The cabbie, an East European judging by his medallion details, ignored him. Either that or it was already up to the max.

It was coming up four in the afternoon, a slow time for The Club. The lunchtime crowd had gone, the after-work drinkers and oglers were still chained to their desks and the bachelor-night-guys were still several hours away from the slow descent into incoherence they had before them. He had timed it well.

Dick shifted in the seat and felt the weight of the metal in his coat. He wouldn't have to tolerate it for much longer. Twenty minutes by cab on a day like today. No more.

No more anything in fact. He thought about all those future women who would never know what his actions today would spare them from. Maybe he would become something of a legend, a bogeyman of the sexual underworld. Dick The Creep, the man who arrived with a sheet and a little box of goodies. The one who left them bruised and crying. And for this, he had given over visas, green cards, had leaked news of raids, and had handed over the timing of the arrival of an Englishman who could threaten Hoek's whole empire.

That guy Krok may have been some sort of hot-shot, but he forgot how insecure the whole system of using shoulder-height cubicles in Federal offices was. You could hear every conversation, glance over at documents, run round and read messages, documents. It was so easy. They gave the guy a corner of the Immigration office, and suddenly everything he did was public knowledge.

Sebastyen, as Hoek had renamed himself, had been smart enough to cut in the Russians when he arrived, to make sure he helped them here and there, and he had made Dick do some visa work for them, too. Now, if you originated from anywhere east of Vienna in Europe, and were desperate to get into America, you were bound to come to Sebastyen's attention. If you were a woman, the chances were your passage would be paid with an indenture. If you were lucky, you'd end up dancing at The Landing Strip, the less fortunate worked in some of the brothels but, if you really lucked out or upset someone, you were sent to the rooms and, bottom of the heap, maybe a visit from The Creep.

The cabbie took the Queens-Midtown Tunnel heading east before turning up to the Grand Central Parkway, while Dick sat and sweated. He hoped Mike, his boy, would be OK. He hoped they would all be OK. But he somehow thought that wasn't on the cards.

The Landing Strip was near the cargo side of La Guardia, a three-storey former warehouse, now with all the windows blocked out, surrounded by airport support services. He paid the cabbie, tipped him well, and went to the entrance.

The spyhole moved and the door lock snicked back. The spyhole was something of an affectation, to make the punters feel like forbidden fruit was on the other side. Dick wondered just what kind of creature would have to turn up not to be admitted into The Landing Strip.

The foyer was square. At the far end, a big red velvet curtain kept the main arena hidden from casual eyes, muffling the sound of Madonna coming from the other side. No goodies till you paid your fifteen dollars cover. To the left was the staircase that led to the various rooms upstairs. At the desk in front of him Tarr sat smoking a cigarette, talking idly to the statuesque blonde with the deep, dizzying cleavage that mesmerised the punters into handing over their money, no questions asked.

Tarr looked up in surprise and took in The Creep's unseasonal dress. 'Hi. Whatsamatter – not hot enough for you?'

'Hoek here?'

'Nah. Not in the country even. I see you brought your stuff.' He nodded at the case. 'You got an appointment?' He looked quizzically at the dirty blonde who examined the ledger before her and shook her head.

'So, no Hoek?'

'I told you. No.'

'Schmee?'

'Nah.'

'Shame. You'll have to do.'

He started with the Glock, which was in his right-hand pocket, pulled it clear and fired two shots into Tarr's face. Dick got a fleeting impression of a big crimson bloom as the man went backwards over the desk, spraying the blonde with an arc of blood. She stood up and screamed and Dick hesitated for a moment before shooting her too. They all deserved to die.

He could hear the sound of glasses smashing beyond the curtain. The music had stopped. Pandemonium was about to break out on the far side of that red velvet barrier. A face peaked through the drapes and disappeared. Dick fired two rounds into the fabric watching it twitch and convulse. He opened the attaché case and took out the brace of MGP-15 Uzi clones in there and dumped the case on the floor. He flicked the safeties on the receivers to the rear position, one after another. Full automatic fire. He unbuttoned his coat so he could get at the two pistols he had on each side and set off up the stairs.

A long time ago, before he became a rubber stamper, he had trained at Quantico and Fort Bragg, learned all about hostile entries. But he was rusty, he knew that. Rusty and old and tired. He pressed to one wall and kept sideways to present a smaller target. He recalled that much. The first shot to hit him passed through the fleshy handles above his belt, ploughing through subcutaneous fat before exiting through his shirt. He had only registered the slapping impact when he swivelled round and let off a long rattling burp at the curtains, where he was sure the shot had come from, and he watched them dance and jerk like they were having a seizure as all of the thirty rounds snatched at the material. He threw the useless weapon down, put the second MGP into his right hand and the Glock in his left.

Then the jagged firestreak of pain from his side hit him. No time to worry about that now, he thought.

Two shots came from above, splintering the stair in front of him, and he leant over and fired upwards, a shorter burst this time. A flurry of plaster and wood sprinkled down on him. As he pushed back against the wall half a dozen more shots thudded around him.

He'd made four stairs, and taken a round. This was not a good ratio of ground taken to losses. Time for a rethink. He placed the MGP at his feet and took out the two Colts from under his coat and put them in his waistband for easier access, then scooped up the machine pistol again. And then he ran.

He took the stairs two at a time, alternating a quick burp from the machine pistol with the lighter bark of the Glock. He made the first landing and saw one body, bent double, head between the knees, gut shot. Lucky, but it'd do.

The second bullet went through the top of his arm and into his chest cavity, carving its way through soft tissue, nicking blood and lymph vessels, churning up his internal geography.

The impact smashed him against the bannister, but he managed to empty the last of the MGP into the offending door as it slammed shut. He paused to catch his breath and felt a ripping and gurgling from within. Shit. There were screams from down below and he fired the Glock down the stairwell until it was empty, then took the Colts in each hand, revelling in their old-fashioned heaviness. Big forty-fives to punch some lights out with. One more floor to go.

He kicked open each of the three doors in turn. One was a corridor, lined, he knew from past experience, with six rooms where the girls waited, probably cowering, maybe even with a john in there. The other two were big rooms, one some kind of office, but both empty, unless you counted the corpse in the one he had sprayed his machine burst into. He recognised the guy from one of the houses on the island and felt a grim satisfaction. The Creep, eh? Well, suck on that, pal.

Pain was coming from all over now, not just the wound areas. Bad pain. Probably close enough to reclassify as agony. He had to shut it out. One more floor. He made the bottom of the next flight when a familiar face snatched into view on the stairwell above and fired at him. Mr Moustache. He felt one bullet whistle passed his ear, but two hit him, sending him down into a heap. The man reappeared, a raised gun in front of him, and he braced himself for the shot, legs apart. Dick managed to fire one round, which hit Mr Moustache's thigh, taking out the main femoral artery in a wild explosion of blood. As he started to fold, clutching at his savaged leg, the man fired again, and Dick felt his vision go, a thick blackness illuminated by strange multi-coloured spirals. He'd been hit in the head somewhere, and severed nerve-endings were sparking like downed cables in a storm.

He lay there, trying to get a handle on what was happening around him. The only sound was the terrified squeaking of his victim and the psst of blood coming out under rapidly diminishing pressure. The guy could see his life draining away. Dick couldn't see anything. One more floor and he would make it to Belle. She was up there. Special treatment room. If he could just get up, climb those stairs, he would be a hero. Not The Creep any longer. They need never know it was him who told Hoek that they would be giving him a duplicate boy. He had made him do it. Threatened to take his own kid, Mike, unless he helped him. How was he to know he was going to grab Belle as retribution for the charade?

He couldn't help himself, he had to scream. He did so, an immense, ragged sound full of liquid frothing and ruptured membranes flapping somewhere inside him, and he must have fainted for a second, because now he could hear footsteps. Close. He had to get up. But nothing would move. He could feel his right arm flailing, and only the scraping of metal on wood told him the gun was in his hand. He suddenly felt it stop, and a new sensation, a pin prick next to the neural fireworks detonating all over his body, but he knew what it was. Someone standing on his hand. He assumed the gun was being levered from his fingers.

He could hear the man breathing, hot exhalations on his face. He tried to brace himself for the impact of the bullet, but even those muscles weren't responding. Systems failure, he thought. Time to reboot.

The voice next to his ear was surprisingly soft. 'Federal Officer, Dick. Quite a mess you made here. He's dead, the guy up the stairs there. You always forget how much blood you got in you. Eh? Like a Niagara here. You're in a bad way. Can you talk? No? Listen we found your note. Don't worry, we will make sure your son gets met from camp and is well cared for. That's what you are mainly worried about. Yeah? OK, it'll be cool. Now this guy you were after. Is he here? Is he one of the stiffs?'

Dick tried to shake his head. He wasn't sure whether it moved or not.

'No. OK. What's upstairs?'

His lips worked hard until the word emerged. 'Belle.' The sound of his own voice was frightening. It had a tremulous scratchy quality of someone well into their second century. 'Belle,' he repeated.

'Belle Barry? OK, we'll get someone up there. She'll be fine, too. Was she who you came for? Good. Good work. Now, one last thing . . . the medics are here, Dick. One last thing. This guy who made the Barrys swap. Sebastyen? We know all about that. Barry told us. What? What was that? Speak up if you can, I know it's difficult.'

'Hoek.'

'Hook? The guy's name is Hook? No? OK, we'll worry about that later. Where is he? Where's the boy?'

The lips had lost it, they were like a couple of earthworms squirming around, trying to mate. 'Lonnnnnn—'

'Again.'

'Luddin.'

'Luddin?'

'Londnnnn.'

'London. London? OK, good. London. Now, Dick, the good news is the medic here is going to fix you up. You'll be in the hospital in no time.'

Special Agent Edgar Shand stood up and looked at Wendy and said none too quietly. 'And the morgue right after that.'

FORTY

New York City

Coogan had thought Wendy had grown strong, but he guessed he had got it wrong. He checked them into a hotel in Midtown New York, near Gramercy, and sat and watched her cry and scream and kick and curse and throw things until she was exhausted and fell into a deep sleep on the bed, while he watched an old Robert Mitchum movie, marvelling, as always at the man's rolling gait.

Two days had passed since the bloodbath at the strip bar, two days in which they had been interrogated by homicide, FBI and ATF, then again by the FBI regarding their role in the various Federal offences that had been committed out of the recuperation facility, then by the State Department concerning anything they could offer up about Dick.

The woman, Belle Barry, was in hospital, being treated for wide-ranging mental and physical damage, the husband was under arrest for abduction, although he might well be out on bail. A decent lawyer might be able to argue some kind of balance-of-mind-disturbed mitigation. Meanwhile Wendy's boy was still missing.

They hadn't been able to get hold of Shepard. All calls to the hospital were now being put through an operator and monitored. Agent Shepard was, apparently, incommunicado. They'd left a message saying where they were, hoping he could get a line out. The silence suggested Shepard was being roasted by the Feds. Coogan couldn't feel too bad about that. Nobody had put his arm up his back to make him help and he had a feeling that any investigation was going to come down lightly on a man in a wheelchair. Besides, he had to remember what Mercy had said all those weeks ago, that ruining a few careers was small beer next to moving the recovery of your child on a notch.

What about Wendy, though? How was she going to survive this one? State Department claimed they would be contacting London, issuing descriptions, getting the boy's picture on news bulletins and with something called Interpol. But it was a big city, with close contacts to Europe. The man could be anywhere. And with him, the boy. She was going to have to face up to the fact that Pete was gone. Coogan felt bad enough about it, he could only imagine what sort of raw wound was going to fester across her soul for the rest of her life.

Wendy stirred. It was nine-thirty at night. They hadn't eaten since a couple of bagels in the morning. They would have to go outside into the concrete jungle with the rainforest-humid atmosphere. Or get room service.

She stretched like a cat and ran her hand through her hair, and Coogan reminded himself this was business. Pleasure had no role to play here. Not with a boy missing. How could he think of such a thing? Because he was a guy, he guessed, and his dick took no account of circumstances. Not now, boy. Back in the kennel. Maybe, just maybe, when all this was over. Then you can think about it.

She yawned. 'How long have I been out?'

'Coupla hours.'

'Sorry. About the little . . . temper display.'

'You're entitled.'

'I feel hollow. Just empty.'

He snorted. 'Hey, don't confuse what you feel with hunger. I could put some French's on that mattress and eat it right now. We ain't had any dinner, remember? I ain't being flippant. You'll feel better.' She came over, knelt down and laid her head on Coogan's lap. He wanted to touch her cheek, her eyes, stroke her head but stopped himself. He patted her back very gently, moving his hand away when he realised he was hitting her bra strap. It was a minefield.

'I didn't think it'd end like this, Coogan. I always thought we'd find him.' She looked up, and he could see that her blue eyes seemed to have taken on a brittle, hard quality, like someone had put flint into them. 'I want to kill them.'

'Who?'

'The couple. The Barrys. How dare they take my child. How *dare* they. Just to save their own, snotty, spoiled kid—'

'I guess they did it because they thought just like you did. I ain't defendin' them. No. It was despicable. But people do strange things—'

'You want to hear something wicked? Really wicked?'

Well, no, Coogan wanted to say, he might just have heard and seen this year's quota of wickedness. 'What?'

'I'm really glad that happened to her. That they did those things to her.'

She moved her body, shifted position and he felt her breasts rub against him. He bit his lower lip but to no avail. He was starting to get a hard-on. And she was sure to notice. He tried to move himself, but he was certain he felt a little pressure from her, a hug almost. Well, not certain. Hopeful was more like it.

'Do you think that's really wicked?' she asked.

Before he could answer there was a knock at the door and they exchanged glances. Wendy asked: 'Did you order room service?'

He shook his head.

'Who is it?'

The reply was muffled. Someone straining to be heard who didn't want to shout. Coogan went over and opened the door. She could tell by the expression on his face it wasn't company of the kind they were expecting. Coogan stepped back, flung the door open wide. There, standing on crutches, but also on his new plastic leg was Roy Krok. 'I checked myself out,' he said. 'I thought you might need some help.'

'With what?' asked Wendy.

Krok looked puzzled, as if this was the dumbest question he had ever heard. 'With finding your boy.'

They ate at a garish Chinese off Broadway, big helpings of greasy carbohydrate, a few light years from haute cuisine, but fine for bodies suddenly ravenous and reinvigorated. Krok spoke as they ate, pausing only to chopstick in a heap of noodles or rice.

'So the leg arrived and I had my first lesson with it. They didn't call it that of course: Supplementary Limb Motor Skill and Balance Tuition. At the same time the Feds had run poor Ernie ragged. He'll be OK, though. Me?' he laughed. 'I told 'em to shove it up their asses.'

'How come?' asked Coogan.

'Well, my department was not really beholden to anyone.' He looked serious. 'Not really. They can't touch us. Not at that level. It would have to go upstairs. And upstairs is busy.' He saw the look in Coogan's eyes. 'I'm not hangin' Ernie out to dry. I'm here with his blessing. Thing is, I can get bigger guns rolling than Ernie can. Off the meter.'

'You back in the saddle then? Official?'

'You kiddin'? I'm here to help you guys like I said. On a freelance basis.'

'Why?' asked Wendy. 'I mean, I appreciate all you did. You got me to how and why it happened, even if it didn't . . . even if Pete's not back yet. But we're at a dead end now. What's your interest?'

'My section of the State Department was not really heavily funded. Not recently. We got the sweepings off the table, the crumbs, the odd few hundred grand here and there nobody would notice. Easy to do, up to a million or so. Especially in government. But it meant we shared offices, resources. And we shared with the Visa and Immigration Service, because a lot of what we do involves overseas intelligence.'

'You're not CIA?' asked Coogan.

'State Department, I told you,' he said irritably. 'I'm not bullshitting you. Listen, CIA got their own recuperation and rehabilitation units. They don't put CIA with FBI to get better together. Not good for the blood pressure. Know what I mean?'

'I know what you mean,' said Coogan, although he didn't really have any idea about the scale of inter-agency rivalries, he just knew that, traditionally, there was no love lost. 'Anyone want this last dumpling?'

'You, I guess,' said Wendy. She was the happiest she had been for a couple of days, and part of Coogan resented it. He had only just realised why. Wendy was happy because there was another man along for the ride now. Coogan was jealous. Again. Recognising it for what it was didn't stop it, but it helped him ignore it. He popped the dumpling into his mouth whole and said: 'Gwn.'

Krok continued: 'OK, so most of our work these last two years was following up on reports of known war criminals or fugitives, either in the US or on friendly soil. Which is how come I know London. It's a friendly capital. One of the guys in the same office was Agent Crichton. So when I hear what happened at the strip club, I get a copy of Edgar Shand's ATF transcript and I see the name Hoek. Hoek and Sebastyen. The same guy. So Dick was in hock to this guy Hoek, the one that wanted the Barry boy. The eye-for-an-eye deal.'

Coogan swallowed and said: 'It's unbelievable.'

'Opportunist. Hoek's kid, his own kid, had some bone disease that would've killed him anyway. So he decided he could combine revenge with a little horse-trading, get a twofer.'

Wendy said: 'These are children he is talking about. My child.'

'Wendy, the man deals in bodies all the time. He brings in illegals, gets them visas, green cards, new IDs, SSNs. Through people like Dick Crichton. He paid him in women. Women he could do anything he pleased with. Does that sound like someone who cares much about other people's kids?'

Wendy nodded. It had all been in Dick's confession, a sorry, twisted document full of half justifications and pleas for mercy. They had found it after Barry pointed them to Dick's place in Bloomsberry and Edgar Shand had organised an ATF chopper lift over to La Guardia – a chopper ride during which she thought Coogan was going to throw up – just in time to find the man dying. She hadn't liked seeing him shot full of holes, but she couldn't say she felt the world had suffered a loss.

'Barry is in shock. Not only has his wife been drugged, raped and sodomised on a daily basis, he now finds out that his chum, the one who helped kill the kid, has set him up all along. Carried out the shooting on his house, told Hoek where Barry was running to, which made Hoek seem omnipotent.'

'You certain Hoek is Sebastyen and your guy? Really sure?' queried Coogan.

'Absolutely,' Krok said dismissively, before continuing: 'And Dick put a tape in the trunk of the car, again to make Hoek seem like he could get to them anytime. And he took potshots at Barry to scare him into not going to the cops.'

'Nice piece of work, this guy,' said Coogan. 'Anyone still hungry? I'll just get some ribs, then. And a beer. Beer?' He ordered a pile of the spicy ribs and three more beers. 'So what now?'

'I have a few friends left in London. They killed the best one, of course. Thanks to Dick. He told them the flight time. I had bought the tickets for the guy. I had the documentation on my desk. Dick must have known what we were up to.' Krok shook his head at his own complacency. He remembered laying into CIA guys for the Ames debacle – never suspecting one of their own. Now that one had come back to bite him in the ass, big time.

Coogan echoed his thoughts and said: 'I thought you guys were *secret* agents?'

Krok stopped himself reaching over and punching the guy. 'Coogan, I pulled your sheet, you know. Just to be on the safe side. Just in case you was the kind of guy who figured the one place I wouldn't look for a kidnapper is at the side of the victim's mother. You understand that? Mog, 1993. Now, I know you guys had it bad. I am just wonderin', are you one of the ones who blames us guys? Intelligence? That we should have known every warlord's location twenty-four seven? Is this what I am gettin' here?'

Coogan shook his head, realising he had let the personal and the political become confused here. 'Not from me.'

'Good. In answer to your sneer, it was a Federal building. What we did wasn't so secret. You just think you're all in it together.' Krok rubbed his forehead like it was a magic lamp. 'That guy Crichton is lucky he's dead, believe me. So, anyway, it is in both our interests to find Hoek. Thing is, as I said, I am unofficial. In fact I think there are people in the State Department would rather not have me out here. I reckon I can pull a few minor favours along the way but it's pretty much us three.'

'So what next?' asked Coogan.

The deferment eased Krok's anger. 'Next is tricky. I need to talk to Barry again. Get some details of any conversation he ever had with Sebastyen. Now, I am used to having to deal with assholes who have done terrible things in order to get to guys who have done worse things. You find a guy who shot a neighbour and let it pass if you can grab the guy who wiped out the village. Understand? It's a trade-off. What I want to know is this.' He looked at Wendy. 'Can I trust you to stay calm about all this? With Barry? After what he did to you and Pete?'

Wendy grabbed a rib and bit a chunk off, smearing sauce all over her face. 'No,' she said with a firm voice. 'Absolutely not.'

Across the East River, near La Guardia, Hoek was sitting in a loading bay a few hundred yards down from the empty, shuttered Landing Strip, in a Grand Cherokee with full Stealth Pack, windows so black they could well have been spray-painted.

There were no cops around now, the mêlée that had surrounded the building for fourteen hours had dispersed. He turned to Schmee and said, 'How many?'

'Four men shot dead. One wounded. Rebeka the receptionist shot dead. Seven guys arrested. None of the documents will stand up, they'll be out. Deported. All but three of the girls – again, they'll be undesirable aliens.'

'And they'll be talking?'

'They're strippers and whores, boss. You think they going to keep quiet to save our necks?'

'Any of them know much?'

'Rebeka was the one. Without her . . .' Schmee made a dismissive gesture.

'And the guys?'

'Drones. Again, The Creep killed the only ones who mattered.'

'Yes. Who would have thought? Everything covered?'

'Except the house in Bloomsberry. Seized assets. Every other avenue we can think of closed.'

'Good. I think this country is finished for us.'

'London?' asked Schmee.

'London,' said Hoek.

Jim Barry had his wife moved to St Ormond's, the hospital where the dead boy had been taken all those years ago. At least it seemed like years ago. He had certainly been young then. Now he felt old and used, as if the last of his youth had been extinguished. Even with Tommy he could manage nothing but a kind of frozen torpor. A game of catch was too much to bear. In the end he asked Belle's sister in Sparta to look after the boy for a few weeks, until Belle could come home.

Not that he was sure when that would be. She hadn't spoken

to him yet, not really. The doctors said she would heal, physically at least and probably in time, mentally, but for the moment they had to sedate her at night because of the dreams.

The full story had not yet been leaked to the press. He knew a couple of investigative reporters were asking questions around town, trying to piece it together. That the *New Yorker*, even, had set Rebecca Wade on a nightmare-in-suburbia exposé. Probably some ten-thousand-word monster that would cover every sordid wart on the story. It would all come out at the trial – possibly trials, he reminded himself – probably later in the year. Which would give the magazine a big, pestilent story for Christmas.

There had been no trouble about bail, once Belle's situation had been explained. Now he sat in the room in Bloomsberry among the packing boxes, the darkness creeping in as the sun slid down, a soft twilight grey falling over the streets and he thought about his inertia. And Belle's. What would bring him back to life after all the damage he had caused? What could make him whole again?

He was still thinking that as the gun barrel pressed against his ear, causing a sharp stab of pain, and the woman's voice said. 'Move and I'll blow your fuckin' brains out.'

FORTY-ONE

Outskirts of London

Hoek waited until the helicopter had fully settled before he flung back the door and took the ear defenders off The Boy. He must stop thinking of him as The Boy he reminded himself. He was now Petyr Gulya, of Hungarian descent, just as he was now Gabor Gulya. He turned Petyr's face to look at him. 'Well?'

'That was neat,' he said, wide-eyed. 'Duke always promised me a ride in his helicopter . . .' A note of sadness came into the voice and Hoek thought he was going to cry again, but he said. 'He never did give me one. Now I've had two. Is this it? Is this the place?' Instantly the spirits were up again and he slid from the doorway and, imitating Schmee who had got out ahead of them, ducked as if to clear the rotors as he ran towards the house.

He stopped next to Schmee and looked around, marvelling at the space. Schmee could see why. There was a good few acres here. A large ranch-style clapperboard house before them, two storeys, with some new extensions at the back. A couple of paddocks for the horses and, to their right, a stand of mixed deciduous trees making a small wood. And that was before you counted the lake and stream behind the house.

'Is this it?' the boy turned and asked again.

Hoek ducked down and ran beneath the slowly spinning blades, feeling the down draught pressing on his shoulders. As he straightened up he put a fatherly hand on the boy's shoulder. 'Yes. This is it.'

'In true life?'

'In true life, Petyr. All yours. Once we put up a basketball hoop, it'll be just like home.'

'Wow.'

Kids, Hoek thought. The most resilient creatures in the world. He wasn't sure where they had found this boy, but his energy and enthusiasm were more than a substitute for the morose, sickly specimen that had been his son. And none of that Cirek baggage. This one had spent a week moping, but the gradual corrupting influence of big shiny gifts, the latest computer games console and, promises of all that his heart desired, made him see that the future here was much brighter than in whichever desert he had been plucked from.

'Can we set up a diamond?' he asked.

Hoek started to walk slowly towards the house, looking for Marta and the servant girl. 'A diamond?'

'Baseball diamond. You got lots of space here. Look we could do it over there.' The boy pointed to one of the paddocks.

'We'll see. But you might be interested in learning another sport.'

'Noooo.'

'Soccer, perhaps?' Hoek had never really got to grips with American sports. Although soccer was played in the States it seemed to be as much a girl's pursuit – his lip curled involuntarily as he thought this – as a man or boy's.

'Eech. Girls play soccer.' There. A nation's manhood polluted by the notion that the greatest game in the world was somehow effete. Still, there was time to change his perception. He would show him the great European teams. Liverpool, Manchester United, Real Madrid, Barca and Dynamo Tblisi would slowly reverse the rot. One day, perhaps, he could tell him of the Pristina Pirates, who had begun life as a football team. Just the way Arkan had recruited from Red Star Belgrade to create the Serbian Volunteer Guard – the Tigers – so Hoek had drawn upon the supporters of the Pirates to form his own militia. He had always rather relished the idea of the Pirates taking on

Obilic, the soccer team Arkan subsequently bought. But that was just a dream, for the grass would have turned red within minutes had the two sides ever met. Besides, the Pirates were either dead, or in captivity, or scattered all over Kosovo now. And Arkan. The final whistle had gone for him, too, and Milosovic. There was a lot of complicated history to teach the boy, it would have to wait.

'Hockey, then,' he suggested. 'That might be more appropriate.'

'Basebaaaaaaaall,' Petyr yelled, sprinting over towards the paddock.

Hoek looked at Schmee, who said, 'At least someone's happy about all this.'

'Relax.'

'Relax? We nearly lost everything back there.'

'You told me we had a limited time in New York. And you were right. The boy thing,' he pointed at the kid who was swinging on one of the paddock fences, 'was just a catalyst. You'll see.'

Schmee opened his mouth to speak but recognised the tungsten set of Hoek's eyes. No arguments. He swallowed the sentence and nodded, but it echoed around his mind, the words refusing to fade away. That boy thing will be the death of us.

Isa Bowman signed in at the entrance to the recuperation facility and showed her badge to the receptionist. There was more security than at Police HQ in Seattle, she thought, as she passed through a portable metal-detector and an electronic door, before being met by a tall, stooping man in a white coat. He held out a limp hand. 'I am Dr Fincher. The Director of the facility.'

'You expecting trouble?' She indicated the various barriers she had passed through.

'Expecting? No. Detective Bowman. We've had trouble. Most of it thanks to your friend Agent Shepard. If you would like to follow me.'

As they walked down the window-lined corridor he said; 'I just need to warn you that a repeat performance will not be tolerated.'

'This is a personal visit.'

'He has placed us in an awkward position—'

'Doctor. This is a personal visit. I put it in writing when I requested permission. Remember? I'm not asking to join the fuckin' Masons here. I just want to see Ernie.'

He didn't bat an eyelid as the profanity. 'And I am just trying to keep this fucking place open, Detective.'

She half grinned. 'As long as we understand each other.'

He showed her to Shepard's room, knocked and let her in. Ernie had his back to the door, watching TV, but he turned the chair round and broke into a wide smile when he saw her. He pressed the remote and the basketball game faded to black. 'Isa. Come in. Close the door. Thanks, Doc,' he shouted, with an edge of sarcasm. 'Sit down.'

He indicated the chair next to the bed. She looked around. The room was painted bright, non-institutionalised colours, with well-stocked bookshelves and a small hi-fi. She was glad to see that. From her bag she pulled out half a dozen CDs and handed them over. 'I thought these might be better than flowers. You always liked to know what was going on over in Belltown. Just some local bands.'

Shepard flicked through and nodded. 'Nope. We don't get any of these in rural Virginia. Who's good?'

'Shok Tactics kinda live up to their name. You know it's my thing. Guitars'n'all.'

'Great. This should piss the Doc off a little more.'

She sat on the bed rather than the chair. 'I don't think that's possible.'

'Ah, fuck him. You look good, Isa. Put a bit of weight on. I don't mean that's bad. You was real skinny, when . . .' He swerved expertly away from going in that direction, 'Coffee? White, no sugar.'

'So what happened? With Coogan and the woman?'

He told her as much as he knew, avoiding the questions he wanted to ask about her and the guy. None of his business, he kept saying to himself.

'Ernie, I thought you were going to give her a little help. Not turn into the Horseman of the Apocalypse. What is this guy Cote doing?'

'The current situation is, I might add losing my pension to losing the use of my legs.'

'Damn.'

'But they are kinda screwed here. They gonna put a whole bunch of guys with bits missing and medals and citations and shit up in the dock? For trying to help a woman find her abducted kid?'

'Well . . .'

'Look. I know enough guys on Washington newspapers to have a good time with that story. So it's reprimands all round, is my guess. At the other end of the line, we got agents suspended and demoted. The ones who helped us in Miami and New York? That I feel bad about, but there you go. It seemed like a good idea at the time.'

'You got that guy who killed your partner.'

'That sack of shit? Someone did it for me. My pal Edgar put a big wadcutter round through the back of the head? Felt good to me. I have these dreams, where it's me pulling the trigger.'

'You take something? Sedative to stop the nightmares?'

'Isa, that ain't a nightmare. It's better than a wet dream. Excuse me, that was uncalled for.' He thought about Alice, his partner who had died on the New Jersey shore parking lot, and the two guys who had burnt to a frazzle in Lucy, the elephant landmark down by Atlantic City. All those dead bodies. And it wasn't over yet.

'Pardon me?' she suddenly asked.

'What?'

'You said something.'

'Did I? Here,' He handed over the coffee. 'Must have been thinking aloud.'

'What's not over?'

'Krok? The other guy? He's jumped ship. He's got unfinished business.'

'What was he? Bureau?'

Shepard laughed. 'Well he never exactly said, as I recall. State Department. That's a big place.'

'Spook?'

'Take it to the bank.'

'What about Cote? How does he feel about Krok going off?'

'Well, far as I know he hasn't found him yet. But he basically said if he breaks another Federal statute, he'll go for jail time, no matter how many legs he's got. Krok's not calling in to me too often because they're monitoring the calls.'

'What unfinished business? The boy?'

'Nah, the guy who's got the boy. He knows him of old.'

'Jesus, wheels within wheels.'

'You bet. Always the way. What goes around . . .'

There was a long pause as they both drank coffee. Finally Isa said: 'You get out soon.'

'Yeah, I get time off for bad behaviour.'

'And what then?'

'I got this place in Silver Lake. Nice.'

Quickly she said, 'You wanna come to Seattle? For a few weeks? I could take some time off. I got a ground-floor apartment, so the chair's no problem.'

She saw his eyes widen.

'And two bedrooms.'

'You hardnosed bitch,' he laughed. 'But what about your boyfriend?'

'I haven't got one.'

'Oh yes, you have. Just so happens he's married.'

It took her a while to put it together. 'John? John Tenniel?'

'Yes, John fuckin' Tenniel. That guy who was always in bed

with us every time we got under the sheets.' She was taken back by the bitterness. 'Maybe not in person, but in spirit.'

'That bad, eh?'

He softened a little. 'Well, pretty rough, yeah. I mean hard for anyone to cope with. I seen a picture. He ain't Keanu Reeves, is he?'

'That's a plus as far as I'm concerned.'

'You know what I mean.'

'Yeah, yeah, I do. OK, the deal is this. You come and stay. We hang out, we see what happens. If it doesn't work out, no recriminations, OK? No blaming it on the chair. We pulled apart last time, could easily happen again.'

'Is this a sympathy vote?'

'Fuck you. Do I look like the kind of girl who gives sympathy votes? Or fucks for that matter? And one thing. John Tenniel. I saw him recently.'

'Yeah?'

'I was with him when I got the call from Coogan. In a bar, before your mind goes into overdrive. He isn't an issue any more.' She said it with a confidence she didn't quite feel, but it was time to take that stance and pursue it for all it was worth.

'In which case it would give me great pleasure to accept the kind offer of your spare room.'

'Great.'

'I gotta warn you of one thing, though.'

'What?'

'These last few weeks? I can get a hard-on again.'

She spat coffee across the room as she laughed. 'Shit. The deal's off, big boy.' But she walked over and hugged him.

Wendy pulled the drapes, turned on a sidelight, and Barry blinked at the sudden glare. She raised the Sig that Krok had given her and said: 'Stay where you are.' She let Coogan and a shuffling Krok in the front door. He was in some pain. The new prosthetic was chafing badly, but he refused to have it seen to. Krok lowered himself stiffly into the couch and looked at Barry.

'I know you two.' Barry pointed at Coogan and Wendy. At least this way he would never have to face a trial. A quick bullet to the head, all scores settled. 'I guess I know why you are here.' He glared at Krok. 'What about you? You just like to watch, friend?'

Krok took out a cigarette. He had started again after five years. You lose a leg, the risk of smoking suddenly seemed acceptable. He lit up without asking permission. 'I'm the cavalry, Jim.'

'Oh yeah?' Barry felt himself stirring a little inside, a lick of anger flaring up, replacing the cold numbness that had seeped through his very being. 'How do you figure that one?'

'Because I am going to get the guy who did that to your wife.'

'Sebastyen?'

Krok pursed his lips in distaste. 'Hoek. His name is Hoek. Actually his name isn't that either. We think it is Savvas. And that he was a cab driver before the war. The Balkan war, that is. A cab driver whose main fares were drug couriers. Your pal Dick knew all this.' He took a long drag on the cigarette. 'It was like they had two lives. Both of them. Here, in Bloomsberry, was neutral territory, a kind of Neverland – Hoek was Sebastyen, a well-to-do banker, not a purveyor of human flesh . . . and Dick was Dick, a regular guy who helped teach baseball. Not some lowlife sex fiend.'

They all saw Jim tense as Krok talked, the tendons in his neck stand out. It wasn't just hatred. It was rage at his own stupidity. 'You still think he's a Hungarian venture capitalist?' Dick's words that should have told him the man knew much more than he was letting on. It was there that the nightmare began, there in that hospital room. Dick could have warned him, warned him that he had just killed the son of a psychopathic mass murderer, the kind of scum that only war propels to the top of the heap. Otherwise Hoek would have been left grubbing at the bottom of any decent society's compost heap, where he belonged. A drug-running cabbie? That figured.

Jim suddenly stood up and turned to Wendy, who instinctively pointed the gun at him. 'I know you hate me. I know that. And my wife. What we did was terrible. But she didn't deserve that? Did she?' He looked for understanding, maybe compassion, but there was none. 'You have to understand. That man, this Hoek, he started the dominos falling, it was him who began this whole chain of events. Him who . . .' He stopped and Krok waited. The man was suffering mood swings. It was to be expected. His next sentence wasn't, not entirely. 'I want to help you. I want to find him, too.'

Krok said quietly: 'Then tell us what you know. From the top.'

'No. No. I mean, of course. But I want to be with you. In the chase, the hunt, whatever. I let them take her. I couldn't do anything. You know – you think when the chips are down, you really are Clint Eastwood underneath. And it's a shock when you realise you're closer to Mr Bean. This guy – Hoek, Sebastyen, whatever – he's got me hatin' myself now. I want to find him and kill him too.' The mood pendulum was right up now, his eyes flaring, the mouth working the saliva onto his lips.

'You can't help us,' said Krok.

'Don't you see? What he did to me and my friends as well as you? He made us – he made us like *him*. What would *you* do? I asked him once. What would *you* do in my position? I'd kill *me* he said. And then he said: the only way to get something done in this country is to do it yourself. No use relying on others. Police, FBI, courts. Do it yourself. That is what you are doing isn't it? Isn't it?' He looked at Krok who nodded. The man was right, the only way Krok could guarantee real satisfaction was this way. 'I deserve the chance after what I've been through.'

Wendy looked at Krok and then at Coogan. Before they could stop her she drew back the barrel of the Sig and swept it across

Jim's cheek, sending him sprawling back into the seat with a shriek. A big flap of skin hung down where the front sight had torn the flesh. For a second Coogan thought she was going to fire and he tensed himself for the detonations.

But her shoulders dropped and she glanced over at Krok. It was that phrase 'after what he had been through' that had triggered the red fury. No thought there for what he had done to her. That he should find space for self-pity. Disgusting. 'I feel better now,' she said. 'Want to continue?'

Jim touched his cheek, winced, and examined the blood on his fingertips. The bullet graze had only just healed, and now this. 'I guess I deserved that, too.'

'No,' said Coogan quietly, 'you deserve the bit where she empties the Sig's magazine into you. I think that was just a little on account.'

Krok said: 'You want to help. Just try and remember anything Dick said about London. Anything at all.'

'London?' Jim shuffled into a sitting position. 'Why London?'

'All we know is, he has decamped to London. Dick told an ATF man. That isn't much to go on.'

Jim looked at Wendy. 'With your boy?'

She nodded.

'Shit. I hope he likes the Blue Jays.'

'What?' Wendy asked.

'The Blue Jays. They're a baseball team—'

'I know that,' Wendy snapped impatiently. 'Toronto.'

'Yeah, but they'd be London's local team, wouldn't they?'

And Krok was with him. He suddenly knew he had to call in the markers he'd put out all over the UK, all those guys checking flights and immigration records.

But Coogan was a step behind. 'I don't get it. Why?'

'Why go there?' asked Jim, misunderstanding. 'London ain't that far.'

Coogan crinkled his brow in puzzlement. 'From where?'

'London, Ontario,' said Krok slowly. 'Not London, England.'

'Canada?' Wendy was incredulous. She'd been facing up to the thought of five thousand miles of water separating her and her son. 'He's in Canada?'

'Maybe,' said Coogan, turning the new locale over in his mind. 'He might be right. If the guy runs illegals like you said, then Canada's a lot more lax than Uncle Sam. He could get them in there, and across the border if need be.'

'And Toronto's got a pretty healthy, if that's the word, vice trade. He could feed into that real easy. Jeez,' said Krok, as if dumbfounded at his own geographical confusion.

Jim said: 'You thought London, England? If you were a war criminal would you go back over there? To Europe? I just assumed it would be Canada.'

Wendy said: 'How big is this London?'

Krok shrugged: 'Nothing compared to the real thing. I'd guess tens, not hundreds of thousands. It's real spread out, though.'

Jim seemed to bark, and it was a while before they realised it was a derisive laugh. 'You guys really do need me, don't you? It'll be easy to find the house where Hoek is. It'll be the one with a helicopter pad.'

FORTY-TWO

Outskirts of London

The Fall had already begun up in the agricultural area between Belmont and London, on the fat isthmus separating Lakes Huron and Erie, and Toronto and Detroit, where they had rented the house. The small clumps of trees that held on between the acres of corn and tobacco were sloughing off their green pigments to reveal the ochres, russets and golds beneath their usual green coatings. As Wendy pulled over the car and Coogan put yet another mark on the map, she looked across to a perfect combination of a red barn next to a small copse, surrounded by a sea of yellow and said: 'Beautiful, isn't it?'

Coogan looked up and nodded.

'I stopped noticing, you know. Stopped looking, tasting, feeling.'

'It's only a matter of time,' he said. 'Be over soon. Then you can get back to worrying about how things taste. Know what I mean?' And perhaps we can go back to where we left off in the hotel room. Well, not left off, they had barely started, but there had been no moments of intimacy like that since. Now it was all focus, focus. Which was how it should be, he told himself. No matter what his prick kept whispering.

Coogan consulted the map. He had a large-scale Rand McNally and a series of aerial photo shots which Krok had come up with. Some were from a local aerial-survey company, but Coogan guessed others might originate in NIO – the National Imagery Office, which controls satellite snooping. 'A few small favours' as Krok called them.

Somewhere out there, Krok and Barry were doing the same

thing, checking every house that might contain Hoek and her son. They had a list of thirty-five properties outside the urban centre of London which had been bought in the last year, and it was just a matter of elimination. Unfortunately, the helicopter pad idea was a dud – folks up here liked a bit of land, which meant choppers could land somewhere on most of these properties.

Wendy had been opposed to bringing Jim along, but she had found it hard to keep up the intense level of hate she had felt at that moment when she whacked him with the gun. His face was healing, and all that was left was a nasty yellow bruise to remind her of the venom that had welled up inside her.

'It seems a long way from Arizona, eh?' Coogan finally said.

She shrugged. 'Yeah. It's getting harder, not easier. I want to go home.'

'We'll get there.'

'No, don't get me wrong. I want to go home with Pete. But sometimes I just feel like handing it over to the professionals.'

'Krok is a professional. Was. He's just off on his own little vendetta. Be grateful both your interests coincide.'

Most of the time, he had to admit, Krok was all businesslike and calm, like he was back in harness with the State Department and his cohorts weren't one Ranger with a bad back, a traumatised mother and a soon-to-be convicted kidnapper. But at other times, Coogan knew that whatever happened on that roof at JFK had scarred more than Krok's body. When he told Coogan the way he wanted this to end, for instance – his idea for a grand finale. Coogan had kept that, and a few other things, from Wendy.

'Coogan . . . thanks for everything. Did I ever say that?'

'Yup. But you can say it again when this is all over. There'll be plenty of time.'

'Listen, Coogan. I think you've done enough.'

'What does that mean?'

'I . . . I was talking to Roy. He was telling me this could get messy. I said good. No, he said, real bloody messy. Good, I said. But I thought . . . you? You're just a guy with the bad luck to have moved opposite me in a trailer park. I can't ask anything else of you.'

Coogan couldn't believe what he was hearing. 'Did Krok – or Roy as it is now – did he put you up to this?'

'To what?'

'Writing me out of the script?'

'Coogan—'

'Look, I spent a long time learning how to do certain things and come back alive. I did things that Krok only sees in manuals—'

'Coogan—'

'And if he doesn't think I'm up to it, he could have the fuckin' good manners to say so to my fa—'

'Coogan. It's me. *Me.* Not Roy Krok. See, Jim Barry, I don't give a shit about. You I do care about. What I mean is . . . I don't want you to feel obliged. Responsible.'

Coogan calmed down a little, took a breath. So she 'cared' for him, Whatever that meant. 'I hate not seeing something through,' was all he said. 'I'm in to the bitter end.' Then added quickly: 'Or sweet end. What happens when you get Pete?'

'I'm out of the park. Couldn't go back there. Maybe show Pete my real home. His real home. Minnesota. I don't know. Anywhere that isn't Arizona.' She put her hand on his leg, briefly. 'We'll keep in touch. Arizona'll just remind me . . . just like seeing Barry all the time.'

He tried to decode the hand-on-leg while he said: 'You manage something close to civility these days. With him, I mean.'

'Do I? I still want to wear his balls for earrings every so often, but . . . Jesus, he's just a guy, you know?'

'So's Hoek. That's what's so frightening. Just a guy with different parameters. He isn't a monster. I hear what Barry says, he thinks we're up against a mixture of Godzilla and Adolf Hitler. Once someone got you thinking that way, they've won.'

She thought about how she'd been close to killing Barry that night when she slugged him, only the promise Krok had extracted stopping her. 'And Roy?' she said, 'is he a regular guy?'

'Krok? You know what they say, "He who walks with monsters" . . .'

'I thought you said Hoek wasn't a monster.'

Coogan laughed. 'On second thoughts, I like it better when he is. It'll be easier that way.'

'What will?'

Before he could answer, his stomach vaulted over as they heard the familiar complex aural signature, a whistle and a whine and a large air-mashing whup-whup as a helicopter came overhead, dropped out of the sky and disappeared from view over the other side of the red barn.

'I'll be damned,' said Coogan softly, feeling his helicopter-nausea overwhelmed by a sudden adrenaline buzz.

Wendy's throat went dry. 'What's over there?'

Coogan consulted the list. 'Uh. It'll be . . . that's East Mence. Let's see . . . a ranch-style house sold six months ago to a company in Toronto. There's a right turn up ahead, goes straight to the town. Well, village, really.'

'What do we do now?'

'What Krok said.' Coogan started the car and engaged reverse, executing a three-point turn.

'Shouldn't we make sure? I mean – you know, there's probably more than one chopper round here.'

'Remember what our Chief Spook said? If they make us, Pete could end up down some well somewhere.' He stopped the car in mid-turn. 'You want to go up there? Risk that?'

She closed her eyes. 'No. He's right. And anyway, I don't have to go up there.' She took a deep breath and opened them, and he could see her face had flushed with colour, as if she was burning with embarrassment, but he could tell from the tremor in her voice it was excitement. 'Pete's close, Coogan. I can feel him.'

✳   ✳   ✳

Coogan and Wendy were sitting on the low wall in front of the four-bedroom house they had rented when Krok's Dodge van reappeared, bumping along the unmade road, throwing up spirals of dust motes to dance into the last rays of the sun. Three days had passed since the helicopter sighting, three days in which Krok had made all the running, telling them to stay put, sometimes going into a huddle with Coogan, excluding her for reasons she couldn't fathom and which made her angry. Finally Krok had disappeared at midday and said he would be gone for a short while. That was seven hours ago.

Krok pulled up and jumped out of the cab. 'Hi. Sorry I'm late.'

'Don't worry,' said Wendy. 'There's no dinner to spoil.'

'We'll get take-out. Anything happen here?'

'I didn't kill Barry . . . again,' she said. She was trying to be calm, but it was clear Krok operated on some need-to-know basis, and she didn't qualify. In his scheme of things, Pete was not the prime objective. As Coogan said, she was lucky he figured in there somewhere. She just hoped she didn't get sidelined. They had promised her a full briefing that night, and she was going to have to ram home what she wanted from all this. Barry and Krok could play hyenas-with-a-carcass all they wanted, picking over the bones of this guy. All she wanted was Pete.

'Congratulations,' Krok said to her. He turned to Coogan. 'She been like this all day?'

Coogan shrugged. 'Well, she's kinda mellowing now. She was much meaner earlier on. How you get on?'

'Good.' He walked to the back of the van and opened the doors. Wendy gasped when Duke stepped out, dusting himself down and grinned sheepishly, 'Hullo, darlin'. Told you I always come in the nick of time.' Coogan felt a jolt of guilt. On the phone to the air park he had convinced Duke that this was the audition for the Grand Canyon job, that once they cleaned up here, Flagstaff was the next stop. Ah well, the Vietnam pilots that the guy worshipped ended up disillusioned. Duke would get a hefty dose of that.

He was followed a tad more stiffly by Nash, carrying the small box under his arm that Coogan had asked him to get from his trailer. He gave a two-fingered salute to Coogan. All the markers were being called in on this one. He'd known Nash'd come. That was what he was getting at when they were at the Canyon. Anything I can do . . . anything that'd make us real again, count me in, that was what he meant.

Coogan touched Wendy's face and tenderly closed her gaping mouth. 'The midges are out, I wouldn't do that.' She turned to look at Coogan, her face forming the dozen questions she had for him. 'I think we better talk,' he said.

He told her. And himself. It is exactly the same. That is the beauty of it. Only this time no fuck-ups. No dust. No crazy quat-chewing Sammies. Who said there were no second acts in American lives? This was Act Two, Scene One.

This time it would be clean, surgical, the way it was meant to be a dozen years ago. This, in a strange way, was a gift from above. A chance to make amends. And he would. Let's do it.

Do it for Russell.

For Riley.

For O'Brien.

For Mab.

And for God's sake, she added, let's do it right.

FORTY-THREE

Outskirts of London

Schmee watched Hoek show the kid how to brush the horse in the paddock. He squeezed the leg to make the hoof come up, and raked each one out in turn. Then, using a stiff bristle brush, he stroked the flank, a softer one for the leg, then the mane and the tail. All the time the boy sat on the fence, watching the animal with intense concentration, while Hoek kept up a running commentary. He then led the horse around the perimeter fence of the corral.

Schmee lit a cigarette and turned to Szento, who would be taking the trip into Toronto with Hoek. They were dealing with some fellow Albanians there. Schmee was best out of it, he was told. 'Kids and animals, eh?' he said, nodding at what could be a touching scene with anybody else being kind to the dumb creature.

Szento nodded: 'Same in Kosovo. Had this fuckin' little puppy. Always yapping. Yap, yap, yap. We hated it. One day, a Serb sniper shot it. Dead. Hoek was crazy. Crazy. Next village he went mad. Killed everyone in it. Women, children. Made us shoot a line-up of six old men.'

Schmee nodded. The stories no longer had the power to shock. Shit happens, as the Americans like to say.

Szento said: 'Thing is, it wasn't the Serbs. We got one of our snipers to do it because the dog was driving us all stupid.' And he laughed a big booming music-hall laugh. It wasn't much of a punchline, thought Schmee.

The servant girl came and fetched the boy, while the new stable kid, a local, took the horse. Hoek came over, taking his gloves off and dusting himself down. 'I'll shower and then we go, eh? Don't want to smell like the Lone Ranger, huh?'

Schmee nodded and fetched a coffee from the kitchen, before he wandered out to watch the pilot make the pre-take-off checks on the Bell helicopter. He wondered what he should do next. He had a feeling that Hoek would settle into some little routine here in Canada, a scaled-down version of the New York operation. He could already feel a sense of cloying dullness close on him. He was no country boy. He needed to be in a city. Berlin, Hamburg, Buenos Aires, New York, they had been his stomping grounds. Maybe he should relocate permanently down in the US, rather than just going back for the container unloadings, Schmee thought. He could act as a liaison for Hoek, have his own little set-up. He'd raise the matter with him.

Hoek came out freshly laundered and smelling of something a bit more sickly and oily than horse flesh. Some kind of Albanian Calvin Klein, Schmee reckoned. He and Szento boarded the Bell and Schmee stayed to watch the rotors start to turn and cone, whisking the air into a frenzy beneath them, and to see the helicopter gingerly, delicately leave the ground, gain height and bank over the woods.

He went in for a second cup of coffee and smiled at the servant girl as she shushed the boy towards his play room. She smiled back. She was one of the lucky ones. Marta had selected her to look after the original Petyr from one of the early batches. It saved the pretty dark girl from the rooms, for she was simply not voluptuous enough to have made it as a dancer at The Landing Strip. The boy disappeared up the stairs, but even so, when Schmee took the gun from his belt holster, he placed it high on a cabinet out of the reach of idle hands. He knew how many kids died from handling misplaced weapons every year. And Hoek's response to losing a second son would probably be on a par with losing that puppy.

Upstairs he could hear that dreadful turbo-folk music that Marta liked to play wondering if it would wake Zeno, the

Albanian who was sleeping it off in the attic. Marta seemed less sure about the new version of the heir apparent than Hoek. Maybe it was because she hadn't given birth to this one, and clearly couldn't produce a replacement. Perhaps the boy reminded her of the Ciret cow shed. Or maybe she thought the whole business wrong. That would be a turn-up for the books. Marta makes a moral judgment about her husband? Bit late for that one, liebchen.

He'd just drained the second cup of coffee, wondering about how to kill time, when he heard the thrum of rotors again. Hoek was back. What now? Forgotten his riding crop to bash against his leg to impress his old peasant friends with his new country life?

Schmee went outside and squinted at the helicopter, waiting for them to emerge, but it sat there on the grass, its blades still spinning, as if it was undecided whether to lift off again.

He put the mug down and walked over. He knew what was expected. Hoek just wanted to give him a message, and he had to trot over and receive it. Why hadn't he just radioed in? Marta always picked up the receiver. Or used the cellphone?

He started to jog across the grounds, and unease only started to leak into his bones when he was halfway there. He could have sworn there were two pilots in the chopper when it left. And the registration numbers of the tail . . . they were in a different place. He froze, unsure for a second of what to do, feeling exposed. His gun was in the kitchen, still on that cabinet.

Schmee flipped round and began to sprint, willing his legs to pump faster than they had in many a year. Instantly his lungs began to burn. He was out of condition. This sedentary American life, all fast food and mindless television. It had ruined him. He heard the helicopter door slide open behind him. He was betting on the fact that they wouldn't shoot a man in the back. He was right. The shotgun blast hit him in the legs, tearing into muscle, just as he had minced that guy on the roof of JFK.

He went down heavily, the wind exploding out of his body,

rolling onto his back, flicking shreds of flesh in bloody arcs. He could see the blue sky, white clouds, and if he raised his head he could see the very edge of the whirling blades. His breath came back, and he managed to get on one elbow. Mustn't look at the leg. He knew he'd faint if he did. There was a woman walking towards him, an automatic pistol in her hand, behind her two guys, a short one and a longer, lankier guy. The short one had some strange sort of gun in his hand, long and bulbous. The other a machine pistol.

The trio drew level, eyes on the house, ignoring him, and he let himself believe they were going to let him live when, almost as an afterthought, the woman raised the pistol and fired at his head. His brain almost had time to register the dreadful force of the entry wound before it stopped registering anything for ever.

Nash looked at Coogan and made a face as he if was going to whistle in disbelief. Coogan shrugged. He'd've let the guy be as well, but she'd done the right thing strategically. He might have had a gun, anything. It had been Krok's Remington pump that had hit the guy initially, but the one-legged man was staying put in the borrowed chopper, at least for the moment. He was back there screwing a McMillan M87R rifle together. Barry was in the helicopter door, the pump across his knees, just in case anyone made a play for the machine.

They reached the house and Nash went in through the open kitchen door first, swivelling the Beretta SMG as he went. Coogan was next, with Wendy last. They could hear music playing at deafening volume. Enough to drown out the shotgun blast? Maybe.

At the foot of the stairs Coogan asked, 'Point?'

'Point,' agreed Nash, and stepped aside. His eyes were blazing, as if he had just done a whole load of poppers. Coogan just wanted to get out, go home. Nash was eating this up.

Coogan raised the suppressed H&K OHWS had picked up for him, a little Ranger souvenir, something he never thought he'd be using again. But then, he had never thought he could face a helicopter ride, and this was his second in a week. If this woman can survive losing her kid, he had told himself, you can bite on a couple more chopper lifts. And he had. Just the return journey now.

Coogan took the stairs fast and low, keeping his body almost parallel to the angle of the risers. When he reached the landing he rolled into a ball, threw himself forward and came up with the gun held out in front of him. Nothing.

Nash came next, same position, but passing Coogan and crouching in the corner. He knew he could blow anyone in half with the Beretta sub-machine-gun. If only Krok had been able to rustle up a whole set of them. But the helicopter was pretty good going, he'd give him that. A friendly Canadian 'government agency' was all he would specify. Canada had spies? It just got stranger.

Wendy stepped over Coogan and he sprang to his feet, pushing her ahead so the three of them wouldn't be bunched on the landing. Four doors. Stair to some kind of attic room. The music coming from the room directly opposite. Nash came up and tapped Wendy on the shoulder, signalling for her to stop. He pointed a position for Coogan to take, waited until he was in place, and then launched himself at the door, turning the handle as his shoulder hit it, spinning and rolling onto a bright red carpet, noting the position of the people as he righted and brought the gun to bear, trying to ignore the ear-splitting wail of strange foreign music filling the air.

'*Stop*,' someone managed to shout over the music.

It was the older of the two women. Kneeling in front of her, clutching her legs was a young girl, and hiding behind, a boy. 'Stop. You want the child? Take him. I knew it was trouble. *Take him*. And go.'

She grabbed the boy's head and pushed him round, causing him to stumble. Wendy lowered her pistol, still suspecting a trick. 'Pete? Pete?' The haircut was wrong, the clothes terrible, and he'd aged, years it seemed, if it was him. 'Mom?' he asked. It was. It was him. She ran in and scooped him up, carefully pointing the gun away, and smothering him with kisses.

'Go,' the woman repeated in her heavily accented English and stroked the head of the frightened young girl. 'Take your boy.'

'Yes, ma'am,' said Coogan.

Coogan and Nash made a sandwich of Wendy and the boy, one front, one back, with the pair as the filling, and they ran down the stairs, not worrying about noise now, and into the open. Coogan could feel the pains in his back where his spine was protesting. It didn't like being back on chopper patrol one bit.

He made the start-rotors signal to Duke, who flashed a thumbs-up. He had never let them stop, but he increased the throttle, cranking up the engine whine. Krok began to shuffle towards the door, while Barry waved and willed them on, looking up nervously as if the other chopper might return any minute.

Wendy, slowed by the weight of Pete, couldn't keep up, and Nash stopped and took him from her, clasping him to his chest, feeling the boy's arms lock around his neck. Coogan had made it to the helicopter, and was taking the rifle out for Krok, who was shuffling towards the door lip. Wendy realised now what Krok was going to do, what part of the plan he had kept from them. This was why he was doing it off the meter, as he liked to put it, completely unofficially.

'One up for Chalk Five,' Nash said to himself with a grin, when Coogan reach the bird. 'At last.'

They were level with the bloodied form of Schmee when the burst of small-arms fire caught Nash in his lower back, a jagged line of impacts, buckling his legs, pitching him forward. He managed to twist and throw Pete clear, sending him rolling over the grass, before he thumped to the ground and lay still. One of the rounds sliced through the upper part of Wendy's thigh, a big ugly gash exploding outwards, showing glistening red meat. She screamed and stumbled.

The body of Schmee jerked as another clump of rounds thudded into it. Wendy frantically scanned the house and located the open window at the top. The attic room. Someone they had missed. She shouted to the others and raised the pistol and fired, her arm flailing backwards with the unexpected ferocity of the recoil.

'Run. Pete, run. To the helicopter.'

The boy was bewildered and winded, tears in his eyes, but unscathed. He took a step towards Wendy. 'Run. That way, Pete. Please.' She managed to heave the sub-machine-gun from under Nash's inert form.

'Come on, Pete. Come on.' It was Barry. Shouting, his arms extended, waving the kid on. Still the boy hesitated. 'Go on,' said Wendy, nodding frantically, 'He's one of us now. A good guy.' Pete started to move, his little legs accelerating into a headlong rush as Barry called to him.

Wendy dropped onto her good leg, pulled the bolt on the machine pistol as Krok and Coogan had shown her over and over again these last few days and fired a burst at the window, grunting with satisfaction as it splintered into a swirling storm of metal and wood and glass. She waited until the magazine was empty, threw down the gun, and went after her son, in a strange galloping limp.

She was about twenty yards away when she saw what was going to happen. Could tell by Barry's crouch. She tried to shout but nothing came. Coogan and Krok were laying down more fire at the window, not paying enough attention. *No*, she said in a croak. *No, you stupid bastard*, shouted her brain faster than her lips could form the words. Her leg gave way and she fell to her knees, a small grenade of pain exploding down her left side. *No.*

Coogan put his suppressed pistol in his belt and emptied the pump at the upper storey, even though he knew it wouldn't do much damage at this range. He had just cleared the last round when he felt the sickly warmth of the blood splatter across his face. He turned to look at Krok next to him, expecting to see a mass of flesh and bone and blood, but the man was still squinting down the telescopic sight, waiting, hoping a head would appear at one of the apertures in the house.

Barry, then. But no. Jim Barry was holding the boy in his arms, unable to comprehend what had happened, staring at the head with the top removed like a bloody hard-boiled egg, at the tissue that splattered his face and arms and the mother on her knees a few yards away, wailing.

Coogan looked beyond him at Nash, and for the first time realised what had happened to a man who'd gone through a crazy war and an even crazier peace and had come out to help an old friend. And now he could hear the hardest pain to bear of all, the kind of agony he would never ever feel, spilling uncontrolled out of Wendy's mouth. He looked again at Jim Barry's slack-jawed face, the face of a man who didn't think, had never considered, that getting a kid under the arms and lifting him up near a helicopter would bring the little cranium into contact with spinning rotor blades.

As Wendy's screams got louder and more deranged, Coogan finally realised why he had stayed on till the end, what his role in all this was to be. Not the White Knight at all. The janitor. The man who sweeps up the mess. He stepped forward, put his silenced pistol to the side of Barry's head and squeezed the trigger, listening to the soft kiss as the round left the barrel and the harder sound of bone parting. He reached out and took the boy in his left arm as the lifeless Barry fell away in a heap. Someone was shouting. Probably Krok or Duke, but Coogan ignored the yelling, went over to Wendy with Pete still in one arm, and, as best he could, pulled her to her feet.

The three of them, one alive, one dead, one in torment somewhere between the two, made it to the chopper door.

Wendy's face was streaked with dirt and blood and tears as

she looked at Krok. 'Me,' she said. Krok couldn't understand what she meant.

'Let's go people. For Chrissake, it's like Mylai out there.' It was Duke, frightened and in so far over his head he wasn't sure which way was up. Just like 'Nam they'd said. A helicopter mission. Good practice for the Big One. If he'd only known just how much like the real thing they'd meant, he'd have stayed in the desert.

Krok shuffled some more towards the door to get out.

'No. Me. I do it. Me,' she repeated.

Krok looked at Coogan for a translation. Coogan put the floppy body of Pete into her arms and she pulled him to her bosom.

'She knows.'

'No,' Krok said firmly. 'My call. He's mine. It is why we are here. Why I helped.'

'Not any more,' she managed to say, the moving air column all around them making the words vibrate strangely, as if she had a metallic voicebox.

Krok went to open his mouth and Coogan put his H&K pistol to the man's head, and pressed it into the flesh. 'Don't think I won't. Ask Barry if you aren't convinced.' Coogan knew he could do it. The equation was seared into him now, confirming what he had felt after Mog. People die around helicopters.

Krok nodded very slowly, as if totting up some kind of score card. Out of the two of them, perhaps she had earned the right most to do this thing. He touched the scoped rifle and said to Wendy: 'You know how?'

'Oh yes,' she said, remembering the hunting trips with her father and brother. She'd missed then, but this was different. This was very, very different. 'Oh yes.'

She lay at the edge of the treeline, covered in a pile of deep red leaves, only her head and shoulders showing. Next to her was the inert form of Pete, also partly concealed. She had managed to arrange a crown of leaves to disguise the terrible wound to his head so he looked like some kind of wood nymph or pixie, caught asleep in a glade, like a character in a fairy story. Every few minutes she reached over and kissed his cooling lips and left another tear running down his cheek, as if it was the boy himself who was crying.

In a strange way, a way she recognised was hugely selfish, she was glad it had ended this way. Having him back, alive, that would have been option one, no doubt. But, if she'd never found him, never known where he had gone, who was watching him grow, feeding him, living his life, that would have been hell beyond imagining. At least with this middle path she knew where he was, what he looked like, frozen for ever, serene and beautiful and ageless. No more growing up for Pete. He had been spared all that pain that chips away at you throughout the decades, like acid rain on a limestone building, melting and distorting and scarring what was once perfect, bringing you, in the end, to dark, miserable places like the one she inhabited now.

Her left leg was numb, the agony reduced to a dull throb by a fistful of painkillers from the chopper's first-aid kit. There were probably all kinds of pathogens crawling into the crusty, weeping wound from the woodland soil. She didn't care about that.

Coogan and Krok had set up covering fire blowing out every window in the house as she had run haltingly to the woods, Pete in her arms, the McMillan slung over her shoulder, making sure nobody would glimpse the one figure who wasn't going to leave the scene of this crime.

She checked the rifle again, squinted through the sights, bringing the crosshairs to bear on the huddled form of the man out in the field, lying lonely and dead. The only movement she had seen was over by the stable, some young kid peeking out before sprinting away. She hoped he wouldn't have time to raise the alarm before she had finished here. Five shots, Krok had said. Big, fuck-off 50-millimetre Browning ammo. So powerful the gun was used as much for equipment destruction as antipersonnel. Well, screw that, this time the .50s were going through flesh and bone.

They had taken the bodies of Barry and Nash with them. Barry would be tipped out over some lake. But, Coogan swore, he'd find a way to get Nash home, to bury him properly. Krok had said he would make sure. He figured he might as well do something useful now they had taken this off him, his moment of lying in the wood waiting for the enemy.

Then she heard it. The other helicopter. The woman would have called Hoek with news of the raid. He would have returned immediately. But she could also hear another mechanical sound, that of police sirens, urgently whooping as the cars sped along.

No matter.

She brought the McMillan up to her shoulder and hesitated, leaning across to give Pete one last soft kiss, before thumbing off the safety and sliding back the bolt to chamber a round. It locked home with a reassuring well-machined snick. Now the metallic chattering noise in the sky was growing, drowning out the sirens. She could feel the pressure of air churned by thudding blades pushing down on her, hear the trees above her rustling in discomfort, see the leaves covering Pete start to rise in the vortex, the grass starting to bow down in supplication. Soon, she thought, putting her eye to the rubber cup once more. Soon.

AUTHOR'S NOTE

I would like to thank Robert Lehner of the Tucson Police Department, members of the Newark PD Homicide, Rick Young, Senior Special Agent with the State Department and Department of Transportation (Retired), Neal Schiff of the Federal Bureau of Investigation in Washington, trumpeter extraordinaire Guy Barker, guitarist and ace photographer Laurie Evans and Martin Beiser, Managing Editor of *GQ* in New York and inhabitant of the nice, non-homicidal town of Montclair, New Jersey, for answering what must have seemed very strange questions at the time.

There was no Chalk Five in Somalia. For a riveting account of what happened to US Forces in Mogadishu – one no work of fiction could hope to compete with – I refer you to *Black Hawk Down* by Mark Bowden (Bantam), one of the great accounts of modern warfare.

Trans Am is a piece of fiction, unfortunately NAMBLA isn't, nor is the National Center for Missing & Exploited Children. Whether you have kids or not, its website www.missingkids.com does not make for easy reading.

Finally, as always, heartfelt thanks to David Miller and Bill Massey, Christine Walker and Susan d'Arcy, and apologies, this time around, to J.M. Barrie.